Would that be marry an
eighteen-year-old virgin than
the aged woman certain to be
his fated bride—if he
married at all!

Rafe Godsol had a position as one of the king's knights, but it didn't provide him with enough income to attract any gentlewoman. Nay, he had but one asset beyond the strength of his sword arm. . .

It was his face that would hopefully gain him a rich widow. But for now, his attention shifted to the crowded courtyard as he sought a woman who'd add that special spark of excitement to his stay at Haydon. It didn't take him long.

She was perfect, her features refined, the smooth oval of her face framed in wings of fiery chestnut hair. Beautiful, young, and rich . . . what more could he want?

The Warrior's Damsel

Denise Hampton

AVON BOOKS

An Imprint of HarperCollinsPublishers

AVON BOOKS
An Imprint of HarperCollins*Publishers*
10 East 53rd Street
New York, New York 10022-5299

Copyright © 2001 by Denise Lindow
ISBN: 0-380-81546-X
www.avonromance.com

First Avon Books paperback printing: May 2001

Avon Trademark Reg. U.S. Pat. Off. and in Other Countries, Marca Registrada, Hecho en U.S.A.
HarperCollins ® is a trademark of HarperCollins Publishers Inc.

Printed in the U.S.A.

10 9 8 7 6 5 4 3 2 1

Chapter 1

July, 1214

"We are gathered here this day in the sight of our Lord God and in the face of this noble company to join in matrimony Emma of Haydon and Gerard d' Essex."

The bishop's announcement thundered out over the priory's quiet courtyard. Every one of the hundred or so watching gentlefolk, Rafe Godsol included, sighed. It surprised him, that he could be so affected; he didn't consider himself a religious man. Then again, for Rafe and many others here, this was the first church-sanctified wedding they'd attended in years.

Until this very month, England had been under papal interdict. That meant no priestly rites, save the

1

first and the last, could be performed. Only when King John had agreed to accept the pope's choice for archbishop of Canterbury and repay the sums he'd stolen from England's churches and monasteries during the period of interdict did the Holy Father again allow English priests to perform their masses.

Rafe watched Bishop Robert as the bishop scanned the gentlefolk gathered below him. Jewels flashed in the clergyman's miter. June's hazy sunshine made the golden embroidery on his vestments glint.

So deep was the silence that Rafe could hear fledgling swallows piping in their nests beneath the church's eaves. A joyous breath of air tumbled over the priory's tall stone walls. It stirred the clinging ivy and set the gentlewomen's brightly colored veils to fluttering.

"Is there any man here who can give reason why this joining should not proceed?" the churchman demanded, his powerful voice shattering the quiet.

Silk and samite rustled as noblemen, knights and their wives all glanced about as if expecting some response. A low rumble rose from the priory's arched gateway. Crowded into that opening were the commoners tied to Haydon Castle, come to watch the wedding of their lord's eldest daughter. Beyond that, no man raised his voice.

The bishop gave a satisfied nod and retreated to stand before the bride and groom, his back to the church's open doorway. Tradition and common sense demanded the couple exchange their oaths out here, where all the world bore witness. Only after their words were said would the bride and groom enter the church and celebrate mass.

In preamble to the speaking of the vows, the churchman launched into the list of properties the couple brought with them into this marriage. Since Rafe already knew what lands and farms the two families were exchanging, he eyed the bride. Dressed in green and gold, Emma of Haydon was a willowy, red-haired lass of eighteen, nearly ancient for a first marriage. But her mother insisted on postponing these nuptials until Emma's marriage could be sanctified by a churchman.

Rafe's mouth twisted in longing. Would that he might marry an eighteen-year-old virgin rather than the aged and barren crone certain to be his fated bride—if he wed at all. He was the youngest of Sir John Godsol's three sons. With his sire naught but a country knight, there had been no inheritance for him upon his father's death last year.

Although Rafe had a position as one of the king's knights, a position he now considered leaving after spending these past months losing battles in France, it didn't provide him income enough to attract any virgin gentlewoman's father. Nay, Rafe had but one asset beyond the strength of his sword arm.

He glanced at his two brothers, who stood beside him. Although all three had black, curling hair and dark brown eyes, Dickon and Will owned their mother's short build, round face and thick features. Only Rafe had inherited their father's height and fine looks. It was Rafe's face that would free him from penury, hopefully attracting him a rich widow, a woman able to choose her own mate by the sheer happenstance of having outlived her previous husbands.

Rafe's stomach soured. Aye, but any such woman was also likely to be too long in the tooth to bear him sons. Nor did it sit well with him that he'd be dependent on his wife for his income.

On the porch, Bishop Robert commanded the bride and groom to join hands, his voice raised so that even those in the gateway heard him. The groom, Gerard d' Essex, faltered as he turned to face his new wife. To disguise his nervousness, Gerard gave his shining blue and red tunic a yank, then ham-handedly grabbed Emma's fingers.

Rafe grinned. Like a number of other young men watching this ceremony, Rafe was Gerard's friend and foster brother, one of dozens of lads from gentle households high and low raised in King John's court as hostages for their fathers' loyalty.

Those among Rafe's companions who had no marital prospects had taken it as their solemn duty to hector Gerard these past weeks, suggesting that the youngest among them hadn't the manhood necessary to appreciate a wife. It seemed they'd succeeded in making Gerard nervous.

The bishop launched into the mandatory lecture about the duty of wife to husband and husband to wife. Rafe yawned, the novelty of hearing a churchman speak already wearing thin. His attention shifted to the crowded courtyard as he sought the right woman, the one who'd add that special spark of excitement to his stay at Haydon.

It didn't take him long. She was perfect, her features refined, the smooth oval of her face framed in wings of fiery chestnut hair. Fine brows peaked sharply over almond-shaped eyes, while her lips owned a lilt that made her seem on the verge of smiling. Rich yellow gowns clung to her slender body. Bright jewels flashed in her necklet and bracelets. Pearls decorated her green cap and veil.

Rafe eyed her cap and smiled, for her headgear proclaimed her a married woman. Not only beautiful, but young, rich and married. What more could a prospectless man like himself want but the opportunity to borrow a rich man's pretty wife for a night or longer?

After waiting years to stage his daughter's wedding, Lord Haydon now spared no expense in its execution. There would be days of celebration complete with nightly feasts including music and mummery, at least three hunts, and even a joust and a melee. Rafe's grin widened. Thanks to Lord Haydon, he had ten full days to pursue this woman and cuckold her husband.

On the porch, Bishop Robert launched into the recitation of the vows. "Gerard d' Essex, will you have this woman to wife, to honor and—"

The ringing words brought Rafe's attention back to the bridal couple. Depression nibbled at him. Oh, to claim his own wife, not another man's used-up castoff. More than anything, he wanted a woman who'd bedded no one but him, one who hadn't borne another man's child.

Trapped in his momentary depression, he

watched as the oaths were traded. When they were done, the bishop gave the groom a ceremonial kiss, then indicated that the new husband should do the same to his wife. On the porch, Gerard pulled Emma close to him. As she came to rest against her new husband's chest, Emma set to hiccuping. Their lips touched.

It was the moment for which Rafe and his friends waited. Rafe put his fingers to his lips and loosed a long, shrill whistle in salute to the first of his companions to wed. Five other whistles joined his.

Gerard jerked in reaction, then shifted, turning his back to both witnesses and hecklers. What should have been but a ceremonial press of flesh to flesh lengthened. Emma's hiccups ended. Her arms rose to encircle her new husband's neck.

Commoners and nobles alike roared their approval. Frowning, the bishop parted the couple, then shooed them through the church door for the mass. The guests followed, surging toward the porch stair.

In no hurry to join the mob, Rafe once again looked for the woman he meant to pursue. She, too, was hanging back from the crush, her gaze scanning the yard as she waited for the crowd to clear. The thrill of the chase filled Rafe. In another instant, her gaze would be aimed at him.

He checked to see his brown cap was at the right angle, then gave his new tunic, a serviceable gray linen with red and blue embroidery at its neck and hem to make it festive, a quick jerk. It wouldn't do to have a single wayward fold mar the powerful outline of his chest.

Standing to best display the breadth of his shoulders, he lifted his lips into the smile that had more than once won him a willing partner in bedplay. At the very instant the beauty's gaze should have alighted on him, Rafe's eldest brother shifted back a step to stand between Rafe and the woman he hoped to impress.

"Move, you lummox," Rafe hissed, and shoved Will to one side. Too late. The woman's gaze swept on past, completely missing him. "Damn you, she was looking for me," he complained.

Will didn't need to be a dozen years older than Rafe or as powerful as his youngest brother to command respect—not when he now held all their father's property. "Don't be shoving me, Rafe," he growled, then peered out into the crowd. "Who's looking for you?"

"Have some respect. This is a wedding, not an alehouse," their middle brother, Dickon, chided.

With the cowl of his habit thrown back, the bare skin of Dickon's tonsured head gleamed in the sun. A year younger than Will, Rafe's middle brother had been given to the church as a child and was now this priory's brewmaster. Despite his scold, Dickon shifted to look in the same direction as his brothers. "Who's looking for you, Rafe?"

"She was," Rafe answered, pointing to the beauty.

Dickon choked on a laugh. "Why, Rafe, you've found just the sort of woman you need. Yon creature is a rich widow."

"She's a widow?" Rafe cried, as the potential of seduction melted into whole new possibilities.

Will dealt his youngest brother a cuff sharp enough to make Rafe's ear ring. "Turn your gaze away," he commanded. "You'll marry a serf's daughter before you so much as look at that one."

Snarling at the insult, Rafe's hand fell to his belt where his sword would have hung had this not been a peaceful wedding. "You'll not strike me for no reason, Will," he snapped. "If yon beauty is a widow, I intend to court her, and there's naught you can do to stop me."

It was an empty threat. Rafe knew well enough that the widow was too young not to have a father or guardian already planning her next marriage. All he wanted was to challenge Will's certainty that as the Godsol patriarch he could control his youngest sibling.

Will's beefy shoulders tensed beneath his blue tunic. He balled his fists. The sun caught on the few silver threads in his black hair as he glared up at his youngest brother. "Defy me, and I'll slit your throat, as is my God-given right," he threatened.

"I'm at your convenience," Rafe returned, his eyes narrowed, his voice low and harsh as he called his brother's bluff. "Try it as you may."

"Enough, Rafe," said Dickon, putting a hand on each brother's arm, "you've proved your point. As for you, Will," he said, glancing at the eldest of them, "can't you see Rafe doesn't know who she is? How could he? Rafe was already fostered with our king when she was born and rarely home after that to have any chance to know her. Aye, and she was but a wee child when she went newly betrothed from our shire. Nor can you blame Rafe for his interest. Despite their filthy blood, the Daubneys breed up fine-looking women."

Shock rattled Rafe. "She's a Daubney?" he cried out, his voice loud enough for nearby folk to send glances his way. He stared at the beauty. How could something so lovely be related to a family so foul?

"Aye, but marriage made her Lady Katherine de Fraisney," Dickon said.

Will spat. "She's not just a Daubney, she's the daughter of Humphrey of Bagot, that bitch's son who murdered our sire." That Will didn't use Humphrey Daubney's rightful title as lord of Bagot was a reflection of his hatred for the head of the Daubney family. That he kept his voice to a bare whisper said he knew better than to utter such insults aloud while unarmed and where a Daubney supporter might overhear.

Wicked amusement came to life in Dickon's eyes. He glanced at his younger sibling. "You're the one women like, Rafe, the pretty one. I dare you. Pursue her. Aye, wed her and you'll be the Godsol who finally reclaims that same acreage those loathsome rat-kissers stole from our great-grandsire. When her brother died last year in Bagot's attack against us, the same attack that killed our sire, yon Daubney widow came into our Glevering. Of course," he taunted, "there's a good chance the Daubneys will see you dead within moments of speaking your vows."

Rather than chastise Dickon for proposing the same thing Rafe had contemplated only moments ago, a harsh laugh left Will's lips. "Oh brother, what twisted thoughts wake in me with your words," he said to Dickon. "Why, I find myself thinking vengeance truly could be ours."

Will glanced between his brothers, the lift of his chin bidding them draw nearer for a bit of private conversation. "I hear Bagot paid our king an earl's ransom for the right to wed his daughter wherever he wishes. That means our royal master cares naught where the bitch marries and won't be taken aback should she make an unexpected match." He kept his voice low and looked at Rafe.

"More than sixty years ago those sorry Daubney excuses for manhood kidnapped our heiress and forced marriage on her. It's our acreage that lifted them into the nobility, while our own family went wanting royal recognition. More than thirty years ago and for spite's sake, yon beauty's sire, rat-kissing nobleman that he is, bought the bride our grandsire wanted for our father."

Will's grin was the mere baring of his teeth. "I now say turnabout's fair play, especially when it also revenges our father's death. What sort of man did our king make of you, Rafe? Powerful enough to steal a daughter from her sire and do it in the less than ten days our families bide together at Haydon for this wedding? Are you strong enough to stomach getting sons on a Daubney?"

Dickon's eyes widened in horror. "I don't want to hear this, Will," he muttered, then turned toward the church. "I'm going within now, so my ears won't be assaulted by any more such nonsense."

Ignoring Dickon's quiet protest, Rafe again looked at Lady de Fraisney. With her face lifted to the sun, everything about her glowed—her skin, her hair, the jewels she wore. Here was beauty and wealth, all his for the taking. Vengeance for his father's death as well. But only if he could keep her and his life long enough to enjoy any of it. Hesitating, he looked back at his brother.

Will's smile widened into a taunt. "Aye, she's worthy of a man's desire, despite her filthy bloodline. I vow to you on my honor, brother. Take her however you can, and I, along with every man sworn to me, will stand with you to see you keep her and her lands as your own."

With Will's promise of support, new excitement stirred in Rafe. After all, what did he have to lose save either a toothless and barren old gentlewoman or poverty?

"She's mine," was all he said.

Chapter 2

Secure in her shadowy corner of the bridal chamber, Lady Katherine de Fraisney plucked a fading flower from one of the garlands decorating the curtained bed. Kate breathed in what remained of its perfume as she watched the women in the candlelit and stuffy room. Noblewomen surrounded the bride at the chamber's center, laughing, pushing, shoving, as they all tried to help Emma disrobe. Kate made a face at their disgusting antics. Shame on them, acting as if preparing a virgin bride for her deflowering were some game!

Given a choice, Kate wouldn't have been within a mile of Emma's bedding. Unfortunately, her father had dragged her to the bedchamber's door, then thrust her inside it. Not that he wanted her to participate. Nay, his only purpose was to display his newly available daughter to mothers of potential bridegrooms.

A wasted effort. Beneath a month's worth of resentment a sliver of triumph glimmered in Kate. She doubted a single woman noticed her standing in this corner, not that any of them would know her. Her twelve-year absence from this shire made her a stranger to all of them and they to her. At eight, her father sent her to the de Fraisneys, to be raised alongside her future husband. Indeed, the only people Kate knew at this wedding were her father and Sir Warin de Dapifer, her father's steward.

In the room's center, the disrobing continued. Shoes and stockings flew. No less a woman than an earl's aged widow crowed as she came away with Emma's belt. Lady Haydon laughed and caught her daughter's overgown as another gentlewoman tossed it to her.

Dressed in scarlet, Lady Amicia de la Beres, the pretty, dark-haired woman who was this wedding's only other young widow, came away with the bride's green undergown. One of Lady Haydon's younger daughters reached for Emma's chemise. Her mother stopped her.

"Nay, lovey," Lady Haydon said, "you can loosen our Emma's hair, but only a married woman or one once married should do this. Who wishes to remove my daughter's last garment?" she called out in invitation. "Is there anyone who hasn't had a hand in this yet?"

Still safe in her corner, Kate grimaced. Lady Hay-

don acted as if baring every inch of Emma to her
new husband was some great privilege and not just
another step leading to the repulsive act of copula-
tion.

Memories of her own wedding night remained
all too fresh in Kate's mind. The unrelenting noise of
the shivaree. Standing nude while strangers made
embarrassing jests, especially about Richard. Poor,
ailing Richard. He'd been naught but a frail, knock-
kneed lad of ten and four at the time, Kate all of two
years his senior.

Once they'd been well and truly humiliated,
everyone left them alone to complete a marriage
that neither wanted. Richard had bluntly informed
Kate he wouldn't touch her, then had rolled onto his
side and gone to sleep, much to Kate's relief. After
living with the de Fraisneys for so long, Richard
seemed more a brother than a husband.

When the guests awakened them the next morning to find no blood on the sheets, there'd been lectures for both Kate and Richard. Then Lady Adele,
Richard's newly widowed mother, had given Kate
explicit instructions on how to touch her young
husband's manhood to bring about her own deflowering. Even after so many years, the mortification of that conversation ached in Kate. The next
night neither she nor Richard dared risk defiance.
Kate did as instructed and touched Richard. It
worked; Kate could still remember every one of
those painful thrusts.

Nor had that been the end of it. Every day after-
ward, Lady Adele nagged Kate to do her marital

duty, always hoping her daughter-by-marriage would come with child before her sickly son departed this world for the next. All for naught. The only things left from her first marriage were her dower—the portion of the de Fraisney property Kate held for her life's time—and the hopeless desire to never again lie abed with a man.

"I think she hasn't helped yet," Lady Amicia called out, beckoning Kate out of her corner with a wave of her hand. "Come and aid us in this, my lady."

Kate's heart jolted as everyone in the room, even Emma, turned to look at her. Between her own foul memories and the strangeness of these women, she couldn't do it. "Nay, not I. Choose another," she cried.

"Are you so shy, then, Lady de Fraisney?" Lady Haydon laughed. "Too bad, for I think me it won't be long before we're undressing you. I've been watching your sire this night, interviewing man after man. At this rate he'll have you betrothed before we celebrate the last day of my Emma's event."

Kate's heart twisted. So everyone knew her father couldn't wait to be rid of her for the second time. It had been only weeks after her mother's death that her sire had arranged for the betrothals of both his daughters and sent them from Bagot to be raised by their promised husbands' families.

Now, less than one month after Kate's return home, he acted as if she were a cheese on the verge of going bad and he a cheese seller eager to foist her onto the first gullible customer through his door.

Lord, but the only time her sire spoke to her was to tell her to open her mouth so that a potential husband could see she still had all her teeth.

Someone pounded on the bedchamber's closed door. Kate started as the sound thundered into the room. "Let us in," shouted the men from the solar that lay outside the chamber.

"Oh, hold onto your cocks," the countess shouted back. "We're not ready for you yet." The old noblewoman squinted nearsightedly at Kate. "Hie now. Come out of there, child, and do your duty."

With so many painful memories of Richard and their marriage bed, Kate blanched at the word. Lady Amicia shot her fellow widow a concerned look, then caught the arm of a small, plump woman.

"Leave her be, my lady, and let's have Lady FitzHervey here do it. She's not yet had the chance to undress a bride, although she's three years wed herself. Let her remove Emma's chemise." As Lady Amicia spoke, she sent Kate a sidelong and reassuring glance. Never so grateful for a rescue in all her life, Kate offered her a tiny smile in return.

A moment later, Emma stood clothed only in the waves of her long, red-gold hair. Lady Haydon moved to the door and laid her hand upon the latch. Her plain face was flushed, while her eyes fair danced with excitement.

"Are we ready?" she asked of the women within the room.

"Aye," all but Kate shouted, as the others formed a wall between the bride and those soon to enter, so none might see Emma before the proper moment.

Lady Haydon threw open the door. Gerard d'Essex flew into the room, borne on the shouts and laughter of those who shoved their way in behind him. The bridegroom came to a halt but a foot from the nearest woman, his cap already off and his belt missing. The men ringed Gerard for what seemed but an instant. Clothing flew in every direction, then they stood back from the naked man.

"Your husband is ready, sweet bride," crooned one young swain. "Now, stand aside, you old crones, so yon wife can see her man and he, her."

At his command, the women parted. Emma's sisters lifted her hair, smoothing the long tresses over her shoulders and down her back. Bright color seeped up Gerard's neck as he gazed at his naked wife.

"I find no flaw," he said, his voice thick and quiet.

"Nor do I," Emma giggled.

Much to Kate's surprise, Gerard's shaft jerked, then began to rise of its own accord. The men hooted and stamped their feet in approval.

"How now, daughter," Lady Haydon cried out with a laugh. "It seems your sire has found you an eager husband. Remember you all I've taught? Let him kiss your lips," she started, only to be interrupted by another round of hooting, this time from both men and women.

"Upper or lower lips?" one man asked.

"Lower is better," shouted the aged countess, "for every woman has an easier time of it when a man kisses her nether lips." Her laugh was a hen's cackle.

Kate's ears burned. She looked in pity at the bride, wishing she had some comfort to offer. But Emma wasn't cringing at all. Instead, she laughed, her eyes brighter than the color on her cheeks.

"It's Gerard, not Emma, we should instruct," Lady Amicia called out, as she pointed to the bridegroom. "He needs to be reminded to stroke and caress until his wife's breath comes fast. He mustn't fail to please her, not if he wants a handsome babe nine months hence."

Despite the bright color blazing on Gerard's face, he glowered at those around him. "I know what to do."

"Do you?" Emma asked, her tone sultry. She strode to the bed and patted the mattress. "My mother has given me her instructions. If you have more to teach me, my liege, come show me now."

Gerard's eyes widened. His shaft saluted. "Out!" he shouted, already pushing his friends toward the door. The women followed, still shouting bawdy instructions.

Kate trailed at their heels, one of the last to leave. She was barely inside the solar, Lady Haydon's private parlor, which occupied the other half of the keep's upper chamber, when the door slammed behind her. It was the sign the dozen or so soldiers waiting in the solar wanted. Each one lifted his shield and began to beat upon it with his sword, shouting like a wild man.

Behind the soldiers musicians lifted their instruments. The piper teased a long, squealing belch from his pipes, the drum banged, the violist sawed his bow across his viol's strings, while the sackbut bellowed. The shivaree had begun. The noise would continue for as long as those in the solar could hold out, their object to distract the bride and groom from completing their marital duty.

Kate covered her ears and raced out the door that led from solar to hall. Here at Haydon the keep tower was too small to accommodate more than the small solar and the lord's bedchamber. Everyone else lived in the massive stone hall that sprang from the keep's side, that space being three times as long and just as tall as the tower.

The chamber was a fine construct, its walls dressed in plaster painted with a brightly colored design, save that there were no true windows. Instead, narrow, cross-shaped openings, meant for crossbows, not viewing, cut through the thick walls at regular intervals. Painted linen panels draped these defensive windows to stop drafts.

Since fabric stopped light as well as air, a bank of torches ran along each long wall and a great fire danced upon a central hearthstone to drive back the room's natural gloom. Just now a pair of jugglers were tossing their balls above the flickering flames, pretending they burned their hands each time they caught one. For all their screams, their voices were barely audible over the roar of conversation in the room, so many guests were gathered here.

To Kate's surprise, Lady Amicia waited for her just inside the hall. The young widow's smile blazed on her face, her green eyes glowing with the promise of friendship.

"Why, here you are at last," Lady Amicia said, threading her arm through Kate's. "I've been waiting all evening to meet you. Now that the bride and groom are settled and you're finally free of your sire, we have some time to become acquainted."

A little startled by this odd introduction, Kate cleared her throat. "My thanks for what you did in there. I just couldn't—" The remainder of her statement died unspoken. She wasn't going to tell a woman she didn't know about her miserable wedding night and marriage.

Lady Amicia dismissed her gratitude with a wave of her hand. "No thanks are necessary. All I knew was that you looked uncomfortable and those old biddies were going peck at you for their own amusement. I'm Lady Amicia de la Beres, but you may call me Ami, if I may call you Kate."

Delighted, Kate smiled. "If you please."

"I do, indeed," Ami said, her smile all the brighter. "I knew from the moment I saw you we were bound to be friends. Come. We'll sit where it's quieter and we can talk."

She paused to scan the hall. With the newlyweds abed, many of the older guests were saying their good-nights to their host. At last free from their elders' watchful eyes, the more youthful folk were wandering the hall as they would. With most everyone up and about, there were plenty of empty tables and benches from which to choose.

"There, back in yon corner," Ami said, pointing to a table that was far from the hall's noisiest area. "We won't hear a word anyone else says over there.

I can't speak for you, but I'm sick of all this talk of rebellion and penny-pinching kings."

"Rebellion?" Kate asked in surprise as they went. Even though she knew it was silly, she shot a glance behind her toward Haydon's door, as if some troop might appear through it this very moment. "What rebellion?"

Ami shot her a sidelong glance. "Folk said you'd been cloistered in your marriage, and I see now it must be true if you don't know that some men call for an uprising against our king." Ami shook her head. "These peers say our monarch will never be content until every knight and nobleman in the realm has an empty purse and no weapons in store.

"But enough of that," she finished, as she took a seat, then pulled Kate down on the bench beside her. "Now, we must tell each other everything," Ami commanded. "I'll start by saying I've been nigh on dying to meet someone of my own age and rank. Even though I'm only a sheriff's widow, I came into the king's custody upon my husband's death. There are a few younger ladies at his court, and all of them are above me in rank. They take great pleasure in snubbing me whenever they can."

"If the royal court is so unfriendly, why don't you leave?" Kate asked.

Ami shot her a disbelieving look. "You have been cloistered, haven't you? If I could, I would, but the king will never let me go. The warden he gave me is busy milking my dowry and widow's portion for every pence that can be wrung from my lands, sharing half of what he takes with his royal master."

Kate stared at Ami in shock. "They can do that?"

"Who's to stop them? Our John is still England's king, even if he's no longer Normandy's duke," Ami replied bitterly. "I should be grateful that he hasn't made a gift of me, as he has some of the other widows, and married me off to one of those crude and hateful hired foreign swords of his. Be grateful you're not in his custody."

Kate stared at Ami for a startled moment. If this was what the king did, then no wonder there were those who talked of rebellion. Still, Ami's call for gratitude teased a breath of scorn from her.

"Don't be thinking me the fortunate one. You heard Lady Haydon. My sire cannot wait to see me out of his home and into another marriage I don't want." As Kate spoke, her gaze shot over the hall until she located her father.

Tall and thin, Humphrey Daubney's shoulders were bowed, bearing as they did the death of two wives, his only brother and nephew, all three of his sons—one only recently, and one of three daughters. Although the hair on the top of his head was gone, the lower half of his narrow face was hidden beneath a rusty bush of a beard. It was disguise enough to make Kate wonder if the only features they shared was their coloring and their gray eyes.

She watched her sire's bearded chin wag as he spoke to a portly middle-aged man. Intensity gleamed from the upper half of her father's face. In the next instant, Lord Bagot straightened, scanning the room until he found his daughter, then pointed rudely at Kate.

She cringed. "Must he be so obvious?"

"What's he doing?" Amicia asked, looking toward Lord Humphrey.

"He's pointing at me," Kate complained. "Lord, but I can hear him now. 'So,' says he to each man he meets, 'I hear your grandsire, son, nephew, brother, is looking for a wife. Would he be interested in my daughter?' Why doesn't he spare me the torment and simply call out 'Wife for sale' for all to hear?"

Ami laughed. "Don't say that too loudly. It may give him ideas." Her amusement died into a smile filled with quiet mischief. "I vow, at least half the eligible men in England are here in this room. What say you? Why don't we choose one of them to be your husband? Then you can tell your sire which man to approach. That way you'll get a decent husband, he'll get you married and there'll be no more pointing."

"I hardly think he'd consider any man I suggest, even though the king supposedly granted me the right to choose my next husband," Kate said, without rancor. After hearing Ami's tale, perhaps it was better that her sire had paid to free her from royal custody. After what it cost him, Kate never even considered that she'd actually be the one to choose her next husband. Then again, no sensible woman beneath the age of two score with living male relatives expected to have a say when it came to her marriages.

Still, there was something tantalizing about this game. What could it hurt? She smiled at Ami. "As you will. Find me the perfect husband."

"First you must tell me the sort of man you want," her new friend replied.

With a happy sigh, Kate let her attention leap to the table where her father's steward sat with other knights his equal. "He should be a man like Tristan or Lancelot, someone slender and strong, not bulky." At three and thirty, Sir Warin de Dapifer was tall, his form long and lean. "He should own a sweet voice and be courteous to a fault." Just as Warin was. "His hair and beard should be fair." As was Warin's hair and mustache. "His eyes should be gray." Warin's eyes were blue; it was his only flaw. In all other ways, her father's steward was the perfect knight.

He was also a man Kate could never have, and not just because he was her father's employee. Warin was landless. Without income, no man could marry. The hopelessness of their love made Kate's heart fill and ache in the same glorious instant. She took the pain as proof that her love for Warin was true, as true and pure and chaste as love was meant to be.

And Warin loved her in return, their affection unsullied by carnal desires. Kate couldn't wait for the joust. Although doing so might well jeopardize his position in her father's house, she hoped Warin would ask to be her champion and wear her token.

"All that in one man?" Ami laughed and shook her head. "I'll do my best."

The sheriff's widow scanned the hall, her gaze flitting from man to man, then she caught her breath. "Oh my," she said, her voice husky, her words barely audible over the thunder of conversation and hazy echoes of the shivaree from the solar. "I think I have just the man for you."

"You do?" Kate tore her gaze from Warin to look where Ami indicated, even though she knew it wasn't possible there could be two such perfect knights in all the world.

In the open space where the wedding party had done its dancing stood a clutch of six young men. Although Kate couldn't hear them, she knew they were conversing, for heads turned from one to another in a way that marked the flow of words. It was the nearest man Ami indicated. Flickering torchlight made his fair hair gleam like gold. Shadows clung beneath the sharp lift of his cheekbones and marked the gentle curve of his brow and his nose's slight hook.

"Who is he?" Kate asked, knowing she'd been introduced to him at some time during the day. With all the folk she'd met or remet today, she couldn't recall his name.

"Lord Haydon's natural son, Sir Josce FitzBaldwin," Ami replied.

Kate gave a quiet snort. "A bastard? My father would never accept a bastard."

"He's not of low birth," Ami protested, as if she thought persuading Lord Bagot's daughter of the man's worth would have any effect on her sire. "His mother was a knight's daughter. Lord Haydon claimed him and saw to his raising. Why, he even sent Sir Josce to be raised at court and knighted by the king."

"None of that matters to my father," Kate retorted with a harsh breath. "Gentle or not, as long as Sir Josce can't inherit Haydon, my sire won't consider him."

"Well, if you won't have him, I will," Ami said, her sigh filled with longing. "I came to know him at court this spring after I first entered into the king's custody." She broke off as across the room Sir Josce threw back his head to laugh. Even from a distance, the sound was merry enough to make Kate smile in reaction.

Again Ami sighed. "No matter his birth or his worth, that is a fine-looking man, one I wouldn't at all mind taking to my bed."

"Ami!" Kate cried, shock reverberating all the way down to her toes. She reared back on the bench to stare in dismay at her new friend.

"Ami, what?" Ami asked, wicked amusement glinting in her pretty eyes. "That Sir Josce isn't fine-looking or that he's not the sort of man I should take to my bed?"

Hot color washed Kate's cheeks. "Say no more! A proper woman doesn't jest about such things," she chided, sounding every bit as harsh as had Lady Adele.

God in His heaven knew that Adele would have beaten Kate for such a comment. Adele divided women into two classes: those who controlled themselves to live pure lives, loving only chastely and from afar, and those who gave way to lust's temptation and paid the price. Kate knew what that price was, because Adele had never ceased to remind her. Either the sinner rightfully died at her kinsmen's hands or she was ruined in the eyes of the world. Of the two fates Adele claimed ruin the worse.

Ami laughed, her brown plaits sliding against the breast of her red overgown as she shook her head at Kate. "How old are you, Kate?"

Sensing there was more to this question than mere curiosity, Kate hesitated. "A full score. Almost a score and one."

"Ah, four years younger than I. And you were married how long?" Ami wanted to know.

"Four years," Kate replied, her suspicion growing that there was some sort of taunt hiding behind these questions.

"As long as that?" Ami asked, pressing a hand to her breast as if shocked. "I'd not have thought it, with you still so innocent."

"I'm not naive," Kate protested, piqued by this assessment of her character.

"As a babe," Ami replied, the corners of her mouth lifting. "If you weren't, you'd know the difference between wishing and doing. I know better than to take any man to my bed, no matter how much I might want him. That doesn't mean I can't dream. Now, since you won't have Sir Josce, what about that one?" She pointed.

Still stung by Ami's assessment of her, Kate glanced at the man Ami meant. He was pudgy and so short that his head wouldn't have topped Kate's shoulder. Relief that Ami had abandoned the dan-

gerous topic of illicit relations, even if it was for a
taunt, washed over Kate. She shook her head and
joined this new game. "Nay, too short."

"That one's probably rich, but he's a wee bit too
old," Ami said, the lift of her chin indicating a dod-
dering ancient at a nearby table. The old man
snored, his head braced on a hand. "Still, the possibility that he wouldn't be a burden to you for long
could be an asset."

As Kate laughed, Ami shook her head, rejecting
the oldster. "Nay, that's no compensation. I know
old men. My husband was over three score when he
died. A good man he was, gentle and kind, but in-
competent between the linens during the last three
years of our union and not much better before that.
If you must marry again, you should have a man
who'll be vigorous in your bed."

The very thought made Kate grimace.

"There, that's the one." Amicia pointed to the
room's center. The jugglers had finished their act,
leaving the area empty save for a page, a lad of ten
or so. "He's handsome and young."

"He's only a child," Kate protested.

"Isn't he just," Ami said, her expression smug. "I
heard your first husband was younger than you. I
thought you might feel more comfortable with another young one."

"Oh, you!" Kate chided with a laugh. "Be serious.
Show me a man I really could wed."

As Ami again studied the hall, the door to the solar opened. The musicians strode back into the
room, playing a merry romp as they came. Cries of

pleasure spilled from those within the hall, gentle and servant alike. Before another moment passed, commoner and nobleman joined hands to form a circle, the hall's raised hearthstone at its center.

When the dancers were ready, the musicians paused a beat, then the drummer found the rhythm on his tambour. As the piper joined in, the ring began to move. The sound of so many footsteps on wooden flooring thundered up into the hall's naked rafters almost loud enough to drown out the music.

"There he is, the perfect husband for you," Ami cried, a strange, sly tone to her voice. She was once again looking at the group of men around Sir Josce. With the musicians returned and the dancers using their space, the young men had moved to stand before the wooden screens that guarded the hall from door-drawn drafts.

When Kate saw the man Ami meant, her lip curled. He was the opposite of her heroic ideal. Although he was tall like Warren, his shoulders strained the seams of his gray tunic, while his gown's sleeves clung to the hard curves of his upper arms. His hair fell in loose ebony curls from beneath his brown cap to frame a wide, clear brow. There wasn't the slightest curve to his black eyebrows or his narrow nose. Unlike Warin and his clean-shaven jaw, this man wore a beard, although not the tangled mat that covered her sire's face. Instead, it was a carefully trimmed narrow band of hair that outlined his mouth then traced a bare line along the length of his strong jaw.

"He's not for me," she said, rejecting Ami's choice with a shrug.

Surprise started through her new friend's eyes. "That's all you can say about him? He's not for you?" she asked, her tone almost a prod, as if she'd expected another answer entirely. "Come, now, I know he's not golden-haired, but a man's coloring is no reason to reject him. Look again, ignoring that about him. Surely then you'll find him worthy of consideration."

To please Ami, Kate did as commanded and once more looked at the dark-haired man. He'd left his companions to saunter in a wide circle around the dancers. "Nay, I won't have him. He swaggers."

Ami blinked, frowned, then looked at the man. A moment later, her head cocked as if in serious study of the arrogant way he walked. "You're right. He does swagger," she said, as if surprised, then added, "but I can't say I find that unattractive."

"Hah," Kate crowed, relishing the opportunity to repay Ami's jab about being innocent. "Thus do you prove you've had little experience with swaggerers in your life. His strut tells me yon man will be naught but an overbearing bully. You only need watch my father walk to know I speak the truth."

Kate's gaze followed her words to where Lord Humphrey had been a moment ago. Her sire was no longer there. Instead, he was swaggering in his daughter's direction, the portly man to whom he'd been speaking at his side.

"Ach, Ami," Kate cried in mock pleading, clutching her new friend's hand. "Here comes my sire with another potential husband who'll want to count my teeth. Save me!"

"Ask and you shall receive," Ami replied with a laugh. Grabbing Kate's hand, she pulled Kate up with her as she came to her feet. "I think it's time we joined the dance."

Chapter 3

❝**I** mustn't," Kate protested, albeit feebly, as Ami pulled her away from their table. "My sire will be angry if I run from him." She started to throw a worried look in her father's direction.

"Don't look," Ami commanded, forcing Kate ahead of her, then pushing her new friend on toward the dancers. "If he catches you peering at him, he'll know you meant to escape him. If you don't turn your head, you can say in complete honesty that you didn't see him coming."

Such a subterfuge hadn't occurred to Kate. A wild laugh spilled from her at the thought of repaying her father's indifference with an innocent hoodwinking. Out of the depths of her mind came the memory of her childhood willfulness. How could she ever have forgotten that disobedience could be so enjoyable? Perhaps it was the vigorous way Lady Adele had plied her belt that had dimmed Kate's desire to misbehave.

She and Ami stopped just outside the turning ring of folk. Calling for Kate to follow, Ami plunged eagerly into their midst, catching the hands of those at either side of her. It took but an instant for her feet to match the others' steps. Lacking the same confidence in her footwork, Kate hesitated, hoping the tune and the dancers would slow a little.

"Katherine?"

Her father's call was barely louder than the music, but it was more than enough to shatter Kate's qualms. She thrust into the ring between two women. Taking their hands, she jogged to the beat while studying the steps of the woman to her right. Just as she was finding the pattern, the woman at her left released her. There was a jostling, then a man's hand closed over hers. His fingers were strong, his palm warm and callused.

Startled, Kate glanced at him, then nearly stumbled. It was the dark man, the one Ami had chosen to be her husband. Beneath his smooth ebony brows his eyes were a deep brown. He smiled at her. His teeth were even and white. Kate's breath caught as she saw now what she hadn't noticed at a distance. Dark and swaggering he might be, but Lord in heaven, he was handsome.

To Kate's surprise, as she acknowledged his attractiveness her heart set to a nervous stuttering. Perhaps it was the way the man's fingers curled around hers, owning her hand more than holding it. Or it might have been the way his gaze seemed to smolder as he watched her.

Unnerved, she forgot to concentrate on the dance. Her feet lost the music's beat and began to move to their own, discordant rhythm. Even as Kate recognized what was happening, there was nothing she could do to stop it. She was going to stumble and make a fool of herself in the process.

Just as she began to fall, the man tightened his grip on her hand and pulled her out of the dance. Those on either side of them cried out, hurrying now to close the gap. Still off balance, Kate staggered backward a few steps until her rescuer caught her by the upper arms to steady her. She came to a panting halt against him, her hands braced on his chest.

"My thanks," she offered in true gratitude. "You saved me and everyone else in the dance. I was falling."

"I know," he replied with a quiet laugh, the sound warm and deep. "And it is my pleasure to be your rescuer, Lady de Fraisney."

Kate blinked, startled that he should know her name. Clearing her throat, she asked, "Have we met?"

His brows shot up. His eyes widened. Embarrassment twisted in Kate. It was written on his face for her to read: she should know him just as he knew her. She racked her brain, but nothing came to mind. Oh Lord, but she'd collected dozens and dozens of new names this day. True, this man wasn't Warin, but surely she wouldn't have forgotten one so handsome if she'd met him.

His surprise died almost as swiftly as it was born, then his lips lifted into a quiet smile. "Come with me, my lady," he said, giving her no chance to refuse as he caught her hand and started toward the nearest wall.

"What are you doing?" Kate protested, her complaint lost in the noisy room. He stopped before one of the painted linen panels, then shoved aside the hanging. The embrasure hidden behind the fabric was more than a cloth yard deep but only wide enough for a single archer to stand comfortably as he shot at besiegers. Moonlight silvered its plastered walls, while cool night air poured through its unshuttered arrow loop.

Before Kate knew what he was about, her rescuer pushed her into the alcove ahead of him. She pivoted, turning her back to the window, but he was already in front of her, blocking her escape. The hanging dropped behind him, swinging slightly as it fell. Oily torchlight disappeared into an intimate and unseemly darkness, broken only by the moon's pale radiance. That weak glow touched the man's brow, the line of his perfect nose and the bow of his lips, leaving the rest of his face in shadow. His eyes were bare gleams.

Kate scowled at him, not caring that he most likely couldn't read the expression on her face any better than she could his. May God chide her a fool! She'd let this man's handsome face so boggle her that she'd forgotten Lady Adele's lessons. Any man who wasn't a chivalrous knight was a lecher. Indeed, even a usually courteous man might give way to temptation and press untoward caresses on his ladylove if she wasn't vigilant against potential sin.

Crossing her arms, Kate put what barrier she could between them. "Just what do you think you're doing?" she demanded.

"A moment is all I ask, my lady." His voice was smooth. He smiled, his white teeth bright in the alcove's darkness. "That and a bit of privacy in which to introduce myself. I'm Sir Rafe—Rafe Godsol."

It didn't escape Kate that he offered her both his given name and its more intimate form. That was to be expected of a man bent on seduction. What did surprise her was the flicker of recognition at the back of her brain as she heard his family name. When whatever she should have remembered about his surname didn't leap to mind, she tapped her toe in impatience.

"Aye, well, you've had your moment, and we're introduced," she said. "Now stand aside so I can depart."

A startled breath left him. His smile was brilliant against the night's blackness. "What, so quickly? Stay a moment longer, my lady, and share a bit of conversation with me. I'd like to know you better."

Kate's irritation soared. What sort of fool did he think her? Indeed, Lady Adele had warned her most strictly against conversations in private places, saying such meetings only led to sin.

"You'll stand aside or I'll scream." This threat was the tool her former mother-by-marriage claimed worked best in such instances.

It was sheer pretense. Adele believed a woman need only scream when accosted by the crudest and most callous of men. Gentlemen, however forward they might be, were still gentlemen. As such, they would behave honorably when a lady made it clear she wanted nothing to do with them, although said lady might need to prod them into recalling their manners.

"Now, my lady, there's no need for that," Rafe Godsol protested, sounding confused, as if he hadn't understood her perfectly clear threat. "S'truth, it's naught but conversation I intend."

Kate's mouth tightened. A promise from a lecher was worth nothing, especially when the man didn't move an inch. Not only was this Rafe Godsol a swaggerer, he was a gentleman with no manners at all. To add weight to her threat, she drew a deep breath. It was sheer mummery. She had no intention of screaming, not when that meant being found intimately closeted with a man.

Rafe made a sound that mingled surprise and panic, then threw his arms around her and yanked her close to him. Kate's breath left her lungs in a startled huff as she hit his chest. His arms tightened around her.

Bracing her hands against him, Kate shoved. Rafe Godsol was no gentleman at all! When she filled her lungs again, it was for a true scream.

Before so much as a peep left her lips, his mouth took hers. Kate froze. The taste of the night's sweet wine lingered on his lips. His skin smelled of soap.

She felt the scrape of his narrow beard against her cheek. Beneath her yet tense hands his heart pounded. His lips were soft and warm.

Caught in the tumble of these sensations, Kate's eyes shut of their own accord. Of the few kisses she and Richard had shared none had ever felt like this. In the next moment, his mouth shifted a little atop hers. That wee movement woke something warm and hidden within her. Heat, wondrous, glorious heat, followed. With it, Kate forgot she should escape Rafe. Everything outside the alcove—the music, the dancers, her father, the possibility of another guest discovering them in this private place—disappeared. All that mattered was the astonishment of this feeling.

Her arms relaxed. Her hands slipped up the front of his tunic, feeling the strength of his chest beneath her palms. She laced her fingers at his nape. His hair was thick and soft where it curled against her knuckles.

Rafe's arms tightened, drawing her closer still until her breasts pressed against his chest. Pleasure washed like a wave over Kate. Rafe made a quiet sound deep in his chest, then his mouth began to move on hers, the sensation at once gentle and filled with longing. With that, Kate lost herself to him. Nothing else mattered, save that he never stop what he was doing.

In the corner of Rafe's mind least affected by the incredible woman in his arms, he chided himself for a fool. Dragging the daughter of his enemy behind this curtain was surely the most idiotic thing he'd ever done. After all, one shout from her, and any chance of stealing her away from her father died. Rafe doubted he'd remain at the wedding long after Lord Humphrey found his available heiress closeted with a Godsol. That was, if Rafe lived through that discovery.

Of course, none of this would be happening had Lady de Fraisney recognized him as a Godsol. The instant he realized she didn't know him, all he could think was to confide his name to her in privacy. How he imagined this might change her hatred of his family was beyond him just now, but it seemed the thing to do at the time.

To his complete astonishment, Katherine de Fraisney, nee Daubney, hadn't even raised a brow upon hearing his family name. Instead, as impossible as it seemed, she'd taken insult at his offer of conversation, acting as if he'd threatened rape! God save him, but his heart had nearly dropped through the floor when she drew breath to shout.

All of which was why he'd kissed her. In his panic, it was the only way he could think of to stop her scream. It wasn't, however, why he was kissing her now.

This kiss, which should have been the second most foolish thing Rafe had ever done and might still cost him his life, had gone wonderfully awry. Kate Daubney fair melted in his arms. Behind the dazing sensation of her breasts pressed against his chest, a flicker of confusion woke.

Aye, melt she had, even going so far as to put her

arms about his neck. But now, when she should have stroked and caressed in encouragement, she stood passive and still against him. Indeed, she acted more like an innocent virgin than a widow long familiar with the ways of bedplay and husbands.

No matter how she reacted, Rafe needed to feel more of her against him. Pulling her closer, he shifted until the mound of her womanhood rested against his shaft. Even with the layers of their clothing between them, the sensation was strong enough to make him shudder. Kate made a quiet sound. Her arms tightened around his neck, then she lifted herself against him.

Rafe groaned. It didn't matter that she didn't follow this with an inviting touch. There was still no mistaking her intent. She wanted him, just as much as he wanted her.

Catching her face in his hands, he pressed kisses to her cheeks, her brow, the tip of her nose. She made a mewling sound of protest, then turned her head to catch his mouth with her own. Rafe's knees weakened at the need that flowed from her to him. If there'd been a way to take her from Haydon through the arrow slit behind her, he'd have done it in a heartbeat. The sooner he married his enemy's daughter, the better for them both.

Chapter 4

⌣⌣

"Katherine!"

Her father's bellow rose from well within the hall beyond the curtain, the sound of it barely loud enough for Kate to hear above the thrumming crescendo of the ending dance. Even as quiet as his call was it still punctured the haze of sensation that held her in thrall. Kate's eyes opened. From this angle, she could see the forceful thrust of Rafe's nose and the fringe of his eyelashes splayed against his cheeks. Although her lips still clung to his, she frowned. What in God's name was she doing kissing this stranger?

As if Rafe sensed the change in her, he made a quiet sound that mingled pleading and disappointment, then cupped her face in his hands. His palms

41

were warm and hard against her skin. The stroke of his thumbs over her cheeks sent another wave of heat flowing through Kate. She forgot he was a stranger and that the only thing standing between her and her sin's exposure was a single curtain. Her eyes closed, her mouth again softening beneath his as she lost herself once more to the pleasure he made in her.

"Katherine! For God's sake, where are you?" Her father's voice boomed into the alcove from just beyond the flimsy drape.

Kate jerked away from Rafe. Mary save her, her sire was about to catch her behaving like some light-skirt. Lady Adele's promise of death at her father's hand tore through her. Instantly, Rafe grabbed her back to him, shifting so his greater bulk would shield her from the hall should the hanging move. At the same time, he pulled her head down into the curve of his shoulder, knocking her headgear askew as he did so.

"Sh," he breathed in warning.

As if she needed to be warned! Trembling, Kate cowered against him and prayed for heavenly mercy. A futile exercise. God didn't grant favors to a woman skipping blithely down disobedience's road toward fornication.

For what seemed like years, she listened to the drum of Rafe's heart against her ear and the rush of breath into his lungs. Outside the alcove, the musicians brought the romp to a screeching halt. Dancers and listeners alike cheered and stomped in appreciation.

"Katherine! Katherine de Fraisney! Where are you?" her father called again, his voice more distant this time.

Kate's head whirled in relief. Perhaps God was a more forgiving man than she thought. Now all she need do was slip from this place without her sire seeing her, and no one would be the wiser over the wrong she'd done. She straightened in Rafe's embrace.

"Release me," she commanded in a whisper.

"Must I?" Rafe asked, with a quiet, shaken laugh, even as his embrace loosened. "I vow, my lady, I'd rather die than live another moment without you next to me. Your kiss leaves me as weak-kneed as a babe."

Shame painted hot streaks across Kate's cheeks. How tactless of him to jest about a moral lapse that she swore here and now she would never, ever repeat. "Not my kiss, but yours. You kissed me," she retorted, squarely placing blame where it belonged.

"I may have started it, but I think me it was you who set us afire," he replied, laughter heavy in his quiet voice.

Kate frowned at such nonsense and lifted his hands off her hips. "Say no more," she commanded. "Only stand sideways so I can pass you. You will wait here a decent length of time before following," she told him, in case he hadn't the sense to understand the need for such caution.

"But of course, my lady," he replied, shifting to the side and holding up his hands as if to show he had no intention of keeping her.

Kate's frown deepened. There was something in his voice that said he was laughing at her. For no reason Kate could name his amusement reminded her of Ami's charge of innocence. Stung, Kate lifted her chin and eased past him. With great care, she peered around the hanging's edge, looking in the direction from which her father's voice had last come. Lord Humphrey stood a goodly distance off to her right, his back to the alcove as he scanned the hall for his missing daughter. Relief surged through her, strong enough to make her vision swim.

"There you are! I wondered where you'd gone to ground," Ami cried from only a foot or so to Kate's left.

With a startled yelp, Kate sprang from the alcove and whirled to face her new friend. Ami's face was yet flushed from dancing. Beneath her veil, fine tendrils of brown hair had escaped her plaits to coil against her gleaming throat. As she eyed Kate, her smooth brows rose. "You've lost your cap, Kate. It's dangling to one side of your head."

Guilt made Kate snatch off her headgear, then scramble for some explanation, only to realize she stood but a hair's breadth from catastrophe. If Ami saw Rafe appear, there'd be no explaining any of this save for Kate to confess she was a lightskirt when she wasn't. Truly, she wasn't. She grabbed her friend's arm.

"Come, Ami, back to our table, where you can help me repin my cap," she said, frantic to lead the woman away from the embrasure.

Ami's body turned to follow Kate, but her head

still looked toward the wall. The young widow's eyes widened. Her mouth opened. Kate looked behind her and groaned. Sure enough, Rafe had slipped from the embrasure, his own cap in hand. With his back to the closed curtain, he eyed the two women in front of him.

"Lady de la Beres," Rafe said to Ami, offering a brief bow as if nothing at all were amiss.

Hopelessness washed over Kate. This was the end of her friendship with Ami. No good woman kept company with a lightskirt.

Ami whirled on Kate, her expression alive with fright. "You were in there with him?" she cried, then shot a frantic glance in Lord Humphrey's direction. When she saw Kate's sire had his back to them, she breathed out in noisy relief, then once more looked at Kate. "Are you mad?"

"Mad?" Kate asked. What had madness to do with being a lightskirt? In confusion, she glanced at Rafe.

As their gazes met, the corners of his mouth quirked upward in amusement. Although Kate couldn't say why, his smile teased a strange little laugh from her. The thought that Ami might be right filled her; insanity was all the explanation she needed for what had happened between her and Rafe Godsol. Indeed, it seemed she was yet mad, for, right or wrong, she wouldn't much mind kissing him again.

That thought struck Kate like a blow. She wasn't mad. She was a betrayer! Rafe wasn't the man she loved. She shot a glance toward the table where

Warin sat not but a few yards distant. Her relief when she saw Warin had his back to her died into a new round of guilt. It should be Warin's kisses she craved, not this stranger's. Lord, but Warin would never forgive her if he learned she'd given to another man what she'd steadfastly refused him. It was her need to see that no hint of her wrongdoing ever reached her love that brought Kate around to once more face Ami.

"It isn't what you think," Kate lied, her words all but tumbling one over the other as she wrung her cap and veil between her hands. "Yon gentleman but saved me from stumbling in the dance. Thinking to give me a bit of quiet and cool in which to recover, he led me to yon embrasure. I found the place too intimate for my taste and left. That was when my cap came loose, I suppose," she finished, only to realize too late that her words were more truth than disguise.

"I mean, my cap slipped when I stumbled during the dance, of course," she amended herself hastily and shot a glance at Rafe, hoping he'd say something to support her tale.

Instead, he gawked at her, his face the very picture of surprise. Irritation cut through Kate. Honestly, if she ever again let herself be swept away by a man's touch, she'd first see to it that the man wasn't a halfwit.

"Oh, but this is all my fault," Ami cried, her face twisting in regret. "Truly, Kate, I meant no harm, but once I realized you didn't know who he was, I only thought to twit your sire a little. I never thought you'd approach him or that he'd—" she broke off and looked at Rafe, then cleared her throat and again looked at Kate. "Or that the two of you would—" again she stopped, this time to draw a calming breath. "Mary save me, Kate," she cried out, "you're a Daubney. You must stay away from him. He's a Godsol!"

Hearing Rafe's family name spoken for a second time stirred deeper ripples in Kate's memory. Godsol. Suddenly she was six again and standing in Bagot's tomb. Her uncle, his son and two of her three brothers were there, laid out upon catafalques, their faces waxen and still in death. They'd lost their lives in an attack upon Godsol property when the Daubneys tried to retrieve stolen stock.

In her childish memory there was no sign of her mother; Kate rarely remembered her, and when she did think on her, her dam's features were those of Lady Adele. Instead, it was her father's image that was clear as ice. He knelt in the chapel, great rending sobs shaking his body as he grieved for those he'd loved and lost.

Feeling as if she were trapped in some horrible dream, Kate shifted to look at the man she'd just kissed. His mouth flattened, the gleam left his eyes. "Godsol," she said, her voice barely loud enough for him to hear over the noise in the hall. "You're a Godsol, one of those who killed my uncle and my brothers."

His expression emptied until his eyes were as black as all sin. "That is who I am, Sir Rafe Godsol, youngest son of Sir John Godsol, just as you are

Kate Daubney, daughter to Lord Humphrey of Bagot, the man who killed my father, and the great-granddaughter of the man who stole our heiress and our property."

With his words, the horror of what she'd done started in Kate's toes and grew until it filled every inch of her. By the Sacred Heart! She'd kissed one of her father's most hated enemies. Nay, she'd not only kissed him, she'd enjoyed every second of it and wanted more. This was worse than behaving as a lightskirt. This was worse than losing Warin's love. If her father ever learned of what she'd done and felt, he'd slit her throat for certain.

"Katherine!" her sire shouted from somewhere beyond the hall door.

Fear pricked Kate like a knife. She whirled, needing to be as far from Rafe Godsol as she could possibly be. "I come, my lord," she called, and raced away from certain death.

Chapter 5

The instant he heard Lord Humphrey's call, Rafe shifted out of his enemy's line of sight. There was no need to borrow trouble. As it was, he was grateful he couldn't see Kate's face as she left him. After the sweetness of their kiss, her horror when she finally recognized his name had been unnerving.

At the center of the crowded room, the musicians began another tune, this one slow and stately. Yet standing before him, Lady Amicia put her hands on her hips and glowered. The urge to laugh took Rafe by surprise, and he struggled to catch back his smile. Lady Amicia wore the same look his old nurse had used whenever she'd chided him.

Had it been any other woman, Rafe would have

ignored her, but Amicia was almost a friend. During the first month the sheriff's widow had dwelled at court, Rafe harbored hopes of marriage to the young, well-to-do, pretty woman.

Over the duration of his pursuit, he'd come to know her as lively, interesting, and sensible. Any expectation of wedlock was destroyed after his dearest friend, Josce FitzBaldwin, discovered the king found the orphaned Amicia's dower and dowry too profitable ever to allow her remarriage. That hadn't stopped Rafe from seeking Amicia out on more relaxed court occasions for conversation's sake.

"Why is Lady de Fraisney lying to me?" Amicia demanded now, trading on their familiarity to pose so intimate a question.

"Is she lying?" Rafe asked. Amicia could chide, but that didn't mean he needed to admit wrongdoing. Not that Rafe didn't want to know as badly as Amicia why his Kate was telling tales.

After her threat to scream, he'd fully expected her to shout out an accusation of assault, not shield what they'd done. That she tried to conceal it could only mean Kate was protecting someone or something. God knew it wasn't him. Then who? More importantly, was there a way he could use Kate's lie to aid him in taking her?

Eyes narrowed, Amicia made a rude sound. "You know very well she is. There was no conversation in yon alcove. Nay, she looks well kissed. No surprise that, since 'twas you with her in there."

"Do you suggest I've misused Lady de Fraisney,

when the lady herself said we did no wrong?" Rafe asked in the pretense of insult. "Why should you make such a charge? Was I ever aught but respectful toward you?"

"Of course you were respectful to me. I'm under the king's protection," Amicia replied sharply, even as chagrin for the affront she thought she'd done him danced across her face. Worry followed, creasing her smooth brow.

"You know as well as I that it doesn't matter what you did, only who she is," Amicia continued. "And don't tell me you didn't recognize her, for I know you better than that. Was it your plan to ruin Lord Haydon's festivities with violence? The truce between your families would shatter if her father knew what had just occurred. Heaven help us, but her sire might well kill her for being alone with you."

This was a reminder of how careful Rafe must be to succeed in winning himself a wife and giving Will the vengeance he needed against the Daubneys. Rather than deter him, it only fired his resolve to keep Kate for himself. As for Amicia, she had no right to an explanation, so she got none.

"Why do you complain?" Rafe asked instead. "Nothing untoward happened, and there was no violence to mar this evening. Perhaps you're the one seeking to make trouble where there is none."

Amicia stamped her foot in frustration. "You always turn my words back on me when you don't want to answer my questions," she complained.

"Well, this time it matters naught what you admit. I'm the one who must take the blame for what happened here."

She sent a quick glance in the direction Kate had gone. "Fie on me for playing so poor a trick on her and sending her your way. I truly never thought she'd tolerate so bold a man as you, upright innocent that she is."

Rafe frowned as Amicia's words recalled the passive way Kate had accepted his kiss. "How can you claim innocence for her when she's been a wife?"

"Poor thing," Amicia said, her quiet words only audible because in that instant the music fell away into the lonely trill of the pipe. "Married she was, but there are those here who say her childish husband spurned her."

The surprise that shot through Rafe was sharp enough to tease him into throwing a quick glance at Kate. She and her father now stood near the hall door. Lord Bagot had his back to his enemy's son. Rafe could see Kate's face just beyond her sire's shoulder. With her cap yet held in her hands, the torchlight found deep red highlights in her hair. The light's golden glow outlined the gentle curves of her profile. Could she truly be the innocent Amicia claimed?

"Turn your eyes away, sir knight," Amicia snapped, her voice hard. "I read your face well enough to see where your thoughts drift. She's not for you, and you know it. Worse, your attention will only lead to tragedy."

"What harm can there be in looking?" Rafe

started to protest, only to be interrupted by Josce FitzBaldwin.

"Why, Rafe, here you are at last," Rafe's dearest friend called from a few feet distant. "I've been looking all over Haydon for you."

Rafe glanced at Josce, then snorted. Josce was lying; it wasn't him his friend sought. Rafe's foster brother's gaze was fixed on Amicia. Amicia watched the tall, fair-haired knight no less intently in return.

"Now that you've found me, what is it you want?" Rafe asked, glancing from one to the other. Josce found Amicia endlessly interesting, mostly because he knew Amicia had formed an affection for him, and he wasn't one to refuse a woman's attention, especially one with an inheritance.

If there had been anything Rafe could have done to win Amicia and her wealth for Josce, even if it meant turning his own back on her, he'd have done it, such was Rafe's love for his friend. More than any other men at court, he and Josce were irrevocably bound to each other. Between Rafe's poverty and Josce's bastardy, the two of them were the least among men of their rank. Only on the tilting field, mounted on their warhorses with lances in hand, did they escape that lowly estate. He and Josce were accorded the most powerful jousters among the king's men, some said in all England, now that the earl of Pembroke was an old man.

Josce's gaze never shifted from Amicia. He smiled. Lady Amicia blushed prettily. "Mary, but I seem to have forgotten, Rafe," Josce said.

Rafe loosed a quiet laugh. "Is that so?"

His words stirred Amicia into finally offering the newcomer the appropriate quick bob. "Good even to you, Sir Josce. It's a fine wedding your lord father stages for your lady sister." Her voice was soft now, all sign of shrewishness gone.

"Indeed, it is," Josce said, catching the widow's hand to bow low over it. "I shall convey your compliments to Lady Haydon."

Rafe grinned at such courtly posturing. As Josce straightened, he shifted to stand beside the widow. She tucked her hand into the crook of his arm and once more gazed up at him, fair moonstruck. It was a triumphant grin Josce sent Rafe's way before he again looked at the sheriff's widow.

"My lady, since it seems my friend has failed to ask you, I won't be shy. Will you share this dance with me?"

Lady Amicia's smile could have melted wax. "It will be my pleasure." She caught herself to throw a chiding glance in Rafe's direction. "But I won't go until you tell yon Godsol I'll be watching to see he behaves himself over the next days."

Rafe's brows lifted. There was no misunderstanding the warning. Amicia thought he meant to seduce Kate and would not stand for her friend's misuse. There'd be no ally for him here, not that he expected one.

Josce bent a pitying look in Rafe's direction. "My lady, I fear any scold you send in his direction is wasted effort. Years, I've lectured our Rafe over his behavior, all to no avail."

That made Rafe laugh out loud. "The blind leading the blind, my friend," he said.

Josce's haughty sniff at the jab was all pretense. "Come, my lady, we're already late joining the dance."

"Then we'll just have to dance a second time to make up for what we've missed," the widow said, leaning coyly against her escort's arm as he led her away from Rafe.

With their departure, Rafe's attention returned to Kate where she stood with her sire near the door. Innocent, Amicia called her, and innocent she was. Excitement woke deep in him. That Kate was unschooled in the ways of love he no longer doubted. The proof was in the guileless way she'd shifted her body against his and the fact that she'd offered no caresses of her own.

Rafe grinned. Unschooled, aye, but not unwilling, not with so much passion in her kiss. By God, her maidenhead aside, it would be he, Rafe Godsol, and no other man, who made Kate Daubney a woman.

As his determination to own her grew, Rafe's gaze shifted to the man beside her, Sir William of Ramswood. It didn't take a scholar to recognize that the shire's newest widower was ogling the lift of Kate's breasts beneath her silken gowns while pretending to listen to her. Rafe sneered. If that paunchy wreck was the best Bagot could do for his daughter, Kate would likely leap to join a Godsol in secret marriage, enemy or not.

"Rafe!" The sound of his shouted name echoed

up into the hall's rafters. Rafe turned to find Sir Simon de Kenifer motioning to him from the opposite side of the room.

"Come join us," Simon called. "We've emptied our own purses dicing and would now like a chance at yours."

Rafe shot a final glance at Kate. Now that she knew who he was, it wasn't likely he'd have another chance to approach her this evening. Not that it was necessary; nay, he'd done enough for one night, and the morrow offered plenty of opportunity. As tradition demanded, the newlyweds would cling close to their chamber for all of the next day. To honor them, the wedding guests would likewise remain close to Haydon. Baldwin of Haydon planned a short hawking excursion into the nearby woods, with a picnic and dancing to follow.

Again Rafe smiled. Summer foliage was thick. The possibility woke of luring Kate far enough away from the others to kiss her once more if not steal her outright.

Content, he made his way to where the remainder of his companions stood. "Dicing already?" he asked, as he came to a halt beside them. "I thought you meant to wait a day or two before you lost your riches."

"We've no choice," Simon said, shooting him a sidelong glance. "There's nothing else for us to do, now that so many here know we serve the king. A good half of Lord Haydon's guests shun us, so busy are they plotting rebellion against our monarch. The other half only want to convince us they're yet loyal liege men, so we might carry the tale to our royal master. Lord, but we grew so tired of listening to them, we were almost sorry that we begged leave to return from France for this event."

Beneath the fringe of Simon's light brown hair, sly amusement gleamed in the young knight's pale eyes. A grin pricked at the corners of his mobile mouth. "That left us naught to do but wager over what you're watching from the shadows." He paused a beat. "So just what were you watching?"

"What am I ever watching?" Rafe asked with a shrug, knowing full well past behavior would lead his friends to assume he once more planned a seduction. Not even they would think him bold enough to plot the theft of the Daubney heiress.

His companions hooted. "What, indeed, save some rich man's wife?" laughed dark Hugh d'Aincourt from beside Simon, pouncing upon the bait left for him. It was whilst the king battled his Welsh son-by-marriage a few years back that Hugh had won the thick scar across his cheek. Rather than detract from his appearance, it lent Hugh's otherwise dour and harsh face a rakish air.

Alan FitzOsbert gave a disgusted shake of his head. "You'll die a castrated man, my friend." Although his fine fair hair and gray eyes made Alan the darling of those ladies at court addicted to tales of courtly love, he was so cautious in his behavior that he'd earned the pet name Priest from his companions. Alan wanted desperately to become a knight Templar, a celibate warrior. Unfortunately, he was his father's only son and was expected to breed up heirs for the family line.

"Rafe will never be castrated, Priest, because he'll never be caught," Stephen de St. Valery retorted, his green eyes merry. He rattled the die in his cupped hands. With his easy nature and ever open purse, Stephen could always be counted on for a drink, a game or a song. Now, this youngest son of an earl offered his friends a broad grin. "Being chased by so many husbands has made our Rafe quick enough to outrun Death, if need be."

Stephen's jest teased Rafe into shooting a final glance over his shoulder. It wasn't Kate he looked for this time, but her sire. If Death waited for him these next days, he'd surely wear the guise of Lord Humphrey of Bagot. Both father and daughter were gone, no doubt retired for the night.

Rafe looked back at his friends, only to have excitement over the morrow once more tug at his heart. It was enough to make him reckless. Opening his purse, he took out a couple of his precious pence to show them to his friends.

"What say you, Stephen?" he demanded. "Do you intend to toss those bones or only rattle them in your hands all night?"

Chapter 6

A cock crowed, then another and another. Geese honked. Sheep bleated, anxious to be milked. Kate groaned and pulled her bedclothes over her head, praying for another hour's sleep.

It was hopeless. One after another, maids sang out their good morrows, while noble guests began calling for their servants. Why, even under all the linens with her eyes clenched shut, Kate could feel the tent walls gleam bright red and blue with newborn sunlight.

Throwing back the blankets, she stared at the fabric ceiling over her head. Like the majority of Haydon's better heeled guests, Lord Humphrey came to this wedding with his own tent and set up camp in the castle's grassy exterior yard. Sleeping out of doors was no hardship in midsummer. Indeed, those camping in the bailey were better off by far than the guests who had to sleep in the hall, all of them packed into that airless room like herring in a barrel.

From outside the tent's flimsy wall a few feet from Kate's cot, one of her father's men-at-arms cleared the dreams from his throat and spat. His voice was a wordless rumble as he muttered his greeting to the few of Bagot's soldiers who accompanied them to this event. As his men stirred, so did their lord. From the opposite side of the blanket that partitioned the tent's interior into two smaller chambers, Lord Humphrey's cot creaked. He groaned, the sound rusty and pain-filled.

"Is it dawn already, Peter?" Bagot's lord asked of his manservant.

"It is, my lord," the man replied. A rustle of straw said that Peter was rolling away his pallet for the day.

"Then I'll bid you a good morrow in our Lord's love," Humphrey said in somber greeting to his man. He followed this with a brusque "Help me to sit up."

There was more rustling, this time of linen. Lord Humphrey released another pained sound. The servant clucked in concern. "Are your joints so bad, then, my lord? I thought with Haydon being drier than Bagot you'd have less aching here. Need you more of that salve?"

"Not now, Peter. Mayhap tonight," her lord father replied, his tone so warm, so filled with gratitude for his servant's concern, that Kate came upright on her cot with a start to stare at the blanket that separated father and daughter. She hadn't known her sire capable of such an emotion.

"For now, all I need is water for washing," Lord Humphrey went on, his voice yet friendly.

"Then that's what you shall have, my lord," Peter said.

The sound of the tent flap opening followed, then there was nothing but quiet. Kate eyed the blanket partition. Dawn's light pricked through its open weave to scatter tiny yellow squares on her side of the tent. She gnawed on her lip in consideration. Was a little concern for her father's ills all it took to win the lord of Bagot's affection?

Although the greater part of her chided that this was naught but foolish thinking, that the way her father treated his servants had nothing to do with how he treated his daughter, Kate's need to postpone her next marriage was the stronger. If she could but end the surly silence that lived between them, perhaps she could persuade him there was no need to hurry that ceremony. Throwing off her blankets, she shrugged into her bedrobe, then went to carefully pull back the dividing drapery.

Sunlight streamed through the tent's opening, bright enough to make her squint. The braided rush matting that served as their floor glowed golden. At the back of the tent, the brass bindings on her father's armor chest glinted. Encased in a nubby sheet, Peter's rolled pallet leaned against the chest's end. A single jointed stool, a seat easily dismantled for travel, braced the pallet in place.

Her father yet sat on the edge of his cot, the tangled linens draping the lower half of his naked body. A long scar marked his bare chest from shoulder to waist, its lips raised and uneven. It was an old mark, having long ago lost its lividity. Her sire's yet nightcapped head was bowed as if in prayer, his beard resting against his chest.

If her father didn't notice her, his favorite hound did. The burly beast's ears pricked as it considered her. Perched nearby atop its T-shaped roost, her sire's hawk turned its head from side to side, knowing she was there even if it couldn't see her. The tiny bells on its blinding hood tinkled with its movement.

The sound stirred Lord Humphrey from his musings. Sighing, he lifted his head. His expression was quiet, his face relaxed as he met his daughter's gaze.

For the briefest of instants, his gray eyes came alive with longing, then hardened into icy slate. "Back," he snarled so sharply that Kate nigh on flew backward into her own half of the tent. The partition dropped into place, leaving her blinking in the sudden dimness, too startled to feel the sting of yet another rejection.

"Albreda, your charge escapes you," her father called, his voice raised, although there was no need to shout. "Rise and see to her, else I'll have you beaten for dereliction of your duty."

On her pallet at the other side of Kate's cot, Albreda came upright with a startled snort. Over the past night, thick dark hair had escaped the maid's plaits to tumble around her meaty shoulders. Eyes wide in her fleshy face, the middle-aged woman glanced frantically around her until she found Kate.

"She's here, my lord," Albreda cried out in relief.

"I know she's there, you fool," Lord Humphrey retorted in irritation. "Wake up. The dawn's come. See that my daughter's dressed appropriately for hawking."

Kate's shoulders tensed until they were tighter than a catapult's rope. Her heart felt just as twisted. "She, her, my daughter," she muttered. "Speak to me," she demanded of her sire. Coward that she was, she kept her voice too low for even Albreda to hear. Her father was the only man on the earth's face with the right to raise his hand to her, and Kate wasn't interested in finding out what he might do if provoked.

"Aye, my lord," the maid replied breathlessly as she came to her feet.

Having never disrobed the previous night, all Albreda need do to prepare for the day was straighten her blue gowns and tie on her headscarf. "Stay here while I fetch your water, my lady," she commanded, her chiding look clearly blaming Kate for her own scolding. Still barefooted, the maid exited around the dividing drapery.

Kate made a face at Albreda's back. God forbade a daughter from hating her sire rejecting her, but the good Lord had nothing to say about despising maidservants for their disrespect. Indignation swiftly devolved into a homesick longing deep enough to make Kate's lips quiver.

Oh, to be back in the de Fraisney household and have sweet Maud at her side once more. Maud, Kate's maid for all the days she'd lived with the de Fraisneys, had been both friend and confidante. When Lady Adele offered Maud to Lord Humphrey, Kate's sire had refused. Humphrey of Bagot said he'd have no strangers in his home.

Kate's jaw tightened. God knew her sire hadn't lied when he told Lady Adele as much. Why, he couldn't wait to be rid of his daughter, a woman who was as great a stranger to him as hapless Maud.

Wishing she could scream out her frustration but not ready to discover just how her father would re-act to such an outburst, Kate dropped down on the corner of her cot and rubbed at her aching brow. The day loomed before her, one long torment. With no hawk of her own, there would be nothing for her to do but watch others hunt. And the picnic promised to be only more of last night—prospective husbands being shoved at her throughout the thing.

"Good morrow, my lord." Warin de Dapifer's deep voice flowed through the blanket partition as his footsteps marked his entry into the tent.

Excitement chased away Kate's headache and her depression. Her heart filling with the affection she bore Warin, she shifted on her cot to peer desper-ately through the blanket's weave. The smallest glimpse of her dear love and all would be right with the world.

"I hear Lord Haydon's foresters have herons for our hawks this day," Warin said to his lord. "At last, a prey worthy of your bird."

"Aye, so it is," Lord Humphrey replied with a pleased grunt.

The squeak of the cot as Bagot's lord came to his feet gave way to a fond murmuring. Again the bells on his hawk's hood loosed their delicate chimes. Kate didn't need to see her father to know he was stroking his bird's feathers. Resentment simmered. What evil could she have done her sire before her eighth year that would cause him to give more care to a bird than he spent on his own flesh and blood?

"I'd expect nothing less of Haydon," her father said after a moment's pause. "He's a good host, careful of the entertainments he offers. Have you news from Bagot? Nay, what news could there be," he went on, sourly answering himself, "when those foul Godsols are here? My property will be safe from attack for as long as I know where they are."

Guilt and not a little fear shot through Kate, a reminder of just how close she'd come to disaster last night. Never again, she vowed to herself. It was an easy promise to keep. Now that she knew who Rafe was, she'd stay as far from him as possible.

"Nay, my lord," Warin replied, "there's no news. I only thought to pass on what I'd heard about the day's hawking." As he spoke, the drapery separating him from Kate rippled as if he'd touched it. His shoe scraped on the rush matting near its hem. "That, and I meant to inform you we're at your convenience, ready to escort you to the hall to break your fast."

"As you should be, Sir Warin," her father said, a touch of laughter filling his voice. "As you should be."

"My lord," Warin said, the simple statement signaling his intention to depart. Disappointment shot through Kate. He was leaving, and all she'd seen of him was his shadow against the curtain.

Again his shoes scuffed on the matting. The blanket jerked. A wee packet of parchment shot beneath it to bounce unevenly across the flooring and come to rest upright where one length of mat met another.

A note! With a happy gasp, Kate snatched it up, then unfolded it, her fingers trembling with excitement.

Warin had a careful, neat hand. The ache of her loneliness and rejection eased at the very sight of it.

My dearest lady,

Another day without your goodness to enlighten this poor sinner is too long to be borne. Take pity upon me, my sweet saint. Once the hawking is done and we're at our victuals, I will retreat into the woodlands. I pray you, follow me. When you find me pining for you 'neath some shady tree, come ease my misery as only your kind words can.

Yours in God's love and mine,
Sir Warin de Dapifer

Kate's exhilaration diminished. Adele's warnings against such intimacy with any man, especially a courtly lover, clamored. Warin wanted her to join him in the wild woods beyond all sight of the others, when they'd never before met in private. Why now, when he'd always before complimented her on her insistence that they remain within sight if not earshot of witnesses?

What was wrong with her? This was Warin, the man she loved. Unlike some men she had the misfortune to know, if Warin wished to meet with her, it wouldn't be to force unwanted kisses on her.

Nay, Warin would never suggest a tryst. All he wanted, nay all he needed, was the simple joy of her presence. The proof of that was in her hand. Kate again studied his last words. For a seducer to claim to love her as he loved God was sacrilege.

Not that any of this mattered. Disappointment ate at Kate as she folded the note back into its tiny square. Her father's plans for her didn't include allowing half an hour's private time to spend with a man she could never wed.

Then a sly and daring thought followed, the sort she hadn't had in years. She could escape her sire for a time, just as she had last night. With the right excuse, he'd be none the wiser as to where she went or what she did. The echoes of last night's wild exhilaration raced through Kate, strong enough to make her smile. No wonder the priests spoke of temptation's lure. Sin was thrilling, indeed.

Caution came swiftly on its heels. If she was to do

this, she'd need to be careful. Unlike her heedless youth, before Adele made a lady of her, if Kate were caught this time, the penalty would be more than a few stripes laid on her back with a belt.

First and foremost, the note must be hidden from Albreda, for the maid would surely give it to her lord. Reaching beneath her cot, Kate pulled out the wee wooden casket that held her jewelry and opened it. Painted parchment lined its lid. Prying the sheepskin away from the wood, she slipped Warin's note into the space between lining and lid, then pressed the skin back in place. When all was safely stored and the coffer returned to its spot beneath her cot, Kate grabbed up her comb and straightened her hair, now waiting impatiently for Albreda's return. With every breath, her love for Warin filled her until she thought she'd burst with it. It was going to be a glorious day.

Chapter 7

"**H**ere she is, Rafe," Will Godsol said to his brother, "Daubney's bitch and Glevering, both here, within your reach."

Although Rafe and his eldest brother sat on the outskirts of the picnickers, Rafe could barely hear Will's voice. It wasn't that the musicians' piping and drumming was overly loud; it was a trick of the surrounding foliage. Towering oak, thick ash and delicate alder, their feet cloaked in heavy tumbles of pink hedgerose and fern, caught the music in their glossy leaves and sent it echoing back into the glade.

It was just as well there was so much noise. The last thing Rafe needed was for anyone else to hear Will even hint at their plans for retaking Glevering through its heiress. Nor did Rafe need his brother to tell him where Kate de Fraisney was. The woman he would marry hadn't been out of his awareness all morning.

He glanced up from the cold meat pie in his hand to the dancers at the center of this grassy spot. Beneath a wisp of a veil held in place with a golden circlet, Kate's dark hair gleamed coppery in the sun as she danced. She was dressed for hunting, although she hadn't done any of it. Made of sensible linen, her upper garment was sleeveless to allow ease of movement. Her undergown sported sleeves wide enough to allow a bow to be drawn, while lacking the extravagant drape of formal attire. Both were dyed a dark hunting green. Plain the gowns might be, but their color suited Kate marvelously well. His wife to be didn't need jewels and silks; she was beautiful in her own right.

Across the field, Kate threw back her head and laughed as she danced. Rafe drew breath in admiration, his lungs filling with the spicy scents of fresh ale, crushed grass and summer air. By God, but she was more beautiful and more alive than any woman he'd ever seen.

The strangest flicker of warmth woke in his heart. His wife. The words resonated in him, and that warmth grew. Soon Kate would belong only to him, his to cherish and protect. Aye, but not if he let his desire to have her make him foolhardy. He shifted on the blanket to look at the Godsol patriarch.

"Folk listen, Will. Have a care with your tongue. As for our prey"—Rafe paused, giving his sometimes thick brother time to realize he spoke of Kate—"I say near enough, but hardly within reach."

Creases formed on Will's broad face. He blinked as he decoded Rafe's meaning, then his expression darkened. "What do you mean, not within reach, when *our prey* is but across the glade? What sort of excuse is this? Perhaps you've discovered you haven't the backbone for the task I set you. Here we are, outside Haydon's walls with horses at hand. Snatch her, man. I'll stop the others from following."

"You're out of your mind, Will," Rafe replied, impervious to so ridiculous a goad. "You and three of Long Chilting's soldiers are useless against so many."

The jerk of his chin indicated the folk teeming in this wee valley, their numbers easily in the hundreds. It wasn't just the invited wedding guests who hunted this morn, but every man or woman from any guest's household wealthy enough to keep a hawk. That included a good number of the bishop's clerics and Dickon's prior. Rafe sent a longing glance at his brother's bird, tethered to its roost. The training and maintenance of such an animal was a luxury he couldn't afford. Yet. His gaze returned to Kate.

"Nay," he told his brother as he watched his future wife dance, "when I take my prey, there won't be a full army following on my heels, eager to retrieve her."

"Perhaps this moment isn't the right one," the eldest Godsol grumbled in agreement, frustration burning in his dark eyes. "But you must vow to me that you won't fail. A year's already passed since our sire's death, and Bagot still hasn't paid for what he did. The sooner you and what you want are safe behind Long Chilting's walls, the easier our father's soul will rest."

"On my honor, you'll have your vengeance, just as I'll have her. But take heed, I'll not go to Long Chilting with her. Our home's exactly where they'll look once they learn it's I who's done the deed." He needed someplace less obvious. Although Rafe hoped it wouldn't come to it, it was possible he might need a little time to convince Kate that marriage to him was in her best interest.

"Just where do you intend to go, then?" Will demanded, his voice dropping into a harsh whisper.

For all his desire to make Kate his, Rafe hadn't actually yet formed a plan. Now, as he considered his brother's question, the answer came to him. He grinned and leaned close enough to Will so there was no chance anyone, not even Will's hawk, could overhear.

"Where better to take her than to Glevering? After all, the property is by rights ours, having belonged to our ancestors before her family stole it from us."

Wicked pleasure filled Will's slow smile. "Aye, that's precisely where you must go." He sent a searing glance at his foe on the opposite side of the glade. "By God, I'd spend every coin I own if it would buy me a chance to see Bagot's face when he learns that we once more have in our possession what his blood stole from us. That and something else he cherishes."

In the next instant, Will's satisfaction died back into concern. He looked back at Rafe. "It won't work, brother," he breathed. "Glevering's priest isn't going to wed his lord's daughter to a Godsol. Nay, you must come home, for only our own priest won't refuse you."

Rafe shrugged. "If all we need is a willing priest, then send a man riding to Long Chilting. Have him bring Father Philip and all the men you can spare halfway to Haydon. There they'll wait for our messenger to bid them meet us at Glevering."

His words sent his eldest brother rocking back on his seat. A laugh exploded from Will, the sound loud enough to make his hawk flap helplessly against its tethers. Will dealt Rafe a hearty and approving slap on the shoulder.

"By God, but you're a devious man! It's all that living at court that's made you what you are, God be praised for small favors."

"Glad you approve," Rafe said, the corner of his mouth lifting.

Content with what he planned, Rafe finished his pasty, then used his eating knife to spear a honeyed plum from the round of stale bread that was his trencher. As he raised the sweet to his mouth, the music stopped. Rafe's gaze leapt to the dispersing dancers.

Across the glade, Kate started back to where her sire sat, a golden-haired man at her side. Rafe sneered. Although this man was tall enough, Kate's companion was wiry, lacking a proper man's breadth of shoulder. True, the knight wasn't as ugly as Sir William, but neither was he fair-featured enough to offer Rafe any true competition.

Then Kate lifted her head to look at her companion. Adoration filled her expression. For another man!

The realization was like a crossbow bolt through Rafe's heart. How could Kate not know what was so clear to him? There was no other man for her save him, just as there was no other woman for him. They were meant to be together. The passion in their kiss last night confirmed that.

Still reeling at Kate's unwitting betrayal, Rafe's gaze shifted to the knight beside her, then he forgot all in a swell of newborn anger. It wasn't just any sort of smile the fair-haired man sent Kate's way. Rafe needed nothing more than his own experience in borrowing other men's wives to recognize the man's expression. The worm-eating lecher was trying to seduce his Kate. God help her, but she was too innocent to realize the man's intent! The need to protect Kate brought Rafe around on the blanket so swiftly that the plum slipped from his knife's tip to splatter onto the fabric.

Will shied back from the staining slop. "Ack, Rafe! Be careful what you do!"

"Who is he?" Rafe demanded, stabbing his knife in the direction of the fair man.

Will gingerly shifted on the blanket and looked where Rafe indicated. "Warin de Dapifer, Bagot's steward. An honest man, by all accounts—that is, until he took employment with the Daubney rat-kisser."

Rafe again looked at the steward and Kate. Damn him and the Godsol name that kept him at a distance. How was he supposed to protect Kate from her father's man of business when the bitch's son had constant access to his liege lord's daughter? Jesus God, but he couldn't even warn Bagot that Warin de Dapifer was a false knight who planned to betray his employer by stealing both Bagot's daughter and her riches.

Across the glade, the seducer and his intended victim stopped near Lord Humphrey. The traitorous steward offered his employer a low bow, then started back across the grassy expanse. Rafe watched de Dapifer's every step until the man reached the edge of the woods. There Sir Warin paused to send a meaningful look in the direction of his lord's daughter. It was an invitation for Kate to join him, nothing less.

Rafe's fists closed. By God, but the man leered at her like a hungry wolf. How could Bagot not see him for what he was?

The urge to race after de Dapifer and kill him on the spot tore at Rafe. He forced himself to stay where he sat. Attacking the man would not only result in his banishment from the wedding, but was likely to encourage Kate's misguided affection for de Dapifer. It was a sour lesson from Rafe's own experience with women. Assault a man for whom a woman harbored even the smallest attraction and, for some godforsaken reason, you often drove the woman right into the other man's arms.

His gaze shifted back to Kate at the other end of the glade. Her face pinched in what seemed refusal, then she sat down on her father's blanket with him. Rafe sighed in relief, then pride's warmth filled him.

Shame on him for doubting his sweet, innocent Kate. His had been the first and only touch to stir her from her upright behavior. There'd be no other for her; she just hadn't yet recognized that fact. A smile tugged at his mouth. His Kate was both passionate and virtuous, just the sort of woman a man like himself craved as his wife. Nay, she was *the* woman he would *make* his wife.

He started when Kate sprang to her feet. What seemed almost pain twisted her face. Rafe's pride dissolved into worry. It wasn't pain he saw. She looked like a woman who couldn't stop herself. Even as Rafe willed her not to, she offered her father a nervous bob and started toward the woodland's edge, following exactly in de Dapifer's wake.

Rafe's need to save her from her misguided emotions ate up all his common sense. He leapt to his feet. What she couldn't do for herself he would do for her.

Kate's heart thudded in her chest, its pounding so loud that she wanted to cover her ears. Her breath caught in her throat. Each step was agony, so badly did her knees tremble.

If only Ami were here. A single glance at the

young widow, to remind Kate of how easily she'd hoodwinked her sire the previous night, would have gone far to bolster her courage. Unfortunately, Ami was yet at Haydon, being one of the women chosen to wait upon the newlyweds today.

A bare three yards from where Warin had stepped into the forest's dappled shade, Kate's feet froze to the sod. Try as she might, she couldn't move another inch. Her vision blurred at the edges. From deep in her soul, Adele's voice screamed that she must stop. Guilt made mincemeat of Kate's will. Mary save her. It didn't matter how much she wanted to spend time with Warin, she couldn't do this.

She turned back to face the picnickers. Across the way, Lord Haydon had joined her sire at their blanket. Her father's tangled beard wasn't thick enough to hide the smile he offered their host. A moment later and her sire threw back his head to laugh. Even from this distance, Kate could hear his heartfelt amusement.

Resentment shot through her. There he was, giving to Lord Haydon the consideration he denied his own daughter. Her eyes narrowed. Warin was waiting. She whirled.

And came face to face with Rafe Godsol.

With a startled cry, Kate took a backward step. Rafe followed, nearly hovering over her. Like most of the men today, her sire's enemy wore a sleeveless leather vest over a dark green tunic that reached to his knees. Soft leather boots, their tops disappearing beneath the hem of his tunic, were cross-gartered to his legs. He'd removed his hat; his curling black hair gleamed in the sun. Resolution marked every line of his fine face.

Deep within Kate, remnants of last night's pleasure stirred. Fear of what her sire would do to her if he saw her near a Godsol slaughtered her reaction. Kate shifted to move around him. "You have to stay away from me," she cried. "We are enemies."

He blocked her path. "You and I aren't enemies," he replied, his reasonable tone belying the insanity of his statement. "It's only our families who hate each other."

Kate shot a frantic glance over her shoulder at her sire. Much to her relief, her father had his back to her while he spoke with Lord Haydon. That wouldn't last.

"Move," she commanded.

"I won't," Rafe replied, sounding determined, indeed.

If he wouldn't move, she would. Kate whirled to the right. Since running would only alert those watching that something was amiss, she strode as fast from him as she dared.

He followed, easily keeping pace. With each step he took, he veered a little more toward her, subtly and surely driving her farther from the edge of the woods. With an impatient breath, she stopped to glare at him. "What are you doing?"

He grinned in the patronizing way that folk save for idiots and young children. "What every line of your body and face begs of me. I'm stopping you from meeting in private with your father's steward."

Kate froze, shock and guilt like living things within her. She stared up at Rafe. Certainty glinted in his dark eyes and the casual bend of his lips. He knew about her meeting with Warin. A wave of confusion followed. How could he possibly know anything? Only she and Warin knew.

"What are you talking about?" she demanded, her voice thready.

"I'm talking about you and Sir Warin de Dapifer," Rafe replied, his tone that of a tutor to a slow-witted student. "I thought I should warn you. No matter what you think he wants or what he may have told you, it's a tryst he expects from you."

"A tryst?" she gasped, once again awash in shock. This morning's misgivings over Warin's intentions stirred. God help her, but she'd known better from the start. Then, even as a part of her sighed in relief and gave thanks to Rafe for stopping her, the guilty need to shield her reputation from wrongdoing woke.

"You're wrong," she cried, her voice squeaking a little against so vain a protest.

"I think not," Rafe replied, his tone conversational, as if it were the weather they discussed and not the blackening of her repute. "But then, neither do you. It's written all over your face. Never has there been a woman so unhappy at the prospect of meeting a man than you."

Another wave of shock hit Kate, this one filled with Lady Adele's strident warnings about straying from propriety's path. Oh Lord, if Rafe had noticed that much, had anyone else? God help her! It didn't matter that her meeting with Warin hadn't yet taken place. All it took for her reputation to be ruined was for others to believe her capable of such misbehavior.

Hiding her worry by crossing her arms, Kate glanced around her. Lady Haydon and the aged countess sat on a nearby blanket but a few yards distant. The bride's mother watched them from beneath the wide brim of her straw hat. Her brows were high upon her forehead, her expression alive with concern.

"Lady de Fraisney, is all well?" Lady Haydon called as their gazes met.

Before Kate could answer, the dowager countess beside their hostess threw off her own hat, baring her thinning hair to the sun's light. The old woman eyed the two members of the shire's feuding families, then let loose a lewd chuckle and looked at her companion.

"What trouble could there be, Beatrice, a handsome lad and a pretty lass like that? 'Tis naught but courtship games they play. Leave them be," she continued, laying her wrinkled hand on Lady Haydon's green sleeve. "Too bad they can't succeed. Think of the peace this shire might have if they were to unite their warring families."

Lady Haydon yet looked dubious. Despite the countess's confidence, the old noblewoman's escort came to their feet, their expressions guarded.

They'd come to Kate's aid if she asked for it.

Aye, but to ask for their help was like unto begging Rafe to spew his accusation of trysting for all to hear. Rafe was her father's enemy. It wouldn't trouble him that what he said ruined Kate's life.

With that new understanding, Kate's concern for her reputation fell before cynicism. Her eyes narrowed. Rafe knew nothing about Warin. Only happenstance and misfortune made his guess correct. This was but a ploy by a Godsol to ruin a Daubney and a Daubney servant.

"All is well," she lied to the ladies.

From her seat on the blanket, the countess grinned. "See, it's as I told you," she told the others. Lady Haydon shrugged and smiled as the men behind them relaxed, once again returning to their places.

Turning her gaze back to Rafe, Kate's jaw firmed. For shame! She'd let her father's lecherous, ill-behaved enemy make her doubt her good and true Warin.

The worst of it was that she was now well and truly trapped. With his course set on destroying her, this mannerless ape would surely follow if she tried to enter the woods. Should he catch sight of Warin, the Godsol would immediately trumpet his lie for all to hear. She'd have to retreat.

Disappointment nibbled at her heart. When she didn't meet him, would Warin believe she wanted him no longer? That meant no champion for her in the joust. As if Rafe read her thoughts on her face, a slow and triumphant grin stretched his mouth. It was enough to make irritation run away with Kate's tongue.

"Lecher!" she scolded. "I've had enough of you and your sordid behavior. But why should I expect anything else from a man who takes advantage of the unwary by forcing touches and kisses? Well, I may have earned your ill opinion through my lapse last even, but my father's steward deserves no such blackening. Sir Warin is too true a knight to ever do as you suggest, and I'll not have you dirtying his name with your false accusations. If you must know why I was entering yon wood, my reason is private, a need for a moment in the bushes."

Amusement flashed in Rafe's dark eyes. "Ah, outrage to bind your wounded pride. My apologies, lady, for exposing your sire's steward as a wretch, thus ruining your day." It was a brief and mocking bow he gave to punctuate his words. When he straightened, he set a fist upon his hip and cocked a brow. "Apology given and received, now retreat to your sire where it's safe."

Kate gaped at him. *He* was telling her what to do! Indignation took fire in her heart. Of all the men in the world, this was the one she was absolutely certain had no right to tell her where she could or couldn't go. Her jaw set. All sense died against her need to put this impossible Godsol in his place.

"How dare you try to bend me to your will? I will not retreat. Now, you stand aside and let me pass."

New light glowed in his brown eyes until they

smoldered. "You'll retreat," he repeated, "even knowing how very frustrated Sir Warin will be when you don't meet him as planned. God knows I'd be frustrated, were I in his place."

Kate loosed a searing breath. "Meet you in private, when I know the sort of advantage you take? Never as long as I live, sir knight."

His face softened. Without moving a muscle, he seemed to shift nearer to her. "You have no idea how deeply I pray you eat those words, Kate," he said, his voice suddenly husky and deep.

His forward use of her pet name should have shocked Kate. Propriety and sense should have screamed that she turn and run. Instead, the memory of their kiss sparked, and Kate's body came to sharp life. Every fiber of her being longed to once more feel his mouth on hers.

Before she knew what he was about, he captured one of her hands, his fingers twining with hers. Kate stared at their joined hands. As it was the dinner hour, they'd both removed their gloves. The feel of his bare fingers against hers made Kate's pulse do the strangest thing. Heat woke in the depths of her body, then surged through her with each beat of her heart until she felt she was ablaze.

Her gaze lifted to his face. Rafe's eyes darkened until they seemed black. His mouth was soft. The longing for the same kiss Kate needed clung to the curl of his lips. Her breath caught in her throat as that realization led the terrible, awesome heat in her.

"Release me." Her words were but a breath, half because his touch so intoxicated her that she couldn't breathe and half because she now craved his kiss with every inch of her being.

Deep within her, Adele scolded. Even if Rafe weren't her sire's enemy, to crave a kiss was immoral. For heaven's sake, folk watched!

Despite that, Kate sighed in disappointment when rather than touch his lips to hers, Rafe brought her hand to his mouth. Rather than press a courtier's kiss to her fingers, he turned her hand in his to touch his lips to her naked palm. Kate caught her breath. His lips were warm, the hair of his beard felt both rough and soft in one glorious instant.

His mouth moved in her hand, turning the simple press of flesh to flesh into a sweet nuzzling. Kate gasped. The sensations sizzling away from his caress made her spine melt.

His mouth moved from her palm to the delicate skin at her wrist. Kate's knees weakened. The need for more of this ate her alive. She shifted nearer to him.

Rather than embrace her as she so craved, he released her hand and stepped a full pace back from her. "Nay, Kate," he whispered in warning. "We can't."

Embarrassment scourged Kate. Where were her morals that she should need a Godsol to tell her what was appropriate behavior? Panic followed. What was she doing?! She'd let her father's enemy kiss her hand right there in the center of everything where anyone might witness!

"Oh, help," she muttered to herself, not a little unnerved. She whirled, more than ready to retreat now, only to stumble back as someone barreled past her.

With a wordless, raging shout, her father launched himself at Rafe.

Chapter 8

Damning himself for letting his longing to touch Kate blind him, Rafe sprang back from Bagot's lord. He wasn't fast enough to completely escape the thrust of the nobleman's hunting knife. The tip of Lord Humphrey's weapon gouged his leather vest at waist level.

Rafe stumbled back from the assault. The old man pursued, his teeth bared. Bagot's next blow was low and fast but not fast enough. Catching Lord Humphrey's wrist, Rafe gave the smaller nobleman, a man thirty years older and two stones lighter, a goodly shove.

Hissing in frustration, Bagot fell back, grabbing a handful of Rafe's clothing as he went. It was a strange, panting dance they did, one attacking, the other retreating, while both fought for footing. A woman screamed. Kate? From all across the glade, men shouted. Relief shot through Rafe. Their voices were the sound of aid coming his way.

Again Lord Humphrey tried to drive his knife into his enemy's gut. Rafe's fingers tightened on the old man's wrist to hold him at bay. It was all the defense he dared. Thief or not, Bagot was still his better. Only a man with a death wish struck his better.

Breath by breath, Rafe's world shrank until it encompassed only himself and the old man. Sweat beaded on Kate's sire's brow, slipping down the grimy lines that tracked his weathered face. Hatred seethed in Bagot's pale eyes. His front tooth was chipped. A bit of pasty clung to the wiry strands of his ruddy beard.

Lord Humphrey's breath wheezed from his lips. The old man's arm trembled. It was the edge Rafe needed.

Another sharp shove sent Lord Bagot spinning back from him. In the same instant, Rafe wheeled in the opposite direction, his hands lifted to show any who watched that he held no weapon. He careered into Will.

His brother caught him by the shoulders to steady him. Panting more from tension than exertion, Rafe let his world once more expand. Men crowded around him and Bagot.

Howling, Lord Humphrey lunged for Rafe, only to come up short as Lord Haydon and three other men grabbed him. The old man writhed against his captors. "Godsol scum!" Lord Humphrey shouted, intent only on the man he hated. "You'll die for what you've done!"

Rafe, his arms yet held clear of his sides, didn't bother replying. He but waited as Josce pushed past his noble sire to join him. His friend reached around Rafe to snatch his hunting knife from its short scabbard. Only when Rafe was thus disarmed did he lower his hands. Turning, Josce held the weapon high for all to see.

"Take heed," Lord Haydon's bastard called out. "You all stand witness that Sir Rafe's weapon was sheathed throughout these last moments. He weathered Lord Humphrey's violence without responding in kind."

It was testimony that although strained, the peace of the wedding hadn't been broken; no man's loyalty demanded he go to war that day. So many in the glade breathed out at this that it was almost a breeze. Whether they did so in relief or disappointment was hard to say. There were plenty of men willing to kill Godsols for Bagot, and a good number of guests would happily loan the Godsols their arms for the sheer sport of making Daubneys bleed.

Beside Rafe, Will made a furious sound deep in his throat. Closing his fists, he took a step toward the man who'd killed their father. Rafe, still giddy from having escaped certain death by the skin of his teeth, stared at his brother in new panic. Will meant to provoke violence when any hope of owning Kate depended on keeping the peace.

Catching his elder brother by the arm, Rafe gave

him a quick shake. "Not a word, Will," he begged in a quiet whisper to no avail.

"You go too far with this unprovoked attack on my brother, Bagot," Will shouted. "Our truce is broken!" The agreement of the Godsol supporters thundered in the air.

"Bitch's son!" Lord Humphrey threw back, again lunging for those he hated. The men who held him strained to keep him where he stood. "Hold that forked tongue of yours, or I'll cut the thing from your mouth."

Will's head snapped back as if struck. His hand dropped to his knife's hilt. Rafe yanked on his brother's arm, stopping him before he could pull the weapon.

"You'll do as Bagot says and hold your tongue, or I'll cut it out for him," the youngest Godsol dared in a panicked whisper to his elder.

Shock flattened Will's face. Eyes wide, he stared at the least member of his family. He growled, but much to Rafe's relief, he held his tongue.

Lord Haydon took a step closer to the Godsols. Although not as tall as his only son, there was no mistaking Josce's parentage. Baldwin of Haydon and his bastard owned the same shade of fair hair, the same jut of the chin and hooked nose.

"Sir Rafe, I look upon you and see no blood. Are you injured?" their host asked, the question command rather than inquiry.

"I am not, my lord," Rafe replied.

"Of course he's not injured," Lord Humphrey

said, his voice suddenly calm, his tone sly. "Cowardly pig refused to fight with me."

The insult sliced through Rafe. His fists closed. Rage tore away all his good intentions. No man called him coward!

Beside him, Will laughed, the sound low and wicked. "So what you thought good enough for me to bear is too much for you, eh?" the eldest Godsol whispered, even as his hand closed about the hilt of his hunting knife in preparation for an attack.

As if conjured out of thin air, Simon and Hugh appeared at Rafe's side. Simon grabbed Rafe's arm, his grip like iron as he held his friend in place. Meanwhile, Hugh lifted his chin and turned his face so all in the glade might see the scar upon his face.

"Look upon me and see I wear my bravery where the world might witness," he called to the crowd. "Of all the knights I know, there's no man I'd rather have at my side in war than Sir Rafe Godsol. Lord Bagot's charge of cowardice is as dastardly as the nobleman's unprovoked attack upon my friend."

At Hugh's testimony, more than gratitude for the restoration of his honor flowed through Rafe. Hugh had not only saved him from his own idiocy, he'd left him with a thread of a chance to own Kate.

Trapped between terror and mortification, Kate let the other guests push past her as they crowded around Rafe and her father. Oh, Lord help her, how long would it be before someone mentioned that Rafe had kissed her hand?

This was nothing more than God's punishment

for daring to breach propriety's bounds. She should never have let Rafe near her again, knowing as she did the sort of spell his touch laid on her. If it had been possible, Kate would have raced all the way back to her father's tent at Haydon, climbed into her cot and pulled the blankets over her head. Since there was no such hope of escape, she put her hand to her heart. Never again, she swore, would she come within arm's reach of Rafe Godsol.

Someone laid a hand on her shoulder. With a startled cry, Kate whirled. It was Warin.

Guilt shot through her. She'd forgotten about him waiting in the woods for her. Her surprise soured. Warin's leather vest lay open over his chest, and he'd loosened the ties at his tunic's neck.

Others might see naught but an attempt to escape the day's heat. Suspicion shot through Kate. Was Rafe right about Warin's intentions? Feeling as innocent as Ami proclaimed her, Kate prayed there was some other explanation. To protect herself from her own foolishness, she amended her vow. Never again would she consider meeting a man in private, not even if Warin begged her on bended knee.

"What happens here, my lady?" Warin demanded, his face tense, his narrowed eyes aimed at her captive sire in the crowd's center.

Kate's mouth opened. Nothing came out, mostly because no combination of words could adequately explain how this situation had come about without making it seem as if she'd done something wrong when she hadn't. At last, she settled for a very bare version of the truth. "My lord father attacked one of the Godsols."

Her dear love's jaw tightened. "May God take all Godsols," he muttered. Grabbing her by the arm, he started into the crowd. "Come."

Panic shot through Kate. Lord help her, but she didn't want to be anywhere near Rafe. When he saw Warin's dress would he repeat his unfortunate conjecture about her destination? The present disarray of Warin's attire was damning, no matter his true intent.

"We can't," she whispered, tugging on her trapped arm. Warin made no reply, only tightened his grip until it almost hurt. Kate gasped, too startled by this to do anything other than be pulled alongside him.

Even though she told herself she mustn't, as they made their way toward the crowd's center, Kate's gaze slipped to Rafe. He stood proudly before their host, day's golden light gilding every handsome line and plane of his face. A hint of gratitude and relief shot through her. He looked no worse for her sire's attack.

Rafe wasn't watching her but Warin. At the sight of Warin's loosened tunic, his eyes narrowed and his fine mouth twisted. Kate cringed. Just as she'd feared, his dreadful and wrongheaded suspicions were confirmed.

It was going to happen. Rafe would spew his belief that Warin planned a tryst, thereby ruining her. Her father's enemy couldn't afford to miss so wondrous an opportunity to destroy that man's daughter.

She and Warin halted but arm's length from her trapped sire. "What is the meaning of this, my Lord Haydon, that you would hold Lord Bagot like some common captive?" Warin demanded, speaking as Bagot's steward. Outrage filled his voice over the insult done his liege lord. "Release him this minute!"

"I cannot, Sir Warin," their host replied, his voice lifted so that it filled the glade, "at least, not until your noble master calms himself. He's attacked Sir Rafe Godsol."

"If there's any fault over what happened here, you can rest assured it lies with the Godsol," Warin dared to retort. The Bagot supporters in the crowd muttered their approval of his claim, the sound rumbling up into the vast and vaultless blue of the sky, while the Godsols' backers shouted that it wasn't true. The noise was enough to set those hunting dogs accompanying their masters this day to belling.

"Sir Warin, I saw you as you came from the woods after the fact," Sir Josce FitzBaldwin called from his stance next to Rafe. His deep voice cut like a sword through the noise. "If you were in the trees, how can you know who's at fault for what happened here?" Those who favored the Godsols roared at this.

"No more, I pray you," Lord Haydon called out, holding up his hands to punctuate his plea. "No one is injured, and the peace of my daughter's wedding continues. Let us all retreat and leave this incident behind us without notice."

"What of my honor?" Lord Humphrey spat out.

Kate watched her father draw himself up to his tallest even as he remained a prisoner. With each inch he straightened, he released rage and reclaimed his noble arrogance. One by one, those who held him stood back. When he was free, Lord Humphrey yanked his leather vest back in place, then stooped to retrieve his hunting knife, which lay at his feet. Sheathing it in his belt, he looked at his host.

"I warn you now, Baldwin," he said, using Lord Haydon's Christian name without his title to make a point of their equality, "Wedding or not, I'll kill that piece of Godsol offal for assaulting my daughter."

The silence in the glade was instant and complete. Kate's senses reeled. The air left her lungs. Her father's words left Rafe no choice save to spill some sort of excuse to protect himself. Aye, and she knew just what he would say.

At the center of the crowd, Lord Haydon whirled on Rafe. "Did you assault Lady de Fraisney?" His question was sharp, promising swift retribution if offered the wrong answer.

Kate's life crumbled as she waited for what would surely come. Rafe shot her a swift look. Hot color crept up her cheeks as she read the message in his gaze. How did he dare question whether the kiss he placed in her hand qualified as an assault!

His gaze shifted back to their host. "My lord, ask

the lady if you must, but I did in no way assault her this day," he said, that and no more.

So deep was Kate's relief that stars swam before her eyes. Something akin to joy stirred in her as she chided herself for misjudging Rafe. Despite his bad manners, Rafe Godsol was an honorable and good man. Not even to honor his father's hatred for the Daubneys would he destroy her.

"A lie!" Lord Humphrey shouted. "My daughter would never willingly remain near a Godsol! He must have held her. Moreover, I saw the way that bitch's son stood before her, giving her none of the respect due her position."

Lord Haydon looked at Kate. "My lady, did Sir Rafe disparage you in any way?"

Kate's heart pounded as she saw the trap close around her. She couldn't lie and say Rafe had done wrong, not after he'd behaved so honorably. But if she told the truth, how could she ever explain to all these people, her father included, just where she was going and why Rafe had tried to stop her? She couldn't without seeming a forward woman or implicating Warin.

She was quiet so long that Warin gave her arm a shake. "Speak, my lady," he commanded.

Feeling like a martyr before Rome's lions, she cleared her throat. "Sir Rafe did me no harm, Lord Haydon," she replied, her voice trembling and soft. "Nor did he do any insult to my title."

"What?" her sire bellowed in outrage. Above the reaches of his beard, outrage painted red streaks on his lean cheeks. "I saw the two of you. If he wasn't assaulting you, then what were you doing so close to him?"

Kate shrank back at the threat in his tone and found Warin's shoulder behind her. The solid strength of his arm against her back went far to bolster her fluttering heart. Against that heady sense of safety and security, her tongue loosened. Her words were out before she even knew they were there.

"He was only trying to stop me from going into the woods without an escort."

As she heard what she'd said, Kate gasped. She willed the ground to open up and swallow her here and now. She'd ruined herself far better than Rafe could ever do.

Warin's shoulder disappeared from behind her. Staggering back in surprise, Kate threw a startled glance at him. Her love stared at her, bright color touching the harsh jut of his cheekbones, his mouth a tight line. Behind the rage clouding his blue eyes, Kate saw he understood that Rafe Godsol had somehow discovered their meeting and stopped it.

In the next instant, accusation filled his gaze. Shock rattled Kate to her core. How could Warin think for even an instant that *she'd* told anyone, especially a Godsol, of their meeting?

Her father caught her by the shoulders. Fury settled into the deep lines of his face, the emotion cold as if it had been cherished for a life's time. His eyes were the color of steel, his mouth a mere slash above his jutting, bearded chin.

"You told me you only meant to walk for a few

moments," he said, his words frigid and hard. "You said nothing about entering the woods."

No matter whether affiliated with the Godsols or the Daubneys, men all around the glade muttered. Kate heard it in the air around her. It was just as Adele had warned. Every one of them believed the worst, that she'd been trying to escape her sire for some illicit purpose. She was ruined.

Just when Kate thought she'd crumple under their disapproval, Lady Haydon pushed past her husband to join her beleaguered guest. Shooting a worried look around her, Lady Beatrice put her arm around Kate's shoulders, subtly shoving Lord Humphrey back a step. Her plain face radiated concern, her dark eyes were filled with commiseration.

"I'm certain what you've said isn't what you meant, Lady de Fraisney," she coaxed. "Come, now, I know you're shy, but don't let fear tie your tongue. Tell us again and say it plain. Why were you going into the woods?"

Kate snatched the rescue her hostess offered and pulled herself back from disaster's brink. "I needed a moment's privacy, my lady, it being almost my time of month," she managed to mutter.

It wasn't quite a lie; she wasn't with child, so she would again have her time. True, it wouldn't be for another two weeks, but that could be construed as *almost*. At least there was no chance this lie would be discovered. In two weeks she'd be far from Haydon. No one, not even her sire, would be the wiser, since her father kept no record of her cycle.

Lady Haydon grinned. "As I thought, my lords," she called out to both her husband and Lord Bagot. "She needed time alone to tend to a woman's problem. Knowing none of the women here, no doubt she didn't feel comfortable asking any of us to be her companion. Seeing how her sire brought no maid to tend her this day, what choice had she save a secret trip for privacy's sake?" It was a chiding look she sent in the direction of Kate's sire.

Lord Bagot shrugged off his hostess's scold. "Be that as it may, there remains one question. Why would any Godsol seek to protect a Daubney?" This was more challenge than inquiry as he turned his sharp gaze on Rafe.

Rafe's only reaction was to lift his brows. "No matter her name, I'd not see a woman come to harm when I can prevent it," he replied. The Godsols and their friends cheered at this.

Lord Humphrey's lips drew back from his teeth in a snarl. "More likely you meant to taunt me through her, pretending concern when in truth you have none." At his comment, men either shouted approval or growled their disagreement, depending on their loyalty.

"Come, daughter," Kate's sire snapped, catching her by the arm to yank her from Lady Haydon's embrace. "I want you away from these bits of Godsol dog offal. Sir Warin," he added to his steward in harsh command.

Rafe watched Lord Humphrey drag his daughter out of his reach while Sir Warin yet remained at her side. Damn him, but all he'd accomplished today was to alert Lord Humphrey and his steward to his interest in Kate. Nay, he'd done even worse than that. He'd managed to leave her unprotected before their anger. His eyes narrowed. If they so much as bruised her over this, he'd kill them both.

"I knew there'd be a simple explanation for all this," Lord Haydon called out, his voice alive with relief and pleasure as he looked out over his guests. "Go on, all you gentlefolk. Let us enjoy the remainder of this day."

Most of the crowd was quick to do as he commanded. Off key and fumbling sounds left the musicians' instruments as they struggled to regroup and find their way into another tune. Calls for servants to refill cups with ale peppered the air. After a few moments, the only ones left near Rafe were Will, Josce and Lord Haydon.

Will made a disappointed sound. "I'd hoped to let a little blood," he breathed to Rafe, his hand still clutching his sheathed knife's hilt. "To be the one who cuts out yon rat-kisser's heart would suit me well, indeed."

Rafe managed a halfhearted grunt in reply. Will started away, only to realize a step later that Rafe wasn't following. Pausing, he shot a look over his shoulder at his youngest brother. "Are you coming?"

"In a moment," Rafe replied, then glanced at Josce's sire. Lord Haydon's face might have been carved from granite. His eyes glinted like steel in their sockets. "I'd offer my apologies to our host first."

Concern swam across Will's broad face, as if he only now realized they'd nearly lost their chance of vengeance. What followed was pure eagerness. His nod gave Rafe permission to say or do anything to see that he wasn't banished from the wedding.

"That would be well done," he said, his tone that of an approving patriarch, then he strode off across the grass.

When they were private, Rafe offered his host a deep bow. "My lord, I humbly beg your pardon for the discord I've caused," he said as he straightened.

Baldwin of Haydon's face thawed like ice in summer. A slow smile stretched his thin lips until his grin seemed to reach from ear to ear. "Lad, I couldn't be more pleased with this day's discord."

"My lord?" Josce asked his father, startled.

Lord Baldwin's low chuckle ended almost as soon as it started. "Mary save me, but it wouldn't do to have anyone hear me laughing when by all rights it's a lecture they expect me to give you," he said. "But how can I complain about you when I was the fool who planned a melee as part of this celebration?" The melee was a welcome activity at any gathering, as the mock battle offered participants a chance to earn coins; the losers had to pay a ransom to the winners. "I know as well as any man that all England is presently torn between those who believe we must curb our king and his excesses and those who feel their oaths will ever bind them to our monarch even if our John leads us into penury. What I heard yesterday from my guests had me quaking in my boots. It seemed my bit of sport would become the first skirmish in open rebellion."

Again Lord Haydon grinned at Rafe. "A thousand thanks, lad, for leading them away from politics. Four days hence, when the melee commences, those who think Bagot wrongly attacked you will align themselves with your brother, while those who believe you misused Bagot's daughter will put themselves at the Daubneys' back. Your families' hatred at the center of our game ought to please your brother right mightily, bloodthirsty man that he is."

Rafe gaped, unable to believe what he heard. "My lord?"

"Go," the nobleman commanded his son, throwing a quick gesture toward Rafe, "take him from my sight before I'm tempted to laugh again."

Josce shot Rafe a bemused look, then shrugged. "As you will, my lord. Come, Rafe."

"By the by," Lord Haydon called after them as they started away, "if you tell any man I said this to you, I'll deny it. And stay away from Bagot's daughter, Sir Rafe. Lord Humphrey will not soon forgive you for coming so close to her. Should anything even slightly untoward happen between you two, Bagot will ask for your hide, and I'll have to give it to him."

Chapter 9

Sir Gilbert DuBois leaned closer to Kate. Barrel-chested and only ten years older than she, the well-to-do landowner had already lost most of his fair hair. The light of the hall's burning torches was just bright enough to reveal a scar on his naked pate. It streaked like lightning down his forehead to split a fair eyebrow. His reddish beard was tangled and thick.

He eased even closer to her. Kate's nose twitched. The knight reeked of sweat and blood. He hadn't washed since returning from the day's sport.

She took a backward step only to find the wall between her and escape. Sir Gilbert smiled at her attempt to slip away, the lift of his mouth more leer than grin beneath a nose bent by some past battle.

He braced a forearm against the wall behind her.

Kate sent a hopeless glance flying over his shoulder toward her sire. Lord Humphrey stood only a few feet distant, his lance-straight back toward his daughter, his gaze directed at the center of Haydon's night-dimmed hall. Kate read the message in the set of his shoulders. Her father meant to ignore what happened between her and Sir Gilbert, the man he most wanted his daughter to wed. Indeed, Kate doubted her father would complain if the knight threw her over his shoulder and left Haydon with her this very moment.

Her father was still livid over this afternoon's events. Along with Warin, they had left the picnic immediately after the incident, riding in horrible silence back to Haydon's courtyard and their tent. Although Kate fully expected some sort of punishment, her father hadn't lifted a hand to her. Instead, he'd pushed her into her side of the tent, then maintained his stony silence until the hour arrived for this evening's feast.

Sir Gilbert reached out to catch Kate's fingers, his grip tight as he pulled her hand toward him. Although Kate did her best to resist without actually seeming to, the knight was the stronger. A moment later, her palm was pressed to his chest. The fabric of his brown robe was soft and thin enough for her to feel the thud of his heart against her fingers.

"Weeks ago, when your sire first approached me regarding an alliance between our families, I refused," Sir Gilbert said, his voice surprisingly high-pitched for a man with so violent a reputation. "You were four years wed and had produced no child. I thought you as delicate and spineless as my previous two wives. All I got from them was a single sickly lass." There was naught but contempt in his voice for his only child.

Kate's stomach knotted. It was rumored that Sir Gilbert's first two wives died at his hand for failing to produce living sons. True, neither the Church nor the dead women's families had leveled charges against him, but those poor women were still just as dead.

"It's a strong woman I'd set my mind on this time 'round," Sir Gilbert went on, "one capable of breeding up even stronger sons."

Uncertain how to respond to this, Kate only stared up into his face. Sir Gilbert offered that leering smile again. "After today, I've reconsidered my original assessment of you," he said, lowering his head.

Panic drove Kate flat against the wall. He meant to kiss her! Placing her free hand on his chest, she pushed. It was useless. His lips touched hers.

Kate gagged and turned her head to one side. "Sir Gilbert," she protested in a harsh whisper, "I pray you no. My father but stands a few feet from us."

The knight retreated bare inches to narrowly eye her. "What is this? Would you deny me the sort of game you intended to play with some other man before a Godsol caught you at it?"

Rather than frighten her with his tone, his insulting words made Kate angry. She shoved him with all her might. Although she succeeded in driving Sir

Gilbert a foot or so from her, his grip on her hand didn't relax.

"How dare you say such a thing to me!" she scolded, then did her best to save her mangled reputation. "I played no game this day. Did you not hear what I told Lady Haydon?"

Her protest was all storm and no substance. Worse, it was pointless. Sir Gilbert was like every other man here, all of them now believing her a forward lass, if not a lightskirt. Despair closed around Kate. She'd stepped outside the bounds of the game of love, and just as Lady Adele had warned, she was ruined.

Sir Gilbert's pale eyes glowed with pleasure. "Here it is once more, that fire of yours. How it intrigues me. I wager you'll be no limp reed in my bed. Nay, I'm thinking we'll have long nights of passion, you and I."

Shocked to her core and not a little sickened by such talk, Kate gaped at him. The heat of her blush started at her breastbone and seeped upward until she could feel it searing her cheeks. "Sir Gilbert, I am a modest woman," she protested.

"God save me, my lady, but I hope not," he replied, his head again lowering as he sought to reclaim her lips with his.

"Why, here you are at last, my Lady de Fraisney!" Ami's overly loud cry came from a few feet away. "Do you know I've fair scoured the hall looking for you?"

Startled, Sir Gilbert pivoted to look upon the interloper, his grip on Kate's hand loosening. Kate yanked her fingers free, then hurriedly slipped away from him along the wall. At the same time, Ami, once again resplendent in her scarlet attire, started toward Kate. Lord Humphrey shifted to stop the widow, but she slithered past him to come to a halt beside her new friend. Taking Kate's arm, Ami turned to offer the men a demure and courteous bend of her knee.

"My pardon, sir knight, my Lord Bagot," Ami said smoothly, "but Lady Haydon says she simply must have Lady de Fraisney for this next dance. Did you know that every other lady in the hall has danced at Emma's side save she?" Ami continued, her face beaming with sincerity as she claimed the Daubney heiress on her hostess's behalf. "You won't mind if I borrow her for a time, hmm?"

Lord Humphrey glowered at the young widow. "Inform Lady Haydon that my daughter cannot join the dancing, as I have other plans for her. Away with you." The wave of his hand dismissed the widow or would have had not Sir Gilbert caught the nobleman's arm.

"Now, my lord, we mustn't insult our hostess," the knight said, his tone mild and his gaze fixed on Kate as he spoke. It was the promise of more hidden touches and forced kisses that filled his eyes and lifted the corners of his mouth. Before Kate knew what she was about, she'd laid a protective hand over her breast. Sir Gilbert grinned at the movement, then looked upon Lord Humphrey.

"It's an honor that your daughter should attend the bride. Let her go, my lord. Let her dance with her friends for the evening. We have much to discuss, haven't we? What say you we do it over another cup of Lord Baldwin's fine wine?"

Lord Humphrey's brows jerked upward, then the annoyance drained from his face. He smiled, his grin so wide it displayed nigh on all his teeth. "That's a fine suggestion," he said, reaching out to clap Sir Gilbert on the back, "a fine suggestion, indeed. Shall we?" The two men left Kate without so much as a backward glance.

Kate's heart sank to her toes as she watched them walk away from her. Ami shifted nearer to her friend, clutching Kate's arm a little tighter. "They aren't doing what I think they're doing, are they?" she asked, a touch of disgust in her voice.

"I fear they are," Kate replied, her voice small and her spirits flat. "The haggling over the marriage contract begins. Oh, Ami, pray for me. Pray that Sir Gilbert wants more for me than my sire is willing to give. Better still, pray Sir Gilbert's demands are so excessive that my sire decides to remarry and get himself a new heir rather than make me half-heiress to all he owns."

"Aye," Ami said with a quiet laugh as she led Kate away from the wall and toward the central hearth where the dancers were gathering, "better that he remarries than you if your only choice is Sir Gilbert. There's but one problem. Who'd have your sire? Lord Humphrey is a bloody prig," she finished with a disrespectful snort.

"Ami!" Kate gasped at the profanity.

Ami's smile was a cheeky grin. "Now you know

why I'm the one Lady Haydon sent to fetch you. I'm a bold lass, not afraid to face any man no matter his consequence.

"Here we are, Lady Haydon," she said as she and Kate came to a stop before their hostess.

Lady Haydon's round face came to life with a quick smile as she saw them. "So you are, my ladies. Glad I am to find you well and whole, Lady de Fraisney," she told Kate with an even quicker wink. "I hope you don't mind me commanding your participation in this next dance. It's only that I think it wise your sire know others here have an interest in your well-being."

Relief and gratitude swam in Kate's eyes at such kindness. Someone cared what became of her. Not that Lady Haydon's sympathy would alter the fact that Sir Gilbert's reputation or brutality meant nothing to her father. If he wanted her married to the knight, then married she would be.

"My thanks," she said humbly.

"Nay, no thanks are needed, lovey," Lady Haydon said, her smile reappearing. "Just enjoy the dance."

"She will. I'll see to that," Ami replied for Kate, already pushing her friend into the milling folk waiting for the music to begin.

As soon as they were out of their hostess's earshot, Ami grabbed Kate's hands to draw her new friend close. "Now, tell me all," she whispered breathlessly, "for I'm quite dying to hear. What really happened at the picnic this afternoon?"

She gave Kate no chance to reply before continuing, "You should know that when I learned your sire attacked Sir Rafe Godsol because that knight came too close to you, I went to him myself. I scolded him just as I had last even, telling him that he must leave you be."

"You spoke to Sir Rafe on my behalf last night?" Kate asked in surprise.

Ami gave a brusque nod, her mouth thinning a little. "Aye, indeed I did, showing him the sternest side of my tongue whilst I was at it."

Kate's liking for Ami grew by leaps and bounds. "I thank you for that, but I fear your effort is useless," she said, then gave breath to a frustrated sigh. Rafe would never ccase his pursuit of her, not after that kiss of theirs in the alcove. Nay, Rafe Godsol thought her a loose woman and wanted very much to collect upon the accidental promise she'd made him beneath the window. Despite her exasperation with Rafe, the memory of his mouth on hers returned. So too, did the recall of the kiss he'd placed in her palm.

How could she call her promise accidental when it seemed she kept making it to him again and again?

A tiny smile played along Ami's lips and gleamed in her green eyes. "I know why he needs to be near you."

Kate gasped as shame tore through her illicit rememberings. Heat prickled along her cheekbones. Had Rafe told Ami what kept happening between them? Please God, but she hoped not.

Ami's smile widened. "Sir Rafe cannot help himself when it comes to you," she said, a taunting tone to her voice.

These words were so contrary to what Kate expected to hear that she was lost in confusion a moment. "What do you mean? Tell me."

Coming close enough to whisper in Kate's ear, Ami said, "Rafe Godsol cannot help himself because he's formed an attachment for you. Last night, I believed he merely meant to use you, mayhap thinking to ruin you in your father's eyes for the sake of the feud between your families. But this evening, when I confronted him, I saw the truth in his face. As he spoke of you, he scanned the hall, seeking some sign of your presence. When he found you, his gaze locked on you and his lips lifted. Ach, Kate, he cannot bear to utter your name without gazing upon you at the same time."

Leaning back from Kate, Ami caught her friend by the shoulders. Her expression was more than satisfied. It was exultant. "Oh, but this serves him rightly after all the women who've pined for him in vain. Daubney or not, Kate, I think Rafe Godsol is in love with you," she whispered.

Kate stared. In love with her?

The very words set a whole stew of emotions to bubbling. A strange happiness surged through her. Love. A smile tugged at the corners of her mouth. The words Rafe had spoken to her just before her father attacked him echoed in her ears. He wanted to be the man she met in the woods.

Kate's happiness grew, bringing with it new insight. It'd been for love's sake that Rafe had watched her throughout the picnic. That's why he'd seen her follow Warin into the wood. Also for love's sake had he swallowed his dreadful accusation of trysting to speak honorably about her when confronted by Lord Haydon. A lover always protected his beloved.

Kate's smile grew apace with her pleasure. Every inch of her warmed. There were two men in love with her! This was better than any of Lady Adele's tales. Why, even Guinevere had only one true love in Lancelot.

Lost in the wonder of it, Kate's gaze shot across the hall to where Rafe sat. She knew where he was; she'd known all evening. He was keeping to the north end of the hall at the fringes of the entertainment. No doubt he meant to lie low until today's incident dimmed in everyone's memory.

She sighed as she found him. His black hair gleamed in the uncertain torchlight. Shadows highlighted the sharp lift of his cheekbones and the length of his fine nose. Rafe might not be golden-haired like the knights Lady Adele adored, but he was a very handsome man. More importantly, Rafe Godsol was in love with her. As her father's worst enemy, his cause was even more hopeless than Warin's. Could there be anything more glorious than that?

Just as it had happened twice since she'd entered the hall tonight, Rafe seemed to feel her watching him. His head turned in her direction. Their gazes met.

Earlier this evening, his expression had been

clouded, as if he were worried over her—but of course he worried, he loved her! Kate swallowed another bubble of happiness. This time, when Rafe saw she stood with Ami, it was pure relief that flowed across his face.

Kate's heart did a little dance in her chest. The sweet jerking wasn't so different from what she felt when she thought of Warin. Could this mean that she loved Rafe in return, at least a little?

"Stop looking at him, or folk will notice," Ami whispered with a quiet laugh. "Come, my lady. Pay heed," she continued more loudly, sounding very much like an irritated tutor. "The dance is about to begin."

It was a courting dance, this one, with twin rings, one male, the other female. While they faced each other, they moved in opposite directions. As the music started, Kate and Ami joined hands with the other young women. The men facing them did the same. Never a confident dancer, Kate kept watch on her wayward feet for the first moments. Only when she had the steps and the rhythm did she dare lift her gaze to the men dancing opposite her.

Warin glared at her as he moved past. Kate's shock over this was followed by a surge of pique. What right had Warin to be angry with her? It was her reputation in tatters, sacrificed for his sake.

'Round and 'round, she and the other female dancers went, then the tempo changed and the rings broke. The women began to wend their way through the men, once, twice, thrice, before taking a partner. Just as Kate stopped before a tall, thin man, Warin stepped in front of him.

"Dance with another," he growled at the hapless fellow, grabbing Kate's hand.

"What are you doing?" Kate cried quietly, disconcerted by such rudeness in her usually courteous knight.

"I'm dancing with you," Warin retorted, leading Kate through the procession as if nothing untoward had just happened between them. His face was a thundercloud, his lips so tight they whitened.

Kate frowned. This wasn't the man she'd come to know at Bagot. Moreover, Lancelot never snapped at Guinevere. There was no room for discourtesy in the game of courtly love. "I think I'd prefer a less surly partner."

Warin's hand tightened on hers so swiftly that Kate yelped more from surprise than pain. "Sir Warin!"

Instantly, his grip loosened. "My pardon, my lady," he muttered, but there was no sincerity in his apology. Kate's eyes narrowed. If Warin thought he could rule her by brute force, he'd best think again.

A moment later it was time for them to return to their respective rings and begin circling once again. Yanking her hand from his, Kate coldly showed Warin her back in punishment for his misbehavior. The next time the rings again broke into partners, he was on the opposite side of the circle. Grateful that she didn't need to encounter him a second time, Kate made her way through the final procession with the scarred young man who'd defended Rafe this afternoon.

When the dance ended, to the cheers of both participants and witnesses, folk milled for a moment. Friends sought out their companions, while couples went looking for their mates. Kate turned a wee circle, waiting for Ami to find her, only to come up against Warin.

He caught her by the arm. "We need to talk," he snapped.

Kate didn't like his tone, nay not at all. Moreover, the last thing she needed was for the hall to witness her walking into some darkened corner with the same man who'd come dashing from the woods after the fact this afternoon, his clothing all undone. "I think me there's nothing for us to discuss, Sir Warin," she told him, jerking her arm out of his grasp.

"Nothing to discuss?" he whispered, his slitted eyes glittering with threat. "I want to know what in God's hell you were doing speaking to that devil-spawned Godsol this afternoon and why the cur looks at you as if you belong to him and no other man."

Irritation flared in Kate. *This* was the knight for whom she'd sacrificed herself? There was nothing of Lancelot in Warin. She crossed her arms and drew herself up to her tallest.

"Sir Warin, I have no control over how others look upon me. As for what I do and to whom I speak, that is none of your concern. You've apparently mistaken yourself for my nursemaid or my keeper, when last I knew you were only my lord father's steward." Her voice was frigid, her words conveying in their every syllable the end of their attachment.

Warin caught a shocked and sudden breath. Even though the torchlight was dim, Kate saw concern flash across his face. He took a swift backward step, then bowed deeply. When he straightened, the seething, arrogant man was gone, leaving in his place the honest and true Warin whom Kate loved.

"I pray you, my lady, forgive me," he begged and prettily so this time. "I've no excuse for my forward behavior save that my heart has run away with my tongue."

Kate's irritation with Warin drained from her in a great rush of emotion as she understood. He was jealous, just as Rafe had been jealous of Warin this afternoon. She savored the sensation. Two men loved her, and each was jealous of the other.

"My lady?" Warin extended his hand, wanting hers in return.

Kate frowned at his fingers. Warin knew well enough that it was only words, never touches, that they dared share. That he would ask this of her where others might witness and after what happened at the picnic was doubly worrisome. She shot a swift glance around her to see who might have noticed his gesture.

Squatting before the hearth only a foot or so away was a wee serving lad. The boy wasn't watching them as he poked uselessly at the wood burning upon the stone. His crouched stance suggested his true purpose was to escape the eye of his master.

Her face alive with interest, Ami hovered at the discreet distance good manners dictated, standing where she could see but not overhear her friend. Beyond her, most of the others had dispersed. That left Kate and Warin alone at the room's center and a possible focus of all attention.

"You know I dare not, good sir," Kate whispered to Warin, striving to keep the reproach from her voice as she reminded him of their relationship's proper form. "Folk watch."

Frustration danced across Warin's fine features, but his hand fell to his side. "Of course, you're right," he agreed, then lowered his voice to a breathy whisper. "My lady, my love, forgive me. Forgive me and tell me you love me still despite what I have done, as I yet love you."

Pleasure washed over Kate. This was the Warin she adored. Surely, there was some explanation for the disarray of his dress this afternoon, for he would never think to misuse her. She smiled at him, grateful to have their relationship back on familiar ground.

"Forgive I can and already have," she told him. "Love you I always will."

Warin's smile was beautiful. "You are a saint, my lady, I know it, aye. Two days hence, I will redeem myself in your eyes when I take the prize in the joust as your champion."

His words sent Kate floating down a wondrous river of emotion. How was it possible for her heart to hold so much at one time? This must have been how Guinevere felt when Lancelot stood as her hero.

He half reached for her before he caught himself. The glorious ache of hopeless, unrequited love deepened in Kate's heart. It was sweet torment to know that he wanted so to touch her yet never could. How she longed to allow him what he so desired, but even the smallest of touches was forbidden to them.

She dropped into a deep curtsy. "I am honored, good knight," she murmured as she rose, keeping her head bowed like the virtuous woman she knew she was.

"If I am to be your champion, then you must give me your ribbon to wear next to my heart," Warin said, his voice soft as he fulfilled Kate's dreams.

Her heart swelled until it nearly broke. With a trembling hand, she touched her plait and the embroidered strip of fabric she wore braided into it. Warin would wear it, despite that to do so threatened his position in Bagot's house should her father catch him with it.

"How can I give it to you?" she asked, her voice breaking against the hopelessness of their cause. "I cannot do it now, not when so many watch. Nor will the morrow be any better." The wedding party hunted on the morrow. While the woodlands offered the possibility of a moment's privacy in which to give him the ribbon, to thrust the gift at him with no chance for the pretty words and phrases that should accompany it wasn't what she wanted.

"Aye, it cannot be the morrow," Warin agreed, "for I must accompany your sire the whole while we hunt. After this day's misadventure, he cannot be left unprotected, for fear the Godsols, dishonorable worms that they are, might attack him under cover of the sport. What of the morn of the joust? Your father will be busy arming. For those few early hours while he prepares, he'll free you from his presence. I'll wait for you near the postern gate outside Haydon's walls. There we can have our privacy."

Kate hesitated. Only hours ago she'd vowed to herself that she'd never again meet any man alone and unchaperoned. Then again, no matter what Warin thought, there was no chance her father would ever release her from his custody. Which meant she'd have no champion when she needed her courtly lover to fight for her more than she craved breath in her lungs. Against that need, her vow dissolved.

"Aye, should my father indeed release me, we'll meet then," she said, nodding to emphasize her agreement.

Warin's smile was glorious. "We shall meet then, my lady. We shall, indeed."

When he turned and strode away across the hall, Ami came to join Kate. The young widow's brows were pinched. "Did Bagot's steward bring you news of your sire's negotiations with Sir Gilbert?" she asked.

"Nay," Kate replied. "Sir Warin but wanted to apologize for his behavior at the picnic."

"Ah," Ami said, the very sound of the word fraught with her wish to have more than that for an explanation.

The desire to share the tale of her hopeless love for Warin welled up in Kate only to die. It was one thing for Ami to know about Rafe's attachment to her, for Rafe's cause was obviously impossible, he being a Godsol. Although Warin's cause was no less futile, Warin was her father's steward. An accidental word about their love could never reach her sire.

At last, Kate only shrugged. "He spoke discourteously before me in the interchange between my sire and Rafe Godsol."

"That's all?" Ami asked, sighing in disappointment. "I hoped for something more meaty than that." She caught Kate's arm. "Come. We're all going out to the garden, it being a lovely night. Emma wants to play a round of Hoodman Blind in the dark."

A moonlit game sounded like pure joy to Kate. She laughed in anticipation as they hurried toward the hall door, only to meet Lord Humphrey when they were but halfway there. Even Ami quailed at the black look on Lord Bagot's face.

Kate's father caught his daughter by the arm, yanking her away from Ami. "A handfast!" he snarled, speaking more to himself than to them. "He suggested that because you'd proved barren in one marriage that the two of you should handfast instead of exchanging true vows! That might have been good enough during the interdict, but for him to suggest it now is insulting. No daughter of mine will risk bearing a bastard on the promise that the child and the relationship might be legitimized after. Come, Sir William of Ramswood has gone to the garden."

So great was Kate's relief that she wouldn't have to marry Sir Gilbert that it was hard to be disappointed over losing her freedom. She threw Ami a triumphant look as her father led her out of the hall ahead of the widow. After all, she was still going to the garden and the game, doing it all the while without the possibility of Sir Gilbert trying to force another touch upon her.

"Here's your coin, lad. Now, what did they say?" Speaking in the child's native English rather than the French of his own class, Rafe handed the serving lad a single pence, one he could afford to spend only because the dice had made the contents of Simon's purse his own.

The boy examined the coin, checking to see that the image of their king decorated one side and the Lord's cross the other. He ran a finger over its edges, seeking missing bits. When he was satisfied, he stuffed it down inside the high collar of his shoe. With his new riches safely stowed, the lad straightened to face the gentleman who'd bought his ear.

"First the knight was angry. Jealous, I think me, since he wanted to know why you, sir, kept looking at the lady. Then the lady got angry and high-handed over him asking her such questions. Then they talked of love, sir," he said, spitting his disgust over such a topic into the thick layer of rushes that covered Haydon's hall floor.

That much Rafe had been able to discern from a distance. Although he doubted Sir Warin's emotion was jealousy over Kate. Nay, it was ownership of Glevering that Bagot's steward meant to protect. As for Kate, her face reflected her every emotion. Rafe had never been happier than when he'd seen her frown at her sire's steward.

Unfortunately, her bad mood had too swiftly given way to the same adoring glow she'd worn this afternoon when looking at Sir Warin. It was an expression that pained him mightily, since he wanted that sort of look all for himself.

"Anything else?" he prodded, scanning the hall for Kate.

A moment ago she and Lady Amicia had been headed for the hall door, no doubt on their way to the garden with most of the other guests. As much as Rafe longed to follow, he couldn't—not this night. He dared not risk some wayward glance or chance meeting that might further enrage Lord Bagot.

Now, the morrow would be different. Once those in the wedding party had broken their fast, they'd all ride out into the royal chase for the hunt. There was no order in the wild racing of hound and horse after the buck. Better yet, men and women would ride together, each to their own abilities. If a man were to come across a woman during such an event, say even keep pace alongside her for a time, he could blame it on the chaos of the sport.

"Aye," the child said, "the knight vowed to win the joust for her."

That teased a scornful snort from Rafe. Sir Warin would be lucky to keep his seat for a single run when they faced each other. The joust and its prize, a purse filled with three marks' worth of pence, was one of the reasons Rafe had teased Gerard into inviting him. Winning the joust wouldn't hurt his career should he truly decide to leave the king's service. He smiled to himself. Once he'd taken that purse, Kate would have no doubt who was the better man, the man worthy of all her smiles.

"Then," the boy went on, "the knight asked the lady to meet him at dawn the day of the jousting outside Haydon's postern so she might give him her ribbon to wear."

Rafe's full attention snapped back onto the child. "He asked her that? Nay, you misheard them. Your French is so poor you've translated wrongly."

"I did not," the lad protested, rubbing his nose on his sleeve. Ashes from the fire spread a dark streak across his cheek. "I speak your tongue as well as any man, sir. I heard him tell the lady that her sire would be busy arming himself and have no time to watch where she went. The lady, she seemed like she didn't really want to meet with him, but said him aye nonetheless."

That sounded too much like Kate's behavior at the picnic to be wrong. Rafe's eyes narrowed. May God damn that bitch's son. He still meant to misuse Kate's innocence. Untouched as she was, Kate didn't know that she should tell the lecher nay.

Gratitude swelled in him. He thanked God he'd had the coin to buy this child's ear. Now he knew both when and where de Dapifer meant to make his attempt. Kate wouldn't be left alone to fend off the wolf.

"You did well, boy," he told the lad, reaching out to tousle the child's brown hair. "What say you? Shall I pay you for keeping your eye upon the knight for me? You'll report to me everything he does and says about the lady and their doings. Consider yourself my servant for the remaining eight days of the wedding. Heed me on this, though, for I'll only pay you if you tell no man or woman what you do on my behalf."

The thought of eight pence all his own made the boy's eyes gleam. He bowed low. "Your servant, loyal and true, good sir. My tongue yours to command," he said, then scampered off into the hall.

Rafe laughed. The lad had expensive ideas about loyalty.

Chapter 10

⌒◠◡◠⌒

Laughing, Kate leaned low over the neck of her horse as she raced with the others through the trackless woodland. Trees streamed along at either side of her, the light through the verdant canopy in joyous flux between sun and shadow. The smells of sweating horses and summer filled her every breath. Men shouted, their voices echoing through the ferny hills and lush dales. Lymers yipped in excitement as they coursed after the prey they'd been bred to hunt. Not too far from Kate, the old countess whooped.

"The buck lodges!" someone called from the head of the pack.

"Faster! He's cornered!" Ami shouted to her, spurring her own mount to an even headier pace.

"I come," Kate cried in reply, digging her knees into the hunter her father had brought to Haydon for her use.

Although she'd never before ridden Pelerin, her sire had assured her the gelding was an amenable mount, given to great bouts of speed and owning the endurance of a hart. Now Pelerin proved his master no liar. He sprang into a breathtaking sprint, shooting past Ami's smaller palfrey.

Knees tight, Kate drew him to a halt amid the milling crowd of horses gathered at the edge of a steep drop. Below the mounted gentlefolk, the hillside was thick with trees, brush and bracken, the foliage close enough to deter a sensible rider. Men and women alike groaned as the buck galloped out of the concealing growth at the bottom of the hill, as unreachable as heaven.

"He wasn't lodged," the countess shouted. "Look at those antlers! He's an oldster, like me, warned and wary. Poor Lord Haydon," she called to their host. "You paid the king a fortune for the right to hunt yon creature, and now we'll never catch him."

"Speak for yourself," Sir Josce FitzBaldwin bellowed, and spurred his horse over the edge. Haunches low and forelegs stiff, his mount slid downward to disappear into the trees.

Sir Josce's idiocy must have been contagious. In the next instant, the horner went over the edge, his instrument lifted to his lips as he called everyone to follow. A goodly number of the hunters, Kate's sire and Warin included, did as he bade, their horses slipping rather than running down the hill. Dogs

seethed along in their wake. Within an instant,
nothing remained of those foolhardy souls save the
sounds of excited barking and the crash and thrash
of horses through the underbrush.

Among the more sensible folk remaining at the
hill's crest, chaos reigned. Some turned their
mounts to the right, others to the left, depending on
their perception of which was the shorter way
down. Horses snorted and cried in complaint.

In the crush, someone's mount nipped Pelerin's
hindquarter. He bucked in reaction. Caught off
guard, Kate dropped her bow to clutch his reins and
calm him. As Pelerin settled, his forehooves touched
down on the wrong side of the hill's edge. Already
loosened by those who'd gone before, the earth
gave way beneath his weight. With no more choice
than a stone, Pelerin started into a headlong descent, thundering down through the thick growth.

Kate had no breath for screaming. Every ounce of
her was focused on keeping her seat. Sharp holly
tore at her gowns, scraping her legs where sitting
astride left them bare. Twiggy branches poked and
pried. An old oak stole her cap, while a leggy
hawthorne tried to yank one plait off her head.

Pelerin screamed. Kate's world whirled, then
came to a breathless stop as she met the ground
with stunning impact. Gasping, she lay where she
fell.

Through the branches above her, a herd of woolly
clouds was making its way across the vastness of the
sky. The rich smell of damp woodland rose from the

ground beneath her. Last year's leaves felt velvety-soft against her cheek.

From too far away came the shouts of the hunters. The horn was a distant blare. A moment later and the sounds faded. One after another, birds began to chirp as the woodland reclaimed its noisy peace.

A whole new concern jolted through Kate. God save her, she was alone in an unfamiliar wood filled with who knew what sort of threats. The sooner she regained the hunting party, the better for her. Drawing a deep breath, she sat up and moved her arms, then her legs. There'd be bruises tonight, but everything worked.

From behind her, Pelerin snorted and blew, the sound distressed. Secure in her own well-being, Kate rose to look to her mount. The horse stood beneath the orderly branches of a beech, favoring his foreleg, while his head hung. Clucking in dismay, Kate went to him. Tucking her gloves into her belt, she ran her hands down his leg, then snorted at herself. All that told her was that if there was a break, she couldn't feel it.

From the hilltop above her, something large thrashed in the bracken. The woodland creatures dropped into an eerie silence. Saddle leather squeaked. Bridle rings jingled. Vegetation crunched.

Dread started through Kate. Even though she told herself it was likely one of the king's foresters following after the hunters to see to stragglers, thoughts of thieves and brigands churned. Adele said a woman alone without the company of her menfolk or trusted male servants faced a horrible and debauched death.

Slipping around Pelerin, she stood between horse and beech so his bulk concealed her. As if such a thing would buy her more than a moment's safety! The thrashing drew nearer.

"Slowly, my lad," Rafe Godsol said, his voice echoing oddly in the silent forest. "Have a care where you step."

Kate smiled, so deep was her relief. Coming around Pelerin, she watched Rafe bring his mount to a halt near hers. Oh, but he looked fine, indeed, even dressed as he had been yesterday, in a green hunting tunic with tall boots gartered to his legs. His leather vest had been mended after her sire's attack. Today, his hunting bow jutted up over his left shoulder.

Something warm, deep and oh so pleasant stirred in Kate. A part of her longed for another of those wondrous kisses, wrong though it might be. Who could have known that a mere press of lips to her hand might set her on fire?

"How did you know I was here?" she asked in an attempt to distract herself from her inappropriate thoughts. It didn't work. Instead, all Kate could think was that Rafe watched her because he loved her.

He smiled at her. "I saw your poor beastie make his dash over the edge. From the look on your face, I guessed it wasn't planned."

Rafe made a show of eyeing her up and down, then reached out to dislodge a clump of forest floor from her shoulder. "You look only a little worse for your wild ride."

That made Kate laugh. "Wild it was," she replied, leaning down to brush in earnest at her leafy and torn skirts. When she was done, she sent a wry smile his way. "There was even a brief moment of flight, which came to a jarring end. Fortunately, nothing's broken, even though I'll soon have bruises on my backside to match those on my pride."

"Brave lass to make so little of such an experience." Approval glowed in Rafe's eyes, then his face softened. "God be praised you weren't hurt."

Why the expression on his face might make her want to wrap her arms around him was beyond Kate, but that's exactly what she wanted to do. She did her best to slaughter the urge. When it refused to die, she turned to pat Pelerin's neck, hoping that out of sight might be out of mind.

"Would that I could say the same for my horse," she said, speaking to Pelerin's mane. "There's something amiss with his leg."

Leaving his own mount, Rafe stripped off his gloves, then squatted to cradle her horse's foreleg in his hands. The gelding shuddered and shifted at his touch. "Nay, now, sweet Pelerin," Rafe said, reaching up to stroke the horse's shoulder. "It's only me, Rafe. You remember me, do you not?"

Surprise drove even the inappropriate thoughts

from Kate's mind. She frowned at Rafe. "How would you know this horse when he belongs to my sire?"

Still holding Pelerin's leg, Rafe looked up at her. There was a touch of bitterness in his gaze. "Your sire hasn't always owned him. Pelerin was bred and born in Long Chilting's stables. I've ridden him myself while home from court on visits. Four years ago, your lord father or some other Daubney stole him from us. I think your sire got less than he expected, for Pelerin had been gelded the month before he was taken."

His words stirred an uncomfortable sensation in Kate. She didn't much like the thought of her noble sire as a horse thief. It didn't help that she only now remembered Rafe saying that her sire had killed his. Then again, a Godsol had killed her brother. She tried to feel some outrage over her sibling's death, but there was nothing. She'd barely known her brother; he was but a lad of two when her sire had sent her from Bagot.

Rafe came back to his feet a moment later with a shake of his head. "Nothing's broken, but I fear he'll bear you no more this day, my lady," he said.

Although his verdict was no different from what Kate expected, disappointment ran deep. "Oh, fie," she cried softly, even as she gave Pelerin's ears a good scrubbing so he'd know it wasn't him she blamed. "The day has just begun, and I was so looking forward to the hunt."

Now, rather than enjoying hours and hours of Ami's companionship, Kate would be making the long walk back to Haydon with some servant as her escort. Haydon would be interminably lonely before the rest of the party returned. Selfish tears stung her eyes. She leaned her head against Pelerin's neck to hide them from Rafe.

"If it pleases you, my lady, I'll lead Pelerin back to Haydon in your stead. You may use my mount for the remainder of the day." His words were heartfelt, making his offer more than simple courtesy.

Kate leaned back from her horse to look at Rafe. There was naught but a desire to do what pleased her in his face. Sweet tendrils worked their way into Kate's heart. Here was proof that Rafe harbored affection for her. Only a man in love would trade away his own pleasure in favor of his lady. The need to hear of his affection grew apace with her joy, although she had no choice but to refuse his offer.

"Would that I could," Kate replied with a sigh, "but somehow I'm certain my lord father wouldn't much like to see me astride your horse, even if you're nowhere to be found."

As if he'd forgotten her sire's hatred for the Godsols, Rafe winced. "About yesterday," he said, his voice low. "I beg your forgiveness for approaching you as I did. I meant only to do right by you. Instead, I left you open to harm. I pray no hurt came to you because of my actions."

Here was more proof of Rafe's feelings for her. That river of feeling again welled in Kate's heart. She went eddying along in its current until she was fair giddy. How she longed to tell Rafe she approved, hopeless though his love might be. She dared not. On this point the rules of chaste love that Adele had taught her were very clear. There could be no word from a lady to a knight about such things until that knight had professed his adoration for said lady. Even after he had, the lady dare not do much more than acknowledge his devotion with pretty sighs and longing looks.

Frustration gnawed at Kate's heart. Rules, always rules. She wouldn't be alone with Rafe for long. Surely, Ami or someone else would miss her before much longer and come seeking her. With time so limited, how was she supposed to win his admission of love, when the best she could do was lead the conversation in the direction she wanted?

"No harm came to me," she said, only just catching herself before she thanked him for his honorable behavior the previous day. To do so would insult him, since it suggested she'd expected otherwise. "As for my forgiveness, it's given."

"What?" he asked with a quick laugh. "So freely does a Daubney forgive a Godsol? Best you never tell your lord sire of this moment. With the animus between our families, I doubt he'd approve of your generosity."

"Of that there is no doubt," Kate replied in impatience. That awful feud. It stood like a wall between her and the confession she wanted Rafe to make. "About this hatred between our families. What caused it?" she asked.

Rafe's brows raised as surprise filled his dark eyes. "You don't know?"

Kate gave a lift of her shoulders. "I suppose I did once, but I've long since forgotten it," she replied truthfully.

The silence that followed lengthened until the sparrows went back to chirping. Rafe's face was the picture of consideration. While he pondered his answer, he scrubbed at the narrow line of his beard. At last, he gave a shrug. "I suppose there's no harm in telling you, but remember this is the tale from the Godsol side of the line.

"Some three score years ago, a Daubney stole one of my ancestresses, an heiress, and forced her into marriage with him. That Daubney had as his friend old King Henry, God rest him, our own king's sire. King Henry was just then coming onto his throne. Thinking to secure his grip on his new realm, old Henry worked to make an ally of every man he could. For that reason did he confirm the Daubney's forced wedding as legitimate. Once the Daubney thief added our Glevering to his other properties, he had wealth enough to justify old Henry naming him baron. And that is why a Daubney is now Lord Bagot while we Godsols go wanting half of what should be ours."

Stunned, Kate stared at him. "Glevering became part of my dowry upon my brother's death," she said, her voice quiet. Aye, but it was stolen no less than Pelerin was. "If the tale you tell is true, then why haven't your family or your ancestors sued to reclaim Glevering from my kin?"

Rafe's smile was swift and bitter. "Believe me, my lady, it hasn't been for lack of Godsol effort that

Glevering is your dowry. We've tried by fair means and foul, but neither court nor war has served us. All our persistence has won is Daubney determination to destroy us for all time." He gave a quiet laugh. "Your sire even tried to break my sire's heart."

At Kate's startled look, he grinned again, the movement of his mouth more natural this time. "Before your parents were wed, my sire courted your dam. Your father paid your maternal grandsire a great sum to have the woman my father desired. We Godsols say this expenditure was simply for spite's sake. Because my father wanted her, your sire made certain the Godsols didn't get her."

Thoughts whirling, Kate struggled to absorb all Rafe told her, then use it to lead the conversation toward the subject of love. Words jumbled in her brain only to fall past her lips before she quite knew what she intended to say.

"How strange that nothing you've tried has worked to restore Glevering to you. Perhaps our Lord has different plans for your family and that property. Do you suppose that since a marriage was the cause of all your Godsol losses, He deems some future marriage will restore Glevering to you?"

As Kate heard herself, she flinched. Oh, Lord, but that hadn't come out even close to what she needed. What had marriage to do with love? Adele had been right to despair over her daughter-by-marriage's propensity for speaking when she shouldn't. Now Rafe would think her a fool, for no one could ever believe their families' feud might ever relax enough for a Daubney and a Godsol to marry.

Surprise rendered Rafe wordless. Dear God, could he have heard rightly? Was Kate proposing to marry him?

Rafe stared down at the woman he'd expected to force into wedlock. Numerous tiny rents played havoc with her sleeveless green overgown. Her undergown, a slightly darker green than the upper garment, had suffered far worse damage; one narrow sleeve had been torn from wrist to shoulder, revealing the full length of her slender arm to him. Her head was bare; she must have lost her cap in the wild dash down the hill. One of her plaits had opened. Thick, dark hair tumbled over her shoulder, reaching well past her waist.

A shaft of longing tore through him, so powerful that it rocked Rafe back on his heels. His mind supplied the image and sensation of Kate's hair streaming over his bared chest. Another image followed, that of a naked Kate lying like some wanton on the bedclothes. Not just any bedclothes, but his. Oh Lord, but the idea of a willing Kate in his bed on their wedding night was as intoxicating as fine wine.

As if she, too, felt the gnaw of his new hunger, heat warmed the quiet depths of Kate's gray eyes. Sudden color brushed her cheeks. Her lips parted.

Rafe's heartbeat lifted to a new pace. It was all the invitation he needed. Cupping her face in his hands, he stroked his thumbs over the slant of her cheekbones. Her skin felt like silk against his naked fingers.

Kate's eyes closed and she sighed. Rafe's blood boiled. He touched his lips to hers, a brief press of flesh to flesh. Again her mouth was soft and sweet beneath his. A moment later and she moved as she had in the alcove, shifting toward him until her body melded against his.

Need blazed in Rafe, pleading for immediate satisfaction. His mouth took hers, his lips demanding the response he knew she could give him. For a moment, Kate melted against him, offering what he wanted and more, then she gasped against his mouth. Bracing her hands against his chest as if to push, although she made no attempt to force him back from her, she tore her mouth free from his and looked up at him. Embarrassment and longing mingled in her expression.

"You mustn't kiss me," she chided, but her words came out breathless and soft. "Indeed, we mustn't even touch. It's wrong."

Rafe's hands closed over hers. "Not to kiss you, my lady, is to die a thousand deaths," he said, the words coming without effort, having been uttered to so many women.

Pleasure washed a pretty pink over Kate's cheeks. What seemed like triumph flashed through her gaze. The corners of her mouth strove to rise. "Is that a Godsol admitting to some care for a Daubney?" she murmured. As she spoke, she cast her gaze downward, her lashes making perfect crescents against her smooth cheeks.

"You know I care for you," he said, only hearing the truth in his words as they fell from his lips. Of course he cared for Kate, he would always care for her. A wife was a man's property to cherish and protect.

That thought brought with it the image of Kate cradled in his embrace and savoring his strength. He needed to feel all of her against him. Now.

Rafe stroked his hand up the length of her exposed arm. Her skin felt smooth to his touch. She freed a shaken breath, then her head lifted until their gazes met. Heat put color in her cheeks. Pleading for more such caresses lived in her gray eyes.

The fire in his belly became an inferno. No matter what words she might spill, her body told the truth. She wanted him.

His arms slipped around her. Feeling her loosened hair against his hands only drove need higher. With but the slightest of pressure on her back, he urged her closer to him. Triumph rushed through him when she did as he wanted and leaned against him. Her hands slipped up and over his shoulders until she laced her fingers at his nape. Rafe damned the thickness of leather. Save for that thick material he might have felt her breasts against his chest.

Again she raised her head to him, once more inviting him to claim her mouth as his own. Rafe lowered his head until their lips were but a breath apart, then couldn't bring himself a whit closer. Need for her flooded him, taunting, pulsing, demanding. And still he couldn't bring himself to touch his mouth to hers.

Kate made a tiny impatient sound. Her eyes opened. Questions filled her gaze.

Only then did Rafe understand himself. Other women he took, using them as he would, but not Kate, never Kate. By his will and her words, she was fated to be his wife, the woman who would share his bed for all the days of his life. He needed to know she desired him and that he alone would be her passion.

"You have told me I mustn't kiss you, my lady. If a kiss is what you want, then it must be you who kisses me," he whispered. With each word, his lips brushed hers, the sensation a most delicious torment. It was true. Not to kiss her was to die, but it was the sweetest sort of death he'd ever imagined.

Kate hesitated, a tiny furrow marking her smooth brow. Then, just when he feared she would retreat, she touched her mouth to his. Rafe groaned against her lips, so wondrous was the sensation. His. She was his, and she wanted him.

Her mouth moved on his just a little, then again. Rafe shivered at her innocent attempt to stir his desire. Oh God, to think that he and no other man would teach her the joy that could be had between them.

That thought was his undoing. Need exploded in him. His arms tightened about her until she was crushed against him. His mouth took hers, demanding, nay, pleading that she yield to him. She gasped against his onslaught, then met his need with her own. His mouth left hers to kiss a path along the slender line of her jaw. Kate's breath came in tiny pants. He pressed a kiss against her ear. She gasped at the caress, then arched against him.

A tremor racked Rafe as the mound of her womanhood came to rest against his aching shaft. Putting a hand at the small of her back to hold her against him, he moved his mouth along her neck, kissing his way down toward her collarbone. Each caress wrung a shiver from her, and each of her shivers drove his own desire all the higher. Again she arched against him as she sought to make herself one with him.

"Kate," he murmured against her skin. "Love me, Kate."

"Lady Katherine! Katherine de Fraisney! Where are you?" Josce's bellow echoed across the woodland to drive a stake through Rafe's desire.

Kate gave a sharp cry and sprang back from him as if pricked. Panting and trembling, she stared at him. Her eyes were as wide as a startled doe's. Rafe groaned in disappointment. Worse, her absence from his arms left him feeling a sudden emptiness, as if a great part of him had gone missing.

"Lady Katherine!" called Amicia de la Beres. "Can you shout to us, so we know where to find you?"

Kate shot a panicked look in the direction of the cries, then caught at her loosened hair as if her mere touch might disguise it. "Dear Lord, but I shouldn't

have—we mustn't," she stuttered, then caught hold
of her panic.

An instant later, she drew herself up to her tallest
and crossed her arms before her, once again every
inch the proper woman he'd taken into the window
embrasure. Rafe's heart twisted as he watched her
shed her desire for him as if it was an unneeded
cloak. Soon, he promised himself, soon she'd wear
both desire and him as he pleased.

Lifting her head, she turned in the direction of
her rescuers. "I'm here!" she cried out, then once
more looked at him. "You must go, but before you
do, I cannot help but say it. What you've done—"
She stopped, a start of guilt shooting through her
gaze. "Nay, what we've done," she amended herself, pleasing Rafe that she owned her part of their
shared passion, "it's wrong, and we daren't ever do
it again."

"Wrong?" Rafe protested, caught off guard by
her accusation. "How can it be wrong for a—" He
caught himself just before he spilled the rest of what
he meant to say: for a husband to desire his wife.
That knot in Rafe's heart tightened. Kate wasn't his
wife, not yet. Nay, she wasn't, but she would be as
soon as he took her for his own.

The thought cut Rafe to the bone. Only then did
he recognize the opportunity he'd just lost. Jesus
God, what a fool he was! For the last quarter-hour,
he'd been alone with Kate. Why hadn't he simply
taken her on his horse and left with her?

Understanding followed on the edges of his retreating lust. Kidnapping the Daubney heiress was

what a Godsol bent on revenge would do. But he wasn't just a Godsol. He was Rafe, who wanted Kate, let her family name be damned. He wanted her as a wife, his loving wife, not as a prisoner to whom property was attached. Aye, and now that he'd had another taste of a willing Kate in his arms, he'd better find a way to take her soon. If not, he swore he'd die for the wanting of her.

Standing less than arm's length away yet well beyond his reach, his Kate shot him another flustered glance. "You know it's wrong. How you can drive all sense from my brain is beyond me, but now that I know you do it, it won't happen again." Her words had the sound of a vow in them, but the desire that yet stained her fair cheeks made them a lie. "Now go. If my sire rides with them, he'll kill you should he find you here, and that I could not bear."

Rafe almost smiled. She couldn't bear the thought of his death. That went far to ease her accusation that there was something wrong about their mutual desire.

"Then I'll leave you, my lady, but only most reluctantly," he replied.

Making his way to his horse on legs that still felt like thread after their kiss, he swung up into his saddle. Kate followed to stand at his mount's shoulder and look up at him. At the back of Rafe's brain lodged the image of a willing, loving Kate in his bed. That's what he wanted.

Kate's expression sobered until it was shy and somewhat pained. "I pray you don't think ill of me.

I tell you truly, I've never before behaved this way with anyone. I don't know why it is that you . . ." Her voice trailed off into silence as she gave an almost embarrassed shrug.

Happiness spiked in Rafe. There was no doubting the honesty of her words. Did she realize that in telling him this she also told him that the affection she believed she had for Sir Warin was no affection at all? Against that, how could she still want him for her champion on the morrow?

The need to beg her to refuse de Dapifer and name him in the steward's stead filled Rafe. He swallowed the words. He wasn't supposed to know about her plans with her father's man, nor was there any way to broach the subject without revealing that he'd spied on her.

"My lady, when I think of you, it is only with the highest regard," Rafe said at last. It was true. How else did a man think of a cherished wife?

Pleasure warmed Kate's face and glowed softly in her smile. "I thank you for that," she said quietly, then shook free of what troubled her to regain a more normal mien. "Since it seems I'll not be there to watch it, I'll wish that you take this day's prize."

Inspiration struck like lightning. Leaning down, Rafe took her hand and raised her fingers to his lips. "If I fail you this day, then I vow I'll take the morrow's prize in your honor," he promised her.

Pretty color again washed over Kate's face. The need to sweep her up into his arms and ride from here with her tugged at Rafe. His hand on hers tightened.

"Call to us again, Lady Katherine," Josce shouted, now no more than three hundred yards distant, "so we can find you."

With a gasp, Kate tore free of his grasp and pivoted in the direction of her rescuers. When she turned back to him, naught but worry for him marked her face.

"Go," she urged, her brow creased as she stepped back from his horse. "Now, before they see you."

With a nod, Rafe set his heels to his mount and started away from Josce's call. It wasn't until he was well out of Kate's sight that he touched a hand to his breast. Coiled beneath his leather vest was one of Kate's ribbons, the one from her open plait. He'd found it dangling from a broken hornbeam branch on his way down the hill. He'd taken it as his own mostly because he knew she meant to give Sir Warin its mate. The thought that Bagot's steward might have more of Kate than he did was intolerable.

Not that anyone would know either he or Sir Warin had Kate's ribbon. Rafe dared not wear his where others might see, especially not his brother. Will would never understand why Rafe hadn't taken Kate at the same time he took the ribbon.

As for the steward, Rafe didn't think Sir Warin bold enough to wear his where Lord Bagot could witness it. At the very least, Kate's sire would be enraged that his steward had formed a relationship with his daughter; at the worst, Sir Warin would lose his position, if not his life, for his pursuit of Kate.

Kicking his horse into a trot, Rafe rode in a great

circle around Kate's position on his way to rejoin the hunt. As he went, his thoughts turned to the morrow's joust. Yesterday winning that competition meant only lining his slim purse; his goal now was to take the prize in Kate's honor. Once he had done that, she'd know he was the better man and her heart would be his. All that remained then would be to marry her.

Confidence welled in Rafe. Nor would it be a forced wedding. After all, by her own words, he was the husband God intended for Kate Daubney.

Chapter 11

"**T**here, my lady," Albreda said, settling Kate's golden circlet on her veil to hold it in place. "You'll be the loveliest of all the gentle-women this day, you will."

Seated on her cot, Kate lifted her precious hand mirror. No larger than her palm, the bit of silvered metal set in a horn frame had been a gift from Lady Adele upon their parting. Starting with the mirror aimed at her middle, Kate maneuvered it to slowly reveal herself from waist to shoulders.

Because no man had yet tendered an offer for her hand, Lord Bagot dictated that his daughter wear a new overgown today, the one he'd purchased for Kate's upcoming and as yet unscheduled second wedding ceremony. The garment was styled in the height of fashion, with a raised waistline and sleeves so long their hems brushed the ground. Made of silk dyed a pretty shade of blue, she wore it over her pale yellow undergown.

Now the mirror reflected Kate from shoulders to chin. One of her ribbons had gone missing after yesterday's riding accident, even though she, Ami and Sir Josce had searched the whole hillside for it. Because Kate needed the remaining ribbon to give to Warin this morning, she'd refused to let Albreda use it in her hair today. At the moment, it was hidden inside the narrow sleeve of her undergown—this even though she very much doubted she'd have a chance to meet with Warin before the joust started.

With no other hair ornaments to use, Albreda had braided Kate's hair into a single plait, then wound this into a great knot. The hairstyle drew the beholder's eye to the thick golden necklet set with amber that Lord Bagot had given his daughter to wear.

At last, Kate gazed upon her face, framed by the sweep of her fine white veil. She smiled, pleased. All in all, she thought herself an elegant affair. In fact, she looked every inch a woman who had two champions, each trying to take the day in her honor.

From the recesses of her memory came Lady Adele's voice warning that a true lady only ever had one hero at her beck and call. Adele claimed that only an ill-mannered woman gave tokens to more than one man. Doing so, she warned, could lead to more fighting between the champions than against their opponents. God knew that there was plenty of animosity between the two men who loved her.

Then again, she hadn't actually given Rafe a token. And she had promised Warin that he would be her champion. Kate made a face at herself in the mirror. She wasn't certain it was Warin she wanted as a hero.

Once again, that whirlpool of emotions set to turning in Kate. All on its own, the need to be near Rafe woke. Before she caught herself, the corners of her mouth had lifted against a sudden, startling and wonderful pressure in her heart.

What was wrong with her? Kate forced her mouth to flatten. She shouldn't be encouraging these sorts of thoughts. It was a lady's God-given duty to keep the relationship between herself and her courtly lover chaste and she'd fallen down in her duty. Why, yesterday, that first rebuke of hers, that Rafe shouldn't kiss her, had been anemic at best. Even so, Rafe had been honorable enough to bind himself to her words. And, what had she done? Why, she'd kissed him!

Confusion stewed in her. How was she supposed to stop herself from touching Rafe when even the memory of his kiss could set her heart to pounding? Lord, but just the trace of his bare fingers up her naked arm had left her lost in the most glorious rush of heat.

Who would have guessed a man's touch could be so pleasing? Not all men's touches. Kate shuddered at the thought of Sir Gilbert forcing his mouth onto hers.

In disgust's wake, wicked curiosity arose. Rafe was a man she barely knew and hadn't yet come to love, at least Kate didn't think she had. If his kiss was so marvelous, shouldn't Warin's kiss be even better? After all, Warin was the man she'd loved for all of last month.

"What do you think?" Albreda demanded, interrupting Kate's inappropriate musings.

"I think I'll do very well, Albreda," Kate replied, banishing as best she could the remains of her sinful thoughts. Fearing Albreda might discern something in her tone, Kate busied herself in returning her mirror to her jewel chest and placing the tiny coffer back beneath her cot.

"Now, my lady, don't you worry," Albreda replied, wholly mistaking her mistress's lusts for disappointment. "Some fine knight will make an offer for your hand soon enough."

Kate sincerely hoped not. As she straightened and brushed her veil back into place, Albreda leaned forward to put her head near Kate's. The maid shot a swift glance at the blanket that divided the tent in twain.

"If I were a bolder woman," the servant whispered, "I'd be telling your lord father that's he's too impatient. These things take time."

"Do they?" Kate asked, turning so swiftly toward Albreda that the servant shied back from her. Oh, how she prayed it would take weeks, months, even years before she had to marry again. "Are you certain?"

"Indeed, I am," the maid replied, offering a confident smile. "Why, years ago, your maternal grandsire kept Lord Bagot waiting nigh on two years before the marriage to your lady mother finally came to pass. Of course, this was partly because there were entanglements with another family that had to be broken. So, too, did your lady mother need time to settle her affections," she added.

The past clouded Albreda's gaze for a moment, then she smiled. "I know it's hard for a young thing like you to believe when you look upon him now, but your sire was quite the stallion then, roaring for his mare. He would have no woman but she. Lord, but I thought he'd eat his heart out of his chest, so deeply did he long for his lady."

Albreda paused, her lips lifted against some long, almost forgotten scene. "She was a beauty, your lady mother. Although your coloring is your sire's, you have the look of her, you do."

That startled Kate, as did her sudden longing to hear more of her forgotten dam, especially about her mother's connection to the Godsols. "You knew my dam well?"

"I did indeed, my lady. I was only one of Bagot's seamstresses then, but—" Albreda fell silent as the drape separating father and daughter lifted. It was Peter, Lord Bagot's manservant.

"Albreda, since you're finished with Lady de Fraisney, Lord Bagot awaits you," he said, a note of warning in his tone. His stern expression left no doubt he'd overheard the maid discussing his lord with that man's daughter and sought to stop any further confidences.

Chastised, Albreda bowed her head. "I come," she said, leaving her charge without a backward glance.

Stewing in frustrated curiosity, Kate slipped around the blanket to stand near the tent's open flap. Once again the rising sun filled the tent's interior, the long, lazy rays reaching all the way to the back wall. Today, the light teased metallic glints from her sire's chain-mail hauberk and leggings where they lay draped across Lord Bagot's armor chest. Since her father had no squire at the moment, Peter did the duty of checking the armor for loose and rusting links.

At the far end of Lord Bagot's cot lay a basket of breads and cheeses, delivered not long ago from Haydon's kitchen to break her sire's fast. A square of greased fabric now covered the tent's rush flooring. Near one corner stood a bucket filled with steaming water. Haydon's tiny bathhouse was too small to accommodate the many knights who wanted to use it this morn. Thus, some men opted to bathe in the river. Others, like her sire, made do with a scrubbing and a rinse in the privacy of their own tent.

Lord Humphrey, dressed in naught but his skin, sat on his stool at the cloth's center, face aimed toward the tent's doorway. Any hope of meeting Warin died. It was as if her father knew his daughter planned to slip out from under his eye this morn and intended to prevent it.

Kate sighed, only to startle herself when she realized she was relieved. She didn't want Warin to be her champion or have her ribbon. Her hand curled about her opposite wrist and the ribbon hidden in her sleeve. Why hadn't she given this to Rafe yesterday?

Rushing now, Albreda grabbed the cloth from the lip of the bucket, wetted it, then laded on soft soap from the wee cask of the stuff they'd brought from Bagot. Moving around her lord, the maid began to wash the nobleman's back.

Without Albreda to block her view, Kate stared at her father. Resentment flared. By all rights, she should have been the one bathing him; it was the duty of a man's nearest female relative, whether wife, daughter or sister, to perform that service. Why, many a time in the past had she bathed Sir Guy de Fraisney, her father-by-marriage, with Lady Adele at her side. That her father didn't require the same of her only proved how little he cared for her.

Across the tent from her, Lord Humphrey's eyes narrowed. His jaw tightened beneath his beard. "Haven't you anything better to do than stare at me?" he demanded, his voice harsh.

Kate started in surprise, unaware that she was still looking at him. More resentment followed. What did he expect her to do for the two hours before the jousting began—sit on her cot and twiddle her thumbs?

"Nay, my lord," she said in truthful answer.

Irritation flashed through her sire's eyes, then he loosed a fiery sigh. "I suppose you don't. Well, the last thing I need is you underfoot when I must concentrate on what awaits me this day. Go on," his wave shooed her toward the tent's open flap. "Take yourself off to the hall and break your fast with the other ladies. Go, waste your time in whatever useless occupation idiot women like yourself use to fritter away their day." There was nothing but sneering contempt in his voice.

Kate gaped at her sire. Just as Warin had predicted, he was sending her away from him. So great was her surprise that the words sprang from her lips, "By myself?"

Peter came upright from his task, his brows raised in surprise. "My lord, Sir Warin has gone to the river to bathe. Shall I escort Lady de Fraisney to the hall in his place?"

Lord Humphrey gave a curt shake of his head. "You have your own tasks to perform. Besides, it's not necessary. What harm can come to her between here and the hall or garden door? With the joust only two hours away, even those snake-eating Godsols will be too busy arming themselves to bother her. Go," her sire commanded, again motioning Kate out of the tent, "seek out Lady Haydon, who no doubt will happily take you under her wing, once more calling me abuser as she does so."

Kate didn't wait for him to change his mind. Turning, she stepped outside the tent, only to find herself in the midst of unexpected traffic. A page pushed past her, his lord's helmet cradled under one arm. Two servingmen swerved to avoid her, buckets of steaming water suspended from the yokes that crossed their shoulders.

Kate stepped out of their way and paused. For one foolish instant, she considered seeking out Rafe instead of Warin. Even as the thought formed, she dismissed it. She could never approach a Godsol without drawing comments that would wend their way to her father's ears. Nay, if she wanted a champion in the joust, it had to be Warin, who was waiting for her right now. Besides, she owed Warin the honor, having promised it to him first.

Kate strode off through a rainbow of tents, their pennants snapping in the breeze. Up she climbed Haydon's hill until she reached the massive inner gateway leading to the castle's heart. Once through that tunnel-like opening, she stopped to catch her breath in the inner courtyard.

Unlike the bailey, which occupied a broad swath of land between Haydon's outer and inner walls, the area within the second of these thick stone defenses was tight and cramped. The scents of baking bread and roasting meat wafted from the kitchen which lay to the right of the gate. In the corner directly across from the gateway, the square keep tower rose a full four storeys above the courtyard floor. A conical roof, its slate tiles gleaming in the new day's light, perched atop the keep's uppermost storey made the tower seem taller still.

Haydon's hall, its roof made of the far less permanent thatch, grew out of the keep's side, using the length of the castle's defensive wall as its back. At the hall's end nestled the garden, a wealth of summer roses tumbling over its low enclosing wall.

The postern gate, the exit outside which Warin waited, cut through the thick wall at the garden's end. Just now its arched oaken door was thrown wide, the customary porter gone for the time being. This allowed any knight who needed it easy access to the river, just as it gave Kate access to Warin.

A cunning smile took possession of Kate's lips. Would Warin's kiss make her throb with joy as Rafe's had? The sinful thought carried her from where she'd stopped in the larger of Haydon's inner gates all the way to the postern, only to abandon her before she exited through that smaller opening.

From deep within her came Adele's disapproval, along with her former mother-by-marriage's many warnings of rape and debauchery for any woman who left the protection of her menfolk and her walls. It was wicked to seek out Warin for the sole purpose of encouraging an intimate interlude, especially when she was no longer certain that she truly loved him. If she did this, how could she ever again call herself a virtuous woman? Better that she retreat to Haydon's chapel and pray that sense be restored to her.

In the next moment, shouts and laughter echoed in through the open gateway. A group of youths appeared, their downy jaws proclaiming them squires, while their shining faces and wet hair pronounced them well bathed. They made their entrance into Haydon's inner yard dressed in naught but their shirts, which left their legs bare from knee to toes. As they passed Kate, they offered her good morrows.

Kate smiled at her own foolishness. This wasn't yesterday, when she and Rafe enjoyed the privacy of the woodlands. There were no trees or bushes outside the postern, and, more to the point, guards always stood atop the walls at either side of the gateway. She and Warin would never be out of someone's sight. It simply wasn't possible to kiss Warin without someone to see them. With her virtue firmly in place, Kate straightened her gown and veil, then left the protection of the inner yard.

Haydon's original builder had set his fortress on the crest of a tall hill. For defense's sake, that long-dead man had left only ten feet between the back wall and the hill's steepest drop. Over time, the need for more water than the kitchen well provided had carved a narrow path down the hillside to the stream below it. Common sense and a desire to protect the walls had dictated that none of Haydon's succeeding lords allow the path to become wider than a single man could use at one time.

Kate glanced to either side of the gateway. Warin wasn't waiting for her. Frowning, she went to the path's head and looked down toward the gurgling water. No one was on the track. Where was he?

Turning, she scanned the wall behind her. From its farthest corner, deep in the keep's shadow, Warin lifted his hand to her. A touch of concern rose in Kate. The spot he'd chosen was far enough from the gate that those coming and going might not notice him at all. Indeed, from where he stood, not even the guards on the walls could see him.

Virtue screamed that joining him there would make it too easy to give way to temptation and invite a kiss. She should wave Warin nearer to the postern. Instead, curiosity powered Kate's feet as they took her directly to Warin's side. Her beleaguered conscience managed to bring her to a stop arm's length from him.

Still wet from his dunk in the river, Warin's usually golden hair was the color of honey. His skin gleamed, all hint of whiskers scraped from his cheeks. His mustache was neatly trimmed. The smile he sent her was meant solely for her.

"Lord, but your beauty fair takes my breath, my lady," he said, bowing like the courtly knight he was, even though he wore naught but his shirt, shoes and chausses.

The thrill of love's game rushed through Kate. Lord, how she enjoyed being adored. "Why, thank you, good sir," she replied with a deep curtsy. As she rose, she smiled up at him. "I am a lady in search of a champion," she said. "See here."

She pulled the ribbon from her sleeve. In idle play, she twisted its length between her fingers to show it to him. "I carry with me this token, but only the knight sworn to win the day's prize in my honor might wear it next to his heart. Are you that man?"

"My lady, I'd walk upon hell's coals for you," Warin replied, his voice lowering a little as he stretched out a hand to wrap the tail of the ribbon around his fingers.

Kate knew this was the moment to release it to him, especially since she'd forgotten her gloves and her hands were bare. Propriety's dictates died beneath her now all-consuming need to know just what sort of sensation his touch would wake. She held her end and waited.

Surprise danced across Warin's face. In the next instant, the corners of his mouth lifted. As if he knew exactly what she wanted, he claimed the ribbon as his own, then raised his hand to place his palm against hers. His skin was still cool after his bath in the river. Hard calluses marked his palm, testimony to his skill as a knight.

Kate waited. Nothing. Where was the breathtaking rush of heat and the thrilling tingles?

Warin's smile widened just a bit. He slid his fingers along Kate's hand until they reached the hem of her undergown's close-fitting sleeve. There he traced the line of fabric against her skin.

Senses straining, Kate sought any hint of reaction to his touch. There simply wasn't anything. How could that be, when yesterday, the barest brush of Rafe's fingers against her arm had weakened her knees?

An instant later and Warin's head lowered. Kate almost sighed in relief. Aye, a kiss was what she needed. After all, Rafe had kissed her before he'd really touched her. Perhaps where love was concerned, a man's kiss paved the way for other sensations.

Warin's mouth came to rest against hers. Kate closed her eyes, wanting nothing to distract her. Unlike Rafe, whose mouth had been gentle on hers, Warin pressed his lips so hard on hers that it was almost uncomfortable. His mouth moved a little, as had Rafe's.

There wasn't even the mildest of quivers inside her. Then Warin's tongue swept across her closed lips. Startled and a little disgusted, Kate shoved back from him.

"Warin," she cried in protest.

A flash of impatience shot through his blue eyes, then was gone. "Kate, my Kate. You say you love me, but offer me no proof of your affections beyond mere words," he said gently enough. Lifting a hand, he traced his fingertips along the curve of her cheek. Again and much to Kate's surprise, his touch stirred nothing in her. "At last this morning, you come to me as a lover should, promising sweetness and softness. Don't retreat now, when I need you so."

All his pretty words woke in Kate was the memory of Warin's loosened clothing at the picnic. Lord help her. Rafe had been right, Warin had expected a tryst that day. Disgust drove Kate back a step from him.

Reaching out, Warin wrapped his arms around her and pulled her close once more. Shocked by his unexpected boldness, Kate didn't even think to strain against his embrace. Warin's mouth once more lowered toward hers. Not wanting to again experience his kiss, Kate turned her head to deny him access to her lips.

"Warin, I am a virtuous woman. I cannot give you the proof you desire," she protested.

"Just a little kiss," he said, releasing an arm from around her to catch her chin and turn her face to his. "Only a kiss, Kate," he crooned, "that's all I want."

"Here it comes!" shouted a man from around the corner of Haydon's enclosing wall, his voice alive with joy.

Warin nearly dropped Kate so quickly did he release her. As she stumbled back in surprise, he whirled toward the echoing sound.

"I've got it, Stephen," another man yelled, his voice that of Sir Josce FitzBaldwin. There was something in the way his words echoed that said he was yet a goodly distance from the corner. "Now to you, Priest!"

Three or four men hooted, some in triumph, one in disappointment. "It's mine," Rafe Godsol shouted.

Guilt shot like a bolt through Kate's heart. God save her, but she didn't want Rafe to see her with Warin. For some reason it made her feel as if she'd wronged him.

Lifting her skirts, she turned and raced like a hoyden for the postern, not even sparing a glance to see if Warin noticed her abandoning him. Once safely concealed inside the arch of the small gate, she stopped to peer around its corner. Warin yet stood where he'd been, staring at the wall's corner from whence came the voices. A moment later, Rafe, Sir Josce and their four companions raced full tilt around that same bend of stone. Dressed only in their knee-length shirts, they all had linen toweling draped about their necks. As they ran, they tossed an inflated pig's bladder from one to the other. The one with the golden brown hair and a merry smile stopped as they passed Warin and bowed low.

"We beg your pardon, sir," this courteous knight said, "but the sport we planned for our bath in the river started a little before time." His apology given, he lifted his heels and raced on to catch his companions.

Once they were past, Warin turned, only now looking for his vanished lover. Shuddering, Kate retreated even farther into the postern's shadow until she stood well inside Haydon's courtyard. God forbid that Warin see her and think she wanted him to rejoin her.

Turning, she dashed toward the exterior stairway that crawled up the hall's side to its guarded second-storey doorway. By the time she set her hand to the railing, confusion had Kate's head reeling. What was she doing, running from Warin, when he was supposed to be the man she loved? When separated from her courtly lover, a lady always counted the hours until they might next meet.

Another wave of disgust ran through Kate. She didn't ever again want to be near enough to Warin to risk another of his kisses. Understanding hit with so much force that Kate gasped and dropped to sit upon the stair, ignoring a servant who climbed up past her.

At last, all Adele's lectures made sense. With every tale she told, Adele warned that a lady had to battle with all her soul to resist the temptation of her lover's touch. Only now did Kate see that what she'd thought virtue was in truth merely absence of temptation. Not once had Kate ever craved Warin's touch. It followed that if she didn't long for Warin, she couldn't be in love with him. In fact, she'd never been in love with him. Given that, it made sense that she'd feel nothing when he kissed her.

Now, she couldn't say the same of Rafe and his touch. A smile crept across Kate's lips. Oh, nay, she couldn't say that about Rafe at all. There wasn't a moment when she didn't long to feel his arms around her. Why, it was as plain as the nose on her face. It was Rafe she loved, not Warin.

As she accepted this, the memory of Rafe's kisses yesterday returned. Kate's eyes closed. The throbbing heat he woke in her stirred at the core of her being. Oh, aye, there was no doubting her temptation when it came to Rafe Godsol.

Kate gasped. Here she was once more lusting after her sire's dearest enemy! This was wrong, terribly, terribly wrong. What sort of lady was she, if she couldn't control herself, tame these untoward desires and leash sin? No lady at all, that's what sort.

Resentment warmed in Kate's gullet. Rules, always rules. It should be wrong that something so pleasant had to be denied.

"Lady de Fraisney?"

Warin's call echoed against Haydon's inner walls, ringing out over the subdued hubbub of busy servants in the courtyard. Guilt twinged. Lifting her head just high enough to peer over the stair rail, Kate watched the man she was now absolutely certain she didn't love step into Haydon's garden.

She should go to him this instant and confess that she'd been mistaken about her affection for him. Aye, at the same time she'd ask for her ribbon's return. A wave of cowardice hit her. As angry as Warin had been after the picnic, he wasn't going to be any happier to learn she no longer cared for him. Lord, but she dared never tell him that it was Rafe who'd replaced him in her heart. The last thing she wanted was for Warin's bad mood to ruin what promised to be a wondrous day. Nay, until she was ready to tell Warin about her change of heart, she'd need a place to hide, a place well out of his reach. Someplace like Lady Haydon's women's quarters, where Ami slept.

Leaping to her feet, Kate fled up the stairs to the hall's exterior door. There was no gauging the depth of her relief when she escaped into the hall without Warin calling after her. Through that big room she went toward the area curtained off for the women.

Aye, she needed Ami, a woman who wasn't afraid to face any man. If only she could find a way to tell Ami what had happened—without mentioning names, of course. Perhaps her new friend would have some advice. At least Kate hoped some of Ami's boldness might rub off on her.

Chapter 12

Although the day was cool enough with occasional cloud, a harbinger of rain this evening, Rafe's sun-warmed helmet made him sweat. Moisture trickled out from under the leather coif he wore beneath his mail hood. One pesky droplet made its way down his brow and into his eye. Rafe blinked away the sting, having learned as a squire just how dangerous it was to rub his face while he wore gloves sewn with tiny metal plates.

To distract himself, he fidgeted in his saddle and purposely juggled his shield. Beneath him, Gateschales chuffed and shifted. His horse seemed as eager as he to claim victory in the Godsol division of the joust so they might face the Daubney winner to take both purse and honor. There was but one man left for them to best before they did so: Josce Fitz-Baldwin.

What surprised Rafe about facing Josce now was that Josce was no Godsol. As he promised at the picnic, Lord Haydon had made good use of the Daubney-Godsol feud; he'd divided the jousters between the shire's warring families. To escape any hint that he favored one side over the other, unaligned families were apportioned to both sides.

Since none of Rafe's companions were yet landed or wealthy enough to take on a squire, for this day they served each other. Simon appeared at Rafe's side, a fresh lance in hand; Rafe's previous weapon had shattered in his first run against Josce. Because Lord Haydon wanted no fatalities to mar his celebration, the potentially lethal lance wore a blunting tip at its end.

Fewtering his weapon for the moment, Rafe looked across the field's width at Josce. His friend took a new lance from Hugh, hefting it as if testing for balance. A moment later, Josce shook his head and returned it to Hugh. Rafe grinned. The Godsol championship had just fallen neatly into the cup of his hand. The only time Josce ever refused his first lance was when he believed he'd lose the match. Now Josce would sort through the available spears, seeking the one that would lend him the confidence he should have had in his heart. All this because Rafe had twice lifted Josce from his saddle when they practiced two weeks past.

With Haydon's bailey occupied by tents, Lord Baldwin had staged the day's contest in a meadow not far from his home. Long and flat, its grasses scythed close to the ground, this wee plain was situated between two low hills and ringed by fields of wheat. There was even a small stream, which offered water enough to sate an overheated horse or man. Today's event had drawn every serf and peasant for miles around, or so it seemed. All of them wore their best homespun clothing, dyed the rich hues of onion skin and nut husk. So many folk sitting behind the lists, dining on bread and cheese while their children played, gave the day a fairlike feel. Why, a few enterprising souls even hawked ale among their ranks.

Although the gentlefolk were scattered about the field's edges, most clung to the meadow's far end, where Lord Haydon had provided makeshift benches, rough wooden planking set upon barrels. A goodly length of tenting canvas had been raised for shade. At first, the only ones on the seats were the gentlewomen, the few churchmen and those oldsters who chose not to participate in the sport. They'd made quite a picture, all dressed in their finery. The scene had grown a little more ragged over the hours. As knights were eliminated from the contest, they shed their heavy armor and hot woolen underarmor, then joined their womenfolk, wearing only their rough shirts, chausses and boots.

Rafe found Kate in their midst with ease. Her pretty blue gown glowed like a beacon next to Amicia's scarlet. He was in time to catch Kate watching him. A brief but oh so pleased smile flashed across her face as their gazes met, then bright color washed her cheeks. An instant later, she looked down into her lap.

That she could gaze at him so after he'd interrupted her with her lover this morning sent a rush of triumph through Rafe. His gaze swept across to the field to where the Daubneys ran. He didn't know which pleased him more, the fact that it seemed he'd already stolen Kate's affections from Sir Warin or that he was about to meet Bagot's steward and prove to Kate he was the better man.

Sir Warin, it turned out, was a fine jouster, although Rafe hesitated to believe him as fine as himself or Josce. Still, Rafe liked the thought of facing the steward as an equal. That way there was no chance that defeating Warin might stir a grain of pity in Kate's heart for the man.

Just as with the Godsols, the Daubney division was in its final round. It was Sir Warin against Sir Gilbert DuBois, Lord Bagot's neighbor and staunch supporter. As the herald gave the sign, the two men, lances leveled and shields high, spurred their mounts. The thunder of galloping horses resounded across the meadow.

Rafe shook his head. The match was Sir Warin's. Even from this distance he could see Sir Gilbert's lance tip drag. So did the steward. Sir Warin subtly shifted his shield to take advantage of the other man's error.

Shield metal shrieked and lances groaned as they collided. In that split second, Bagot's steward gave a twist of his arm. Sir Gilbert's lance tip dropped so suddenly that it caught the sod. With his horse galloping on to the alley's end, the effect was to lift Sir Gilbert out of his saddle.

The crowd cheered, the Daubneys roaring as they welcomed Sir Warin as champion. After all, he was Lord Bagot's representative in business. Why shouldn't he be his proxy in war games? Even Rafe offered his rival mental congratulations on the well-played trick. Aye, it would be a fine thing, indeed, to meet and defeat Sir Warin.

With the Daubney champion revealed, it was time to determine the Godsols' representative. Rafe looked back at Josce. His friend had finally decided on a lance.

The herald, played this day by a knight too old to participate, rode back across the field to where the Godsols ran. Reining in his horse, he called out the names of the contestants, not that anyone didn't know who either Rafe or Josce was. With his announcement, folk all around the field dropped into a breathless silence.

Rafe hefted his lance. His knees tightened on his horse. It wasn't necessary. Gateschales, well-trained beast that he was, was more than ready. There was nothing that this horse liked better than the joust, being a marvelous sprinter.

The herald retreated. Rafe positioned his shield. His hand tightened on the lance's hilt. At the sign, they were off.

Gateschales breathed like a smith's bellows as he threw himself into his fastest stride, his hooves tearing up great chunks of soft sod. As always, Rafe's world constricted until all he saw was the spot on

Josce's shield he intended to hit. Leaning forward, he allowed long practice to lead his body where it must go.

Lance met shield in an explosion of noise and thrust. Every muscle in Rafe's body strained as he absorbed the force of both Josce and his horse. He gave no inch, nor did Gateschales, who strained to stride on when all nature tried to drive him back.

As had happened two weeks ago during practice, Josce's heart betrayed him. Rather than drive forward, he let Rafe's lance shove him back in the saddle until he tumbled out of it heels over head. His horse veered to one side, trumpeting and raising in trained response to an empty saddle. Grooms raced to catch the dangerous beast.

Rafe drew Gateschales into a quick turn and rode back up the field to his fallen friend. Dropping shield and lance, he threw himself off his horse. Hugh and Simon were already kneeling in the torn dirt at the knight's side.

"Josce!" Hugh shouted, lifting Josce's head.

Simon tried to remove Josce's helmet in case of injury, but the metal headgear clung to the mail hood beneath it and refused to give. "Damn me, but what if we have to bring him to the smith to have it off?" he muttered.

Rafe crouched at Josce's side in time to see his friend's eyes open. "God's pain, Rafe," his friend breathed. "Why do I keep letting you do this to me?" That he spoke was enough to make all three of the waiting men grin.

"He'll yet live to spite his father," Rafe said in abject relief, his hand closing over Josce's shoulder in what was meant as a comforting touch.

Josce winced. "Only as a broken man," he said, managing a laugh. Simon and Hugh put their arms beneath him to aid him in sitting. "I concede to you. Now go on and take the prize, as is your due. As for me, I'll slink back to my father's house and lay poultices upon my bruises, hoping I'll be limber enough for the morrow's melee, so I might make my fortune ransoming horse and armor."

With a grateful laugh, Rafe rose, only to find Lord Haydon standing behind him. It was a tiny, satisfied smile the nobleman sent in Rafe's direction before he knelt at his son's side. However short the glance, Rafe read the message hidden in it. Lord Haydon couldn't be happier at his son's defeat, for it meant the Godsol responsible for the uproar at the picnic would face one of the Daubney participants in that same event. Lord Haydon had what he so needed. The morrow's mock battle would have nothing at all to do with politics.

Pleased with his victory for his own reasons, Rafe strode toward the groom who held Gateschales. As he went, he threw a glance at Sir Warin. The steward had removed his helmet and now stood beside the defeated Sir Gilbert. Sir Warin offered his opponent a friendly hand, but smug satisfaction filled his face. Rafe smiled a tight grin. Sir Warin best gloat while he could. In a few moments, he'd be sitting on the ground in Josce's place.

"Well, now, if it isn't our Godsol champion," Will called, striding out to meet his victorious brother.

Having long since shucked his mail in defeat, blood and dirt stained the hem of Will's rough shirt where he'd used it to wipe his face. Sweat traced the outline of his helmet's eyepieces in the dirt on Will's face. "Yon benighted horse is worth every pence our sire spent on his breeding and training," Will laughed, pointing to Gateschales, complimenting the horse's skill before acknowledging Rafe's talent.

"Good work, man," the eldest Godsol continued, offering Rafe a pat on the back. "Now go and take the purse from yon rat-kisser. Show all the world that the Godsols are the better men. In fact, you have my permission to kill the worm-eater, if you so desire." His grin was wicked. "One less Daubney, even a servant like de Dapifer, is far better for this world."

Rafe laughed as he picked up his discarded shield, shrugging it into place on his forearm. He left his used lance where it lay. There'd be fresh weapons for the final round. "I think I'd be better off saving the steward's murder for the morrow, when I can disguise so dastardly a deed behind the chaos of the melee."

Will opened his mouth to reply, but Rafe held up a forestalling hand. "No more, Will," he said, needing to hurry into his meeting with Sir Warin. Rafe knew well enough from sparring with Josce that sometimes the only edge a man had over his competition was what he held in his heart. If Rafe delayed even an instant, Sir Warin might well garner confidence from the belief his opponent was reluctant to meet him.

Nodding, Will gave Rafe another congratulatory

pat. "Go now and take that prize for the Godsols and our honor."

"That I shall," Rafe vowed, then mounted Gateschales.

As he started for the middle alley, where the run for the purse would be held, the Godsols bellowed their approval. When he neared where Kate sat in a place of honor beside the bride and groom, he dared a quick glance at her. She glowed as she gazed back at him. It was something better than desire for him that filled her smile and softened her face. She was proud of him and what she felt for him, the way a wife should be proud of her husband.

Rafe's heart twisted sweetly. Images flooded him, none of them having to do with lust. They were pictures of mundane future events, such as sharing a meal with Kate, and holding her hand as they walked the lands they'd own. It was this, the quiet, domestic bliss he'd never expected to own in his life, that he wanted from his marriage to Kate. Lord, but he couldn't wed her soon enough and begin sharing his life with her.

Priest and Stephen, who'd ridden with the Daubneys, met Rafe as he drew his horse into position at one end of the alley. Both men grinned as they offered him their congratulations.

"Well run," said Priest.

"Never doubted the Godsol champion would be you this day," Stephen said, his voice filled with true pleasure over the achievement of a well-deserving comrade.

"My thanks for your confidence," Rafe replied

with a quiet laugh, grateful to have friends such as these. "Now, what can you tell me of Sir Warin?"

Stephen pulled a sour face and shook his head. "He runs like you, Rafe, sitting in his saddle as if he were a piece of it."

"I'll add, for what little it's worth, that he holds his shield low and tight," offered the sober, priestly Alan. Then he shook his head. "His confidence is supreme. Unless you shake him on the first run, Rafe, I think you'll fight hard to take the purse from him."

Rafe grinned. "Then shake him I shall," he said, "doing the deed with all my heart, just as I always have. Being a third son, it's my lot in life to vie for the scraps that other men, those who are their father's only heir, leave behind them."

Alan grimaced at Rafe's gentle taunt. "You may have my life if you want it, Rafe, even the wife my uncle wishes to press on me. Let me take yours."

Stephen laughed and clapped Alan on the back. "Don't look so glum, Priest," he said. "Your time to join Gerard in the marital estate hasn't yet come. Until then, lift your spirits far enough to help me sort through the lances they've brought Rafe."

As the two of them turned to inspect the weapons for these final runs, Rafe dared reach inside his left glove. With a finger, he rearranged Kate's stolen ribbon into the cup of his palm. He hadn't intended to bring it with him this morning, but there'd been something about keeping it on his person he couldn't resist. It was like a promise to himself. Now that he owned this much of Kate, the rest of her would soon follow. It felt like a talisman, a guarantee that he'd take the purse and her heart along with it.

Stephen and Priest reappeared, Stephen holding the weapon they'd settled on for the first run. Rafe took the lance.

"Come what may," he said to them, "I promise you this will be a match to remember. Inform the herald that I'm ready when my opponent is."

Chapter 13

It was all so thrilling Kate could hardly catch her breath. She watched Rafe ride past her. Her two champions, one acknowledged and no longer wanted, the other unacknowledged and definitely desired, were going to vie for the day's prize! She might as well be one of the ladies in Lady Adele's tales.

Almost better, her sire had been so busy that he hadn't had time to thrust suitors at her. For the whole of this glorious morning, she'd enjoyed Ami's uninterrupted company. The only mar, slight as it was, was that she and Ami hadn't been alone from the moment Kate entered the women's quarters. Once at the field, Lady Haydon had sat Kate and Ami near Emma, now joined by her new husband. Kate hadn't dared even the most innocent of questions regarding how to gracefully—or rather, painlessly—detach herself from a man she no longer loved.

"Poor Sir Josce. I hope he's not injured," Ami said, her gaze yet aimed at her hero as he was helped from the field by his friends and sire. Then she smiled and reached over to catch Kate's hand. "Well, if my Sir Josce must be defeated by someone, it's just as well it was Rafe Godsol who did it. They are the best of friends."

"Are they?" Kate asked, stunned that Ami would know something so intimate about Rafe. "How is it you know that?" she demanded.

Amusement sparked in Ami's green eyes. "About Sir Josce?" she teased, knowing full well that wasn't who Kate meant. "Why, I learned it at court. You might say Sir Josce and his life are of interest to me."

From her place at Kate's right, Emma giggled and shifted to look at the women beside her. Now that Kate knew Emma better, she saw that all the bride had from her lady mother was her red hair. Just as with Sir Josce, it was Lord Haydon's stamp Emma wore upon her face, with her high cheekbones and the slight hook to her nose.

"What's this, Ami?" Emma asked, her tone taunting. "Are you still pining for my half brother, even though you know full well he's too cautious to return your affection the way you wish?"

Ami laughed, not in the least embarrassed by

Emma's pronouncement. "Cautious he may be and with good cause, but this only presents me with a challenge I cannot resist. I will have his heart as my own, will he, nill he."

Gerard's laugh was a quiet huff as he sat beside Emma. Wearing naught but his shirt and chausses like the other defeated knights, his brown hair flattened by his helmet, he looked out of place next to his new wife in her pretty green and yellow gowns. "Don't think to play the matchmaker between our Josce and Lady Amicia, my love," he warned his wife. "There's no hope for them, especially not while Lady Amicia thinks all men are but mountains to be climbed and conquered," he said, his statement forthright and with such a hint of lewdness that it was just this side of good manners.

Ami had the grace to blush. Emma giggled again. Leaning near to her new husband, she touched her lips to his ear.

"Are you content to know I want to climb but one mountain?" she murmured loudly enough for the two ladies beside her to hear.

Gerard shuddered and groaned softly. "Is that so?" he replied, catching his wife by the waist. Much to Kate's surprise, Emma squealed with pleasure as her husband lifted her into his lap. Yet laughing, the new bride wrapped her arms around her husband's neck, then rested her chin upon his shoulder to lay kisses upon his cheek.

That Emma could be so obviously pleased by Gerard's pawing, given her newly-wedded state, truly astonished Kate. Lady Adele had been very clear that all a woman could expect from marriage were the twin aches of consummation and birth. It was womankind's doom, the price they all paid for Eve's sin in the Garden.

God knew Kate had more than paid her price in her union with Richard, although only in consummation pain. At least Richard had never beaten her; he wouldn't have dared, as his illness kept him smaller than her. Lady Adele hadn't had that much comfort in her marriage. Twice Adele's age, Sir Guy de Fraisney had been a crude man who beat his wife when it suited him. Beyond that, he had no interests save his sword, his horse and his hawks.

Fanning herself with a hand to hide the fact that her cheeks had reddened with Gerard's comment, Ami vented a mummer's great breath of disgust. "Lord preserve us from the newly wed," she said, although her tone was fond rather than irritable. She came to her feet. "Come, Kate, let's wander. I've had enough of these two and their lovemaking."

Kate gaped at Ami. Lovemaking was done with chaste words, never touches, and only happened between a lady and her courtly lover. Everything else was lewdness or marital duty. Kate shot a shocked glance at Gerard and Emma. There was nothing chaste about what they were doing and there was nothing pleasurable about marital duty, so it certainly wasn't lovemaking. Ami must have misspoken.

"Can I help it that I desire my wife?" Gerard muttered, turning his face as he tried to catch Emma's lips with his own.

"Don't apologize to her," Emma laughed, managing to avoid her husband's kiss. "It's not our fault that we happen to find joy in our duty."

Coming to her feet, Kate blinked away a second wave of shock. Emma couldn't be serious. She *enjoyed* the awful intrusion of Gerard's shaft into her most private part?

Ami gave a snort. "All I can say is that if a babe doesn't come from this union nine months hence, it won't be for lack of trying. Come, Kate," she said, taking Kate's arm.

Together they left the awning's shade for the day's bright sun and strolled in silence for a moment. It was no surprise to Kate that the direction of their steps led them ever closer to Sir Josce. The bastard knight now knelt on the ground not far from them, his friends helping him to creep out of his mail shirt.

As they walked, Kate stewed over the idea of anyone finding pleasure in the marriage bed. Try as she might, she couldn't reconcile what she knew to be true about the act of procreating with Emma's comment. She gave it up when her head began to pound. The day was too fine to be wasted on such a morbid subject, especially when she could be watching her love.

Her gaze leaped to Rafe. Oh, but mounted on his massive warhorse he looked every inch a hero. The Godsol colors on his shield and surcoat were jewel-bright, while the sun made his mail gleam silver where his surcoat didn't cover it. Better still, he was watching her in return.

Kate's heart turned a circle in her chest as he smiled at her. All on their own, her cheeks took fire. The sinful temptation against which Lady Adele had so strictly warned her rose like a wave to engulf her. It didn't matter that she knew it was wrong or that feeling this way made her a lightskirt. There was no stopping it. She longed to feel Rafe's arms around her and his mouth on hers once more.

Agony followed. If her need to touch him was so strong now, it would be horribly hard to resist him when next they met, especially when she knew their time together would soon end. Once the wedding was done, she'd never again see Rafe. Oh, this was most definitely love, tragic, deep and never to be requited love.

Beside her, Ami laughed. "Best you stop staring at him before your father notices."

"You needn't worry on that account," Kate replied with a small smile. "My father has eyes for no one but Sir Warin, God be praised." As she spoke, her gaze shifted from Rafe to the other end of the field. Her sire stood near Warin, his pride in his steward measured by the sheer width of his grin.

"Ladies," Sir Josce's scarred friend called to them, motioning them closer still as they drew near. "We'd be honored if you'd join us to watch these final runs."

"Why, we'd be delighted," Ami replied so swiftly that it was clear she'd hungered for the invitation.

She dragged Kate with her as she closed the distance between her and her love. "Sir Josce, how do you? I was sorely disappointed to see you fall," she said.

Kneeling, his head and shoulders still caught in his chain-mail tunic, the big man fought his way out of it. Gasping as he dropped back to sit on his heels, he yanked off his leather coif, then raised his head to look at Ami. His blond hair stood up in spikes around his face. Chagrin twisted his face.

"Would that you hadn't witnessed that. This is the third time I've let Rafe pry me from the saddle. I fear it's become a habit. Lady de Fraisney," Josce said, acknowledging Kate. "Do you know my companions, Sir Simon de Kenifer and Sir Hugh d'Aincourt?" The two men aiding in his disarming offered Kate brief bows. Kate nodded to Sir Simon, then smiled at the scarred Sir Hugh, recognizing him as her dancing partner from the previous evening.

"I, for one," Ami said, drawing Sir Josce's attention back to herself, "was certain you'd take the purse for your half sister's honor."

"Against Rafe?" Sir Simon scoffed. "I think not."

Leaving the acquaintances to argue over whether Sir Josce's fall was mere chance or due to Rafe's superior skill, Kate went to stand next to the temporary fencing that surrounded the field. At the Daubney end of the grassy expanse, Warin had remounted. Her father stepped away from Warin's horse. A page, one Lord Haydon had loaned to her sire for the day, the same lad that Ami had pointed out as a potential husband on the wedding's first night, lifted up a long spear to Warin. Once Warin had it in hand, he signaled the herald.

"They're ready to run," Kate called to the others without looking away from the combatants. Excitement shot through her. It was Rafe, not Warin, she wanted to take the day. Aye, he was her sire's enemy and it was wrong to want what her sire despised, but she couldn't help it.

Ami came to stand beside her, while Sir Josce, yet wearing his mail leggings, stopped behind her. As the other two men joined them, the crowd hushed until the only sound was the odd horse's snort and the trickle of water in the stream. Riding to the center of the field, the herald held up his hand in an unnecessary grab for attention.

"For the Daubneys, Sir Warin de Dapifer. For the Godsols, Sir Rafe Godsol. Ride with God," the old man shouted, then gave the sign.

The two horses sprang into motion, moving so swiftly that their tails flew straight out behind them. Every muscle in Kate's body tensed. Her fingers dug into the soft, green wood of the fencing.

Wood met metal in a thundering retort. In that split second, Rafe rocked back in his saddle. With a resounding bass snap, Warin's lance broke. He teetered atop his horse but didn't fall.

"Only a draw for the first run," Sir Josce cried in disappointment over his friend's failure to score. His words were nearly drowned out as around them the crowd roared out its appreciation for such a show.

"Lord, but they're evenly matched. Did you see the Daubney steward shake our Rafe in his saddle?" Sir Hugh shouted out with a worried shake of his head.

"No matter. Rafe will take the day," Sir Simon said, his voice filled with complete confidence. He turned to look at Josce. "I think there'll be time enough to remove your chausses before they're ready for the second run."

"I'll undo your cross garters," Ami said, speaking of the leather strips that kept Sir Josce's loose steel stockings from sagging about the knight's calves. The group of them backed up a few steps to do their chores.

On the field, Warin continued riding down the alley, his course taking him directly toward Kate. When he was but a few yards away, he drew his big black warhorse to a stop. He laid a hand against his heart, a reminder of where he carried her hidden ribbon.

Guilt seared through Kate. Why, oh, why couldn't she have realized she didn't love Warin before she'd given him her token? The very idea that to retrieve her ribbon she might have to confess to him that she loved him no more made her stomach knot. She hoped she'd never have to confess that she now doubted she ever loved him. The very thought made the coward in her recoil in horror.

Despite the shadows Warin's helmet cast on his eyes, Kate saw them narrow. His jaw tensed beneath his beard. She started. Oh, heavens, but she'd been so lost in her own quandary that she hadn't given him the sign he'd expected in return.

Powered by guilt, her hand flew to her breast, only for shame at pretending something she didn't feel to bring it back down just as swiftly. Every line in Warin's body tightened, until anger screamed from him. Jerking his horse's head around, he kicked the beast into motion.

Kate cringed as she watched him go. He knew. Somehow Warin knew she loved him no more. Just as she feared, he wasn't taking it well.

Like a tiny breath of relief, a single thought tumbled through her. A true knight, a man like Lancelot, would never be angry with his lady if her love for him ended. Nay, his heart had no room for such emotions. Instead, he remained constant even if his lady rebuffed him all his years. That Warin could glare at her so only proved he wasn't that sort of knight, despite his similarity in appearance to Lancelot. Given that, perhaps a single ribbon wasn't so great a price to pay to be quit of him.

Gateschales walked on toward the Daubney end of the field as Rafe dropped his lance and shook his head. It didn't help. His ears still rang. Worse, somewhere back behind him lay the shattered remains of his confidence.

Saints above, but running his lance into Sir Warin's shield had been like hitting a stone wall. Never mind the purse. Another meeting like that, and they'd both die, blunted lance tips or not. Since death wasn't what Rafe had in mind for his future, especially when he hadn't yet bedded Kate, he needed to find a way not only to survive this contest, but also to best his opponent. At that very instant the ribbon hidden in his palm shifted, as if to call his attention to it.

Rafe's confidence roared back to life, fully reborn. Aye, it was Kate's ribbon he needed. One glimpse of it, and Sir Warin was sure to be incensed. An angry man made for a careless jouster. That's all the edge Rafe needed right now, the chance to take advantage of a simple mistake on Sir Warin's part.

Needing a few extra moments in which to recover, Rafe let Gateschales walk all the way to the temporary fencing before he turned the horse. His confidence took another leap as he again faced the alley on the way back to his starting point. Sir Warin was only now turning his own horse and starting back. That meant but one thing: Sir Warin was in the same star-spinning, ear-ringing state as he.

In the next moment, Rafe grinned. Better and better! The smug assurance that had infected the set of Sir Warin's shoulders—indeed, the whole line of his body—was gone. In its place was a new and uncomfortable tension. So the steward now doubted his easy victory, did he? Aye, the time was nigh to show Sir Warin the ribbon.

Fishing a good foot's length of the thing from his glove, Rafe let the wide strip dangle from his cuff. Just before he and Sir Warin crossed paths at the center of the field, Rafe pulled Gateschales to a halt and smiled at the worm-eater.

"I vow, Sir Warin," he called, "you'd have had me if your lance hadn't broken." It was the sort of nonsense a man was expected to spew to his competitor.

Sir Warin didn't even glance in his direction. Instead, he kept his narrowed eyes aimed into the distance as his horse walked on. Rafe swallowed a foul curse, then tried, "Better luck with your next run."

As he spoke, he held up his hand in a friendly gesture, all the while praying Sir Warin's eyes would follow the motion. God was good. In that instant the breeze lifted, the moving air sending the ribbon fluttering in Sir Warin's direction.

The knight's gaze shifted as he caught the motion, then his whole head snapped toward Rafe. Sir Warin's eyes flew wide. His jaw dropped, but surprise swiftly gave way to a snarl. Nearly lunging out of his saddle, the knight snatched for the rippling ribbon. Rafe yanked back his arm as Gateschales danced to the side, taking him out of the steward's reach.

Sir Warin's lips drew back from his teeth. "Bitch's son, if you value your life, you'll tell me how you come to have that," he commanded, his hand dropping to his side where his sword would have hung if this hadn't been a friendly match.

Anger surged in Rafe at his insult. He strove to quell his reaction. It was Warin he wanted careless, not himself.

"What, this?" he asked, nonchalantly stuffing the ribbon back into the body of his glove. "Why, it came from a lady at court. I use it as a talisman when I joust. It's worked so far. I've never been defeated whilst I carry it." That was true enough. He hadn't been defeated yet today.

"Liar!" Warin shouted, his word so vehement that spittle flew from his lips. His eyes were wild as he wrenched himself around in his saddle to stare at Kate. "Aye, and you're not the only one telling falsehoods. She didn't lose that ribbon, she gave it to you. That little whore's playing me for the fool!"

Rage tore through Rafe. No worm-eater was going to call his Kate a whore! Harsh words formed on his tongue, but before he could spill them, Warin dug his heels into his mount's side and sent his big horse cantering off to the Daubney end of the field.

The need to split the steward's skull, not just bash wood against the man's shield, exploded in Rafe. He kicked Gateschales into motion, reaching his end of the field a little ahead of Sir Warin. As he turned his horse, he thrust out a hand for a lance without a word. Priest laid a new spear into his palm as Stephen stared up at Rafe, astonished.

"What on God's earth did you say to him?" Stephen demanded. "I couldn't believe it when yon ice man burst into flame out there!"

Rafe only shook his head and drew his shield into position. His blood boiled. By God, he'd lift the rat-kisser from his saddle this time.

At the other end of the field, Sir Warin rode his horse in a circle around the page and Lord Bagot. Instead of stopping to take the lance, he but leaned down in his saddle and snatched his new weapon from the arms of the page.

Rage ate up all Rafe's other concerns. The worm-eater was cheating! It was the speed of the horse that determined a jouster's power. From a standing start a horse needed half the length of the field to reach its fastest stride. If he didn't go now, Sir Warin would have the advantage.

He dug his heels into Gateschales. His horse was ready. Even after so long a day, the gelding threw himself into his long stride.

At the center of the field, the herald called out the foul, commanding the two men to stop. No such complaints bothered the crowd. They cheered this unorthodox turn.

Rafe's world narrowed until all he saw was Sir Warin's shield. Again the impact was tooth-jarring. This time Rafe's blow hit true.

Not so Sir Warin's. The steward's weapon slid across the face of Rafe's shield with an ear-shattering shriek. Sir Warin followed his lance, twisting in his saddle. Triumph shot through Rafe. The point for this run was his.

His world didn't expand again until he'd reached the end of the field. The crowd roared in approval over the trick they'd played. Some of the gentlemen had migrated to the ends of the field. All of those at Rafe's end shouted out their congratulations over his point.

Rafe ignored them. Tossing aside his used lance, he pulled Gateschales into a tight turn. All the accolades in the world meant nothing if Sir Warin tried the same trick twice and started ahead of time.

Sure enough, as Rafe turned, he could see Sir Warin pulling his own horse around to return to the run's starting point. Back to their respective ends of the alley they rode almost as swiftly as they'd made their way down it.

The herald sat upon his horse in the alley's center, his face dark with disapproval over their breach of etiquette. As they neared him, he lifted his arm in a demand that they halt. Neither Rafe nor Sir Warin slowed their horses a whit as they passed the old man. Approval exploded from the audience for such a drama.

This time, Rafe did as Sir Warin had done in the previous run, guiding Gateschales in a circle at his end of the alley. Priest and Stephen were ready for him. Together they held up a lance so Rafe could take it without slowing or leaning too far from his saddle when he reached them.

As he came about, Rafe threw a glance at his opponent. Sir Warin was well into his own circle, but unlike Rafe's friends, the page serving him hadn't expected his temporary master to ignore the herald. The lad's hands were empty. Warin screamed for a lance. Lord Bagot shoved the page aside and raised the lance he carried to his steward.

New outrage tore through Rafe. The lance's blunting cap was gone. That God-bedamned Daubney snake-eater was trying to kill him! Even across the width of the field, Rafe could see the grin that stretched across Sir Warin's face as he snatched the lethal weapon from his master's hands. Screaming like a wild man, the steward started down the alley.

It was too late to stop, not that Rafe would have done so anyway. No man threatened his life and walked away unscathed. He leveled his new weapon and touched his heels to Gateschales's sides.

From some hidden reserve Gateschales found new strength and flew into a gallop. The crowd screamed, some in excitement, others in protest as they noticed the uncapped lance. Defiance and exhilaration took fire in Rafe. Let them scream. He'd pluck the bitch's son from his horse and ride about the field with the man hanging from his lance in punishment for his perfidy. When he was done, there'd be no one in the world brave enough to challenge him, not even Lord Bagot after Rafe had taken that shit-licking Daubney's daughter from him.

Kate stood frozen in horror as she watched Warin race toward Rafe. The herald howled his command that they stop. Lord Haydon, already halfway across the field after Rafe's and Warin's first breach of etiquette, now lifted his heels into a run.

Chaos erupted around her. Every Godsol in the crowd rose to his feet, cursing the Daubneys for their treachery. Screaming charges of attempted murder, Sir Simon crashed through the flimsy willow fencing that stood between him and his comrade. Sir Hugh followed, his mouth grim, while Sir Josce, yet too shaken from his fall to run with them, set himself to kicking an even larger hole in the fence standing between him and his friend.

Unable to watch Rafe for fear that she'd see him die, Kate locked her gaze onto Warin. With all her heart, she willed her former love to stop. Warin didn't slow, not even a whit. Then just before they met, his lance tip lifted just a little.

It was enough. With the lance off center, the weapon's sharp tip slipped away from Rafe on the slight curve of his shield, gouging a deep crevice in the metal as it went.

Not so Rafe's lance. His met Warin's shield dead center. Warin tumbled backward out of his saddle, just as Sir Josce had done.

Cheers, jeers, bellows of rage and whistles of appreciation rang from all across the field. Kate's senses swam. Rafe lived.

Her knees weakened, and she collapsed to sit upon the ground, heedless of the damage she did to her new gown. She gulped in a great breath of air. Out on the field, the herald and Lord Haydon, as well as a good number of other knightly guests, all converged on the fallen Warin. Every one of them screamed accusations at him, when Kate knew the uncapped lance wasn't his fault.

Someone else had removed its cap, and Kate's wayward glance had caught the villain at it. Tears stung at her eyes. Her father, horse thief and murderer that he was, had just used Warin and his weapon to try and kill the man she loved.

Chapter 14

L ord Humphrey leaned back on the bench he shared with his daughter in Haydon's hall. Beside him, Kate toyed with what remained of the day's feast on her bread trencher.

"My steward is an honorable man," her father said to Sir Ronald of Witton, one of his liege men, who stood behind them. He had to raise his voice a little to be heard. With the day's champion decided, everyone had retired to the hall for a midafternoon meal. Now, as the last course was finished and the conversations were beginning to flow, the noise level rose.

"So he has always been in his dealings with me," agreed Sir Ronald. Kate made a face at her meal. Sir Ronald's voice held all the sincerity of a man whose livelihood depended upon the good will of his better; the knight held his lands from Bagot's lord.

"Of course he has," Lord Humphrey said. "I tell you, those who blame Sir Warin for what happened on the field this day are full wrong. I'll say it again. That cap must have fallen off when I transferred the lance to my steward. So swift were our movements that I doubt he could have noticed what happened. God knows I didn't."

Kate shot her sire a scathing, sidelong glance. Neither man noticed. It shamed her that her father could so easily and boldly lie. The deeper shame was in how little honor he had, allowing another man to suffer for what he'd done.

Poor Warin. Although she knew she didn't love him, Kate's heart ached over the wrong being done him. A mob of onlookers had accosted him after he fell from his horse, every man calling him scoundrel or villain. Warin's protests that he hadn't noticed the lance's state fell on deaf ears. In the end, he'd been banished from the wedding. Why, at this very moment, he was in their tent, packing his meager belongings. The bishop had arranged for him to stay at the priory for the remainder of the celebration so that he needn't ride the full way back to Bagot on his own.

Outrage grew. Why didn't someone else cry out that he'd seen her father removing that cap? *Hypocrite*, a small voice within her chided. Why should it be someone else, when she'd seen what happened?

Another wave of shame surged through her. Coward. It was fear that held her tongue. Were she to admit what she knew, everyone here would spurn her as a traitor to her own blood. No honest knight would ever offer for her hand against the possibility that she might one day betray him as she had her sire. That might well leave her sire no choice but Sir Gilbert for her mate. The very idea was enough to keep Kate's tongue from wagging.

There was but one flicker of grim satisfaction in all this. Although no one else admitted to seeing what her father had done, neither did his usual supporters rally to him this time. Only those men like Sir Ronald, who owed their living and their allegiance to him, had joined in his demand that Warin not be censured. Why, not even Sir Gilbert had said a word in his favor.

"Well spoken, my lord," Sir Ronald replied. "Every man should recognize Sir Warin de Dapifer for the good knight he is. I ask you now, what of the Godsol? Where does his responsibility in this lie? He, too, must have noticed the missing cap. Why didn't he call the fault when he saw Sir Warin hadn't noticed and pull out of the run?"

Her sire grinned broadly at this attack on a Godsol. Righteous indignation tore through Kate. Of course her sire would enjoy hearing Rafe blamed for what was truly none of his fault.

"Aye," Lord Humphrey said. "If the Godsol had felt himself in any danger, he could have withdrawn from the run. Since he didn't and he took the purse, we can all assume he saw the uncapped lance as no threat. Another reason Sir Warin shouldn't be blamed."

"Indeed." Sir Ronald, every inch the lackey, nodded. The movement of his head was a shade too vigorous. "Know you, my lord, that I'll miss Sir Warin in the morrow's melee. Your steward is a stout-hearted warrior, and battling won't be the same without him at your side."

"My thanks for that," her father replied. For the first time, a hint of regret showed in his voice. "I shall miss him as well."

With his required show of loyalty at an end, the knight offered his lord a small bow, then turned and strode back down the hall's length to his own seat. As he went, every man along the opposing line of tables across the room watched, their expressions black with disapproval. So many men all glowering in her direction was enough to dampen even Kate's indignation.

No doubt to prevent a riot in his house, Lord Haydon had rearranged the mealtime seating for this day. Rank no longer determined where his guests sat. Instead, the Godsols and their defenders were on one side of the room; the Daubneys and those connected to them peopled the other. That hadn't stopped the enemies from biting their thumbs at each other throughout the meal. A shiver shot down Kate's spine. So much animosity promised a vicious melee on the morrow.

Beside her, her father turned his attention to the last of his meal, wholly unconcerned by the looks aimed at him. Her appetite gone, Kate's gaze shifted until she looked at the high table. There, seated between the bridegroom and the bishop, who was leaving the table, was the day's champion.

As if he felt her gaze, Rafe's head turned toward her. When he saw her watching him, his lips lifted. That was all it took for need to etch a channel through Kate. Forbidden or not, she wanted to feel his mouth on hers once more.

In the next instant, his smile ebbed until only longing touched his fine features and filled his dark eyes. Kate's heart tore in twain. The truth she already knew was written on his face for her to read. Never again would she feel his touch or the glorious press of his lips to hers. Any chance of ever again being close to him was gone, killed by her father's misdeed. Godsol and Daubney would mingle no more at this event.

Someone touched Kate's shoulder. Startled, she jerked around on the bench to look behind her. It was Sir Gilbert.

Her skin crawled. Unable to bear that her vulnerable back was to him, she eased around on the seat, all the while slipping as far from him as possible on the bench. A tiny smile flickered to life on his mouth at her retreat. Something in his expression said he knew she found his touch repulsive and her reaction amused rather than upset him.

Alerted by her movement, her father shot a glance over his shoulder. The narrowing of Lord Humphrey's eyes was enough to convey that he hadn't forgiven his neighbor either for his lack of support this afternoon or for his offer of a handfast with Kate. He afforded Sir Gilbert a mere grunt of acknowledgment.

Unperturbed by his lordly neighbor's rudeness, Sir Gilbert offered Kate a courtly bend of his head in greeting. "My lady."

"Sir Gilbert," she replied, the words slipping out from between clenched teeth as she willed him gone and swiftly so.

"It was another fine meal, wasn't it?" he asked.

"Fine enough." Kate shrank back against the table. God preserve her! He intended to make small talk when her heart was broken and her life in ruins. She shot a frantic glance around the room, seeking some avenue of escape.

Just as she had done before, Lady Haydon again came to her rescue. At the head of the room, both Emma and her mother were on their feet. Lady Haydon came around the high table's corner and raised her hands to catch her guests' attention.

"My ladies, the bride has decided to retire to my garden and enjoy the remainder of the afternoon in the presence of the musicians. What say you all? Shall we leave the men to their talk of battles and their dicing, while we make merry on our own?" That she was excluding the menfolk from her invitation along with the chiding tone of her voice left no doubt that Lady Haydon was unhappy with the sour turn her festivities had taken.

Kate fair bounded to her feet. "If you'll excuse me, Sir Gilbert, my lord sire."

Her father shot her a harsh look. "You've not

asked my permission to go, nor have I given it," he told her.

The amusement in Sir Gilbert's gaze redoubled. "What a pity, my lady. It seems you won't escape me so easily after all." He reached out as if to take her hand. Kate snatched her arm behind her and tried to take a backward step, only to find herself trapped between the table and the bench.

"She stays with me, not you," her father said, once more eyeing Sir Gilbert. There was no mask for his hostility this time. "You've made your offer and been refused. I'll warn you to keep your hands to yourself where my daughter is concerned."

Sir Gilbert only shrugged off his neighbor's bluntness. "My, but the two of you are out of sorts this afternoon."

Out of sorts! Aye, Kate wanted to scream, she was out of sorts. She'd just discovered she was daughter to a lying cheat.

All around the room, women left their male companions and came to join their hostess. Ami stopped abreast of Kate's table, waiting for Kate to join her. Kate sent her sire a pleading look. Her father ignored her.

"She stays," Lord Humphrey said, waving the young widow on her way.

With a regretful shrug and a worried look, Ami moved on to join the other women as they filed out of the hall. Kate's longing to go with them rose to desperation. She twisted her face into the expression that had ever won Lady Adele's pity. "My lord, might I please join the ladies? I cannot bear another moment in this room, what with so many men angry at us."

Her words were out before her good sense had a chance to catch them. Kate's heart sank. She gave up any hope of escape. Surely her father would interpret her words as chiding for his wrongdoing.

Rather than rage, her sire only grunted again. "It's only the Godsols who glare, and what care we Daubneys for that?" he asked. His tone was even, as if he discussed the vagaries of the weather, not a whole family's hatred for his kin.

From his stance beside Kate, Sir Gilbert's sly little smile widened into a full grin. "I'd say it's more than just the Godsols who disapprove of your steward's behavior, my lord." New shrewdness lurked in the depths of his eyes. "Indeed, even now there are some among your closest supporters saying you should release Sir Warin from your employ. These same men suggest keeping one who stooped to such a trick only blackens your good name. I wonder if these men might also rethink their connection to Bagot should you refuse to rid yourself of this supposed loathsome individual."

"What?" Kate cried, this new and unfair attack on Warin stinging all the deeper because it was Sir Gilbert who mouthed it. So, too, did her own sense of shame grow. Coward, coward! She should speak the truth and save Warin, even if it meant destroying her own life.

Kate expected outrage of her sire. Instead, the hostility drained from his face. He leaned back a little on their bench and scratched idly at his bearded chin. In silence, Sir Gilbert and her father considered each other, their moment of quiet stretching as Haydon's ewerer stopped to refill Lord Humphrey's cup. Once the servant had departed, taking Lord Bagot's nod for his thanks, Kate's father once more looked at Sir Gilbert.

"Does any man in particular say this?" he asked, his words careful and slow.

Sir Gilbert's brows gave a pleased upward jerk. "Sir William of Ramswood is one man of that opinion."

Her father's eyes narrowed to slits. Shifting on the bench to face the table, he leaned forward to see around his still standing daughter. His glance flew down the room's length to where Kate's likeliest suitor sat. Kate's look followed his.

Sir William watched them in return, his round face creased. When his gaze met that of Bagot's lord, he flushed bright red. In the next instant, he turned on his bench as if to speak to his seatmate, effectively showing his potential bride and her father his back. Even Kate recognized the rejection for what it was. There'd be no marriage contract with Sir William.

"Damn me," her father muttered as he shrank into himself. In the next breath, he added, "It seems I must needs begin my search again after the wedding is finished."

Shame's shackles shattered as Kate's heart nearly danced from her chest. Could it be that no man who'd seen that joust would have her to wife? If that was so, then it was naught but God's miracle. Nay, it was better than a miracle. Here was how God would punish her sire for the wrong he'd done, even if all mankind blamed Warin for the doing of it. As wrong as it was to take pleasure from Warin's unfair treatment, Kate couldn't stop her.

Surprise flashed across her father's face as he watched her, then his expression darkened. "Do you dare to look at me so?" he demanded.

Sir Gilbert loosed a quick harsh laugh. "By God, but she's a bold thing." Reaching out, he caught Kate by the chin and forced her to look at him. "Bold and beautiful."

Loosing a harsh breath, Kate jerked her face from his grasp. "My lord sire told you to leave me be."

Again Sir Gilbert laughed, this time the sound naught but amused. "Lord, but what sons we'll have between us, sweet Kate," he crooned.

At the suggestion of a future between them in the knight's words, the pique left her father's face. In its place came new eagerness. "If you're so enamored of her, then ask for her. But no handfast. You'll take her before a church, speaking vows of wedlock for all to hear."

Something akin to triumph took fire deep in Sir Gilbert's eyes, then his face flattened, all emotion draining from his expression as he made his offer. "Remember, my lord, that she was four years wed to de Fraisney with nary a flicker of life in her womb. If I must risk her potential barrenness, then I want more in return than just Glevering. I want Bagot and the title."

"That you cannot have," came her sire's swift retort. "Bagot goes to her sister, who's already borne her husband two sons, hale and hearty, who can take that title should our king agree to pass it to them."

Kate's elation collapsed into shock. This couldn't be happening. Why, they were haggling over her right here.

"And the title will still go to those lads if Lady Katherine bears me no boy children," Sir Gilbert replied swiftly. "But if she does, it's the title I want for my line. If you need some sop to offer her sister's husband, then remind him that Glevering is the better property. I doubt he'll complain. After all, his wife is the younger sister. Consider it, my lord. You can have me as her bridegroom in three weeks' time if you so choose, or you can begin again to find a mate for her."

Kate's shock devolved into depression as dark and deep as she'd ever felt. Her father wouldn't agree to this. He couldn't, because she couldn't bear to be wed to Sir Gilbert.

Every muscle in her body tensed as she watched her sire, waiting for his response. For a long and thoughtful moment, he sat perfectly still. Then he tilted his head to one side.

"What if I need to offer him a little of Bagot's acreage along with Glevering?" he asked.

Sir Gilbert's eyes narrowed. His jaw tightened. "I'd part with a few virgates in that instance."

Kate's head spun. The need to escape grew until she simply had to move. She backed away from the two men, easing out from between bench and table.

"Where are you going?" her father snapped, reaching out to grab her, even though she was already out of his reach.

"To the garden," Kate replied, her voice small against what was happening to her. "You no longer need me in this stage of your discussions."

Her father's face cleared, and he shrugged. "Aye, that's true enough. Go, then." It was a pleasant command.

Kate nearly stumbled as she started toward the hall door. So lost in inner blackness was she that she didn't notice the serving lad standing before the tall wooden screens at the hall's door until she was upon him. The boy stepped forward to block her path. Stopping short, Kate eyed him in surprise. It was the same lad she'd seen at the hearth a few nights ago. Shifting to one side, Kate started around him, only to have him move to block her path.

"Stand aside, child," she demanded, but in her present state her voice lacked any of the rebuke his impertinent behavior warranted.

"Pardon, my lady," the lad said in heavily accented French as he offered her a sketchy bow, "but I have a message for you."

A flicker of hope rose in Kate. If ever she'd needed a kind word from one who loved her, it was now. She shot a guarded look at Rafe and the high table, only to have her hopes deflate. Her dearest love was speaking to Gerard d'Essex, the bridegroom. The message couldn't be from him, else he'd surely be watching to see how she received it.

Kate looked back at the lad. "Who is it that sends me this message?"

"Your knight, my lady," the boy replied. "So, too, does he ask that I see you receive what he says in private."

Her knight? Kate eyed the child in bewilderment. Which knight was that?

The boy beckoned her to follow him as he retreated into the space between the screens and the door. Kate followed him. Once around the screens' corner, they were hidden from the hall's view. Only one of Haydon's porters stood outside the door to witness their conversation. He paid them no heed as his head nodded and his toe tapped to the music wafting up from the courtyard and garden below him.

"Tell me," she demanded.

The boy closed his eyes and began to speak. With the uncanny talent of the illiterate, he put the very cadence of Warin's voice in his words. "My dearest Lady de Fraisney," the lad intoned, "I beg you to meet with me. I know you've no reason to trust me, since my behavior over these last days has been appalling. For that I have no excuse save that my heart aches for you day and night. So, too, do I know that the events of this morning make me seem lower than a villein. I vow to you on my honor and my soul that in the heat of the contest I noticed nothing amiss with the lance I carried. Please, my lady, meet with me as you did this morn, outside Haydon's postern. If you cannot come for my sake, then come to retrieve your ribbon, which yet lies near my heart as I send you this message. As always, your servant in God's love and mine, Sir Warin de Dapifer of Bagot."

The boy paused, nodding to himself over successfully repeating what he'd heard, then continued. "The knight says he'll wait for you along the stream below our postern, where the trees will shield him from view of our guards atop the walls. This he does for fear that our men be commanded to drive him from the estate should he linger."

It was this last comment that did it. Between her shame over not vindicating Warin and her outrage over the wrong her father had done him, Kate's heart broke. It didn't matter that she no longer loved Warin. He needed to hear at least one person say that she knew beyond all doubt he wasn't a scoundrel.

"I'll go to him," she told the child.

Chapter 15

⌒◯⌒

How could it be that he'd won the contest, taken the purse, basked in Kate's admiration, but was still the loser? Rafe didn't think his spirits could get any lower. Across the room, Kate left her father and started for the hall door, belatedly on her way to join the women in the garden. He watched her go, knowing that with every step she beat any chance of him marrying her into dust beneath her feet. As it was, it'd be a miracle if he ever again got within a mile of her.

For this he had no one to blame but himself. Why hadn't he realized using her ribbon would goad Sir Warin past all sense? His stomach knotted. He hadn't realized because once again he'd let his heart rule his head. Only this time, unlike at the picnic, when he'd only almost lost everything, his impetuous action had destroyed all hope and all chance of his future.

"You shouldn't stare at her so," Gerard said.

Rafe blinked, startled by his friend's unexpected comment, then looked at the bridegroom. Occupying Lord Haydon's massive chair at Rafe's right, Gerard yet had his head bowed over his trencher. Now that his new wife no longer distracted him from his meal, Gerard was plying his spoon with all the efficiency of a starving man.

"Who do you mean?" Rafe demanded.

"Why, Lady de Fraisney, of course," Gerard said between bites, still not lifting his head from his meal.

Shock rattled Rafe. If Gerard, with his gaze fastened only on his wife or his meal, had noticed his interest in Kate, had anyone else seen? He shot a glance to his left, where Bishop Robert had been sitting only the moment before, then gave thanks that the churchman had excused himself. The departure of his hostess left the prelate free to join his own family near the table's end.

Grinning, Gerard shot a sidelong look at his comrade. "Don't panic. Beyond me, I don't think any of the others have noted that you cannot keep your gaze off your enemy's daughter."

"Are you mad? Interest in a Daubney?" Rafe sputtered in a futile attempt to shield himself. The effort sounded false, even to his own ears. That he should be so obvious about a lie would go far to confirm Gerard's suspicion.

Sure enough, his friend straightened, resting his spoon hand, and stared at the day's champion. The simple amusement gleaming in Gerard's blue eyes deepened into astonishment. "Lord help me, Rafe, but tell me what I see in your face isn't true!"

"There's nothing to see in my face," Rafe retorted, barely managing to keep himself from lifting a hand to hide his features from view.

Gerard's grin was slow and wide. "Looks like infatuation to me," he said over Rafe's useless protest. "God help you, but when the rest of our mates finally catch you agog over a woman, especially a woman not even you can get near enough to seduce, your repute as a swain will be destroyed for all time. Oh, the tweaks and taunts you'll suffer when they learn you of all men are besotted. Captivated, no less." Laughter tainted Gerard's voice.

"I'm not besotted," Rafe protested, but even as he spoke, his gaze once more shifted in Kate's direction.

Too late. She'd already slipped outside the hall, gone as far from his sight as she was from his reach. A strange ache took root in his heart as he stared at the screens at the door. It was an instant before he recognized it as longing—hopeless, never to be requited longing. Rafe sighed. Gerard was right; he was besotted.

A strangled sound escaped Gerard. Rafe looked at him. The bridegroom beamed.

"Only a heartsick man stares at the place he's last seen his love standing," Gerard said. Then his expression sobered. "Enough jesting, Rafe. Take no insult with what I next say, but I'm praying you'll not follow where your heart would lead. After today's events, there's trouble enough between your two families. I'd not have my lord father-by-marriage turn a harsh eye on me because the man and family I insisted he invite caused the ruin of his event."

Stung by his friend's plea, Rafe glanced past Gerard to where Lord Haydon sat. The nobleman had his elbows braced on the table. He held his head in his hands and stared out at his divided guests. The morose twist of his mouth suggested he'd gotten far more than he expected out of the day's joust.

"Would that it had been Josce in that final round," Rafe said and meant it, much to his astonishment. Aye, better to still have the chance to at least touch Kate than to know he would never again even speak with her.

On the Daubney side of the room, someone slammed his hands down on his table. The sound reverberated up into the hall's exposed rafters and echoed against the plastered walls. It was Lord Bagot. As the whole hall watched, Rafe's enemy's face blossomed with a grin so wide it was like to split his face.

"So be it! I shall happily call you son!" Kate's sire crowed to Sir Gilbert, who stood beside him, smiling like a cat in a dairy.

"Well, that settles that," Gerard said, watching Lord Bagot. "Judging from yon happiness, I'd say your heart is doomed to break and Lady de Fraisney won't be a widow for much longer. All the better for us and these next days, I think," Gerard went on, a touch of relief in his voice as he looked at Rafe. "What do you want to wager that Lord Bagot leaves Haydon this very night? I doubt he'll risk the melee on the morrow with all you Godsols hot for his blood. Nay, he'll hurry home now that he's got his daughter's wedding to plan."

Gerard shook his head. "Poor Lady de Fraisney. Sir Gilbert's a pig." With that, he again picked up his spoon and began to eat.

Rafe's spirits oozed out of the heel of his shoe, sank through the floorboards and dripped down onto the stores in the cellar below. Kate was his. The very thought of another man bedding his woman made his stomach knot.

"Hsst, sir," came a child's call.

Turning on his bench, Rafe found his little spy standing near one of the curtained alcoves. Young Watty was the name the boy claimed as his own. Watty gestured for Rafe to join him, the look on his face decidedly frantic.

Rafe's brows shot up. What sort of news could the lad have now that Sir Warin had left Haydon? When Rafe hesitated, the boy frowned and stomped his foot. Once more he gestured, this time the movement of his arm imperious.

Irritation ate up Rafe's depression. If nothing else the child needed a lesson in manners. He came to his feet.

"Excuse me, Gerard. I think I'll join my brother for a while."

"Suit yourself," Gerard said around what was in his mouth, then motioned a waiting servant to fill his trencher with more of the day's lamb.

As Rafe made his way to the wall, irritation ebbed into the beginnings of hope. Perhaps the boy did know something. After all, Young Watty had turned out to be an apt spy, intent on earning every one of the pence Rafe promised him. Why, without the lad, he wouldn't have known when to begin the race around Haydon's walls this morning to disturb Sir Warin's seduction of Kate.

The drapery still swung where Watty had ducked into one of the alcoves. Lifting the curtain, Rafe followed him into the window embrasure. Outside the arrow loop, clouds gathered, promising a shower tonight. Until then, bright sunlight yet painted itself on the alcove's plastered walls. A swallow swooped past the cross-shaped opening, making free with the wealth of flying insects that called Haydon home. From the armory in the bailey below came the noise of the smith restoring dented shields and armor in preparation for the morrow's mock battle. Louder still and rising from the direction of the garden was the melody of a swift dance. Twined into that sound was female laughter. Even as he told himself it was useless, Rafe's ears strained to pick out Kate's voice from all the others. When he couldn't, he bent a stern look upon his temporary servant.

"What is so important that you must interrupt me at my meat, Watty?" he demanded, speaking in the English tongue.

"It's the knight, sir," Watty hissed, his dark eyes

wide with excitement. "He's plotting to steal your lady, he is."

Shock slammed into Rafe like the smith's hammer against his anvil, only to die away just a quickly. If a man planned to kidnap his lord's daughter, he most surely didn't tell a serving lad what he intended. He gave a shake of his head. "I doubt that."

"Oh, but he is," the boy insisted, unintimidated by his better's pessimism. "I stopped outside of the lord's tent, just to see what the knight did after he returned from the joust. Whilst I was there, the lord came to him, telling him that he must leave for the priory. From the knight there came naught but sweet *aye, my lords* until the nobleman left him. Then such cursing did I hear. The knight condemned his noble master right to hell and swore vengeance for the honor that the lord had cost him. So evil were his words, sir, that I thought I might drop dead right then and there," the boy said, his eyes round from the remembered threat to his soul.

The corner of Rafe's mouth lifted a little at such a protest from one so crude. Young though Watty was, the very rudeness of the lad's estate made it likely that there were few curses he hadn't heard.

"A man promises himself things in private that he never intends to do," he told the boy.

"But you don't know all yet," Watty protested. "When the knight finished his cursing, he put his head outside the tent and, seeing me, called me to him. Just like you, sir, he offered me coins to be his servant."

Watty lifted his tunic's hem. Over the last days the lad had procured a purse, surely someone's castoff, for it was a well-worn leather sack. Its strings were knotted to the braided lacing that held Watty's chausses at his hips. What caught Rafe's interest was the way the purse drooped, for it suggested more than the few pence Rafe had given him.

"And what were you to do to earn these coins?" Rafe asked.

"My last task for the knight will be to run to the priory," the lad replied, "where I'll tell the monks he won't be joining them as they expect. My first task was to tell the stablemaster that both the knight's horses were to be saddled." Here the boy paused to give a scornful snort. "I ask you, what need has one man of two saddles, when he can ride but one horse at a time?" he scoffed, his tone cocky, indeed.

Only Watty's good service these past days kept Rafe from boxing the child's ears. "You're bolder than your station allows, brat. If a man owns two saddles, he takes two, and better to carry them on a horse's back than any other way," Rafe replied, yet unconvinced by what Watty deemed a plot. "Now, unless you've more proof than that to offer, I'll call you mistaken, and you'll think it a kindness that I don't beat you for your impudence."

The boy only lifted a insolent brow. "There was a middle task, sir, a message that I've just now delivered to your lady."

Rafe stared at the boy for an astounded instant before his thoughts skittered back into motion. "Tell me," he demanded, reaching for his belt and his own new and very pleasantly heavy purse. Opening it, he sifted through the coins it contained. The clink of metal on metal was meant as a promise of payment to Watty, encouraging the lad to divulge every word.

Young Watty grinned; he understood the message. With his eyes on his better's fine kidskin pouch, he said, "The knight begged your lady's forgiveness for all the wrongs he's done her, then pleaded with her to meet with him"—here, he shot Rafe a look far too knowing for his years—"in the trees that line the stream below our postern."

Watty's smile dimmed into an intense look. "Since you bathed there this morn, sir, you know how thick the willows are along that stretch. If the knight does intend evil, then none of the guards upon our walls will see what takes place below their very noses."

With that, the bits Watty had given Rafe congealed into a plot, the same plot that Rafe had failed to realize. He snarled. That snake-eating bitch's son was stealing his woman!

Rage closed in on him like a red cloud. His purse still clenched in his hand, he turned to dash from the alcove. The lad caught a handful of Rafe's tunic.

"If you would, sir," he said, "I'd have the pence you promised me for today."

His words, along with the dirty streaks his touch left on Rafe's new tunic, punctured Rafe's anger like a crossbow's bolt. That left room for sense to rise.

Rafe planted his feet to the floorboards beneath his shoes. Not this time. This time he was going to think before he acted.

Only as he released a long, slow breath did he realize what Watty had done for him. Had Rafe dashed through the hall, everyone within the room would have known something was amiss. Most would have followed him. Rather than turn Sir Warin's plot to his own advantage, all he'd have accomplished would have been to save Kate from Sir Warin so she could marry Sir Gilbert.

Gratitude over this unexpected rescue made Rafe generous. Watty had earned the sum he might have owned, had he spied on Sir Warin until the wedding's final day. From one hand to the other, he counted out the coins. "Is there anything more the knight told you?" he asked, yet holding the payment in his palm.

"Would that he had, sir," the boy said, happy avarice gleaming in his eyes as he realized what his better intended.

Rafe gave a brisk nod to show that he wasn't upset by this lack of knowledge, then held out his hand. It had been but an idle hope that the boy might have some inkling as to where Sir Warin meant to take Kate. The boy offered an eagerly cupped palm. Rafe dropped the coins into Watty's filthy hand. Quick as a cat, the child wrenched open his threadbare purse and stowed his riches.

"Well, lad," Rafe said, "it seems I'll need your service a little longer. Go you after the lady, taking care that neither she nor the knight see you. If the knight does make her his prisoner, say nothing. Instead, follow them for a quarter-hour or so, long enough to learn in which direction they ride. Once you're certain, return to Haydon to tell me. I'll wait for you on the field where we jousted this day."

New greed brightened Watty's gaze as he reknotted his purse strings. "Now, sir, you know that if the knight does take her, I ought to raise the hue and cry, not skulk after them. Should the knight be caught at what he does or I be found out, I might lose my place or if I run, become outlaw." It was a not so subtle suggestion that what Watty did now was beyond the scope of their original agreement.

Rafe grinned. "Have no fear, my little spy. No one will ever know what you do for me. When you and I meet again upon the jousting field and you tell me where they've gone, vowing to never reveal what you know, I'll give to you double what the knight's already put in your purse."

Young Watty's eyes widened until they were round as plums. "But the knight gave me two more pence than I have fingers, he did." His tone made a mere shilling's worth of coins sound like great wealth indeed.

"So be it," Rafe agreed. "Do as I ask, and you'll earn twice that from me." He grabbed the boy's thin shoulders and thrust him toward the curtain end of the alcove. "Off with you, now."

"As you will, sir," the boy cried out, the curtain dropping behind him almost before he'd finished speaking.

Rafe waited a moment, then slipped back into the

hall. It took all his will to keep his stride at an easy
pace when what he wanted to do was race like the
lad, screaming out his excitement as he went. Down
the table's length he strode to where Will sat with
one of Long Chilting's neighbors, Sir Ivo de Kyme.
The disappointed droop of Will's shoulders said
failure sat no better on him than it had on Rafe; his
brother knew well enough that the mishap at the
joust meant the vengeance he desired for their sire's
death was now out of his reach.

As Rafe stopped beside the two men, he laid a
hand on Will's shoulder to catch his attention. "My
pardon, Sir Ivo," Rafe said, "but I've need of a private moment with my brother. There's been some
distressing news from Long Chilting."

All Rafe intended was to lay groundwork for the
excuse they'd need to make an unexpected departure from Haydon. His ruse went awry. His brother
came roaring off the bench.

"May God damn those Daubneys," Will shouted.
"They've broken the peace of the shire and attacked
our home whilst we are here and unable to protect
what is ours!"

Heads turned from every corner of the room as
all attention settled on Will. Rafe cringed. Rather
than the circumspection he needed, they were now
the focus of everyone's interest.

"Not that kind of news," he snapped, grabbing
his brother by the front of the tunic and almost
dragging him over the bench.

Too startled to resist, Will let himself be manhan-
dled for a few more steps before he shoved at Rafe.

"Let me loose. You're creasing my tunic and it cost me four pounds."

"Forget your tunic and listen," Rafe whispered, impatience adding bite to his words as he pulled his yet resisting brother closer to the wall.

Will glowered at him. Rafe grinned. "The time has come to take Lady de Fraisney."

After a shocked breath, emotions flew across Will's face: relief, gratitude and finally exhilaration. "When? How?" he demanded, his words so low they were barely audible.

"Now," Rafe replied, then held up a forestalling hand. "As for the how, there's no time to tell you all this moment. Only listen and do as I command. First we go to Lord Haydon and bid him farewell."

As he spoke, a twinge of guilt shot through him. What he planned might well cost him Josce's and Gerard's friendship. He shook away the thought. Far worse for Kate to end up wedded to Sir Gilbert when she should belong to him.

Will's smile was crooked. "I doubt he'll shed any tears over our going, when we take today's hostility with us as we leave. Let the damned Daubneys crow that they drove us off, for they'll be eating the same bird later when they find their heiress and her lands are ours. What reason will we give Lord Haydon for our going?" he asked. "If we don't have one, etiquette allows him no choice but to insist we stay. Forcing our departure after that will insult him."

Rafe snorted. His brother was worried about insulting their host over an unexcused departure? Better that he worry over how to keep Lord Haydon and his guests from razing Glevering and killing them all when they were found out.

"Our excuse will be that there's been an accident at Long Chilting and our bailiff is laid low," Rafe told him.

Worry flashed through Will's dark eyes. "This is just a ruse, eh? There's not been such an accident, has there?"

Frustration twanged inside Rafe. "Of course not," he snapped, his voice yet held to a whisper. "It's but a tale. Remember, you must be as a mummer when you say it, pretending worry and distraction. Lord Haydon must believe our need for haste is overweening."

Will offered an approving nod in response. "Aye, that I can do. Should I send a man to warn our priest and the troop from Long Chilting that it's time for them to move on Glevering?"

A grin teased at Rafe's mouth. It was strange to find himself in command of his elder. Strange but somehow right, for soon he'd be master of his own house and men.

Rafe leaned closer to Will as he continued, "You can warn them that the time is near, but they mustn't arrive at Glevering before we do. We can give Bagot's bailiff no opportunity to send word to Haydon of an attack. Is there a place near Glevering where our men might bide in safety and secrecy while they wait for us?"

Will's smile was smug. "There is, indeed, and a pleasant little valley it is, caught between two good-sized hills. More than once, I've ridden from that spot to take a few of Bagot's sheep and kine."

The possibility of success grew in Rafe, the sensation strong enough to make him want to laugh. "Aye, then, send your message to your men, while we and those men with us here retire to our tent. We'll arm ourselves as best we can, there being no time for donning mail, and pack only those belongings we can carry on our saddles."

"Nay," Will cried softly, rearing back from his younger, taller brother. "I won't go leaving my tent and chests behind me. What if Bagot confiscates what's mine after our deed is revealed?"

Rafe held a warning finger to his lips to urge his brother to quiet. "We've no choice," he whispered. "To take the tent and its furnishings, especially your armor chest, means an ox-drawn cart that moves at a snail's pace when we need haste most of all. If you're concerned, ask Lord Haydon if he'll send our belongings back to Long Chilting in our own cart with one of his teams. That way, our belongings will be well away from Haydon before anyone realizes what we're about. Tell our host we'll pay the cartage."

"You'll pay," Will retorted, his jaw suddenly tense and his eyes narrowed. "I'm not so wealthy a man that I can afford to waste coins on what my own folk owe me in service. You, on the other hand, have just won three marks."

Rafe's teeth clenched. They didn't have time for this. "I'll pay," he snarled.

It was a satisfied smile Will sent his way. "Then all I must do is warn Dickon at the priory of what we plan. I'll not leave him unaware when he may take the brunt of our actions."

With his brother's words, an idea hit Rafe like a blow, the whole of it so perfect that he grinned. "You're right. You must ride to the priory and see our brother, not only to warn him but to beg him for a monk's habit." The priory was so close that Will could ride there and back while Rafe waited for Young Watty at the field.

Will's eyes flew wide. "A habit? Whatever for?"

"A disguise," Rafe replied, still grinning at his own cleverness. "What better way to take a woman than to make her seem a man? If anyone sees us between here and Glevering, they'll notice nothing save a knightly contingent escorting a monk on the road."

With that, exhilaration took hold of Rafe, consuming his depression in a great blaze of excitement. Before long, he'd hold his Kate in his arms, just as God intended. So huge was the emotion that woke in him with this thought that he grabbed his brother by the shoulders to keep from flying off the hall floor.

"She's mine, Will," he told his brother as he gave the smaller man a quick shake, then turned his brother toward the head of the room and Lord Haydon.

Chapter 16

A new breeze filled with the promise of evening showers tossed Kate's veil as she stepped off the keep's stair into the courtyard. Although it was past midday, barely a shadow clung to the sheds and storage barns that lined the narrow yard. With summer days long, the sun was only now beginning its descent toward the western horizon, where it would do battle with the great troop of clouds gathered there.

Given the many hours yet left until nightfall, Haydon's servants should still have been rushing about, hard at their tasks. But no industrious sound echoed within Haydon's inner walls beyond the ringing of the smith's hammer. Instead, everyone who should have toiled danced just outside the gar-

den's wall. Laughing laundresses clasped hands
with grinning stable lads, while seamstresses, out of
the housekeeper's sight for the dinner hour, ran
rings about off-duty soldiers. Why, even the guards
on the walls turned their backs to their watches to
observe the merriment of those below them.

Such frantic gaiety out here was but the promise
of even more happy activity in the garden. Kate's
stomach twisted. The thought of plastering a smile
on her face and joining the women when she had to
marry Sir Gilbert DuBois was more mummery than
she could manage.

Skirting the crowd, she started for the postern
gate. Whereas this morn she'd hesitated to meet
Warin, there wasn't the tiniest speck of worry over
doing so a second time. She had no intention of sin-
ning now. All she wanted to do was absolve Warin
of the wrong her father had laid upon his shoulders
and send him on his way to the priory. Once he was
gone, she'd have what she most needed: time alone,
so she might come to terms with her fate, and the
privacy to scream against the unfairness of having
been born a woman.

A few yards from the postern she stopped short,
her skirts collecting the curls of wood that escaped
the carpenter's shed at her elbow. Although the
gate's little door stood wide, just as it had earlier, it
was no longer unattended. Dressed in Haydon's
colors of green and yellow, the porter had reclaimed
his post, although his attention was on the dancers.

Disappointment drove deep, indeed; there'd be
no solitary moment for her. Even if Kate demanded

to pass, the gatekeeper would never allow his lord's well-to-do female guest to exit alone when his continued health and livelihood rested on protecting her. So Warin would leave without ever hearing that Kate knew him wronged.

Just as Kate was ready to retreat, a young woman broke from the dancing servants. Her feet keeping the pattern of the steps as she came, the lass capered her way to the porter. As she reached the gatekeeper, she began a new sort of dance, with much movement of her hips as she stroked her hands down the porter's arms. Kate eyed her in surprise. There was something about the woman's manner that reminded Kate of Emma caressing her husband this morn.

The porter, as young and handsome as his companion was pretty, grinned. The woman caught his hand. A moment later, the two joined the others in their merriment.

Not willing to lose her chance, Kate threw herself into motion faster than she had ever believed possible. As she raced through the gate, her heart took flight, fluttering like a pennant in the wind. For all she knew, the guards on the walls had seen her exit and would call the alarm.

Out she went, crouching as she started down the path toward the stream at its base. For defense's sake, this hill was but a grassy mound without a tree upon it, which made her the tallest thing in sight. With every step, the music faded until it was nothing but a strident memory. No shout, not even a word was launched at her back.

After what seemed hours but surely was no more than a moment, Kate stopped. The chirps of birds were the only sound. Turning, she looked behind her. She'd descended so far that not even Haydon's rooftops were in sight. She breathed for what felt like the first time since exiting. She'd done it; she was free, at least for the moment.

Grinning, she lifted her face to the sky. Above her, swallows and sparrows were specks against the darkening clouds billowing up from the horizon. Kate's heart caught. Oh, to be like the birds. No one ordered their lives, telling them who to wed and where to go.

Such foolishness! Kate lowered her gaze until she stared at the ground at her toes. Better that she spend her brief freedom cherishing these precious moments than wasting them in futile longing for what could never be.

Continuing her descent more slowly now, she reached the hill's base. A wide clearing had been carved from the trees that lined the stream. This was to make room for Haydon's laundresses, so said scrub boards, a great iron pot and piles of ashes set aside for the soapmaking. She scanned the clearing. There was no sign of Warin, but then he'd said he'd conceal himself against the possibility of Haydon's soldiers driving him from the estate.

"Sir Warin?" she called.

Willows rustled to her left. A horse snorted. A bridle jingled. Twigs crackled. But Warin made no reply.

Kate started toward the sounds. "Sir Warin?" she

called as she strode into the shade of the nearest tree. "It's me, Katherine. Know you that I come not for my ribbon but that you should hear me. I saw my father remove the lance's cap," she said, pushing through the willow's leafy drapery and stepping out on the tree's opposite side.

Silent and tall, Warin appeared so suddenly that Kate gasped. He yet wore his armor, even to his helmet. Framed in the brow curve of his helmet's nosepiece, his blue eyes were cold and hard.

Kate took an instinctive backward step. "Warin," she cried, "you startled me."

"What else did you give that Godsol besides your ribbon?" he snarled, grabbing her by the arm. His grasp was so painful that Kate squeaked. She wrenched her arm, trying to free herself.

"Nay, you'll not reject me again. I need you and your riches now more than ever," he told her, jerking her toward him as he spoke. "Your sire intends to be rid of me to shield himself, and for that I'll see he pays."

Blinding pain shot up Kate's arm, the hurt so intense it ate up her scream before the smallest sound left her mouth. Her shoes slid on the moist foliage carpeting the stream's bank. As she fell, Warin once more yanked on her arm, forcing her back to her feet.

Kate swore her bones all separated one from another. Pain exploded into a great vortex of hurt. Black spots danced before her eyes. With every ounce of her energy, she fought to keep the darkness from overtaking her. That left no strength to resist

Warin as he used her veil to gag her and the lacing torn from her overgown to bind her hands.

Kate's hope of a quick rescue from Haydon came and went with the sunset, the only sign of which was the barest mauve and apricot stain to the thick cloud layer that now owned the sky. Shadows closed around her. In the newborn darkness, this wild wood's ferny bracken, oak and the occasional beech, copsed into a thicket to provide some carpenter with wood, became hulking shapes. Panic rode hard upon her spine, and not because outlaws, brigands and debauched men inhabited such wild places as these.

If her father already followed them, any pursuit would halt with night's onset. The trail would be impossible to follow in the dark. And what if her sire didn't yet know she was missing? It was a possibility, especially if Haydon's ladies had lingered until darkness in the garden and were only now rejoining their menfolk in the hall. In that case, there'd be no searchers on her trail until the morrow and that would be hours too late.

Fool that she was, by meeting Warin alone and unchaperoned, she'd offered him a temptation he couldn't resist after her father's insult. Warin meant to force marriage on her once they reached Glevering, her dowry property.

Just as she'd done so many times over these last hours, Kate conjured up an image of her future. Warin would bind and gag her, then drag her into Glevering's chapel. Given Kate's present mood and the fact that she'd never once been to the manor that was her inheritance, she let her imagination turn that holy chamber into a barn rather than a sanctuary, with chickens pecking at a packed-earth floor and some flea-bitten, English-speaking priest at the altar. Warin would yet wear his filthy mail and reek of sweat as he held her helpless at his side. When the priest called out the vows that Kate should speak, her erstwhile lover would force her head to move and, will she, nill she, she'd become his wife.

Tears threatened to rise. Kate blinked them away. Why had she ever begrudged a union with Sir Gilbert? At least, marriage to her father's choice of husbands was an honorable estate, making of her a legitimate wife. After Warin's disheveled appearance at Haydon's picnic, no man or woman in the shire would ever believe Kate had been forced into wedlock with him. Nay, they'd all think she'd hoodwinked her sire and married her lover to escape a rightfully planned union.

Such a marriage would do worse than ruin her. She'd be shunned. Fathers and mothers would forbid their children contact with her, fearing their offspring might believe they, too, could escape their arranged marriages by such devious means. All this, just when she was beginning to make friends among the shire's women.

Kate choked back self-pity. If there was no one left to save her from a fate worse than death except herself, then she had no time to waste in winning her freedom. This was especially so now that her first two escape attempts had failed.

Both she and the palfrey she rode were now tied to a saddle. Her mount's reins were knotted to Warin's warhorse's saddle, while Kate's gown-lacing bound her wrists to the palfrey's saddle through an ornamental bend of bone trim. As the lacing was made of the same thin fabric as her gown, it should have been a simple thing to tear it, or so Kate had told herself hours ago.

One more time, she forced her arms as far apart as they would go, which was about the span of two hands. Slowly, carefully, so as not to attract the attention of her captor, she scraped the narrow strip of fabric across the saddle's pommel.

The material slipped back and forth more easily now, no doubt because her efforts had polished the wooden saddle to a new slickness. Moments passed. Three new flecks of blue lint danced up to join their brothers in the palfrey's dark mane. Beyond that, nothing.

Hissing in frustration, Kate pulled on her bound wrists until her arms trembled and her hands throbbed. How could it be so hard to do this? At this rate, she wouldn't be free until long after they reached Glevering.

Startled by Kate's noise and movements, the palfrey, too highly strung for his own good and none too pleased by his rider's strange behavior, danced skittishly to one side. His nervous prancing prodded Warin's warhorse into loosing a worried neigh. It was all the big black had strength to do. Already exhausted by this day's labors, the steed's head hung as he plodded ever northward toward their destination.

"Whatever you're doing back there, stop it," Warin snapped.

Kate instantly leaned forward. Her hair, free of its knot after her first escape attempt, slid over her shoulders and down her arms to enshroud her bound wrists and the result of her efforts in a dark brown curtain. "I'm not doing anything," she retorted. "It's this stupid horse of yours, jumping at shadows. Since I have no control of him," she added, "I can do nothing to stop him."

Each word tore at her aching throat. Instinctively, Kate's hand lifted toward her neck as she sought to ease the hurt. Her movement came to an abrupt halt, the lacing once more cutting into an already raw wrist.

Simmering anger rose back to a boil. May God take Warin! He, who had no right to even touch her, had assaulted her not once but three times!

Of course, he wouldn't have had the chance to lay bruises on her if she hadn't been such a fool in her first attempt at freedom. They'd still been within walking distance of Haydon then. Her hands had been bound and she, gagged, but nothing held her to the saddle. If only she'd taken a single moment in which to form even the most rudimentary of plans. Instead, the instant her senses steadied, she'd thrown herself out of the palfrey's saddle and dashed back toward Haydon. By the time she'd loosened the lacing, then torn off the gag so she could scream, Warin was upon her. She'd shouted, but he'd closed his hands about her throat until no air reached her lungs and she saw stars again.

Now, ahead of her, Warin turned far enough in his saddle to shoot her a narrow-eyed look. For comfort's sake, he'd long since removed his helmet. In the twilight, his golden hair gleamed white, while his eyes glinted out of night-darkened sockets.

"By God, but you're a bold bitch," he complained. "It's a wonder your sire hasn't beaten you to a pulp for your impertinence."

"Feel free to finish what you've started and do what he has not," Kate goaded him, knowing full well it was an empty dare.

His smile was narrow and swift. "Tut, sweet Kate, provoke me at your will and you'll still fail. Nay, I took care to see I laid no marks on you. Bruises suggest coercion. I'll not risk the annulment of our marriage after all I've gone through to take you."

Kate sneered at him, wishing she were as confident as her expression implied. "My father won't care if there's proof of force or not. If you marry me, he'll demand an annulment, especially now that he and Gilbert DuBois have agreed to a marriage between their houses. My sire's not likely to let you steal Glevering and me from him."

Yet facing her in his saddle, Warin laughed. There was no hint of amusement in the sound. "Not only do I think your father will allow me to hold Glevering, I am convinced that once he knows I'm within

Glevering's walls and between your thighs, your sire will see the value of having me as both his son and his steward. You see, I know for a fact that he removed the lance's cap with the full intention of murdering the Godsol, for he admitted just that plan to me before the Godsol and I jousted. Were I to call out this truth for all to hear, his name would be doubly blackened, for he's now publicly lied about that same event."

His words pierced Kate to the core. With the tide of opinion turning against her sire since the joust, her father might indeed crumple before Warin's threat. Ach, but if her father supported this wedding, then all was lost. She was truly trapped. No matter if it ruined her in the eyes of the shire, Warin would be her husband.

The very thought of being abandoned to Warin's tender mercies fed Kate's panic. Beneath the shield of her hair, she again worked her lacing against the pommel. This time the fabric gave an odd little jerk, the tension on her wrist relaxing just a little bit. Kate sucked in a pleased breath. Could it be a rent had started?

Ahead of her, Warin frowned, his gaze dropping to her bound hands. Kate started in concern, then threw words at him, hoping to distract him.

"It won't be only my father who comes seeking us, but every man now within Haydon's walls, including the bishop. The churchman will want to see that no sin happened between us. This I vow. I'll speak to the prelate, telling him how you forced me." She took heart from her own pronouncement. It was possible the bishop would listen to her. What a churchman wanted, he got, even if her father protested.

Warin grinned, his teeth gleaming white against the deepening gloom. "Do, my sweet. Do run to the bishop. Tell him whatever you please. Then, after you've seen him, I'll privately reveal that your complaints are only a ruse, a way to evade your sire's anger over our hasty deed. Nay, there's no one to stop me, not when royal writ grants you the right to marry where you will.

"Now that we've settled that," he continued, his smile fading and his eyes narrowing, "you'll hold your tongue, or I vow I'll cut it from your mouth and make of you a perfect wife. Don't think I won't. Just you remember, the tap you took was a gentle caress by the standard of my beatings."

Again Kate's hand tried to rise, this time seeking to cup her jaw, and again her hand came up short. He'd slapped her after her second escape attempt, when she'd yanked the palfrey's reins from his grasp and kicked the horse into a gallop. That attempt had been better planned, failing only because the palfrey was a horrid, stupid creature. Rather than race in the direction Kate aimed it, the foul beast circled and dashed right past Warin, who'd caught the reins with ease. His blow had been only strong enough to startle her, giving him the chance to overpower her once again.

Thunder rumbled in the distance. Nearer to home, the earth loosed a long sigh, a chill breath filled with the promise of rain. Above Kate, tree branches rattled; the greenery blanketing the forest floor tossed. Never intended for riding, the skirts of her finery weren't wide enough to cover all of her legs as she sat astride Warin's palfrey. Fingers of moist, cold air snaked up her indecently exposed skin, waking gooseflesh where her stockings, gartered below her knees, didn't cover her skin.

It was one more humiliation in a day of humiliation. The unfairness of how Warin misused her ripped through her, all the stronger because she'd intended to protect him from the others' scorn. Anger followed, growing until it ate up all her sense.

"Gentle?" she scoffed, her hoarsened voice ringing up into the trees around them. She lifted her jaw to a defiant angle. "There is nothing gentle about you. Such a word applies to men of quality. You're naught but a sham of a knight, a traitor, who betrays his oath of loyalty. Any fate is better than marriage to you."

As she spoke, she boldly yanked on her trapped wrists. She needed him to know that she wasn't cowed by his brutality, that despite his threats, she wasn't afraid of him. Not even the gathering shadows could mask the way Warin's face darkened at her slurs.

"I told you to hold your tongue, bitch." His voice was low and dangerous.

Above them, a streak of lightning flashed across the sky. The thrumming of God's drum followed, then rain pattered onto the leafy canopy above them. Droplets found their way earthward, splashing against Kate's uncovered head and ruining her expensive attire. It was this last insult, the destruction of her finery, that did it. She leaned forward in her saddle to make certain her next words did Warin as much damage as possible.

"More fool me for ever thinking you worthy of my affections," she taunted him. A wee part of her warned that provoking him wasn't wise, but she was too irate to heed so small a voice. "I say that if what you claim is true and Sir Rafe Godsol carries my ribbon, then I'm glad of it. All you and your foul trick at the joust did was sully my token and prove Sir Rafe in every way the better man, Godsol or not."

"Whore!" Warin screamed, the raging word shooting upward to pierce the low-hanging clouds. Lightning flashed in its wake.

He yanked the palfrey's reins loose from his saddle and turned his big steed. The two horses stood shoulder to shoulder, the palfrey dancing nervously to one side. Before Kate knew what he meant to do, Warin struck. Her neck wrenched. Her head snapped to the side. She slid in the saddle, her cheek on fire, this blow more than strong enough to leave a mark.

The palfrey bucked a little at this new and even stranger behavior. Gasping, Kate clutched at the pommel, her ears yet ringing as her fingernails dug into the wood. If she fell while yet tied to the stupid beast, the foul creature might trample her. A moment later, the horse calmed. Kate straightened in the saddle to glare at Warin.

"Beg my pardon," Warin demanded, his hand raised for another blow, "and know that if you ever again speak the name of that bitch's son, I'll kill you."

Even as the brutal words left his lips, his head turned to the woods behind them. He lowered his hand a little. Only then did Kate hear the crack and snap of something moving through the bracken. Hope surged that this was her rescue. Kate wrenched herself as far around in her saddle as she could to see.

"I have them!" The man's howling shout rang through the trees, the sound of it both joyous and vicious in one instant. "To me, to me," he shouted, suggesting others followed.

In that instant, whistles and shouts erupted from the woods around Kate and Warin. Even as Kate grinned in relief, God's fire lit up the clouds. In that brief flash of unnatural light, she saw her rescuer's sword raised on high. His cloak hood was pulled low over his brow, the sides of the garment flying back from his body as he raced toward them.

Hope and relief died into horror. It wasn't Haydon's green and yellow or a knight's mail he wore but mere leather. An outlaw! God help her, but she was done for and in the most horrible way possible.

With a growl, Warin drew his weapon and spurred his horse to face the oncoming man. From some corner of his tired heart the black found new strength, only to use it to strike out at the palfrey beside him. Warin cursed, then released the smaller horse's reins to shoulder his shield.

Kate gaped at the palfrey's dragging leather leads. It was a cruel mockery of the freedom she so needed, come both too late and before she could make use of it. With no controlling hand on him, the palfrey bucked, wanting only to rid himself of his loathsome rider.

Holding tight and praying, Kate heard metal clash as Warin's sword met that of his attacker. Again lightning flashed, bright enough this time for it to blind her. Thunder crashed from directly above her so loud that it sounded as if the sky had split. The palfrey screamed. It circled, pawing at the air, then tore off across the rugged landscape.

Cursing herself, Warin and her sire all at once, Kate lay low against the saddle and held on with all her might. Rain pelted her face. Trees loomed up before her, bushes rushed past, branches tearing and scratching.

Of a sudden, there was another horse running alongside her. Cloaked against the rain, its rider caught the palfrey's dragging reins. Even so short a freedom was too fearsome for the palfrey; he readily relented and slowed, not caring that his new owner was an outlaw.

Awash in terror, Kate came upright in her saddle. Every horrid act Lady Adele claimed befell errant women rose up to torture her. With all her might, she yanked on her trapped arms. The fabric gave. Her hands flew apart, one fist striking her attacker.

He grasped at her hand. Kate shrieked, the sound ripping at her poor aching throat. She thrust away from him and more fell than dismounted. Scrabbling to her feet in the moist earth, she raced off on legs made rubbery by so long a time on a horse.

In that moment, the clouds above her released everything they held. Rain poured down in torrents. Kate aimed for the nearest and thickest of the shadows around her, praying for some sort of hiding spot.

Her feet slid in newborn mud. Crying out, she caught at a tree trunk to keep from falling. Rough bark gouged her palms. A hand closed on her shoulder.

Bounding away, her heart in her throat, Kate sprang over a bushy fern, then around a thick bole. Fingers curled into the neckline of her gown. She screamed, flailing as she fell. He caught his arms about her waist, and together they tumbled to the ground. Turning in his embrace, Kate scratched and clawed, fighting for her life.

"Stop, Kate," a gasping Rafe Godsol said as he turned his face from her attack, "it's me."

Chapter 17

Kate's relief and joy were so great that she fair melted into the earth beneath her. It was Rafe. She was saved. Tears burned in her eyes. As she blinked them back, every one of her aches began to throb and her cuts to burn.

Lord, but she was soaked through and through. Her hair was a muddy mass streaming across her face and tangling about her body. And she was cold.

Her teeth chattered. Her shivering spread until she quaked. The only thing keeping her from rattling to pieces was the wondrous warmth of Rafe's body as he lay atop her.

An instant later, Rafe rolled to one side and sat up, taking both his warmth and the shield his body had offered against the rain. Icy droplets stung her face. With a tiny cry, Kate reached out, wanting his warmth once again. Instead, Rafe caught her hands and stood up, pulling her to her feet after him.

Kate threw herself at her rescuer. Wrapping her arms about his waist, she burrowed beneath his cloak, ducking her whole head beneath his outer garment and pressing her face into the protection of his shoulder. Oh, but he was warm. Droplets pattered against his outer garment, but none of it reached her. She breathed. His leather vest smelled of wind and rain.

More than that, he had rescued her. The man who loved her was also her savior. Craving his strength and the safety she found next to him, Kate curled closer.

He made a surprised sound even as he closed his arms about her and held her against him. "What are you doing?"

"You're warm." Her teeth yet clattered. "I'm cold."

"No surprise that," he said, a touch of amusement in his voice. "You're soaked."

Kate only murmured her agreement. Her eyes closed. Nothing else mattered save that it was heaven to stand so close to him. He took a step.

"Don't move," she commanded, her arms around his waist tightening as if she could hold him in place.

"I'm not going far," he replied, "only into the shelter of this tree. Hold tight," he warned.

Kate clung to him as he lifted her just so far as it took to lift her feet off the ground. He stepped backward until the pattering on his cloak died into the occasional drip. He leaned just a little, the movement suggesting he used the tree trunk as a prop. When he was settled, he pulled his cloak around them both, leaving but a narrow strip of her back exposed to the air. One of his hands slid up that expanse, as if he meant to warm her with his touch.

"I have a garment you can wear," he offered. "It's not much, but it will warm you and shield you from the rain."

"Not yet," Kate replied, pressing her cheek against his vest until she could feel the beat of his heart through it. With every breath, his heat flowed into her, driving away the cold. "Mayhap in a few moments."

His laugh was as warm as he. "Don't hurry on my account. I must admit I find your closeness more than pleasant."

As he spoke, his hand again moved along her back in a slow caress. Kate shivered, but this time it had naught to do with being cold. What was it about love that woke such wondrous sensations? More to the point, it was a terrible shame that such sensations were to be resisted and not indulged.

Still pondering this conundrum, she lifted her head out of his cloak and pushed wet strands of hair from her face to better see him. His face was a pale gleam in the night, but not even darkness was enough to conceal his smile. Kate's heart quivered. Oh, how she liked the way his lips curled when he grinned.

From the depths of her mind came a new image

to take the place of the one of forced marriage that had haunted her these past hours. In this one she was mounted on Rafe's big steed as he led that horse through Haydon's gates. It was early, mayhap dawn. In her imagining, Rafe wore his gleaming mail. She looked as fine as she had this morn, before Warin kidnapped her and ruined all.

She smiled. This was vindication, indeed. Not only would Warin be punished for what he'd done, but her father would face his comeuppance for his wrongdoing. On the morrow, her sire would have to admit to every man at Haydon Castle that Rafe Godsol was an honorable knight. It was a frisson of triumph that trembled its way down Kate's spine this time, but her rescuer mistook it for another shiver.

"Here," Rafe said, turning her until she lay against his chest, half tucked beneath his arm. He rearranged his cloak so it covered all of her but left half of him exposed to the elements.

"You'll be cold now," she warned him. From miles away, thunder rumbled, the sound but an echo of the storm's earlier rage. The rain slowed to a bare patter in the leaves above her.

"Not with you against me," he said, his voice low and suddenly hoarse. "Never with you at my side," he whispered, bending his head as he prepared to kiss her.

Kate told herself there wasn't time enough to consider resisting him. It was a lie. She wanted his kiss.

His mouth came to a rest on hers. Soft and warm, his lips moved on hers. Kate loosed a shaken sigh, relishing the taste and feel of his mouth on hers. It was all the more precious because she hadn't expected to ever again enjoy the sensation.

Even though his caress was quiet and gentle, her skin took fire. Her heart lifted to a new beat. Kate's eyes closed as a spark flared in that hidden place deep within her. Its heat was strong enough to shake her.

Of its own accord, one of her hands slipped up his chest and over his shoulders until her fingers rested against the warm, bare skin of his nape. Shielded by the hood of his cloak, his hair was only a little damp. She caught a curl, winding it around her finger. Rafe made a quiet, pleased sound at her play.

That tiny flame at Kate's center throbbed in the most extraordinary way. She toyed with his hair, this time using her fingers as a comb. Rafe caught his breath against her lips. Again the heat at Kate's core reacted. Lord, how was it possible that touching him could make her feel as if she was being touched?

A need for more of this teased Kate into tracing her nails down the length of his nape. A sound like unto a growl rumbled deep in Rafe's chest. His arms tightened around her as a shiver racked him.

"Jesu!" he breathed, then pleaded against her mouth. "Do it again."

A strange sense of power washed over Kate. She hadn't considered that she could give him the same sort of pleasure that he gave her. As commanded, she again traced her nails down his nape. Rafe trembled against her. The movement of his body against hers woke a throbbing deep within her.

His breathing rough and ragged, Rafe caught her face in his hands as he drew back from her. With a wee sound of disappointment, Kate opened her eyes and stared up through the darkness into his face. His thumbs stroked across the fullness of her cheeks.

"God help me but you cannot know how much I need you, Kate," he whispered.

His words tore at the glorious sensations that held Kate in thrall to make room for another round of Lady Adele's many warnings. Kate slammed the door on that voice. She didn't want to think about why she couldn't have Rafe. She didn't even want to think about why it was wrong to touch Rafe. All she wanted was more of the pleasure they made together.

Joining her hands at his nape, Kate pulled herself closer to him. This time it was her mouth that claimed his. He groaned against her assault, then kissed her in return. All gentleness was gone. Instead, his mouth slashed across hers, demanding something from her that Kate couldn't identify.

That spark within her exploded into blazing flame, the heat's intensity so stunning that Kate lost herself in it. She didn't feel them move, but of a sudden, it was she who leaned against the tree trunk, his cloak caught behind her. His mouth left hers to blaze a trail of kisses across her cheek to her ear.

Every inch of Kate's body came to life. She prayed he'd never stop.

His free hand closed over her breast. Soaked silken gowns were no bar to sensation. His hand was warm, nay, hot. So thin was the fabric that she could feel the calluses that marked his palm against her flesh. All on its own, Kate's body arched to press her womanly fullness more completely into his hand.

From deep within her a tiny voice screamed that this would lead to sin, that she'd rue what she did here. Rafe moved his thumb across the crest of her breast. Pleasure washed over Kate in a great wave, drowning the voice, along with all caution and concern. All she could do was cry out and again arch into his caress.

Rafe's mouth returned to claim hers once more. His hand stroked down the ruined silk of her garments until his fingers rested against the base of her belly. Shock rattled Kate. Even as her mouth yet clung to his, her hands came to splay against his chest and stop him. Before she had a chance to push him away, Rafe's fingers slid between her thighs to rest against her nether lips.

Even with cloth between her and his touch, the sensation was white hot. It stabbed through her, weakening every muscle in her body. Kate cried out against Rafe's mouth.

His fingers moved. Kate gasped. She melted; she could feel the wetness between her legs.

Again his fingers moved. Kate's knees gave way. Together, their lips still joined, she and Rafe slid down the tree trunk and came to rest in a bed of last year's leaf mold, Kate beneath Rafe.

His vest's leather lacing bit into her breasts. His legs straddled one of her thighs. Ah, but none of this mattered as his fingers once more stroked her nether lips.

The heat in Kate grew to an inferno. She gasped. She shook. Her body arched. On their own, her legs spread.

She panted. So did Rafe. His mouth left hers to press a kiss to her brow, then ply a line of kisses down her neck. Kate trembled when he didn't stop at her collarbone but lowered his mouth to the peak of her yet fabric-clad breast. At that same instant, he stroked her nether lips.

All Kate's capacity to think died. There was nothing left within her now save wave after wave of glorious pleasure. It left her naught but liquid at her core. Lost in this hopeless state, she tore her mouth from his and cried out.

Groaning, Rafe sat up. Kate moaned at the loss of his caresses, missing the warmth and rightness of his weight on her. She started to sit up, meaning to catch him back to her, when suddenly his fingers returned to her nether lips. But this time, her gowns were no longer in the way.

The feel of his bare fingers against her naked flesh was so startling, so shocking and so wonderful that Kate sank back to the ground, her whole body quaking. An instant later and Rafe once more lay atop her. His vest was gone, as were his tunic and shirt.

The heat of his bare flesh seared Kate. Gasping, she wrapped her arms around him, then exulted in the feel of her breasts pressed against the strength of his chest. Rafe made a sound that tangled yearning and need, then shifted so that he no longer straddled her thigh but lay in the V of her legs. It was the head of his shaft Kate felt at the entrance to her woman's core.

Shock tore a great rent in Kate's pleasure. Rafe meant to mate with her! The memory of pain ate up all her joyous heat in great, gulping bites. Even as she stiffened and began to cry out against the intrusion, his shaft found its way into her.

Gasping in astonishment, Kate relaxed back onto the ground and looked up at him. "There is no pain," she cried out, yet dazed by this unexpected turn.

Rafe braced his elbows on the ground at either side of her to lift himself a little above her. His face was a pale gleam in the night. "There's never pain when it's lovemaking," he murmured, touching tiny kisses to her lips between his words. Then he sighed. "Love me, Kate. Love me, the way I love you." It was a raw plea, as if her refusal would mean his death.

Kate stared at him, beyond speech. Love Rafe she did, but lovemaking? What they did here was lovemaking? With this thought, the sensation of holding him within her grew beyond mere fullness into something even deeper.

When she said nothing, he once more claimed her mouth as his. With his kiss, he moved a little within her. Kate gasped as a sensation like as she'd never known raced through her. Again he moved, and again that wondrous pleasure shot through her. At the center of her being, an unnamed need woke to clamor for something Kate couldn't name.

When Rafe moved this time, Kate's body lifted all on its own to meet his thrust with her own. Rafe groaned against her mouth, his kiss deepening until his lips once more slashed against hers. The urge to thrash beneath him rode Kate hard. That need of hers set to howling. And still he moved.

Of a sudden, what Rafe did sent pleasure into something more. Consuming everything in its wake, it spilled through her, then grew and grew. Kate dug her fingers into Rafe's shoulders, fearing that she might well explode against what filled her. His breathing grew ragged. His movements quickened, and then Kate was adrift on a sea of joy.

Rafe gave vent to a panting cry filled with the same pleasure that owned Kate, then relaxed atop her. Every inch of her alive with the feeling of him, Kate clasped her arms around Rafe, accepting his weight with a contentment she never dreamed possible.

It wasn't until pleasure's haze ebbed that Kate finally heard Lady Adele's distant voice. It screamed that Kate was now ruined for all time. What she and Rafe had just done was wrong, awfully, horribly wrong, and there would be a price to pay for it.

Kate ignored her. Not one moment was she going to waste in such thoughts. All she wanted to do was cherish Rafe and his lovemaking. Again astonishment rolled over her. There had been no pain, indeed, nothing but pleasure and more pleasure.

In that instant, she recalled how Emma had encouraged Gerard's touches. Understanding made Kate smile. Of course Emma desired her husband's touches if this was the sort of joy coupling could make between them.

Joy dimmed into a new and terrible ache. Nay, she would never call what she and Rafe did here wrong. How could she when on the morrow she and Rafe would be back at Haydon and forever beyond reach of each other?

Sighing, Rafe rolled to one side, leaving Kate longing for his return. Propping himself up on his arm, he lay beside her, studying her in the darkness. With his free hand he traced her cheek, the line of her throat, then let his fingers run along the generous curve of her breast. Kate shivered at his play, savoring it, even as the awful knowledge that she'd have no more of Rafe ate at her.

"Wed with me, Kate," he said, his voice deep and yet warm with the passion they'd shared.

The hopeless longing to be Rafe's wife rose until it nearly owned her. Not even her desire to have him could change reality. "Would that I could be yours," she replied, the taste of the words bittersweet in her mouth.

Again Rafe's fingers traveled around the curve of her breast. Kate's breath left her in a shaken sigh as her hunger for him reawakened.

"But you can be mine," he said softly. "We'll but

go to Glevering and be wed. Thus, is marriage accomplished."

His words were more shocking than any touch could ever be. Kate shoved herself back from him and sat up. The hems of her dresses were yet raised to her thighs. Humiliation tore through her as she slapped them down over her legs. She shifted back from Rafe until the tree trunk would let her go no farther.

Across from her, Rafe sat up. Even in the darkness, she could see the crease that marked his handsome brow. "Kate?" he asked, sounding confused.

"Say it again, what you just said to me," she demanded, her voice trembling. It wasn't that she hadn't heard him, she just couldn't believe she'd heard it.

Rafe sucked in a quick breath, then combed his fingers through his hair. "I said, wed with me, Kate. Let's do as you proposed at the hunt and end this feud between our families with our marriage."

Every mote of pleasure left in Kate died, leaving in its place icy nothingness. "Are you mad?!" she cried. "My father would kill me if I wed you."

Across from her, the crease smoothed from Rafe's brow. "He'd have to kill me first," he replied, naught but arrogant confidence in his voice.

"Aye, and that he'd happily do," Kate retorted, still aching over this betrayal.

He smiled. It was a cocky grin that even night's darkness couldn't hide. "I'm not so easily vanquished. Marry me, Kate, and let me hold you safe from your kinsman."

How could he persist, when each word was like unto a knife thrust in her heart? "I won't," she cried out. "I've just escaped ruin through an illicit marriage to Warin," she started, only to catch her breath as a new pain stabbed through her. Ruin came in many ways, one of which was to fornicate with her father's enemy. As the whole of her sin came to sit heavily on Kate's shoulders, the thought woke that Rafe had used her in order to manipulate her into a secret marriage. Kate's shame grew.

"Nay, I won't wed you," she cried out. "I'll go nowhere with you save back to Haydon."

Rafe's smile died. "You'd refuse me after what we've just shared?" he demanded, sounding right angry, too.

His words made Kate's heart twist. She caught her hands to her chest to stop the ache. It was true. This lovemaking of his was meant only to bend her to his will.

"Nay, you will not," Rafe went on. "I think me we'll go on to Glevering, where it'll be me you marry and no other. That is, unless you prefer Sir Warin as your mate. If that's the case, say so now, and I'll leave the two of you here to complete your journey as you will."

Pain ate Kate alive. She gaped at her erstwhile rescuer. He wouldn't leave her here in Warin's custody! Her eyes narrowed. Of course he wouldn't. Now that one manipulation hadn't worked, he was trying another.

In that instant and with a horrible crack, every one of Kate's cherished illusions shattered, leaving her staring at a world she hated. Tears sprang to her eyes. Lady Adele and her tales were wrong. There was no such man as a courtly knight, nor should a lady give any man, no matter his appearance or behavior, her heart. She especially shouldn't give him her body.

Men were all of a kind, every one of them willing to use a woman any way they could if it meant getting what they wanted. All men were like her father and Warin. And like Rafe Godsol.

"You didn't come to save me from Warin," she said at last, her voice flat in defeat. "You came to take me for yourself."

Dawn found Kate still mounted on that horrid palfrey, only now she was surrounded by fifty Godsol men, more than forty of whom had been waiting for Rafe in a hidden dale. Over her yet damp gowns she wore a monk's habit, the garment Rafe had offered her. It didn't help. She was beyond cold, beyond exhausted, beyond humiliated and desperately hungry, since for pride's sake she'd refused the oatcakes and smoked meat Rafe had offered whilst they waited for the dawn to come. Most of all, she truly was beyond the reach of any rescue this time.

So deep was her hopelessness that she swayed in her saddle. It hadn't helped to discover a whole Godsol troop waiting for them in a hidden spot. That his men were so near to Glevering proved Rafe planned her kidnapping long before her sire's behavior drove Warin to take her.

"My lady," said the soldier, a plain man, round of face and nose, who held her palfrey's reins. Dawn's light made the concern in his blue eyes seem true, although he was a Godsol and she a Daubney. "Are you well?"

Kate peered at the man from beneath the edge of the habit's cowl. She was keeping the hood low upon her brow to conceal as much of her as possible. It was fear that her loss of virtue might somehow show upon her face that made her do it. She wasn't going to give any of the Godsols, who were every one odious men, the chance to judge her a lightskirt, even though Kate now knew full well that's what she was.

"I'm as well as can be expected, considering I've been kidnapped twice in the last day and slept naught at all in that time," she snapped, her voice as rusty as Warin's mail.

The soldier blinked, then shrugged. "Pardon, my lady," he said, no rancor in his voice, "but there's no help for it. Sir William is honor-bound to reclaim Glevering for the Godsols once and for all. If the doing of that means Sir Rafe must take you from your sire, then take you he needs must."

With the man's words, the wound Rafe's betrayal had left in her heart opened anew. Despair ran deep, indeed. What a fool she was. She'd conjured up affection in Rafe's gaze when all he ever wanted of her was Glevering, just as she'd imagined honor in

Warin who wasn't honorable at all. At least Warin was paying for his insult.

She glanced at her sire's steward, who rode on her left. Rafe's men had gagged him, binding him by the neck, hand and foot to the saddle of another man's horse. But at Rafe's command, Warin wore his cloak to protect him from the elements and his wounds had been bandaged.

Such evidence of Rafe's kindness tried to temper Kate's new hatred of all things Godsol. She squashed the sentiment. Better that outlaws had attacked Warin and taken her. Then she wouldn't have the reminder of her wanton behavior with Rafe scourging her with every breath.

Her gaze shifted to the man she now despised with all her heart. Rafe rode at the head of this troop beside his eldest brother, Sir William Godsol. Now that he had captured her, Rafe didn't even bother keeping her near him. Instead, it was Warin's big black warhorse that walked at his side. The black was livelier now that his saddle was empty. He'd eaten and rested over the last two gray hours before dawn, while the Godsols waited for dawn's light to finish their conquest of Glevering.

Glaring at Rafe's becloaked back, Kate willed with every ounce of her being that he should die. By God, but she hated every inch of him. The great oaf! The big twit! She'd die before she married him. Nay, it would be better still if she could thwart him at his own game.

With that thought, the need to find a way to escape the fate he planned for her grew. It twisted and twined around her heart like the morning fog. There was still hope. Glevering's walls had yet to be breached, and that was no certain thing. Every furlong of these lands was her father's. No man who owed him an oath would ever open his gates to a troop of Godsols.

Kate's eyes narrowed. Her mouth tightened. Glevering had to hold. By God, but it'd please her to dance on Rafe Godsol's grave once her father finished him.

Ahead of her, Rafe held up his hand to signal a halt just before he and his brother reached the crest of a low hill. Throwing back his hood, he turned to look at those who followed him. Kate's brows rose in surprise. When had Rafe donned a knight's helmet?

Beside her, Warin made a furious sound deep in his chest, then strained against his bonds. Startled, Kate glanced at him. At great cost to himself, Warin glared up at Rafe as best he could with his bonds, forcing him into a meek pose. His eyes were bright with fury.

Rafe paid neither of his captives any heed as he scanned those following him. "As all of you know, Glevering lies on the other side of this hill," he announced. Nodding and loosening their swords, Godsol soldiers murmured in excitement as they shouldered their shields.

"Heed me well," Rafe called out, warning filling his voice. "No man draws a sword or deals a blow unless he's attacked. I want not a word from any of

you until we're all well within the walls. The first
six through the gate will ride no farther than a yard
or two from it. Wait there while the others pass you.
If there's any sign of trouble, you'll storm the machinery and see to it that the gate doesn't close on
us. Adelmar, Rob," he said to the men that rode
alongside Warin, "you're to take our knightly guest
to the back of the troop and hold him there. Should
things go awry, there's no sense in giving Glevering
a well-trained sword to use against us."

As he fell silent, he handed his eldest brother the
reins of Warin's warhorse, then thrust out his hand
to the soldier who rode beside Kate. "Old John, I'll
take my lady's horse."

"I'll never be your lady," Kate snapped as her
guard led her and her mount closer to Rafe. "And
you're mad if you think Glevering will ever open its
gates to you."

For the first time since he'd halted his troop, Rafe
looked at her. It was a cheeky wink he sent her way
as he shouldered the shield that hung from his saddle. "They're not opening the gates to me."

Behind his gag, Warin screamed in rage and
thrashed against his bonds. Kate gaped. It was
Warin's shield he carried. Only now did she recognize that it was Warin's helmet upon Rafe's head.
With Warin's warhorse at his side, those on Glevering's wall might well think he was their steward
making an unexpected visit.

"There, now, calm yourself," said the soldier
holding Warin's now fretting horse as he led the
straining man and dancing creature back to the

troop's end. "You'll both only do yourself more damage this way."

"This is dishonorable," Kate protested. It was a futile effort, for God knew appealing to Rafe's honor was useless. She knew full well he had none of that.

"Nay, just expedient," Rafe replied, but his smile was tense and tight. Just as well. To once more look upon the grin she'd so admired would only be salt in her yet very raw wound. "Now, Old John," he prodded Kate's guard.

The Godsol man tossed the palfrey's reins to him. Rafe caught them with ease, then held up his hand to show her that he now controlled her. "Glevering will be mine, just as you already are."

"Never," Kate snarled at him, hating him with all her might.

Something akin to disappointment swept across his features, then was gone. "Forgive me, Kate, but you leave me no choice," he said quietly, then gave a nod to the soldier at her side. "Do it, Old John."

Old John sent Kate a quick, regretful look, then dug into his hauberk. What he pulled out was a length of cloth—another gag. So too, was there a coil of thin rope. She was to be bound and stoppered once again.

"You wouldn't," Kate cried to Rafe, only because shouting a warning was exactly what she'd counted on doing. She gave him no chance to respond. "But of course you would. You're a Godsol. Now I know why my sire so despises your family."

Rafe flinched at her comment. "Kate, it needn't be this way between us. Godsol I am, but I vow now before all these men that I'd never be uncaring toward you because you're a Daubney. I thought you cared for me. So said your kisses and all else that passed between us. Why do you refuse me now?"

Kate squeaked as he exposed her immoral behavior before all these men. Shame burst to fiery life on her cheeks, and she jerked her cowl even further down upon her head to hide it.

"How dare you speak so to me!" she cried out. More to the point, how dared he try to use her idiotic infatuation with him against her. She turned in her saddle to face Old John and thrust out her hands.

"Bind me and be done with it, man," she demanded. "As you do it, remind your master that I've no feeling at all for him save the hatred a captive feels for her captor."

"Kate," Rafe protested, sounding sorely aggrieved.

Kate did her best to show him her back. A strange sound, something that might have been a laugh, left the soldier beside her. Kate shot him a sharp glance. There was no sign of amusement on the man's plain face. Instead, he clucked with concern when he saw the raw marks left by Warin's bindings. Because of that, he didn't make the rope about her wrists as tight as it should have been. As he reached to tie on Kate's gag, she pulled her arms as far as she could into the too long sleeves of the monk's habit, to hide the fact that the rope loops slid far down her hands.

Beneath her new gag, a wee, tight smile tugged at Kate's lips. By his own man's doing did the chance to destroy Rafe loom before her almost within reach. It was more than possible that Glevering's defenders wouldn't be tricked by Rafe's ruse. After all, the Daubneys and the Godsols met in battle often enough, someone within the walls might well recognize a man or two in this troop. When that happened, battle was sure to follow, and while the men fought, there'd be no one to watch her. She would be ready to take the advantage.

Chapter 18

Once Kate was bound and gagged, Rafe turned in his saddle to lead his soon to be wife's horse and his brother's men over the top of the hill. In his mind's eye he drew an image of what his and Kate's wedding night would be. The pleasure he'd imagined for that event was replaced by Kate's cold reaction to his lovemaking.

Nay! He knew better. After last night, he knew without doubt that she longed for him, indeed, craved him, as much as he craved her. How could she refuse the happiness they might have together when all that waited for her at Haydon was marriage to Sir Gilbert DuBois?

He shot another sharp glance over his shoulder at his bride to be. Her head was bent, her face almost completely hidden in her cowl. His stomach soured.

This was what came of a man giving free rein to his imaginings: he left himself room to be sorely disappointed. Now, rather than riding up to Glevering's gate with a happy Kate proudly at his side to demand entrance to her dowry property, he worried over her hatred, wore another man's armor and only prayed he could talk himself into the manor.

"Looking at her won't make it sting any less," Will said. However quiet his words, there was no mistaking the laughter in his brother's voice.

Rafe straightened in the saddle to narrowly eye Will. From the men behind them came various chokes and coughs. Every Godsol man was chortling up his sleeve at their leader's sibling. All because of Kate. With a grin, Will clapped a hand on his younger sibling's back.

"Well, what did you expect?" his brother asked, then lowered his voice so the lady behind them wouldn't hear. "Did you fancy that she'd still be pleased with you once she knew that it was only Glevering you wanted?"

Rafe flinched as what Will said drove through him like a stake. But of course that's how Kate saw what was happening right now, especially after being kidnapped by both him and Warin. She was only rejecting him because she thought he was using her. Rafe sighed in relief. If that was the crux of the matter, then all he need do was convince her that if it was Glevering he wanted for his family, it was her he wanted for himself. That was, if he could get her to listen to him.

Will laughed again. "Ah, well, in a few more moments you'll trick our way into Glevering," he said, his tone conversational once more. "As long as the Daubney heiress is already bound and gagged, you may as well take her to the chapel and marry her on the spot. I say do it swiftly and be finished with it. That'll leave you plenty of time, years even, to repent the deed whilst she chars your ears over it for an eternity."

Bile rose to burn the back of Rafe's throat. Will was right. If he forced Kate into wedlock, their marriage would be naught but misery, and that wasn't what he wanted from his Kate. There had to be a way to soothe her into marrying him of her own volition.

"There it is, Glevering," Will said, poignant longing in his voice.

At the center of a long, flat plain, a length of tall, solid wall rose up, black against dawn's gold and pink sky. Unlike Will, Rafe hadn't ridden into battle time and again against Bagot; he had little memory of Glevering. He studied the place that would be his new home with sharp interest.

From this western side, he could see none of the several hundred cottages that found protection near its walls. A small, squat tower lifted a fool's cap of a roof at the north end of the wall, while the sun, only now cresting above the horizon, sent brilliant beams of light between the great stone blocks that stood like giant's teeth atop the gatehouse at the wall's south end.

As light returned to the earth, every bird in the

woodlands offered up its song in riotous celebration of daybreak. From within Glevering's walls, a cock crowed, then another. Those animals penned within and without the walls joined in this raucous chorus. Cows lowed and sheep bleated as they waited for their milking. Where the tower met the wall, water spouted out of a drain. The stream glinted and gleamed in the newborn light.

Rafe counted the men stationed on the manor's walls, one, two, three, then more, outlined by the sun. All of them faced the oncoming troop.

"How many men does Glevering house?" he asked Will, now worrying that they hadn't brought a big enough force with them.

"No more than two dozen during times of peace," Will replied. "What you see above us is surprise because we're unexpected. Thank God, visitors are all they see." Will grinned at his younger sibling. "I'm wondering to myself why I never before thought to have our men remove any color that names us Godsol when we came knocking at their door. Clever of you, Rafe."

Rafe only grunted his response. With his confidence already on insecure footing, he studied the walls before him. Unlike other manor houses that girded themselves in wood, years of feuding over its ownership had left Glevering's residents protected behind expensive stone. A dry moat mined with sharpened sticks encircled its defenses. Framed in the gatehouse's arch was a set of doors leading through the walls. Made of thick oak, they

were bound with iron and twice a man in height.
Metal studs, meant to shatter battering rams, peppered their fronts.

The only flaw Rafe could find was that Glevering
had no drawbridge. Instead, there was but a flimsy
wooden span crossing the man-made ravine that
defended it. True, such a bridge was easily dismantled and hauled within in case of attack. Far better
that his new home have the additional strength of a
drawbridge between his gates and a besieger's assault.

Drawbridge or no, the gates were still stout
enough to resist fifty Godsols, especially since they
had no ram and likely had no longer than a day to
make their way into the walls. Worry grew. If Glevering held, he'd still have Kate, along with the wee
income from her de Fraisney dower, but he and his
wife would be landless until the courts settled the
issue of her inheritance. Nay, he couldn't afford to
give Bagot the chance to hold up their lives for
years. He wanted his home and his wife, and he
wanted them now.

He brought his horse to a stop at the edge of the
bridge before Glevering's gatehouse. His hand
dropped instinctively to his sword hilt. He caught it
back into his lap. Daubney's steward wouldn't
come to Glevering's gate looking as though he
meant to attack.

With those who followed gathering close behind
him, he arranged his cloak against his jaw to hide
his beard, then turned his face to the men above

him. The watchers were no longer looking his direction. Instead, their gazes were aimed at the gatehouse roof.

The bang of wood against wood cut through the quiet of dawn's arrival: the sound of a trapdoor hitting the floor from which it was cut. A new man appeared against the sun's light. The newcomer yet wore his bedrobe, a thick, red gown. It looked rich enough to suggest it had been his lord's before he owned it. The man's gray hair stood up in sharp spikes and gleamed as if it was wet. It seemed their arrival had disturbed him at his bath.

"That's Ernulf de Glevering, Bagot's bailiff," Will hissed from beside him, his own cloak hood now pulled low over his forehead to disguise his face, like all the hoods of the men behind them. The Godsols were well known to the men within these walls.

"Sir Warin," the bailiff called down from the gatehouse roof. The man crossed his arms, the very picture of skepticism. "Is that you?"

"Aye, 'tis," Rafe called back, doing his best to sound like the man he pretended to be, only to grimace, certain he'd failed. To cover himself, he coughed into his hand. Pulling his cloak more tightly about his face, he gave a mummer's shiver. "Pardon, the rain caught us last night, and I fear I'm feverish with the wet."

Ernulf de Glevering nodded slowly. "I know your message said to expect you, but what are you doing coming here when you should be with our own gracious lord across the shire at a wedding?"

Glevering had received a message telling them to

expect Sir Warin? Hope took flight as a wild grin tried to stretch Rafe's mouth. Lord, but Sir Warin was as determined as he to keep Kate as his own. How it must eat at the knight now, knowing that he'd paved the way into Glevering for his enemy.

In the next instant, Rafe's newborn optimism crashed. He didn't know what sort of excuse Sir Warin had put into his message. The hours Rafe had spent concocting a tale that might explain why so many men rode around a single churchman were all for naught, depending on what Sir Warin had written. Ach, but there was nowhere to go but forward.

"For the moment, your lord and mine finds it convenient to lend me to Bishop Robert. We escort yon priest"—a jerk of his thumb indicated Kate in her borrowed habit—"now turned monk at the bishop's decree to his new monastery. Our man here erred badly when he diddled with the bishop's niece."

Coughing once again to hide his nervousness and disguise his voice, Rafe forced himself to continue. "At any rate, we're road-weary and wet to the bone. With Glevering so near, I brought them here to rest our horses and sleep an hour or two before proceeding."

He carefully peered up at the wall as he finished spilling his lie. A new man appeared beside the bailiff, having followed his better up by the gatehouse stairs. Thick and stout, this one was a soldier; so said the steel chips sewn to his leather hauberk and the metal cap upon his head.

From beside Rafe, Will gave a quiet sound of recognition. "That's Glevering's sergeant-at-arms. He's a canny one, a good soldier and a man not easily tricked," he offered, unaware of how his words shattered his younger brother's hopes.

Rafe stared at the soldier. He wasn't going to have his home, because none of this was going to work. Glevering's gate wouldn't open because of whatever Sir Warin had written in his message, and Kate would never forgive him for taking her, even though he kidnapped her after Sir Warin. In another moment, the men on the walls would begin shooting crossbow bolts and slinging stones down on those beneath them as they recognized another attempt by the Godsols to reclaim what was theirs.

On the wall top, the bailiff conferred with his sergeant. From time to time, the two of them paused to look out at those beneath them. In what was surely a futile attempt to turn the tide in his direction, Rafe leaned over to pat Sir Warin's warhorse on the shoulder. Unlike the riderless Gateschales, who was being led at the rear of this troop because he tolerated no man save Rafe atop him, this horse was less chary, especially after a hearty meal of hand-fed oatcakes. Even so, all Rafe's caresses won from Warin's steed was a huff of annoyance. At last, the sergeant threw up his arms and backed away from his better.

Ernulf turned to face those waiting outside his gates. "So it's a fallen churchman you bring calling, is it?"

So stunned was Rafe by the man's friendly tone that for an instant he could but stare. When he caught himself at it, he forced another cough to cover his reaction. "Aye, so he is. The way I see it, he's lucky the bishop let him keep his balls."

Even before the last words left his mouth, chains rattled and clanked. Wood groaned. It was the sound of the bar lifting. Rafe's heart took flight as beside him Will sucked in an astonished breath. They were in!

Beneath the concealment of his hood, Will's face took light in unholy fire. "God be praised for you, Rafe. Never would I have conceived that such a ruse might work," he told his younger sibling in a soft voice. Grinning, he offered his landless brother a quick salute. "Go. Lead us as we do what our forebears could not and take back what is ours."

Nowhere near as certain as Will that Glevering was already theirs, Rafe buried his bearded jaw in the folds of his cloak and led Kate toward her dowry property. Will and Sir Warin's warhorse followed, the weight of four horses and three riders making the flimsy span beneath them groan. Aye, this place definitely needed a sturdy drawbridge.

Ahead of him, the gates moved steadily inward as the machinery groaned on. Rafe peered past the doors to scan the yard within the walls. The garden that kept Glevering's stewpots savory with turnips and leeks took up a good part of the area within the walls, while to his left were the stock pens. Standing tall among the huddled sheep, milkmaids gawked at their unexpected guests. Crosswise from the gate was a small keep tower so narrow that it could only be a defense of last resort. Rafe doubted more than twenty people could be housed in it and then not for more than a week before they all ailed from too much closeness.

The house sprang into the yard from the keep's side. Rising off a stone foundation almost a storey in height, the house was built of wood with naught but thatch for roofing and a smoke hole to guide the fire's breath outside its walls. Still, it was neatly whitewashed, and the roof looked in good repair. A sturdy wooden stairway reached to its raised entryway.

At the opposite end of the yard from the house stood a tiny chapel, God's cross marking its doorway. Exactly halfway between house and chapel was the kitchen shed. A man and two lads stood in its doorway—the cook and his assistants. Knives glinted in their hands as they watched the newcomers. Despite that, Rafe's hopes rose. All in all, Glevering would make a comfortable, even cozy home, for a man who never hoped to have one of his own.

As he rode beneath the gatehouse itself, Rafe glanced warily above him. It was strange how his mind worked. At the very instant he knew relief that there was no hole through which boiling oil might be poured down upon intruders he added construction of just such a device to his list of changes. Perhaps it was just that the house and wife he took today he meant to keep for his life's time.

The bailiff and the sergeant waited for them just inside the gateway, both men clinging close to the gatehouse wall. The old soldier held his bared sword in his hand. Rafe managed a nod terse enough that he didn't need to lift his head much to give it as he rode by them.

"Sir Warin?" the bailiff called out when he was denied the face he needed to confirm the man who entered was, indeed, the steward.

Unwilling to risk even a glance at the bailiff until more of his men were within the gate, Rafe kept his gaze on his saddle. "I'll speak with you at the house, Ernulf," he said.

Only when he was a good four yards beyond the gate did he dare to shift in his saddle, keeping his back to the bailiff, as he looked to see how many of his brother's men were now within the walls. On her palfrey behind him, Kate's head was bent so low that he could see nothing of her face. Her shoulders worked beneath the folds of her borrowed habit, as if she was trying to loosen tenseness from her back. Behind her, Will and Sir Warin's horse were already within the walls, as were the four men following Will. Two abreast, since that was all the gate or bridge would allow, the rest of the troop filed steadily into Glevering.

Kate made a sound. Rafe's gaze shifted back to her. Her head lifted. When their gazes met, she grinned. It was a vicious, triumphant smile.

Rafe blinked. She grinned? Where was her gag?

Again her shoulders shifted, only this time he could see it wasn't muscles she eased. Nay, she was returning her arms to the sleeves of her habit. Her hands appeared out of the cuffs. In one was the length of cloth that had stopped her mouth. The rope that trapped her hands was gone.

All hope of owning Glevering shattered. Even as his hands tightened on the reins to turn his horse, he knew it was too late. She lifted her head.

"Attack them! These are Godsols!" she screamed. "Attack!"

The satisfaction Kate felt as her call echoed out over the yard was beyond measure. In the breathless, startled instant that followed, the astonishment on Rafe's face gave way to grim determination. In one smooth movement, he dropped her palfrey's reins and drew his sword, then kicked his horse back toward the gate.

"Hold the doors!" he shouted to the soldier who had been Kate's keeper.

Even as the Godsol men within the yard turned their horses to race back to the gatehouse, the burly little soldier at the gate sprang forward to block their path. "Close the gate!" he bellowed as his weapon rang against that of one of his enemy's.

Behind the little man, Glevering's massive exterior doors jerked to a halt, then the grinding began anew as they moved in reverse. The Godsol men outside the gates spurred their horses and poured through the ever-narrowing opening, their shields held high. Crossbow bolts sizzled down upon them from the wall above the gatehouse as they rode. Screaming out of the kitchen came the cook and his two lads, their knives at the ready. At the sheepfold, the milkmaids shrieked. Buckets flew. With a flurry of skirts, the women left their bleating charges and raced for the safety of the house, the same sanctuary Kate needed.

Winding her hands into the palfrey's mane, Kate drummed her heels against the foul beast's sides. For once, the idiot creature did as she willed and chased the milkmaids to the stairway at the house's forefront. Slipping off its back, Kate dashed up the steps, pushing past the last of the screeching women.

At the center of the portal was a heavyset woman, her hair covered with a neat white headcloth. Beneath her water-stained apron, her green gowns owned style enough to suggest she was the bailiff's wife. As each milkmaid sprang into the hall, Glevering's housewife gave the hapless girl a shove to speed her on her way—until Kate came abreast her.

The woman grabbed Kate by the habit's shoulder and shouted something in the English tongue. Kate needed no translator to tell her she was being refused entry. She threw back the garment's cowl.

"I am Lady Katherine de Fraisney, the kidnapped daughter of Lord Humphrey of Bagot and heiress to Glevering," she shouted at the woman. "I command you to let me in."

Whether it was her French, revelation of her womanhood or her claim to relationship to Glevering's lord that was the key Kate didn't care. With a startled sound, the portly woman shoved her on into the hall. To Kate's surprise, there was no screen between this hall's door and its main chamber. Instead, she was thrust directly into the body of the room.

As the final weeping girl followed on Kate's heels, the door thundered shut. Huffing beneath the bar's weight, two maids dropped what was nigh on a treetrunk into the thick brackets at either side of the door. The brackets rang like bells.

Almost before the echoes died away, a shouting Sir William Godsol pounded on the door, demanding entry. Every woman in the hall cried out in surprise, including Kate. She backed away from the portal. What if the Godsols took the day and the women opened the hall to them? A single door wasn't enough to protect her from the fate Rafe intended to force on her.

Pirouetting, she scanned the hall that belonged to her, seeking a secondary sanctuary. At the far end of the house, half a tree bore the weight of the roof's crossbeam. Sturdy rafters held the thatch above her head. Whitewashed walls gleamed blankly back at her, offering her nothing in the way of hiding place.

A raised hearth filled the chamber's center, new-born flames leaping on its flat ash-filled stone, smoke drifting up to exit through the guarded opening on the roof. Six sets of trestles sat around the fire, ready for the planks of wood that turned them into breakfast tables. Those planks, along with the benches used for seating, yet rested against the walls.

There was nowhere to hide! Her feet slid on the thick layer of rushes that covered the wooden floor as she finished her turn and faced the room's opposite end. Kate breathed out against the miracle when she saw it.

Cut into the stone wall that divided house from keep tower was a single wooden door. Glevering had a private chamber. In the de Fraisney home, the only room that had a door, other than the cellar, was the master's bedchamber. Because Sir Guy kept his treasure in a special chamber located directly beneath his bed, his door had a bar.

Praying that what was true for the de Fraisneys was also true here, Kate lifted her filthy skirts and ran across the room to the stone wall. The door was ajar. Throwing it open, she raced inside the chamber and whirled. The bar was already halfway in place, held crossways against the door by some foreign mechanism. In the back of Kate's mind the oddness of this arrangement niggled, its meaning something she couldn't place. Who cared! She was saved.

Grinning, she started to shut the door. As she once more faced the hall, she found Glevering's womenfolk yet at its center. Every one of them watched her in wordless surprise, even the bailiff's wife. Kate's need to repay Rafe for his misuse of her as well as to lay one more barrier between her and the man who thought to force marriage on her brought a falsehood flying from her lips.

"Whatever you do, don't open the hall door to anyone," she warned in her sternest voice. "The Godsols out there want to eat your hearts."

Those maids who knew the tongue of their betters shrieked. One swooned. The bailiff's wife whitened, her jowls quivering.

Content that their fear would serve her well, Kate slammed the door. It took a moment before she could work the strange bar down into its brackets, but it finally fell into place with the most satisfying of thunks. Eyes closed and hands braced against the thick, cool wood, Kate drew her first free breath since the previous afternoon.

Safety wrapped its warm arms around her. She leaned her forehead against the door. Despite the heavy panel and the keep's stone walls around her, she could hear sounds of weeping from the hall. So, too, could she hear the distant screams of men in battle. The occasional clash of metal was barely louder than the groaning of the gate doors.

A long, slow breath left her. It no longer mattered what happened in Glevering's yard. Even if Rafe managed to take the day, it would surely be hours before the women opened the hall door to him and hours more before he pried open the door to this chamber. That would give her father plenty of time to find and rescue her.

Yet savoring her freedom, Kate turned to see what sort of room this was, only to smile. She'd done Glevering a disservice in imagining it rustic and rude. The keep's lower storey had been converted into a small but serviceable bedchamber.

It was through an arrow slit cut into the tower's east-facing wall that sound from the yard entered as well as a sliver of dawn's light. A simple bed of wooden posts and a rope network to support a straw mattress laid its head against one wall of this tower chamber. The only other piece of furniture was a great, brass-bound chest to the bed's right, no doubt containing the bailiff's personal effects. The rents he collected for Kate's sire along with the contracts and fee agreements that bound Glevering's peasants and serfs to its master would be in the cellar chamber beneath this one. The room's other corner was empty.

Ah, but what lay at the bed's foot filled Kate's heart with joy. Set on a greased cloth to protect the rush matting covering the floor was a large wooden tub filled with water. A pot of soap stood at its side, while a yet-dripping cloth dangled over its edge. Judging by the puddles on the floor and the damp apron worn by the bailiff's wife, the Godsols' arrival at Glevering had interrupted her husband's weekly wash.

Kate's grin widened. His loss was her good fortune. Nay, it was nothing more than God's compensation for the horrible experiences of last night.

Two steps took her to its side. The water within it was yet warm, but it wouldn't have mattered if it had been ice-cold. In one instant, Kate stripped off the monk's habit Rafe had forced on her, then what remained of yesterday's finery.

Stepping in, she sank beneath the water's surface with a sigh, then rose again to sputter happily as the mud that caked her dissolved. Even as she reached for the soap, she yawned. With safety, there was no longer a reason to stave off exhaustion. Once she was clean, she'd sleep. Indeed, she was so tired, she would likely slumber until her father arrived.

With that, a bit of darkness cast its shadow over her hard-won contentment. Rescue meant no escape from the marriage her father planned for her. From the depths of Kate's mind came a tiny, traitorous voice. It dared suggest that, forced or not, marriage to Rafe was far preferable to a legitimate wedding that made her Sir Gilbert's mate.

Kate slaughtered the thought, but not before her eyes stung. She scrubbed at them. She wouldn't cry over Rafe. He'd used her affection to his own advantage. Rafe Godsol was a rogue who abused trusting, good women. She would never marry him, not even if he managed to break into this chamber and threatened to kill her if she didn't comply.

Chapter 19

L ess than an hour after he'd first breached Glevering's gate, Rafe stood at the base of the stairs
that led to the hall's door. Beside him stood the
nervous little priest who served Will at Long Chilting. Father Philip had a narrow, pointed nose, a
sharp chin and a fox's face to go with the red straw
that was his hair.

Ernulf, Glevering's erstwhile bailiff, stood at
Rafe's other hand, looking only a little worse for the
battle. His now dry hair stood out from his head in
stiff spikes; his fine bedrobe was torn at the shoulder. The blood of Glevering's sergeant, the only
man to give his life in their brief engagement, spat-
tered his face.

As Rafe's gaze met his, Ernulf's expression hard-

ened into stone. Rage lurked in his gaze as he stared
at his Godsol captor. Rafe took no offense. Ernulf
had lost more than his stewardship of Glevering this
day. At his age and after losing the property he was
supposed to protect, Ernulf knew full well he was a
man without hope of further employment, no matter that it wasn't Ernulf's fault Glevering fell.
Spurred by panic, the men turning the gate machinery hadn't kept their movements synchronous, and
the gates had jammed. Without a way to keep the
horde of Godsols out, Ernulf had no choice but to
cede the manor or lose every man.

One last time, Rafe scanned the yard, seeking
any remaining hint of battle signs. Gone were the
Godsol horses, led off to the far reaches of the
demesne. Will and the rest of his troop had herded
Daubney defenders into the nearest barn. There the
men would be held until they either gave their oath
to Rafe or were ransomed by Lord Bagot. Along
with them had gone the bound Sir Warin, although
Rafe doubted Bagot would give so much as a groat
to ransom his betraying steward.

All this preparation in the hope of breaching the
hall before Kate was certain which side had taken
the day. Rafe feared that if the hall doors opened
and she saw evidence of his victory, she might well
hold the house against him. He freed a slow sigh at
the great hurdle yet facing him. It was only a matter
of time now before Lord Bagot and men from Haydon found their way here. Although Will's engineer
was studying the gate machinery, the man couldn't
say when he might free the works and close the

gates. If Kate didn't let him in, they'd have to resort to Glevering's ram to breach the hall. With the hall door broken, Glevering would be rendered defenseless and Rafe along with it. Rafe had no desire to lose his new home as swiftly as he'd come to own it.

All of which was why he needed more than ever to make Glevering his by right of marriage as well as by his sword. Only then would the manor truly be his. Rafe looked at Father Philip.

"To be legal, must vows be said before a church door, or can you conduct a marriage in the hall?" It felt strange to ask this question after so many years of interdict. During that period, priests had been forbidden to make marriages, so many a union was formed before locked church doors, the bride and groom speaking their parts without the benefit of clergy. Still, Rafe wanted to leave no issue that Lord Bagot might use to dissolve his union to Kate. Moreover, taking Kate out of the hall might well mean binding her once more. If Rafe didn't already own it, that would surely guarantee her eternal hatred.

The priest blinked rapidly, as if startled at being addressed, then cleared his throat. "As long as there are witnesses to the saying of the vows, then the marriage is legal no matter where the event takes place."

Witnesses Rafe had in plenty. The thorny issue was finding a way to wring vows from Kate. He looked at Ernulf. "Do it, then. Call for your womenfolk to open the door. Remember, say nothing as to the outcome of the battle."

The bailiff turned his sullen gaze to the steps

leading to the house's door. It was still another moment before he could bring himself to start up the stair and another still once he'd reached the roofless porch before he could spill the words.

"Wife, it is I, Ernulf. Come, open the door," he shouted. "The battle's done."

Female cries, all sounding relieved, escaped through the hall's slitted windows. Wood banged against metal more than once as the maids within wrestled the bar from its home. The door gave a low growl as it moved.

Arms outstretched, a plump woman well into her middle years and dressed in aproned green started out of the door, only to stop short when she saw Rafe at the stair's base. "Ernulf?"

The bailiff gave a rattling sigh, his shoulders drooping along with his head. "Stand aside, wife," he said to his mate in English. "We've lost the manor to the Godsols."

That brought Rafe up the steps in a hurry, all the while praying Kate either hadn't heard or spoke no English. On the porch, the bailiff's wife gave a single keening cry and stumbled back into the hall. Rafe followed her, slowing to let his eyes adjust to the dim room.

Screeching women scattered before him, one whole group of maids falling back into the house's far corner, where they eyed him as if he were the devil's spawn. He scanned their faces. Kate wasn't among them. Frowning, he turned on the bailiff's yet dazed wife. The woman leaned against the wall behind her, her hands clutched together as if in prayer. Tears trickled down her cheeks. Her expression was flat, her gaze dull.

"Where is she?" he demanded in her native tongue.

"Who?" the woman asked, her tone as empty as her expression.

"Lady de Fraisney. Bagot's daughter. I saw her enter when the battle was first joined."

Ernulf gave a startled cry at this, then glanced from his wife to his home's new owner, hope returning to his gaze. "Glevering's heiress is here?"

His wife ignored her husband as she frowned at Rafe. "Do you mean that woman dressed as a monk? She barred herself into the bedchamber." She pointed toward the stone wall shared by house and keep tower.

Rafe almost groaned. The door on the chamber looked as stout and thick as the hall door. He'd be hours breaking it down.

Even as he damned himself for not finding a way to win Kate's heart before circumstances demanded he take her, he congratulated Kate on her pluck. Never had he known a woman with as much courage. If her cuts and bruises told the tale, she'd not meekly given herself over to Sir Warin. Nor had a second kidnapping dulled her spirit. Of course, she'd wouldn't be pleased when she realized her warning shout about the Godsols had contributed to the defeat of her sire's forces here. Oddly enough, his growing admiration for her only fed his desire to make her his own. Jesus God, but time was running out for him!

He turned to Glevering's housewife. "Is there any way past the bar that doesn't include the ram?"

Life returned to the woman's pale face, followed by sly comprehension as she realized it was only one woman the Godsols wanted. The very set of her jaw told Rafe that there was, indeed, another way into the room. It also said that he'd have to pay something to learn what it was. He didn't care. Whatever the cost, it was worth the time saved.

"There is," she replied, even as her husband sprang toward her, his hands waving, to warn her to silence.

"Say no more, Joan," he commanded her. "If our lord's daughter is here, it's our duty to protect her."

His Joan set her hands on her meaty hips. "You'd protect Bagot's get, knowing full well our merciful lord has no mercy in his soul? Nay, after this he'll turn us out to face starvation and penury, even if we should return his daughter to him. The Godsol needs Bagot's heiress if he's to own Glevering right and true, while we need to live on past this day. What we won't get from our own lord, we can have from him," she gave a jerk of her head in Rafe's direction.

"Joan!" Ernulf cried in horror, but even as he protested, practicality ate away at a lifetime of honor. As the truth of what his wife said wrapped its arms around him, his back bent. In one instant, he aged ten years. "Give him the lady, then," said the old man.

His wife looked at Rafe. "Vow that you'll secure us a pensioner's cottage with the Blackfriars, paying our rent and buying our daily bread until our lives are finished, and I'll show you how to crack yon door right now."

A few shillings a year to support this couple with the monks so he might have his Kate? It was more than worth it. He set his hand upon his sheathed sword's hilt. "Upon my honor and Saint George, you have my vow to support you as long as I own Glevering."

Content, Glevering's housewife straightened. Her head proudly held, her skirts jerking with each step, she crossed from the doorway to the hall's hearthstone. There she crouched to remove a loosened stone from the fireplace's raised base. Reaching into that hiding space, she pulled out a single massive key. This she carried back to Rafe.

"Lord Bagot hoards what little treasure Glevering owns beneath that chamber. At his command, we keep the door locked when no one is within it," she said, laying the key in Rafe's hand.

Rafe smiled as he closed his fingers around the key. Kate was his. Better yet, she was trapped. There was never more than one way into a treasure chamber. But that didn't change the fact that she'd hate him for the rest of his life when he stood her before his brother's men and Glevering's women to force marriage on her.

The answer hit him with such impact that he caught his breath. He simply wouldn't force her. If he wanted her to marry him willingly, it was a seduction he needed, and seduction was the one thing he did very well indeed.

He touched his brother's priest on the shoulder. "Father, fetch my brother, telling him I need my better clothing from my saddle pack. He should also bring all of those men who aren't needed to guard our prisoners. I want this marriage well witnessed. That means the rest of you," he called to the whimpering maids, "will remain here until I've released you."

To the bailiff's wife he said, "I need soap and water to wash."

A tiny smile touched the corners of the woman's mouth as she understood his intent. "As you will, my lord," she replied with a bend of her head, then called to her maids to do as he required.

Even though Rafe knew she offered the honorific as a sop, it pleased him greatly indeed. The desire to have all—a wife he loved, a home that gave him succor and the lands to support him—firmed. Indeed, if he succeeded in this, he wouldn't sit idly by and wait for Bagot to find him. Nay, he'd send a bold message to Haydon, telling the whole wedding party where to find him and his new wife.

Something startled Kate out of her dreams. She blinked. There was nothing to see but linen. At some time during her nap, she'd pulled the bailiff's bedclothes over her head.

Not yet certain why she was awake, she lay still and listened. No one screamed or shouted. No arrows sang through the air, no swords clashed. Indeed, there was nothing to hear save the chittering of birds, the peaceful bleat of sheep and someone's distant whistle.

Kate made a satisfied sound. It seemed the battle of Glevering was finished. Surely the defenders had triumphed, else Rafe would be battering at her door right now, demanding entry. She rolled over, meaning to reclaim sleep's embrace.

Someone sighed. She froze. As impossible as it seemed, the sound came from within this very room. Throwing back the bedclothes, she sat up, only to shriek.

Rafe stood at the foot of the bed, watching her. Clutching the blankets to her naked body, she catapulted off the mattress and into the chamber's empty corner. It wasn't far enough. She could still see every fine line of his face.

Damp from washing, Rafe's hair gleamed like the finest ebony. Except where his beard clung to his jawline, his lean cheeks were shorn of whiskers. Gone was the leather vest he'd worn last night. In its place was the gray tunic he'd sported throughout the wedding festivities.

Her gaze flew from him to the door. It was still barred. "How did you get in here?" she demanded.

With neither smile nor sneer at his victory over her, he held up a massive iron key. "There's both a lock and a bar on this door."

Again Kate's gaze flew to the door. Only now did she understand what she'd been too tired and panicked to comprehend earlier. That was why the bar sat half cocked in its brace. Hidden behind it was a flat iron panel, the insertion point for the key. When the key turned it lifted a lever, pushing one end of the bar out of its bracket so that the door could be opened. Lady Adele had spoken of such devices, although there weren't any in the de Fraisney home. Once more Kate named herself a fool for thinking Glevering unsophisticated.

Rafe started around the end of the bed. Kate squeaked. He was coming to claim her, and she was trapped without so much as a chamberpot to throw at him. Not that she could have thrown anything at him. Releasing the bedclothes meant baring herself to him, and that she dared not do when his touch had so much power over her. Her only recourse was to force herself as far back into the corner as she could go, shivering as her naked flesh pressed against the cold stones.

"Leave me alone," she commanded, utterly certain he wouldn't.

He stopped less than an arm's length in front of her. For a moment, his expression was quiet, as if he was considering her demand. He shook his head.

"I can't, Kate."

All Kate could do was glare. He lifted a hand to touch her face. Panic jolted through her. God save her, but what if the pleasure his caresses gave her returned despite his betrayal? If so, she was done for; she'd give him whatever he asked of her without so much as a slap. She turned her head to one side. Feather-light, his fingertips brushed her aching jaw where Warin had struck her.

"I should kill him for what he did to you," he said, his voice low and harsh. "Would that I'd found you sooner, before he laid his filthy hands on you. My poor Kate."

The false endearment rallied Kate's anger. She turned her head just far enough to shoot another glare at him. "I am not your Kate. I will never be your Kate. You used me." Damn her voice for quivering.

The smile he offered her was small and sad. "So I did. Would that I never had."

That brought her around to squarely face him. Kate lifted her chin to a haughty angle. "Hah! Whatever regret you pretend is surely well assuaged now that you have both Glevering and me. Spare me your flowery words and sugared phrases. Bring your ropes and gag to bind me. I'll have this wedding of yours over and done with, so I can return to despising you in peace."

His face tensed with her words, then he shook his head. "I'll not insist on marriage."

"What is this?" she demanded with new suspicion. "You drag me all the way here, threatening forced marriage at every step, only to change your mind at the last moment? I doubt that. Nay, you're but trying to use my emotions against me once again. What else could I possibly own that you need to steal it from me in this way?" Although she tried mightily to hide it, her voice filled with more than a little of the hurt he'd caused her.

He had the grace to flinch as he heard it. In the

next instant, a pretense of sincerity claimed his expression. "I'll *take* nothing more from you, Kate," he said quietly, "including marriage."

Kate's anger deflated so swiftly that it left her gasping. He really wasn't going to force marriage on her? The realization hit her like a blow. Of course he wasn't. He didn't need her now that Glevering was his, made so by the strength of his sword arm.

Humiliation swam in the tears that filled her eyes. Now that he knew she was a lightskirt, he meant to discard her. He'd give her back to her sire, and she really would have to wed with Sir Gilbert—if Sir Gilbert would have her.

Only then did the reality of her new position hit Kate. Now that Rafe owned what had been her dowry, all she had to attract potential husbands was her dower portion from the de Fraisneys. That was but a third of the value of the few lands she'd taken with her into her first marriage. She was impoverished and without prospects.

That wasn't all of it. She'd also spent the night captive to both Warin and Rafe. Even if she didn't come with child because of what she and Rafe had done, there wasn't a soul in all the world who'd believe her yet a chaste woman. If Rafe cast her off without marriage now, she'd be worse than ruined. She'd be humiliated, abased, shamed for all time. Her sire might well discard her, so useless was she to him now, leaving her to beg for her daily bread.

"How can you do this to me?" she cried in new panic.

Something Kate couldn't decipher flashed through

Rafe's gaze and was gone. His eyes darkened until they were nearly black. He placed his hands on the wall at either side of her head, then shifted forward, closing the gap between them.

Kate flattened herself against the wall behind her. It didn't help. His nearness made her heartbeat lift until her pulse sang. He smelled of soap. Even with the bedclothes wadded before her, the heat of his body reached out to embrace her.

No matter that she knew Rafe was intent on destroying her life just as completely as he'd destroyed her illusions. She wanted to feel his mouth on hers again. "Don't touch me," she warned, but it was more plea than command.

"I cannot help myself, Kate," he replied, his tone the one that Kate had previously mistaken for love. His mouth was but a hair's breadth from hers.

She wouldn't let him use her again, she just couldn't. It took all her will to turn her head to one side, hoping to deny them both the kiss they craved. His lips came to rest on the corner of her jaw just beneath her ear. Heat, tainted by the longing for something more, flowed through her from the spot his mouth touched.

His lips left her jaw, then came to rest against her throat. Her skin took fire. Once again a throbbing started in the core of her being. Kate tried to lean away from him, but she was trapped between his hands. He pressed his mouth to the jut of her breastbone.

"Don't," she protested, her voice barely louder than a whisper, then groaned inwardly. For someone supposedly trying to save herself from further humiliation, it was a pathetic defense she staged.

"I can't help myself," he repeated between kisses as his mouth traced a path to where the bedclothes met her breasts.

Even as she chided herself for a wanton, Kate's knees weakened. Mary preserve her, but she needed him to touch her as he had last night. The very thought made her breath come faster.

Disgusted with herself, Kate held the bedclothes in place with an arm and shoved at his shoulder with her other hand. Although he moved not an inch back from her, her resistance did disturb him enough to make him cease his sweet torment. Straightening, he caught her face between his palms. His head lowered until his lips touched hers. Although it was but a gentle press of flesh to flesh, Kate's mouth clung to his. How was it that when he kissed her she felt fevered and more alive than she'd ever dreamed possible?

Then his mouth left hers, and he eased back a half-step. Only by mustering all her will did Kate keep herself from reaching out to draw him back to her. For a quiet moment he studied her, his thumbs stroking pathways across her cheeks, a tiny crease marring the perfection of his brow.

"Would you forgive me the wrong I did you if I fell to my knees and begged for it?" he asked at last.

Even as Kate's head insisted that this was some new ploy meant to further abase her, her wayward heart demanded she give him what he wanted. The battle between the two extremes left her speechless.

In the end all she could do was shake her head in refusal.

He sighed at that. "I suppose it's no more than I deserve. I should never have misused you as I did," he said as he slipped one arm around her. The weave of his linen sleeve felt rough against the bare skin of her back. His hand was warm against her naked shoulder. "As God is my witness, I never intended to cause you pain."

So false was his claim that even her heart ceased its clamor. The floodgates of her anger opened. "Wasn't what you intended?" she cried. "Liar! Kidnapping me was always what you intended, else there wouldn't have been an army of Godsols waiting but a mile or two from Glevering. You planned this long before Warin took me. Don't you dare insult me by claiming you didn't. Even I, who have proved myself a fool many times over these last days, am not so great a fool as that. Now let me go!" She once more shoved at him with her free hand.

Rather than do her bidding, Rafe wrapped his other arm around her and pulled her into an embrace tight enough to make Kate's breath huff from her. With the bedclothes held in place by the pressure of their bodies, she dared release her hold on them and brace both hands against his chest as she tried to put a decent distance between them. She might as well have been pushing at a brick wall for all he moved.

"You're right. I did plan your taking," Rafe said, sounding truly regretful. "The idea occurred to my brother in the very hour that Emma and Gerard exchanged their vows. I agreed, without thought or care for the consequences you might bear, only because I found you so lovely I couldn't resist the idea of making you my wife."

Rafe thought her pretty? He couldn't resist the thought of her as his wife? Kate's arms relaxed a little at his compliment. There was no sign that he noticed her defenses breaching.

"That night, needing to see the sort of woman I meant to take for my own, I sought you out. You cannot imagine my astonishment when I realized you didn't already hate me for being a Godsol, that you knew nothing of the feud between our families. You see"—he paused to sigh—"to have Glevering I knew I'd have to force marriage on you. I couldn't bear the thought of an unwilling woman as my bride. I wanted your affection. I wanted you to desire me. And you did, or so said your kiss."

Shame seared Kate's cheeks. "Please God, don't remind me of that night. Never, until I met you, have I ever behaved so improperly with a man."

Rafe's smile was slow and pleased. "Is it solely me who does that to you? Tell me that it is," he pleaded.

It was a lover's question. Joy tumbled through Kate, only to stop short, slaughtered by the reminder of how Rafe had used her. Still, the need to answer him wouldn't be denied. "I cannot understand how you do it," Kate offered grudgingly, "but you overwhelm all that I know is right to seduce me into doing what I shouldn't."

"God be praised, I hoped you'd say that," he murmured, his hand shifting up her back until it rested at her nape. There his fingers worked and caressed Kate's tense neck muscles. She savored the sensation, even though she knew she shouldn't.

"It's only fair I tell you that you do the same to me," he said. "Indeed, so powerful is your effect on me, you very nearly ruined my plot to have you." There was a new touch of amusement in his voice. "Before God I vow I've never been so jealous of another man as I was when I saw you at the picnic with Sir Warin. That your heart might be given to another ate me alive, since that meant I didn't own it. I'd have died at your sire's hands before I allowed you to meet Sir Warin in the woods."

"What?" Kate cried softly, easing back in his arms to better stare into his face.

His expression was soft. "Kate, I am besotted with you," he said. "My heart is given, yours if you should want it."

How Kate damned her need to believe him even after all the wrong he'd done her. Rafe's hand at her nape slipped upward until his fingers threaded into her hair. Cupping her head in his palm, he tilted her face until he could brush her lips with his.

"Kate," he begged in a whisper, the movement of his mouth against hers provocative, "when I asked you last night, it was a question from my heart. Now I ask it again. Marry me. Be my wife and the mother of my children. Share with me whatever joy comes our way and be my comfort in times of trouble. In exchange, take my heart and my vow to hold you safe for all the days of your life."

His words stunned her. Rafe owned Glevering in his own right now. He could seek out some other heiress, one with more than a pittance to her name. If he was offering her marriage, it could mean but one thing.

Pushing herself back from him, Kate stared up at him in astonishment. "You love me!"

"I fear I do." Rafe's brows rose a little, as if he were chagrined. His shoulders lifted, then a flicker of concern flashed through his eyes. "With all that has passed between us, I'll understand if you cannot tell me my affection is returned. Only tell me that I might hope for the future. Our future?" It was a plea, no less.

With a laugh, Kate threw her arms about his neck. "I am a fool, I know it, aye, but I cannot help myself when it comes to you. You may do far more than hope for my love," she assured him, then caught his mouth with hers.

Rafe's arms tightened around her until every inch of them touched. His kiss deepened, his mouth slanting across hers, demanding. She yielded and happily, as all the glorious sensations she knew he could make in her returned.

Then he released her and took a backward step. Kate gave a quick cry as the bedclothes bunched between them slid. She snatched for them.

Too late. Down her body they went, past her hips, to puddle on the floor around her feet. Frantic to cover herself, Kate bent. Before she reached them, Rafe caught her hands. Twining his fingers with hers, he drew her up so he could better see what she hadn't intended to show him.

"By God, but you're lovely," he said, his voice suddenly hoarse.

Even as his words made a whole new pleasure thrust through Kate, she fought it. If she'd learned one thing beyond the fact that there was no pain in coupling last night, it was that coupling without vows could lead to humiliation. And that she'd had enough of these past days.

"Turn your head," she commanded in a shaken voice, tearing free of his hold to grab up the blankets. She threw them around her shoulders, pulling them here and there until she was swaddled from neck to toes. "We aren't married. You mustn't look upon me until we've traded vows."

"Then marry me," Rafe managed, his gaze yet aimed at what he'd seen, his voice strained and quiet. "Marry me this very moment, ere I eat myself alive for wanting you."

He raised his gaze to look at her, his eyes lambent with desire. "I said I would not force you, Kate," he told her, his voice yet full of longing for her. "You must tell me that you'll marry me, entering into our union because it is your choice to do so, just as our lord king granted. But if you agree to wed me, know that I'll demand a hasty ceremony held this very moment. Delay even so much as an hour, and our chance to marry may well disappear. If the deed's not done in its entirety before your sire finds us, I cannot keep him from claiming you as his property once more."

Happiness started as a quiet glow beneath the heat Rafe had already made in her. That he made this her decision more than washed away the stain of the wrong he'd done her and the wrong they'd done together, for he risked the chance she would refuse him. An obedient, well-behaved daughter, the sort that Lady Adele had tried to make of Kate, would have instantly refused, no matter what affection she might hold in her heart for this man. A good lass never questioned her father's choice for her. However, Kate now knew that she was neither obedient nor well behaved. She smiled. Aye, and because she wasn't, she'd claim a worthy husband, one who honored and respected her, one who offered her his heart and begged to own hers in return.

In that moment, Lady Adele's tales loosed their hold on Kate as she recognized them as shallow, even laughable. Not even for honor's sake should a woman marry a man she despised only to pine hopelessly for the man she loved. Well, if that's how other women meant to live, Kate would let them. For herself, she'd have the one man who was courtly lover and husband all in one.

She smiled. "Then I will marry you this very moment."

Chapter 20

Rafe's smile was wide and pleased. "God be praised! I won't lose you."

Reaching out, he tugged at the edges of her blanket, as if to cover some tiny patch of skin she'd left bare, then turned and crossed the room. Kate frowned, watching him lift the bar. The door opened, and he took a single step out into the hall beyond it. "Father, she's agreed to wed with me," he called out into the hall.

Kate gasped. She hadn't realized he was serious about wedding her this very moment. "Nay, Rafe," she cried out, hurrying over to him as quickly as her swaddling would allow. "Not yet. I need to dress."

Another tiny cry left her, and she whirled to face the filthy remains of yesterday's finery where they

lay near the tub's end. She couldn't wear those
clothes, not the way they were, and it would take
hours to see them clean and hours more before they
dried. That left borrowing a gown. Kate's skin
crawled at the thought of wearing some maid's
well-worn, flea-ridden attire on her wedding day.

Rafe stepped to her side. Wrapping his arm
around her, he turned her back to look out of the
bedchamber's doorway. "You vowed. No delays."

Kate's heart quirked. Before her the hall was full,
Glevering's womenfolk on one side of the room,
Godsol men filling the other. Rafe's brother's eyes
widened when he saw the blanket-clad bride, his
lips twitching as he fought a smile. From the hall's
back came a feminine giggle, while amusement
rumbled from the men.

Embarrassment warmed Kate's cheeks. She
turned her head into Rafe's shoulder to hide her
face from those who watched. "I can't stand in front
of them in only a blanket," she whispered to him.
"My hair's uncovered and undone." Not even on
her wedding day did a widow uncover her hair;
that was for virgins. "They already think me a
strumpet for this."

"They'd best not," Rafe said, his voice lowered to
the depths of a threat. His arm around her tightened, then he said something to the hall in the English tongue. There was instant silence.

"Hold up your head, my sweet," he urged her in
her own language. There wasn't a whit of humor in
his voice. "I've told them that your attire is ruined
and that if I hear another sound, I'll drive the one

who makes it out the gate for not treating my wife with all the respect due her."

Rafe's words wove a joyous web of security around her. Kate lifted her head to look into his face. He smiled. She sighed, well pleased with the man she'd chosen. From this moment on, Rafe would see to it that she was well treated. Oh, but there was much to value in becoming his mate.

Kate turned to look out over the room. The amusement was gone from every face. The Godsol priest stepped forward with Rafe's brother at his back, then the ceremony, such as it was, began.

It stunned Kate that one moment she was Katherine de Fraisney, and the next she was Katherine Godsol. Of course, the priest had pared the rite to barely more than the oaths. All that needed doing now was to share the kiss that sealed the ceremony.

Rafe turned her in his arms. Naught but silence owned the room. His lips were soft and warm on hers. However gentle his caress, that heat she'd discovered last night returned. She sighed against it, her eyes closing.

Kate let her mouth soften beneath his. It was an invitation, a reminder of the pleasure this sort of sharing between them woke. She felt his jerk of surprise, then his embrace tightened. The intensity of his kiss deepened until new heat flooded Kate.

Someone applauded. Approving laughter, both male and female, broke the silence that had owned the hall throughout the trading of the oaths. Kate felt Rafe's smile against her mouth. Yet holding her in his arms, he straightened, his forehead leaned against hers. Emotion darkened his eyes.

"My wife," he whispered, his voice deep with wonder. "You are my wife."

Stunned by the intensity of what showed in his gaze, Kate let him take her back to the bedchamber. Not until the priest, Rafe's brother, the bailiff and his wife followed them into that wee room did her shyness reclaim Kate. Lord, but she didn't like exposing herself to others. To distract herself from the discomfort of it, she reminded herself of the pleasure she found in Rafe's arms.

Across the chamber, Rafe disrobed on his own. There really wasn't room for his brother to help him, especially with the bathtub yet in the way. Instead, Will Godsol remained just inside the doorway alongside the other witnesses to this rite.

Once Rafe had hung his tunic on a bedpost and tossed his shirt on it, he bent to remove his shoes. His chausses followed in swift order, the stockings left to lie beside his feet after he had stripped them from his legs. As he straightened Kate stared at her new husband, beyond words.

How could she ever have thought his frame too bulky or unattractive? Day's light gleamed against the powerful lines of Rafe's body. Shadows marked the masculine rise and fall of his chest. His hips were lean, his legs long. Indeed, so powerful did he look that Kate might have been intimidated, save that the heat his touch always made in her returned. This was all the more stunning because he wasn't even touching her yet.

"Kate?" Rafe prodded, the quirk of his brow reminding her that it was her turn.

At least there was nothing complicated about her disrobing. Keeping her gaze fixed on her new husband's face, Kate drew a bracing breath and let the blanket fall. Only the fact that there wasn't a single ribald jest from those who watched made the moment tolerable.

Across the bed from her, Rafe swallowed. His expression softened, his eyes closing part way as he studied her. His gaze felt like a caress against her skin.

"I see no flaw," he said, his voice thick.

"Nor do I," Kate whispered, saying her part.

"Good enough," the priest said, his tone businesslike. "Once the consummation is complete, this marriage will be legal in all ways. Come," he said to the other witnesses, "we'll leave them to their duty."

Duty. Kate's stomach tightened. It was the sound of Lady Adele's voice she heard in the priest's words. Kate glanced at Rafe. His gaze was yet fixed on her. It was anything but Lady Adele's description of marital duty that she saw reflected in the gleam of his eyes. Deep in Kate, the embers of yesterday's pleasure stirred with violence enough to make her shudder. Her trembling made Rafe's expression soften until the longing to touch her glowed in his face.

The door closed behind their paltry four attendants. There wasn't so much as a jest or shout from those on the other side. Instead, the sounds of normal conversation rose from the hall. Wood banged against wood as tables were erected in preparation for the breaking of the fast. Relief rushed through Kate as she realized there'd be no shivaree for her.

Rafe came around the bed to stand before her, his eyes as black as night. "God help me, but you're lovely," he breathed, "and you're mine."

Reaching out, he traced a finger along the outer roundness of her breast, then his touch blazed a path down the inward curve of her waist. Kate quaked against his caress. How could the mere brush of his fingertip set her skin afire?

His hand descended to her hip, then returned to cup her breast in his palm. His thumb brushed its crest. It was as if she'd swallowed a candle's flame. Heat jumped and darted within her. The throbbing at her woman's core owned her, once more demanding the pleasure he'd given her last night.

Driven by that need, Kate reached out to touch him. Out of the depths of her memory came ancient warnings. Both Lady Adele and the de Fraisneys' priest had allowed that she might touch Richard and his shaft only as much as was necessary to put seed into her womb. Any touch beyond that, they nightly lectured, was prohibited by God. She caught back her hand.

Impatience flared. What was she doing, denying herself? Hadn't she already determined that she was no dutiful daughter, but a lightskirt bent on passion?

With that goal fixed in her heart, Kate laid her hand against her husband's chest. His heartbeat was strong and certain against her palm. The dark hair that covered his skin was springy beneath her fingers. She smoothed her hand against his flesh. The warmth in her grew warmer still. Lord, but touching him made her feel as if she was being touched as well.

A deep, dark sound rumbled from Rafe. Kate fought a smile. It was a lion's purr.

Once again his thumb moved against her breast. Sensation darted through Kate, leaving her gasping in its wake. She fell against him. Rafe's arms closed around her, pulling her closer still until Kate swore every inch of their bodies touched. The fullness of his shaft pressed against her belly.

He was ready for her too soon, when there was so much more they might do between them. Even as Kate lifted her head to beg that they wait a little, Rafe's lips laid claim to hers one more time. The dance of his mouth atop hers was demanding and pleading all in one instant. Kate again melted, feeling the wetness seep from her woman's core. So lost was she in sensation that she barely noticed when Rafe lifted her in his arms.

A tiny sound of complaint left her when he laid her upon the mattress. It was cold without his body next to hers. A moment later, and he lay atop her. He lowered his mouth to kiss her breast.

This time there was no fabric between his lips and her flesh. Kate gasped as he suckled, crying out with a pleasure beyond all understanding.

Then, as he'd done the previous night, his fingers found her nether lips. Again his touch sent Kate reeling. Although someone in the hall might hear her, she couldn't stop her cries. Just when Kate thought for certain she might die, from sheer enjoyment, she caught his hand.

Rafe raised his head from her breast. "What? Will you complain already, wife, that your husband doesn't please you?" he whispered, the corners of his mouth twitching against a smile.

Kate laughed, the sound broken and panting against his sweet torment. "You know full well you please me," she managed. "But what of you? How can I let you give me so much pleasure when I don't return the favor?"

Rafe's eyes lit up in astonishment. "Return the favor?" he asked, sounding almost confused.

Twining her fingers in his, Kate brought his captive hand to her lips and pressed a kiss to its back. "I am ignorant," she complained softly. "Until last even, I didn't know there could be pleasure in bedding. Now I must educate myself. I would touch you until I find the way to make you cry out as you make me."

As she spoke, she freed his hand to lay her own on his shoulder. She stroked her palm up the length of his neck, then traced a finger around the circle of his ear. Rafe shuddered. His eyes closed.

"Jesu," he breathed as he slid off her to lie at her side.

Kate combed her fingers into his hair. Yet cool and damp from washing, the strands curled about her hand. Shifting on the mattress until she faced him, she traced a fingertip down the length of his nose, then outlined the curl of his lips. He caught her hand and pressed a kiss into her palm. Kate gasped as his tongue touched that sensitive flesh, then laughed and jerked her hand from his grasp.

"Nay," she chided. She pushed Rafe until he lay upon his back on the mattress, then she raised herself upon her elbow to look down on him.

"Nay?" Rafe asked, his gaze afire with need of her.

"Nay," Kate repeated, leaning to place a kiss at the place where his neck met his shoulder. Just as he'd done to her, she touched a line of kisses down his chest until her mouth rested against his nipple. "I am touching you, not you me," she breathed against his sensitive flesh.

Rafe shuddered. His hands came to clasp at Kate's waist. "Jesu," he whispered, his voice breaking.

Kate smiled. Laying her head upon his chest, she slipped her hand down Rafe's abdomen to his shaft. Her first husband had needed to be coaxed into readiness to take her. Not so Rafe. Still, Kate curled her fingers around that part of him most male. Gently, carefully, as she'd been taught, Kate stroked.

Rafe bucked a little beneath her, gasping, then caught her by the wrist. "Jesus God," he panted, "don't."

Only now did the worry that she'd gone too far, that Rafe didn't want so bold a wife, prick at Kate. Lifting herself off him, she looked at her husband. A frown touched his brow, hot color marked the line of his cheekbones and glowed in his eyes. The line of his mouth was impossibly soft.

"Kate, I'm fair dying for you." His voice was rough and hoarse. "Touch me again like that, and I may well spill my seed."

Confusion tugged at Kate. "That is bad?"

That slow smile Kate so loved once more tugged at Rafe's lips. "It is when I want our first lovemaking as man and wife to please you as well as it does me. Once we've shared our pleasure, I vow—oh God how I vow," he added in a heated whisper, "that you may make your acquaintance with every inch of me at your leisure." Anticipation of their future joy colored the fine lines of Rafe's face.

Understanding that Rafe meant to indulge in this sharing of sensation for as long as they both pleased weakened Kate's elbow. She slid down to lie beside him on the bed. No longer interested in postponing this moment, she caught him by the arm to urge him atop her. "Come," she begged him, "show me again that there is no pain in coupling."

Rafe shifted atop her with a quiet growl. His shaft came to rest between her thighs. Kate held her breath, but there was no need. Just as had happened the first time, he easily found its home within her.

For a long moment, Rafe held himself still within her. The delay only gave the alien fullness within Kate time to become something far more enjoyable. The need to move as she had the previous night grew with every breath, but even as heat again throbbed in her, she waited for Rafe.

His eyes closed. His brow pinched in a frown. Still, he delayed.

At last, Kate could bear it no longer. She lifted her hips and was rewarded by a shimmering taste of the joy to come. Rafe gasped. He dropped to lie full upon her.

"God help me, but I cannot stop myself. I want you so badly," he growled. Then, once more claiming her mouth as his, he thrust into her.

The heat at Kate's core exploded with his motion. It drove her to meet his next thrust. Rafe moaned against her mouth. Panting now, he began to move in earnest.

With each shift of his body on hers, Kate's pleasure swirled higher. Her fingers dug into his back. Her arms tightened around him. Her hips clung to his. Every inch of her body clamored that she again find the joy she knew Rafe could make in her.

Rafe's breathing grew ragged and hoarse, then he cried out and arched above her. Kate swore she could feel his seed enter her even as she once more lost herself in that sea of joy.

"My God, my God," Rafe breathed, relaxing atop her. He caught her face in his hands, then pressed sweet kisses to her nose, her cheeks, her eyelids, her lips. "Kate," he demanded softly between kisses, "tell me that you love me."

That he needed to hear her words of love turned Kate's joy into something far deeper. She clasped her arms around him, her heart aching as she held her husband against her. "I love you and only you," she told him, yet breathless from their wondrous play, their lovemaking.

As if nothing in the world could have pleased him more, Rafe groaned and caught her mouth with his. His kiss was warm and sweet. The pressure in Kate's heart grew until she had to smile. Her husband. Oh, to have Rafe and this happiness he made in her for all the rest of her days!

Rafe raised himself on an elbow above her. Kate cried out at this, needing his closeness almost more than she needed to breathe. He but smiled at her, his grin languid, the slow curl of his mouth sending another shiver through her.

"My kiss amuses you?" he asked, his brows raised as if this was a serious question.

"Never," Kate replied. "Your kisses do nothing but stir my passion and remind me that it is you who owns my heart. Never leave me," she commanded him, her arms tightening around him.

He laughed quietly. "Ah, now that I've convinced you that procreation is but a wee part of lovemaking, you intend to keep me, is that it?" It was a gentle taunt, delivered with a kiss to soothe any sting his words might offer.

"In a nutshell," Kate replied. The idle thought that Lady Adele had known there could be this sort of joy between a man and a woman stirred in her. Adele's tales and rules now seemed a way to keep Kate from ever seeking out the joy she would never have had with Richard.

A sudden, wee smile touched Kate's lips. She knew even more than that. Because she'd tested what she'd learned with Rafe on Warin, she knew that only Rafe's touch made her heart sing and her pulse race. There was no other man for her. Rafe surely was her one true love.

Once again her arms tightened around the man who was both her lover and her husband. "Vow to me that you'll never cease to love me with your body and your words."

Rafe laughed. "I so vow, but only if you promise the same."

Kate smiled. "I do," she told him, then her stomach growled. She glanced at the tray on the chest beside the bed. "We should eat before the bread dries."

"I suppose you're right," he said, then stifled a yawn, reminding Kate that he'd had even less sleep than she since they had left Haydon. "And after we've eaten, we should probably sleep a little."

Despite his words, he didn't roll off her but lowered his head to touch his lips to the curve of her neck. The very heat of his breath against her skin sent a whole new wave of sensation shooting through Kate. Hunger and exhaustion died as that wondrous craving for his lovemaking reawakened.

A moment later, when he did shift to the side, Kate followed, until they lay face to face. He raised a hand to trace a finger along the curve of her cheek.

"Shall we eat in bed and sleep among the crumbs or leave the bed and feed the rats with our leftovers?" he asked.

She reached out to stroke her hand down the strong planes of his chest, wondering if she might use what Lady Adele had taught her to wring what she wanted from him. "I think we should wait a bit before we eat. Are you certain that we've done all well enough to make this marriage truly legal?"

He shuddered a little at her caress, the softness of desire returning to his face. A breath of a laugh left Kate. Oh, but there was pleasure indeed to be found in this lovemaking. Her hand descended past his waist. Again he shuddered, this time catching his breath. There wasn't much life left in his shaft, but Kate knew how to rectify that. Again she curled her hand about his shaft and, just as Lady Adele had instructed, began restoring strength to that part of him most male.

Rafe gasped. His eyes flew wide. Rather than grab her hand to stop her, as Kate expected, he caught the sheets in his fists. Kate smiled. So he didn't wish that she should stop this, eh?

"Who taught you that?" he demanded, his voice hoarse as newly restored desire flickered in his gaze.

"Adele de Fraisney," Kate replied around her laugh, "so I might make a man out of her childish son. Until now I never realized how useful this particular lesson might be. Do you mind?"

Rafe shivered. The same need that once more burned in her took fire in his eyes. "God, no. Come, wife, surprise me. Show me what else you know."

Chapter 21

"Aye, it's armed men coming, right enough."
Will Godsol's call echoed down from
Glevering's walls into the morning-brightened
yard, then flew like a bolt past Rafe through the
hall's open door to pierce Kate. Although she'd expected this moment—indeed, had believed it might
arrive yesterday, the day of her marriage—the bread
in her hand crumbled like her heart. Terror closed
its burly arms around her as it had in the middle of
last night, when the enormity of what she'd done
came home to roost.

Legitimate or not, her marriage to Rafe wouldn't
stand before her father's hatred of the Godsols. If
her sire wanted to regain control of his daughter
and her dowry, all he need do was make her a

widow for a second time. And he wouldn't hesitate at that. He'd already tried twice to kill Rafe.

"How many?" her new husband called back to his brother.

"There's a hundred of them if there's ten," came Will's reply. "I can but read the shields of the foremost. It's the bishop who leads, with Bagot, Haydon, and the countess's marshal behind them."

The certainty that she was going to lose the happiness she'd just found brought Kate up from the breakfast table. With the laundress still working to remove stains from the fragile silk of her blue overgown, she'd borrowed a red gown from Dame Joan to wear over her freshly laundered yellow undergown. Although the outer garment was belted tightly about her waist, it was still far too large.

When she joined her new husband in the doorway, Rafe extended an arm, inviting his wife into his embrace. Wrapping her arms around his waist, Kate leaned her cheek against his shoulder. The weave of his gray linen tunic felt nubby against her skin. The heat of his body embraced her. Tears rose. She couldn't lose him; they'd had but one day together.

How was it possible she had come to care so deeply for a man she'd met less than a week ago? Then again, how could she help but love him? Last night, between wondrous bouts of lovemaking, they'd talked, trading secrets and stories of their pasts. Rafe confided his dreams for Glevering, dreams that included her at his side at every step of long and happy years. That he should imagine such a life with her did more to secure Kate's heart than any touch he laid upon her. And there it was, her love for him, well and truly lodged in her heart. This was how marriage should be between a man and woman, a husband and wife, not what Lady Adele had taught her. Kate couldn't, wouldn't let her father cheat her of what she'd won simply because he hated Rafe's name. Her arms tightened about his waist, as if her touch could somehow keep him safe.

"You're worrying again," Rafe said, a touch of amusement in his voice.

"Of course I'm not," she lied, blinking back her fears. Her grip was tight enough for her to feel his laughter against her own heart.

"And you're lying again."

"I can't help it," she cried softly, looking up into his face. "My father will kill you when he learns we're wed."

"He will try," Rafe agreed, a smile lingering at the corners of his mouth. "But shame on you, wife, for thinking me so weak that an old man like your sire might easily dispatch me. I should be insulted that you have so little faith."

"How can I have faith when I know my father's no honorable man?" she protested. The tears she'd managed to quell so far now started boldly into her eyes.

Crooking his finger beneath her chin, Rafe studied her face. Confidence glowed in his gaze. "Trust me. We're married, and so we'll stay. You own my heart, and because of that, I will never let you go."

Even as his words fed the love she now harbored for him, hopelessness hissed from Kate like steam from a covered pot. "It's not you I don't trust. I simply know that my father will never accept our union. How can he when you're a Godsol?"

"So are you now," Rafe replied as if that settled the matter, then released her chin to look back at Glevering's repaired and closed gates.

Kate frowned a little as his words lodged in her brain. If she was Godsol now, would her father hate her, as well? Not that his hatred would be so different from his previous disinterest. Still pondering this, she turned her attention to the gate in time to see Will Godsol appear at the gatehouse door.

Rafe's brother started toward the porch and his younger sibling. Unlike her husband, who wore his better clothing, Will was dressed in the same hauberk and short tunic that he'd worn while capturing Kate. His sword was buckled at his side. Climbing the stairs to join them, he offered Kate a nod, then cocked his head to eye his brother.

"So, my clever, crafty sibling, what do we do now?" There was more of amusement than concern in his voice.

Rafe shrugged. "What else but open the gates and let them in."

Shock tore through Kate. "You cannot," she cried, shoving herself away from her husband.

"Are you mad?" his brother echoed, just as startled as she.

Rafe glanced from one to the other. "What choice have we? Even if I wanted to, I couldn't hold the walls against so many, with Glevering's cellars yet laid bare by the winter past. Moreover, we have nothing to hide, and I invited them here."

"You did what?" Kate cried, stunned. He might as well have invited Death to come calling.

Her husband looked at her. "I sent a messenger to Haydon yesterday, announcing our marriage and my ownership of Glevering. In all truth, the sooner our marriage is acknowledged by all the shire's gentry, the safer we'll be from your sire."

As he spoke, he smoothed a hand down her back, as if his touch could soothe her into thinking what he'd done was the deed of a sane man. It didn't work. If her father knew all, then he most surely would enter yon gates planning murder.

"Can either of you think of a better way to gather so many witnesses all at once?" Rafe asked, glancing at her and his brother as he spoke. "Think on it. It's not only Bagot who comes. It's the bishop and Haydon, along with some of the shire's most powerful landholders. They'll be here when I remind them and your sire that by royal decree you were free to make your own marriage. So you have," he looked at Kate, the memory of his smile yet clinging to his lips. "When they accept our marriage as legitimate—and they will, for there's many a man who wishes the feud between our families was no more—then your sire will have no choice but to do the same."

Kate frowned as his words stirred the memory of

the old countess's comment at the picnic. Would the rest of the shire see this union as a chance for a lasting peace between Godsol and Daubney? The barest hint of hope flickered to life, burning on even as her certainty that her sire would end Rafe's life tried to extinguish it.

Rafe once more pulled Kate close to him. "Both of you take heed. If you're asked to speak before these men, say nothing but the truth. A single lie will make all else we say seem a falsehood."

Her new brother-by-marriage shrugged his agreement. Kate nodded with less conviction. What if these barons asked about Warin's kidnapping of her? The thought of having to reveal to so many men just how foolish she'd been over Warin didn't sit easily on her heart. Cynicism owned her. Why worry about something that would never happen? Rafe wouldn't live long enough for the conversation to get as far as that.

"All this is well and good, but it doesn't change the fact that my sire wants you dead," she told her husband. "You're wrong if you think any number of witnesses might prevent him from attacking you."

As Rafe started to reject her warning with a shake of his head, Kate leaned back in his embrace to look up at him. "Why do you think witnesses will stop him? My sire first attempted to kill you at the picnic before all the wedding guests, then tried again at the joust before even more onlookers. Little good so many watchers did you then! Why, at the joust no one even noticed that it was he who removed the cap from the lance."

Rafe's mouth lifted into a crooked smile. "No one noticed? Hardly so. Of the men who watched that run every one knows your sire attempted to end my life."

Kate shook her head in disbelief. "How so, when no man cried out that my sire's claim of happenstance was untrue?"

Will Godsol offered his new sister a quick wink. "What, and call a nobleman a liar to his face? Not likely, unless the accuser wishes to be attacked for the supposed slur. Nay, every man there held his tongue to save the fragile peace of Haydon's wedding, which was already strained nigh unto breaking over the possibility of rebellion against our good and gracious king." The harshness of Will's voice suggested that he thought his monarch neither good nor gracious. "As long as my brother made no complaint, no other man needed to raise his voice. As for Rafe, he took the day without injury. What reason had he to complain?"

Will gave his taller brother's shoulder a companionable slap. "In that, our Rafe was trapped. He didn't dare speak when he'd caused so much trouble at the picnic."

She frowned, still confused. "But, if all men knew my father was at fault, why then did Lord Haydon banish Sir Warin from the wedding?"

"That was the best retribution that Lord Haydon had at hand," Rafe replied. "I daresay that he believed denying your father his powerful steward for the melee guaranteed Lord Bagot would be taken. It would have cost your sire a healthy sum to ransom

his horse and armor. These days, opening a nobleman's already beleaguered purse is sometimes the
best vengeance of all." His grin was wide and easy.

"Of course, Sir Warin made it simple for Haydon
to turn on him by his obvious collusion," Will Godsol added. "An innocent man would have called the
foul and pulled out of the run. That he didn't
showed that Sir Warin knew and agreed to his lord's
plan."

Which was just what Warin had told her. Kate
frowned as she worked to digest this. Rafe pulled
her close once more.

"Do you see now from whence my confidence
springs?" he asked. "My message begged these men
to come under a banner of truce. Thus, a good number of them accompanying your sire come to see
that Bagot doesn't try once more to harm me. They
will be my shield."

Catching her face in his hands, Rafe touched her
lips with his. The kiss was sweet, lacking any of the
heat they'd made between them in their bedchamber. Kate's lips clung to his, then she gave a tiny cry
when he ended the caress. He watched her for another moment, his thumbs stroking across her
cheeks, then he smiled.

"Go within now, wife. Leave the hall door ajar, if
you like, but no matter what you hear, do not come
out unless the bishop or Lord Haydon calls for you.
Whatever you do, do not respond to your sire."

"Nay!" Kate cried in new panic, once more catching her arms around him. "I won't be left blind and
dumb. Let me stay."

Her husband only smiled. "Here we come once more to the words *trust me*. Trust me, my love. Now go inside and wait as a decent woman would."

That stung her. Kate frowned at him. "I am a decent woman."

It was the memory of their lovemaking that set hot lights to flickering in Rafe's dark eyes. He leaned forward to put his mouth near her ear. "Nay, by God, you're not, and that fact pleases me well, indeed," he whispered, then straightened. "Now go, so I can do what I must without worrying over you as well."

Rafe watched bright color flood his new wife's cheeks for all the wrong reasons. She gave a squeak of embarrassment, then whirled to retreat into the house. Oh, but there was pleasure to be had even in watching the swing of her skirts. He'd gotten far better than he'd expected in his impromptu wife. She didn't yet understand how much he valued her fiery nature. Lord, whether she was escaping a captor, betraying him or touching him with the boldness of a whore, there was no other woman in the world for him. The memory of her sitting astride him last night as she drove him into pleasure's arms stirred desire's embers back into flames.

But it wasn't just for lust's sake that he wanted Kate ever in his arms. Last night had been beyond wonderful. Not for an instant had he needed to listen for another man's tread upon the floorboards or worry over discovery. Nor had he needed to guard his heart against affection because the woman in his bed belonged to some other man. For the first time in all his life, he'd slept within his own walls, in his own bed, with his own wife at his side. Heart and soul, Kate belonged to him and him alone, just as Glevering now did. He'd die before he gave up either of them.

Beside him, Will choked on a chuckle, then once more assaulted his taller brother's shoulder with a friendly buffet. A wee teasing glint took fire in his brown eyes. "Not even Glevering's walls are thick enough. Imagine my surprise at learning that a Daubney had it in her to make a Godsol cry out. More than once, I might add."

Rafe grinned. "You're just jealous," he retorted, then pointed toward Will's weapon. "Now remove your sword."

"What?" Shock brought Will's brows high upon his forehead. His gaze dropped to the belt at Rafe's waist. When he saw his younger brother was unarmed, his surprise evolved into concern. "Where's your sword?"

"In my bedchamber, where every host leaves his weapons when greeting all but besiegers," Rafe replied, keeping his tone confident when that wasn't exactly what he felt.

Kate was right. Her sire would try to kill him. Rafe could only pray he hadn't angered the other notables of the shire so deeply that they'd let Bagot do as he pleased before Rafe had the chance to say his piece.

Will's eyes widened until they were nigh on cir-

THE WARRIOR'S DAMSEL 321

cles. "You mean to meet them unarmed. By God, but you must have balls of iron."

Rafe laughed. "I'll take that as a compliment, Will."

"I'm not certain that's how I meant it," his brother muttered, then shook his head. "Nay, Bagot is an enemy long of my acquaintance. I wouldn't join him in a crowded room without a dagger at my belt, much less make myself a quintain in Glevering's yard for him to bash. Rather than remove my sword, I'll tell you to go fetch yours."

It was a helpless lift of his shoulders that Rafe gave. "Tell me how to do that, Will. Bagot is now my father-by-marriage. Do you know any man who greets his wife's relatives with the promise of violence? As for you, if I'm Bagot's son, then you're his relative as well."

Will's mouth twisted as if he'd bitten into something sour. "Jesu. I hadn't thought of that when I dreamed of you wedding your Kate for vengeance's sake."

For a moment, Will pondered the riddle facing them, then once more shook his head in refusal. "Nay, relationship or not, I won't do it. Knowing the history of our families, no man among those who come will think ill of us if we meet Bagot armed. Go you and fetch your sword."

"Others might forgive our lack of trust, but what of us?" Rafe persisted. "When do we begin to heal the rift between our families, if not now? Nay, if it doesn't start here it won't start at all, and for all the days of my life I'll have to guard Glevering's walls against my own family. I won't live that way, Will. If you won't disarm, then go within and wait with my wife while I meet those who come. After all, I'm the one who married Kate, not you."

Angry color flushed Will's face. "Do you call me coward? Watch yourself, lad, or I'll beat you bloody for your insult."

"You know full well insult wasn't my intent, Will," Rafe protested.

His brother's anger was gone as quickly as it came. "Damn me but I do," he said at last. "And damn you for making sense."

With an uncertain breath, Will's hand dropped to his sword's belt. A moment later and the sheathed weapon lay upon the porch floor. Unencumbered by the tool of his trade, Will pivoted to face the gatehouse.

"Open the gates," he shouted to his men. Then, as the newly repaired machinery began to grind, he added in an underbreath, "so Bagot can come kill both my brother and me."

Chapter 22

Rafe shifted uneasily in his stance at the center of Glevering's yard. Will was right. He needed balls of iron to stand unarmed before the man from whom he'd snatched both property and daughter. They were alone in the yard. All Will's men had been sent to the barn with the prisoners, not to guard their hostages but to keep Godsol men from overreacting to what might happen next.

Although no man had yet breached the gates, the movement of so many horses and the rattle of just as many shields was a daunting sound. Will spat nervousness from his throat. The noise ate up Rafe's confidence. The best he could do was cling to the miracle of what he'd accomplished thus far.

After all, it wasn't every penniless knight who

won himself a willing bride and a new home in one
day. A man who could do that much would surely
survive his first encounter with his new father-by-
marriage.

His voice ringing in from beyond the walls,
Bishop Robert called the army to a halt. What followed was the sounds of men dismounting, shouting to one another as they set to making camp. Rafe
waited to see who among those outside the walls
would come to challenge his right to keep Kate and
this manor.

It was Bishop Robert, his mail gleaming like silver beneath a heavily embroidered surcoat, who
first appeared beneath the gatehouse's arch. His helmet hung from his saddle, and he'd removed his
leather coif. Fair hair long since gone to gray lay
flattened against his narrow skull.

At the churchman's back rode his personal escort
of five knights. Behind them came Lord Haydon
with Gerard and Josce as his companions. Knowing
that if he could see his friends, they could see him as
well, Rafe waited. There wasn't so much as a lift of a
shield from either of them to acknowledge him.

One set of worries peeled back to expose another.
Never mind that common sense had long since suggested that loss of their affection was the rightful
outcome of his actions. A part of Rafe had counted
on his friends to support him no matter what he'd
done.

Bagot followed Haydon. He brought with him
only the scant troop that had accompanied him to

the wedding less one—Sir Warin was imprisoned in Glevering's barn. From his stance beside Rafe, Will freed a breathless curse as he saw his ancient enemy. Instinct made him reach for his weapon. When Will's hand came up empty, he leaned close to Rafe.

"Faugh," he whispered harshly, "but I don't like the idea of being that man's kin. What idiot dreamed up the idea of you marrying his daughter, anyway?"

Rafe fought his grin. "It's too late for regrets, Will," he retorted. "More importantly, I'm not giving her back, no matter what you now feel about your plan."

"Aye, I suppose it's too late for that. No accounting for a man who'd let himself become smitten with a Daubney," Will said as if disgusted, although the amusement in his voice ruined his attempt at scorn.

It was jest enough to restore both of them. Easier now, they watched Bagot follow Lord Haydon's party onto Glevering's bridge. Not even the thick beard that covered the nobleman's chin was enough to disguise the vicious set of Lord Humphrey's jaw. Their former enemy was barely past the open gates when Kate's sire shifted in his saddle. An instant later and just as Rafe expected, Bagot's sword sang from its scabbard. He jerked his horse's head to the side, aiming the creature around the bishop's men. At the touch of his master's spurs, the beast charged.

"Here he comes," Rafe warned Will and planted his feet. Together they held out their arms to display their weaponless state.

"Sons of worms!" Bagot roared, his sword set for a killing blow as he raced toward his Godsol foes.

Rafe waited for a reaction from the others, but every man in the yard sat like a statue on his horse. Time slowed. Clots of mud flew at each strike of Bagot's horse's hooves on rain-dampened earth. Kate's sire was near enough for Rafe to see hatred's glint in the man's gray eyes.

Still no one moved. Disappointment flooded him. He'd guessed wrongly. Rather than hear him, these men would condone murder to be finished with the issue.

Rafe's jaw tensed. Well, then, if he was to die, he'd do it with honor, giving no man a chance to call him coward. Aye, and in his going he'd take Bagot's repute with him, making a murderer of him. As if in reaction to that thought, the eerie stillness that held the courtyard in thrall shattered. Noise and life exploded back into being.

"Stop him!" Bishop Robert bellowed.

Near the gate, Josce and Gerard raised their shields and spurred their horses. The bishop's men were faster and closer. They circled their horses around Glevering's new ruling family.

Will's breath of relief was audible. Rafe let his arms drop. Heart pounding, he stared at a horse's shoulder and a man's mail-clad leg in front of him. Sweat matted the creature's brown hide; mud speckled its owner's boots. The tail of the knight's surcoat was sodden.

Outside the circle, Bagot yanked his mount to a sharp stop. "Out of my way, sons of bitches," Kate's sire screamed, his horse's hooves drumming a prancing tattoo against the earth as the nobleman rode this way and that about the bishop's men.

"Enough, Lord Bagot," the churchman commanded, his voice thundering out over the yard. "I told you when we received the Godsols' message that we'd only accompany you under a banner of a truce. I'll not have you destroy that peace before we've even heard a word of their tale."

"Best you heed me as well, Humphrey," Lord Haydon shouted, sounding almost outraged. "I won't stand for violence being done under these conditions. No guilty man stands before an attacker without a weapon to defend himself, as these men have done. Moreover, that they opened Glevering's gates to us before we asked and met us unarmed says they have something worthwhile to impart. I, for one, want to hear what that is." The muttering that erupted at this suggested that more than one man in the yard agreed with him.

An arrogant shake of Lord Humphrey's head rejected their warnings. "You'd have me stay my hand when yon snake-eaters admit to capturing my property while we should have been at peace?" So great was his rage that Bagot's voice rose into the realm of shrillness.

"Nay, I'll not twiddle my thumbs and hold my

justice against such an insult. Mayhap you and yon churchman are deceived into thinking them otherwise, but I know the Godsols for the liars and thieves that they are. If you aren't men enough to punish them for kidnapping my daughter and forcing illegal marriage upon her, then leave them to me. I'll kill them, as is my right!"

Although Rafe hadn't intended to speak so soon, the opportunity was too perfect to be ignored. He lifted his head. "I am no thief," he called back. "My taking of Glevering has naught to do with the wedding peace. That truce, such as it was"—this he added in case any needed a reminder of how Bagot had tried to murder him—"ended when my brother and I departed Haydon yesterday afternoon."

Will shot him an incredulous look. Rafe ignored him. True, they'd plotted from the wedding's first day to take Glevering and Kate, but no one knew that. All that mattered was that his marriage to Kate hadn't been illegal or forced. Bagot couldn't call his property stolen.

"As for my lady," Rafe continued, his claim to possess Kate winning a growl from Bagot, "it wasn't I who first took her from you, Lord Bagot. When I came upon her, she was miles from Haydon and the captive of your steward, Sir Warin de Dapifer."

"What?" Bagot screeched, his horse coming to a standstill at a place where he could peer at his enemy over the rump of another horse. His ruddy skin paled to an ashy hue. His sword hand's knuckles were almost blue, so tightly did he grasp his weapon's hilt.

"I knew there would be more to this story when we learned Sir Warin was missing from the priory," Gerard called out to his betters. That his every word was filled with deep satisfaction said he and Josce had already protested their friend's innocence to the others.

Relief tore through Rafe, the emotion strong enough to make his eyes swim. All was not lost. His friends were still his friends and would support him. With that, true confidence finally blossomed within him. Rafe grinned at his brother and gave thanks to God. The miracle continued. He would keep what he'd already claimed.

"So you said, Sir Gerard," Bishop Robert agreed. "And to hear confirmed that there is more to this than first met the eye is but turnips for this pot of stew. All the more reason to hear the whole of the tale before reacting." Turning in his saddle, the bishop turned a steely eye on Kate's sire. "Now, sheathe your sword and dismount, Bagot, else I'll have my men disarm you." This was a stark command.

Kate's sire started and shifted sharply in his saddle to stare at the prelate. "You wouldn't dare," he retorted, sounding more distressed than angry over the threat.

"I would, indeed, and have you bound as well if you force the issue," the churchman replied, his voice cold and hard. "Now, dismount, else feel my wrath!" He filled the command with every ounce of power owned by his position.

A moment's silence followed. Birds chirped, harness rings jangled. From outside the walls, the business of setting up camp continued, the noise of so many men at work snaking in through the open gateway. At last, Bagot jammed his sword back into its scabbard. His shoulders taut against being chastised like some schoolboy, he dismounted.

Judging the threat at an end, the knights surrounding Rafe and Will retreated. With his vision honed by his need to discern who was an ally and who a foe, Rafe scanned those now within the yard, trying to read each man's face. The churchman had chosen his jury with care; less than two dozen men followed Bishop Robert into the bailey, one representative of each of the shire's finest families along with their retinues. Rafe's hope grew apace as from the old nobleman who'd served as herald at the joust to the countess's marshal, they watched him in return, not in anger but in consideration. He would be heard and fairly so.

"What say you, Sir William?" The bishop, still astride his mount, looked across the yard at Will. "Do you and your brother place yourself in my hands for justice's sake?"

Will glanced at Rafe. The message in his gaze was clear. When it came to matters of Kate and Glevering, he would defer to his younger brother. To see such respect in Will's eyes was heady, indeed. Rafe savored the sensation as he turned to face the bishop.

"We do, my lord. Indeed, that was my intent in sending you the message that brought you here."

He strode forward to stand near the churchman's horse, Will trailing behind him. The expression on the bishop's narrow face was sour as he dismounted. When the churchman was afoot, Rafe reached for the bishop's right hand. Dropping to one knee, Rafe kissed the glittering stone fixed to the churchman's steel-sewn glove, the jewel a symbol of the prelate's power. As if to aid him back to his feet, Bishop Robert cupped a hand beneath Rafe's elbow.

Although Robert was the smaller man, his grip didn't lack for strength. The steel of his glove bit into Rafe's sleeve as he almost lifted the larger man off the ground. Startled, Rafe looked at him.

They stood toe to toe, near enough to speak privately without fear of being overheard. Tense lines marked Bishop Robert's brow. His blue eyes narrowed. Beneath his beard, his jaw was tight, a muscle working along its line.

"From your message to this very moment, your glib and twisting words leave me no doubt that you've suckled well and truly at our king's devious breast, boy," he whispered harshly. "Know you, I recognize your efforts to manipulate me and this situation. Right now, I've no choice but to accept your dubious honesty at face value, but be you warned." Here he paused to let the corner of his mouth curl up in threat. "If you did force marriage upon the lady, you'll rue the day you misused a wedding truce to steal another man's daughter. If that's what you did, I'll help Bagot castrate you, then annul your marriage against your newborn impotence. *If* that's what you did," he repeated.

Feeling as though he'd just tottered back from a cliff's edge, Rafe gave thanks that he hadn't needed to force Kate. "My lord, that's not what happened, as the lady herself will tell you." Even to his own ears his words rang like the truth they were.

Surprise flickered in the bishop's eyes and jerked across his brow line, then ebbed. He shot a sidelong glance at Josce and Gerard, his look saying that Rafe's friends had been vehement in their protest of his innocence. Once again gratitude washed through Rafe. To have such friends was wealth, indeed.

In the next instant, the churchman released Rafe from his biting grip and took a backward step. "Well, then," Bishop Robert said, his voice once more raised so all might hear, "now that we are all bound by the terms of this truce, such as it is, where is Bagot's missing daughter? We'd hear the tale of how she came to be at this place and wed to you."

"She's not married to him," Bagot spat out from his stance at some six yards' distance, "at least not in any true marriage. Of this I am certain: no daughter of my blood would ever willingly wed a God-sol."

"My lady is within. She waits eagerly to answer all your questions, my lords," Rafe replied to the yard. Then, even though he knew that doing so was bound to provoke, he added, "Good lords, will you all enter my hall and take your ease?"

"Not your hall," Kate's sire snarled.

Rafe didn't spare him even the briefest of glances. There was no need. Before another hour passed, everyone here save Bagot would agree that Glevering once more belonged to a Godsol and so did its heiress.

Chapter 23

When Kate heard Rafe invite the searchers to enter their hall, her heart took to hopping like a hare in her chest. God help her, but not even to save her marriage was she ready to face these men. She edged backward from the dais set up along the long inner wall until she stood well inside the bedchamber's doorway.

Fool! There was nowhere to hide at Glevering; she knew that well enough from yesterday. Despite that, she shifted until she stood half concealed by the door's frame. It didn't help. No matter how dim the shadows here, there was no escaping what lay before her. Like it or not, these men would put questions to her that Kate wasn't certain she could bear to answer.

Lord, but if her father didn't do it first, they'd crucify her once they heard how foolishly she'd behaved. They'd accuse her of being too bold, which was naught but true. Worst of all, the very existence of her and Rafe's affection doomed them. These men would never believe that Rafe and she hadn't planned a secret marriage to escape the wedding her father intended for her.

Well, if she wasn't ready for this meeting, at least the hall was. It was in preparation for the search party's arrival that Kate, Dame Joan and Glevering's maids had labored this morn. From the cellar came the chair Joan said Kate's sire used during Glevering's hall moot. This they'd placed on the dais against the back wall.

The breakfast tables still stood, although now cleared of the potage and hard bread that had broken Glevering's fast. Each table was laid with an array of the precious sweet cheeses made from the milk that came after the stock consumed the first of a spring's grasses.

Fresh breads, their yeasty aromas filling the hall's air, waited in baskets at each table. There were pitchers of watered wine, while the village alewives had provided barley water and their freshest brew for any who preferred a simpler drink. Later, if the matter was settled in Rafe's favor—and even if it were not, Kate supposed—there would be a meal of lamb.

Once all was in readiness, Rafe had sent the maids to the manor's chapel. There they would wait along with the Godsol priest until called to bear witness to the wedding. Rafe claimed their stories would be better believed if they weren't within the hall to hear what had come before their testimony.

Of those who came seeking Kate, Bishop Robert entered first. Sunlight sparked off his armor, haloing him in light. Even with that aura, he looked far different dressed as a warrior than as a priest. Without his miter, he seemed smaller, his face that of a weasel instead of a saint.

Rafe and Will followed at his heels. The instant Will was within, he turned to the side and stopped a few feet from the doorway, as if he meant to guard the opening. Rafe looked well pleased with himself. As hard as Kate tried, she couldn't take heart from his confidence. A thousand churchmen could call this marriage legal and still her father would fight to see it dissolved.

"Will you sit, my lord bishop?" her new husband asked of Bishop Robert, sounding every inch the host as he led their exalted guest to the dais and the chair.

One by one, those who would listen to Kate's tale entered. Of the judges there were only six, each a man of quality or, in the case of the countess's knight, the agent of a powerful woman. However, each brought with him his own wee army as he came.

Safe in her shadowed spot, she studied them, seeking some sign that might indicate if they were friendly to her cause. When Lord Haydon entered, he removed his gloves and went immediately to the table nearest the door. There he took a seat and helped himself to a goodly slice of cheese. Sir Josce and Gerard followed him into the hall, but neither man sat—not because they didn't wish to be comfortable in a hall Rafe claimed to own but because they weren't here as judges. Neither were they of a rank to sit with the other men.

Behind them strode the countess's marshal carrying his helmet in the crook of his arm as if he expected to need it in the hall. Disapproval marked his face as he shunned the tables and made his way to the bishop, who now sat in the great chair. Taking a position a few feet to the right and behind that seat, the silent knight crossed his free arm over the breast of his sullied surcoat. Every surly line of his body shouted that she and Rafe had no friend in him.

The old man who'd played herald yesterday made himself comfortable on a bench near Lord Haydon. He tore off a hunk of bread to break his fast, then offered what remained of the small loaf to his middle-aged heir, who, like Lord Haydon's sons, stood at his father's shoulder. The easy way they both studied the room suggested this family had no axe to bury in the Godsols.

But they and Haydon's family were the only two. By the time her father entered, he being the last man into the room, the four men and their parties yet afoot solidly outnumbered those who favored the Godsols. Had any crumb of hope yet existed in Kate, it would have died at this point. Even if she survived the coming interrogation, she was going to lose her precious husband.

Aching over what was sure to come, Kate watched her sire stride into a hall that was no longer his. So stiff was his spine that he might have worn a lance beneath his mail tunic. His face was black as he glanced about the room, his expression so fearsome that Kate edged farther behind the doorframe. Only now did it occur to her that there were two people her sire could murder to end this marriage and regain control of Glevering.

Lord Humphrey's gaze caught on Dame Joan as the hapless woman filled the old nobleman's cup with watered wine. Her father's surcoat snapped about his knees as he strode across the hall to confront the wife of his erstwhile bailiff.

"Where is that betraying husband of yours, woman?" her sire raged. "By God, I'll have his heart out, I will! My property ceded to the Godsols when there's not a mark of battle damage on a single wall! What did that traitor do, open the door and invite these foul worm-eaters to come in?"

The poor woman loosed a pitiful cry and dropped to her knees. Wine slopped over the edge of her pitcher as she set it on the floor in front of her. She folded her hands in supplication. Her ashen face said she expected a death blow at any instant.

In his borrowed chair, the bishop slammed a fist against its thick arm. "We have a truce, Bagot! Leave off her," he shouted in reprimand.

But Joan was already speaking, her tone that of one pleading for her life. "My lord, what were we to do? We knew not that they were Godsols, for no man among them wore a stitch of that family's colors and every face was hidden beneath a cloak's hood. When my Ernulf stood upon the wall yestermorn, it was Sir Warin's horse, shield and helmet he saw. Aye, my dear husband opened these gates, but for your steward, not the Godsols." The room was silent, every man straining to catch each astonishing word.

Lord Humphrey threw out his arms in frustration. "Sir Warin's horse! Are you so gullible? You knew well enough that my steward was across the shire at Haydon's wedding."

"But my lord," Joan cried in a voice stronger than her meek posture suggested possible, "only the previous day we'd received a message marked by your own seal, warning us to expect Sir Warin's arrival in the near future."

Bile stewed in Kate's gullet as the extent of her foolishness over Warin settled heavily upon her shoulders. She'd thought his kidnapping of her a spontaneous reaction to her father's misuse of him. Instead, just like Rafe and his brother, Warin had had a larger plan. Aye, and he'd laid his trap for her with care. No doubt he'd played the part of her courtly lover in the hope of winning her compliance to his scheme. No wonder he'd been so enraged when Rafe showed interest in her. By the same token, the thought of Warin fawning over her for nearly a month's time when he wanted nothing more than Glevering made disgust shimmy down Kate's spine.

Across the room, her sire reeled as if struck. His mail jangled harshly in the hall's breathless quiet as he stumbled back to collide with a table. There he stood, panting. Other than the steady snap and crack of the fire on the hearthstone, his rasping breath was the room's only sound. On his drawn face Kate saw that her sire understood very well what had given Warin the confidence to finally play his hand.

She freed a scornful breath. That made her father double the fool she'd been. So completely had he trusted his steward that he'd made Warin a partner in a murder attempt, thus leaving himself vulnerable to betrayal.

"Nay, he couldn't have plotted so," her father said, his voice thready, his words quiet enough to suggest he spoke more to himself than to the room. "I was good to him, treating him more as a son than one merely oathbound to me."

Mutters rose from his peers, echoing up into the rafters. No matter their affiliation, the good dame's story discomforted them. No man cared to think that those he trusted might turn on him.

At the head of the room, the bishop's eyes narrowed as he looked at Rafe. "Do I assume 'twas you who carried de Dapifer's shield to trick your way into this place?" It was a dry and pointed question.

"It was," Rafe agreed, then held up a forestalling hand. "My lord, I think it hardly matters how I came to own Glevering now that I'm wed to the manor's heiress." He glanced at the men about him, his look meant to collect their attention. "Only if Lord Bagot chooses to disown his daughter will I put to your scrutiny the events by which I can now claim Glevering as mine own."

Across the room, Lord Haydon sucked in a swift breath. The countess's knight lifted his chin with enough sharpness to indicate surprise. Even Sir

Josce and Gerard stirred uneasily at his words.

The bishop looked no more pleased than they. "In that you are right, Sir Rafe," he replied, his voice as tense as his face. "Best that we discuss the marriage first, hoping to leave the other where it lies."

"No marriage," her father rasped out, his face as colorless as a dead man's. He held a fist against his heart as if that organ pained him and dragged in a ragged breath. "No marriage," he tried again, but his words hardly came any louder.

For the briefest of instants, concern for her sire jolted Kate, but the emotion swiftly ebbed. This was the man who cared so little for her that he wouldn't have her in his presence, the same man who wanted her husband dead for no greater reason than that Rafe bore the Godsol name. Her sire had stolen Pelerin from the Godsols and killed Rafe's sire. He'd even destroyed Warin's honor in order to shield his own misdeed. Nay, he neither wanted nor deserved her care.

Concern marked Bishop Robert's narrow face. "Do you ail, Bagot? Sir Reginald." He gestured to one of his knights. "Aid Lord Bagot to a bench and help him sit."

His face impassive, the young knight named by the churchman started toward the bent nobleman. Before he reached Kate's sire, her father's fist opened. Although his head yet hung, Bagot's lord waved off the man, then struggled to reclaim his composure, just as he had done at the picnic. He wasn't as successful this time. When he finally managed to straighten, his face was yet gray.

"I need no aid," he told the room, his words louder now, but his voice still hoarse. "Not from any of you. All I need at this moment is my daughter at my side. Katherine?" he called out, an overly sweet tone to his voice.

Kate's feet froze to the floor. Her father didn't want her, only control over her person. Aye, and once he owned her again, he'd find some way, fair or foul, to keep her from Rafe.

"Katherine," he called again, more power in his voice this time, "come to me."

When still no movement stirred in any corner of the hall, her father frowned and glanced about the chamber, seeking her. So, too, did those four judges who'd chosen to stand. Not so those who sat. Lord Haydon waved a miraculously restored Dame Joan to him to fill his cup, while the old nobleman made his way, slice by slice, through the cheese.

At the center of the room, Rafe turned without hesitation toward the bedchamber's door. The corners of Kate's mouth lifted. Of course he knew where she was. Love bound them, soul to soul, and so it would continue until the moment of death's parting, even if they were separated today.

Yet clinging to the shadows, Kate studied the man she'd wed, cherishing every line of his fine body and handsome face. Rafe's stance was proud, his shoulders held in a way that only days before she might have called arrogant. Now she knew it for what it was, a reflection of Rafe's boundless conviction of success.

Their gazes met. Rafe's mouth softened. Pleasure

warmed his dark eyes, his reaction both a reminder of his love and an encouragement for her to do as she thought best.

Whereas Rafe owned hope and confidence, grim resignation claimed Kate's heart. Unfortunately, what she knew was best to do was what she least wanted to face. No matter what she wanted, it was time to face these men and pay the piper for her misdeeds. If her condemnation as ill mannered and a lightskirt actually bought her marriage to Rafe, then it was a small price indeed.

Giving her borrowed overgown a nervous brush, Kate took a single step outside the bedchamber door to attract the attention of the room. Every head swung in her direction, including that of her sire. Mild surprise touched her father's face as he took in what she wore. As he found the lingering redness along her jaw, all that remained of Warin's blow last night, satisfaction lit his gray eyes. His mouth curled upward in a grin beneath the concealment of his wiry beard as he interpreted the mark as proof of Rafe's force.

"There you are, daughter. Come to your sire's side," he bade her as if she were like unto his dog.

"That I shall not do, my lord," she replied, her voice raised so that all the men could hear.

Aye, and she might well have been a talking dog, so great was her sire's surprise at her refusal. For an instant he wore a mask of startlement, brows sharply peaked above his eyes and mouth round. Then his mouth snapped shut, and he closed his fists. Bright red spots marked the centers of his lean cheeks. All sign of his previous weakness dissolved.

"What do you mean, shall not?" Gone was his false warmth. Instead, his words were strangled and hoarse.

Across the room, the bishop's hand flicked, the gesture bidding her sire to silence. True, her father said no more, but Kate thought it was the greatness of his rage that held his tongue, not any command. The prelate glanced from sire to daughter, a single brow lifting as he studied them.

"Why is it you refuse your noble sire, my lady?" he asked, his tone surprisingly mild.

As was due to one of his rank, Kate offered him a deep bend of her knees before speaking. "I do so at my husband's instruction, my lord. He commands that I respond only to your own call or, barring your protection, that of Lord Haydon."

"What is this?" her father growled, once again in control of his tongue. "You'll come to me as I demand, or I'll have a piece of your hide for disobedience, girl," he threatened, taking a step toward the child he'd spawned.

"Hold where you are, Bagot," the bishop commanded, his tone sharp, indeed.

Her father whirled on him. "You cannot control me in this," he cried, truly aggrieved. "This is my daughter." His tone made it clear that he equated kinship with possession, as if she were a piece of furniture, like Glevering's chair. "It's my right as her sire to correct her when she's errs."

"No longer is she your daughter, but my wife,"

Rafe called out, his voice riding over his better's. "The loyalty and obedience she once gave to you she has now vowed before God and man to give to me."

"Not your wife!" Lord Humphrey screeched.

"Enough, both of you!" the bishop shouted.

When her sire's mouth opened as if to protest, the churchman rose to his feet. "This is not yours to decide, Humphrey, and no amount of shouting on your part will change that. Any more of this sort of argument, and I vow here and now I'll decide in the Godsols' favor to be done with you."

Even though rage yet seethed in her sire's gray eyes, his mouth snapped shut. The bishop dropped into the chair and rubbed at his temple as if it ached. He turned his sharp gaze on Rafe.

"What cause have you to command her to disregard her own kin?"

Rafe took a half-step nearer to the churchman. "My lord bishop, as you see before you this day, it's an ancient hatred shared by Godsol and Daubney," her precious husband said, his voice calm and sincere. "It will take time before Lord Bagot accepts me as his son-by-marriage."

"Never!" Lord Humphrey muttered, but even whispered, the word held emotion enough to be a curse or a vow. Both the bishop and Rafe shrugged away the quiet interruption.

"Considering that," her husband continued, "I'd ask your lordship to offer my lady wife your custody, as she is for all purposes the crux of this dis-

pute. Possession being nine-tenths of the law, I'd
not willingly let her within reach of a man determined to keep her from me at all costs. I warn you
all," he added, turning now to look across the faces
of the men gathered in the room, "she's come to be
precious to me and not just for Glevering's sake. If
you take her from me, I'll spend my life's blood to
reclaim her."

A quiet rumble of amusement broke from the
men sitting at the tables. Behind Lord Haydon, Gerard cupped his hand over his mouth as if to conceal
a smile. Sir Josce stared in open astonishment at his
friend.

"Aye, listen you well to my brother," Will sec-
onded Rafe from his post near the hall door, speaking over the fading echo of their laughter. The
smaller of the Godsols strode along the hall's outer
wall until he stood near to Lord Haydon's kin.
"Know that I'll spend all I own to support my
brother in reclaiming his wife. Take this as my vow.
If she is wrongly separated from my kinsman, there
will be no peace in this shire until she is returned to
him."

Rafe pivoted far enough to shoot his brother a
smile, then returned his complete attention to the
bishop. "Now if you wish to hear the tale of how the
lady came to be wed to me, call for her, my lord
bishop, and she will come."

"Nay!" Her father's refusal was a high-pitched
cry. Emotions flew across his face—fear, hurt, jealousy, then determination. His mouth twisted into a
snarl. He strode to stand abreast of Rafe as if near-

ness to the bishop somehow guaranteed success.

"If my daughter will not come to me, then I say she shall not speak at all. By the Godsol's own words does he reveal that he's already destroyed a daughter's natural affection for her parent." He held out a hand to the prelate as if pleading. "It isn't right, my lord, to ask her to speak when no matter what question you put to her, she'll answer in the Godsol's favor.

"Moreover, if she's so easily turned against me," he went on, his voice gaining angry power with each word, "then she is no longer any daughter of mine. I am done with her."

At his words, the four standing men near the bishop's chair shifted in conspicuous agitation. At the table, the old nobleman's face whitened to the color of his hair, a morsel of cheese held partway to his open mouth.

"Nay," Lord Haydon cried out in what almost sounded like a frightened protest.

The bishop came slowly to his feet. "Have a care with what you do here, Bagot," he warned. "Disown your daughter, and I've no choice but to hear the whole of how Sir Rafe came into possession of Glevering."

Kate caught her breath in understanding. Rafe was right. To a man, these peers all knew what her father had done. They worried that Rafe's tale might begin with the joust or that Sir Warin's would, which would completely damn her sire.

Confusion was a pin's prick. True, what her sire had done was heinous, but no one had been hurt by it, not even the man he intended to harm. What drove them in their fear? It surely couldn't be the risk of war between Bagot and those who called its lord a liar to his face. Not even in her sire's hatred for the Godsols could he be so blind as to challenge six of his neighbors at once.

"Did I mention that I hold Sir Warin de Dapifer prisoner in Glevering's barn?" Rafe offered to the room in a quiet aside.

Lord Haydon jerked back on his seat as if struck. His bench shrieked against the floorboards. With a quiet gasp, the countess's man took two swift steps nearer to the bishop's chair, as if he meant to protect the prelate from attack. Of those standing with him, one man bowed his head as if in prayer.

Her father froze, his face blank. His eyes blinked rapidly. Even at that, there was a stubborn jut to his bearded jaw.

Startled by yet another round of strange reactions, Kate glanced at their faces. All this to protect her sire from his own misdeed? It couldn't be.

At the room's center, Rafe shifted just long enough to send her an optimistic glance. For reasons Kate couldn't comprehend, the very look in his eyes teased Ami's voice out of the recesses of her memory. It was a different sort of war her new friend had mentioned, one against their king.

Only then did the jumbled pieces in her brain solidify into a whole. It wasn't a war waged by Bagot's lord against the Godsols or against any one of them that the men here feared. Nay, they worried that the dispute over her marriage would become the spark that ignited a rebellion against England's king.

Shock jolted through Kate. She stared wide-eyed at her husband. Surely Rafe wasn't mad enough to think he could exploit their fear of civil war to force them to confirm this marriage?

Across the room, Rafe's smile was slow and pleased as he saw she understood. Oh, but he was. Kate wasn't certain if she should faint in fear or scream in rage. Wishing her reeling head would steady, Kate again surveyed the men in the room.

What she saw stunned her. For this one day these noblemen would bow to a single knight. Aye, so they would but only if Rafe and his new wife were very careful in how they played their hand.

"Call my lady wife and hear her tale, my lord bishop," Rafe prodded, his soft voice sounding like a shout in the tense room.

"Nay," her sire once again tried to protest.

The bishop paid him no heed as he fell back into his borrowed chair of state and turned his raging gaze on Kate. His expression left no doubt that he knew the sort of manipulation Rafe was using and liked it not one whit.

"Lady de Fraisney, come and tell me how it is you became captive of Bagot's steward, then wife to your lord sire's dearest enemy," he demanded, the boom of his voice great enough to fill every corner of the room.

Chapter 24

Her knees knocking, Kate started toward Bishop Robert. God help her, but Rafe was going to be the death of them both! Odd, but even as she cursed her husband for what he attempted, she longed to feel his arms around her. So strong was the desire that it carried her across the room to his side.

When her father saw where she intended to stand, he made a deep and raging sound. That only hurried Kate's step a bit. If nothing more, she needed Rafe as barrier between her and her sire if she was to speak at all.

She stopped at Rafe's left hand, then glanced up into her husband's face. Rafe frowned as he read the fear in her gaze and gave a brief shake of his head, as if to tell her there was no cause for concern. Kate's breath hissed from her in irritation. No cause? He was worse than mad. He didn't know her well enough yet to realize she owned no talented tongue. This would fail, all because she wasn't as glib as he.

"My lady?" the bishop prodded.

It was a none too gentle hint that she'd best begin her tale. At the same instant, her father shifted in his stance to look across his enemy at his daughter. His icy gaze bored a hole through her.

Kate's nerves twanged. His look left her as disconcerted as he no doubt meant her to be. How was she going to explain any of this without mentioning the uncapping of that lance? The story she had to tell was complicated enough without worrying over a stray word upsetting the delicate balance in the chamber. Mary save her, but they'd all blame her if this came down to war.

"My lord, I fear it was all my own doing," she said in preamble, then couldn't think of another word to say. The silence lengthened. The bishop drummed out his impatience on one arm of the chair.

"Today, my lady," he commanded.

Her heart clip-clopped. She told herself to take comfort that she started at the middle of her tale. That meant no mention of her idiotic infatuation with Warin. At last her mouth opened. Words dropped from her lips.

"You see, I was heartsore over what happened at the joust."

There was a wary, worried rumble from the men around her. The confidence in Rafe's gaze slipped a little as she stumbled too close to the truth. If it hadn't been so frightening, the irony of it would have made Kate smile. All these men, afraid of what she might inadvertently reveal. The thought of so many powerful nobles holding their breath against what she, one insignificant woman, knew flooded Kate with a sudden sense of power. And that went far to clear her thoughts.

"So much anger and hatred over what was surely an accident, I mean," she said, her clarification winning many a relieved sigh. "After the meal, my father released me to join the other women in the garden. Before I reached the hall door, I received a message from Sir Warin, bidding me to meet with him outside Haydon's walls before he departed for the priory."

"Outside the walls?" her father snapped, his voice a whip's crack. "What sort of woman agrees to meet any man, alone and unchaperoned, while beyond the protection of walls? Moreover, what cause had my steward to believe you would agree to such a request?"

As he spoke, he leaned forward to look past Rafe at his daughter. What Kate saw in his face sent irritation leaping through her. It wasn't curiosity or concern over her misbehavior that filled his face. He didn't care that she might, or might not deserve the title *lightskirt*. All that mattered to him was reclaiming Glevering. Since his peers wouldn't allow him to disown her, at least not here, then he meant to destroy her to win what he wanted from them.

The very unfairness of this, especially when his murderous attempt was the cause for all that happened, put steel in Kate's heart. Let the battle be joined. She wouldn't pay for his sin. She had sin enough of her own to worry over. Head high, she fixed her attention on the churchman.

"My lord bishop, Sir Warin and I had spoken a time or two at Bagot, as those who live in the same place are wont to do, no matter their rank. Never in private, of course," Kate added. Which was true; they'd never had a closeted conversation at Bagot.

"As to what we discussed," she went on, anticipating the next sort of question her sire might ask, "our conversations were naught but pleasantries."

That wasn't a lie either, according to Lady Adele. Adele had insisted that what courtly lovers said between them must always be pleasant. Of course, what these men assumed were pleasantries and what Lady Adele had claimed as pleasant subjects weren't likely to be the same thing.

From the corner of her eye, Kate saw Rafe's jaw shift as if he fought a smile. So he would grin, for she'd told him the whole of her tale last night. She hurried on before Rafe's reaction infected her.

"As for why I left Haydon's walls, my lords, I took my lord father's trust of Sir Warin as my guide. The knight's message begged me to come so that he could assure me he wasn't the villain the joust made him seem. With no reason to doubt him, I went.

"My lords"—she looked at the men standing behind the bishop's chair, for they were the ones she needed to convince—"in that moment, my only thought was to soothe the pain of my sire's esteemed and trustworthy steward, a man I believed too harshly punished over what was sheer accident."

How they would have groaned and gasped if she'd revealed her true purpose in meeting Warin was to confide that she'd witnessed her sire's misdeed. What she next must say would cost her just as dearly. Kate drew a bracing breath, even as the heat of shame flamed in her cheeks.

"Here, my lords, is the crux of mine own foolishness. My lord father is correct to say I should have asked maid or man to accompany me. God knows Adele de Fraisney taught me that. I didn't ask because the animosity toward Sir Warin was so great that I was certain I'd be denied the chance to see him if I did. Thus, I knew I had to go alone and unseen from Haydon's gates."

At her admission of wrongdoing, more than one man nodded, condemning her with the mere movement of their heads. But at the same time, new consideration filled the faces of her critics. They were listening even as they disapproved. Against that, she no longer minded the intensity of her sire's continuing glare.

"How was it you accomplished that, my lady?" Lord Haydon asked. "The Lord God knows my folk have been taught better as well." His stern tone said someone, most likely that handsome porter, would pay a price for what was not entirely his fault. That Kate couldn't bear.

She faced her former host. "When I arrived in your courtyard, my lord, I found the servants dancing to the music from the garden. I waited in the shadows out of your porter's sight, hoping for a chance to escape unquestioned. Just when I began to think my chance would never come, your man's attention was diverted by the dancers. It was then that I slipped past him."

"Jesus God!" her sire shouted, stepping around Rafe to face his erring daughter, and waved a chiding finger in her direction. "It shames me to call you kin. No honest woman would ever have conceived such deviousness. But you, you speak about doing it with such ease that it makes me think you've done it more than this once," he charged.

"Enough, Bagot," the bishop warned again. "This is no church court to pass judgment upon your daughter's morals. I only wish to know how she became your steward's captive. She's answering my question in full knowledge that what she says is to her detriment. Now, no more interruptions. My lady," he said to Kate, "do I assume that when you met with him, Sir Warin made you his prisoner?"

"Aye, my lord," Kate replied, once more turning to face him before launching into her tale.

By the time she'd recounted her attempts to escape Warin as well as his abuse, not mentioning the discussion of Rafe owning her missing ribbon, of course, all but the countess's marshal had slipped away from the bishop's chair to take seats at the tables. When she told of escaping Rafe's bonds to warn Glevering's defenders against the Godsols, something she might have sworn was respect took fire in the eyes of the countess's man.

"Which brings us to the question we most need answered," the bishop said. "After so steadfastly resisting a wedding that was against your sire's will, how can Sir Rafe claim you came willingly into your union with him?"

So stark and bold a question demanded an equally frank answer. Kate glanced at Rafe. He watched her in return, the confidence in his gaze having returned and grown three fold. Aye, but here came the difficult part of the tale. The last thing she needed was for these men to think she'd used marriage to Rafe to avoid a union with Sir Gilbert, which was certainly part of the truth.

Marshaling her tongue along with her courage, Kate started into her answer as if tiptoeing through a field of toadstools. "My lords, I knew nothing at all of Glevering when we arrived, having never seen the place that was my dowry. Still, I was determined to put barriers between myself and a marriage I knew my sire would despise. I barred myself into yon bedchamber"—she threw a gesture toward the doorway that had been her haven—"not realizing that there was a key that lifted the bar. Thus when Rafe"—she caught herself—"Sir Rafe opened the door, I knew all was lost. The Godsols now owned Glevering, which meant I was impoverished, as Glevering is, or was, my dowry."

Here she paused to look about the room at the

men who were her judges. They watched her in return, most in consideration, but others with a glimmering of respect upon their faces. Only her sire still glared, and that he did for his own reasons.

"Without a dowry," she continued, her voice softening against the terror impoverishment had set in her, "all I have to my name is my de Fraisney dower. That's hardly wealth enough to attract any landed man, much less the man my father had settled on as my next mate."

At the head of the room, Bishop Robert nodded. "By the same token, if Glevering was confirmed as his by right of conquest, Sir Rafe might well have looked higher than a widow with a few virgates and a mill to her name." He knew well the property she owned, having dealt with the de Fraisney estate.

Kate's sighed and boldly met the churchman's gaze. "Exactly, my lord. Needless to say, it was no longer forced marriage I feared. Nay, I believed the Godsols were finished with me and would return me to Haydon and my sire."

Rafe shifted at her side. Kate glanced at him in time to catch the slight shake of his head. In his gaze glowed the message that he'd never once considered rejecting her for another. The corners of her mouth lifted as his assurance only deepened the love she knew for him. In the end, he'd wanted her more than Glevering, and that was wondrous for its own sake. She returned her attention to the room.

"Think on it, my lords. There was no chaperone to vouch for my virtue during my experiences. Who would believe me still a chaste woman? I was worse than impoverished and useless to my sire. From that time on, I'd be a millstone around his neck, an embarrassment and a black spot upon his name." Her voice thickened with the horror of the fate she'd only narrowly escaped.

All around the room, eyebrows rose and heads nodded in agreement. Even the countess's man's face softened. He knew well enough she was right to fear ruin, even to this moment, for these men might yet render her marriage to Rafe illegal, no matter how Rafe tried to twist them to his will. For hatred's sake, her sire would never let her remarry Rafe. After what she had revealed here today, no other man would want her. Not even her father would keep her. Calling her a traitor to his name, he'd happily cast off his betraying daughter. If that happened, Kate would soon be dead.

The lift of the bishop's chin bade her to continue. Drawing a shaken breath, Kate did as commanded.

"You cannot imagine my surprise when Sir Rafe offered marriage to me. He did so suggesting our wedding would heal the rift between our two families, saying that it was past time for the animosity to cease. I didn't accept solely to protect myself or my sire from abasement. To me, it seemed the best solution. After all, if I come to bed with an heir for my new husband, that child will have Daubney as well as Godsol blood in his veins. In this way, my sire never loses Glevering, for one of his bloodline yet owns it."

As the last word left her lips, Kate congratulated

herself. Why, she'd even convinced herself that marriage to Rafe was a boon, not a slight, to her sire. Beside her, Rafe's eyes glowed with approval. A pleased murmur rose from about the room.

"Well said, my lady," Lord Haydon called to her.

On the dais, what remained of the tension in the countess's marshal drained from him. Setting his helmet at the chair's foot, he took a step to the platform's edge and looked out at the room. "My lords, as you well know, I come this day as witness for my noble lady. It would be well for you all to know that naught but a few days ago at the picnic, my own lady voiced this very opinion. Before Lady Haydon she wished there might be an alliance between Daubney and Godsol and through it peace might be restored to our shire."

That startled Kate, for it was more support than she'd ever expected from him. His piece said, the knight retreated to stand behind the prelate's chair. No longer did he seem an unforgiving judge. Instead, his stance made him look like Gerard or Sir Josce as they stood behind Lord Haydon.

"What say the rest of you?" Bishop Robert asked of the room. "Sir Guilliame has offered his opinion as well as that of his lady. I'd hear what you think before rendering mine own judgment."

"I say Bagot's better off accepting this marriage," the old nobleman replied, his voice as cracked as his face was lined. "Take it from me, Lord Humphrey," he said, waggling a chunk of bread at his peer as if to drive home the point, "better that your daughter's married, no matter what you think of the union, than that she makes no match at all. I've three girls for whom no man offered, they having no inheritance, despite my efforts on their behalf. Now it's my purse that pays the price, supporting them as they reside in barren uselessness with the Benedictines."

He shifted on his bench to look at Lord Haydon. "I daresay Lord Baldwin here feels the same. He has four lasses for heirs and not enough property to divide between them."

"I expect I do," Lord Haydon replied quietly, a note of sadness in his voice, as if the thought of any of his precious daughters being left without husband or home pained him.

Her father's harsh snort dismissed both the men and their hapless daughters, then he turned his back upon them to study the others in the room. His mouth took a sour twist at what he saw. "You've decided, all of you. Each and every one of you sits ready to trade away my property on a cobbling of lies told by this foul woman." With each word his voice rose.

Circling Rafe, he came to stand before his daughter. The cords of his neck stood out as his fists clenched. Deep rage glittered in his eyes. Kate took a frightened backward step. There was something unholy and ancient about that emotion.

"By God," her father roared, "but she stood before you and admitted she was a woman of no morals! For that you reward her with Glevering? Nay, you do better than that. You'd have the spawn of my worst enemy someday take my property through her."

He whirled once more to look at his peers. "You're thieves, all of you, and I won't stand for it!" His hand dropped to his sword's hilt.

Terror ran roughshod over Kate. Not certain who he meant to kill, she threw herself at Rafe, as if nearness would save them both. Her husband caught his arm around her, shifting until he stood between father and daughter.

"My lord, your protection," he called out to the bishop, but the prelate was already out of his chair and off the dais. The countess's knight came with him, staying close to the churchman's back. An instant later, they closed on the nobleman. As Bishop Robert grabbed Bagot by his shoulders, the knight reached around his better to yank his sword from his scabbard. Kate's sire shouted in outrage and whirled to face this new threat. The bishop gave the peer a stern shake.

"I warned you, Lord Bagot. There is a truce, and I will brook no violence here! Now, calm yourself and think. If you'll but do that, you'll see that this is a reasonable match, especially given that you lost Glevering because of your steward's treachery. My God, man, this is in your best interest."

Rather than heed the churchman, her father pulled free of the smaller man's grasp. "Damn you all! You're stealing Glevering from me to give it to my enemy." His cry was a pained roar.

"Bagot, what choice have we?" one of his erstwhile supporters called to him. "By your daughter's words, the marriage is made, the deed done. She was free to wed. You yourself bought that right from our king."

Fists clenched against his brow, her father squealed in frustration, then threw back his head to shout to the rafters above him, "You know damn well I didn't pay a fortune so she could play whore to my greatest foe!"

As if called to it by his words, Rafe stepped away from Kate to the center of the hall. He held out his arms as if to gather all attention. "My lords, it's a good point Lord Bagot makes. He did, indeed, pay a fortune for the right to choose a husband for his daughter. Since what he did was to my profit, I deem it only fair that I shoulder half my father-by-marriage's debt," he offered.

At once more hearing Rafe name him kin, her father's face twisted until he looked mad. "I will be no relation to a thieving snake-eater!"

He lunged at the man he hated. Kate managed a tiny scream. Her hands clutched at her chest, as if protecting her own heart would save the man she loved.

As he'd done at the picnic, Rafe caught her father by the arms to hold him at bay. Together they wrestled their way down the hall's length. Gerard and Sir Josce raced around the table to aid their friend, while Will nigh on catapulted over a bench to reach his brother. Every peer within the room was on his feet, bellowing for his fellow to cease.

Naught but a moment later, her sire was caught between the two younger men. Will stood panting at Rafe's back, his hands opening and closing against his need to strike out at his enemy when he knew he mustn't. Around the room, not one man reclaimed his seat. Indeed, two of them went so far as to draw their swords.

"You pigheaded noble fool!" Bishop Robert shouted at the recalcitrant baron. "To attack Sir Rafe when he offers to take on half your debt says your hatred of this family goes too deep. For that sin can our precious Lord damn you. But here, through this wedding, has He given you the chance to release what eats at your soul. I beg you. Heed your Lord. Confess to what fouls your heart, bear your penance and heal. For the sake of God and this shire, make your peace with this marriage!"

"Nay," Bagot's lord howled to the rafters, "better that I die damned!"

Then, as if what he said shocked even him, he sagged between his captors. "Better that I die than let that Godsol have my daughter," he sobbed, his tone that of a friendless man alone and adrift on an empty sea.

Already looking uncomfortable at holding their better against his will, both Gerard and Sir Josce took his defeated stance to mean the end of any threat from him. Releasing him, they shifted to stand guard about their friend, should Bagot's lord consider another attack.

For an instant, Kate toyed with the idea of crossing the room to join them, then discarded it. Her father's behavior was too unnerving. Better that she kept her distance, just in case.

At the far table, one of the men who'd entered the hall as a detractor laughed. There was no amusement in the sound. "Take heart, Bagot. You've no need to strike another blow against the Godsol if you want him destroyed. He's just dealt himself a heart wound by taking on half your debt. Why, in no time our greedy king will suck Glevering dry of every coin, leaving him as impoverished and broken as the rest of us."

Gasps and groans filled the air as every man looked toward the speaker. Eyes flashing, the bishop whirled on the man. "No more of that, my lord," he chided harshly. "Not here or now."

In that instant of inattention, her sire exploded into motion. Teeth bared and eyes wild, he raced past the bishop and the countess's knight, barreling toward his daughter. Even as Kate started to cry out, it was too late. Her father's hands closed about her throat, choking off all sound. It wasn't hatred that filled his gaze but pain and jealousy, which leaked from the corners of his eyes, burning hot streaks down the harsh line of his cheeks.

Fighting for breath, Kate dug her nails into his steel-sewn gloves. She kicked at his legs, her shoes bouncing off his knitted metal leggings. Rafe's shout was afire with rage and worry. Men bellowed in protest.

She needed more help than that and right quickly, too. Blackness began to edge her vision.

"Betraying whore," her father whispered, his words searing her cheek. He gave her a shake. "I married you, lifting you above the Godsol when I made you my lady, and still you pined for him. Why?" he hissed in breathless demand. Madness and heartache tangled in the word.

The blackness circled in on Kate. Her hands fell away from his gloves. Her eyes shut. God help her, but he was mad. He thought he was talking to her long-dead dam.

"I loved you," he went on, the words reaching her now as from a distance, "and still you lusted after my pretty enemy. Well, you died once for loving the man who killed our sons. Now die again."

Horror was the last thing Kate knew as the darkness claimed her.

Chapter 25

Never had it occurred to Rafe that Bagot would try to kill his own daughter. Roaring against his terror for Kate, he launched himself across the room to save his wife, all the while grabbing for a weapon he didn't wear. At his back came Josce and Gerard. Bishop Robert was there before them, as was the countess's man. As the churchman grappled with Bagot, trying to break the nobleman's hold on his daughter, the knight drew back a fist for a stunning blow.

Kate hung like a child's cloth poppet in her father's grasp. Not his Kate. He wouldn't lose her now.

Hands joined, Rafe raised his arms over his head to deliver another blow. Before he could drop his arms, Bagot made a gurgling sound. His eyes widened. His hands opened. Like a stringed puppet without a hand to guide it, Kate collapsed in a heap on the floor.

Clutching at his chest, Bagot's mouth opened and closed like that of a beached fish. He staggered to the side and dropped to his knees. An instant later, he crumpled. Life drained from his eyes until they were but soulless stones, once more becoming the dust from which they'd been created.

"Kate!" Rafe shouted, squatting to scoop up the woman who owned his heart. His friends crowded around him as concerned as he. When she was cradled in his arms, Rafe laid his hand against Kate's breast and felt nothing.

A horrified breath left him. Tears stung at his eyes. His heart tore in twain. "Nay," he cried, but the word lacked volume.

"Rafe, be easy," Josce said gently, grabbing his friend's hand to place Rafe's trembling fingers against Kate's throat and what Rafe most needed to feel. "You see? She yet lives."

As the strong and steady thud of Kate's heart battered at Rafe's fingertips, every muscle in his body weakened in relief. He stumbled backward until he meet a table behind him. Leaning against it, he cradled his wife close to his heart. With his forehead resting against her, he gloried in the ragged puff of her continuing breath against his cheek.

"You were right," he told her, the joy that now filled him almost more overwhelming than the terror of the last moments, "it was God's will that you should be mine, for He took your sire to make certain that I kept you."

Something startled Kate out of the darkness that held her prisoner. In that instant, she drew in a deep breath. It was like swallowing sharp stones. The agony beyond bearing, she twisted and fought, gagging as she tried to escape it. Tears blinded her

"Nay, Kate," Rafe said, his voice gentle and filled with care for her, "it's me."

The sound of Rafe's voice was all it took. Kate relaxed against what tortured her, only to find the next breath more tolerable, if not easier. Blinking back the pain, she looked around her.

No longer were they in the hall, but in Glevering's bedchamber. She lay in her husband's arms as he sat upon the bed. Concern twisted his handsome features and darkened his eyes until they were nigh on black.

That he ached over what hurt her only fed the care Kate knew for him. With that came the need to soothe. She lifted a hand to trace her fingers down the line of his jaw, ruffling the short hairs of his beard as she went.

His smile was that slow curl of his lips she so loved, bringing with it the need to feel his mouth on hers, no matter what it cost her. As if he read her thoughts, his head lowered until he touched his lips to hers. Her arms lifted to encircle his neck. Kate savored the sweetness of his kiss.

God and all his saints be praised. She was alive and in Rafe's arms, where she belonged.

Even as the new value she placed on her life came rushing home to her, a thread of caution woke. This moment was worthless if her sire yet breathed. Having discovered his madness, she knew for certain his hatred and harassment would last to his life's end. Or theirs.

Freeing her mouth from Rafe's, Kate leaned back in his arms. "My sire?" she said, then gasped. Speaking was like spitting up daggers.

"Bagot is no more," said Bishop Robert from the bed's far corner.

With a jangle of metal, he stepped into Kate's field of vision. The sliver of day's light that shot through the narrow window burnished the churchman's armor and found threads of gold in his thatch of gray. There was a sad twist to his mouth. "Your lord sire has gone unshriven to meet his Maker, with only hatred to fill his heart. May God have mercy on his soul."

Relief and gratitude rushed through Kate, only to be followed by a new sort of caution. It was a sin to wish ill on the dead. Releasing her hold on Rafe, she crossed herself, praying fervently that her father's thrice-damned soul, denied a heavenly home, wandered far from Glevering.

The churchman nodded in approval of Kate's gesture. "Aye, my lady, his death is a terrible reminder to us all that we must make peace with our Lord at every opportunity," the bishop said, misinterpreting her reaction. "The only boon in all this is that no man here bears the stain of his death on his soul. It was God Himself who stopped your sire's heart and prevented your destruction."

As if he intended to protect her from that now past threat, Rafe's arms tightened around her. A tangled bolt of rage and pain danced through his gaze, then was gone. It was enough to tell Kate that her husband wouldn't have minded bearing the stain of her sire's death, not for the sake of the feud but because of the hurt Bagot's lord had done to one he cherished.

Once again the wonder of Rafe's love washed over Kate. To think he was her husband and she would keep him for all time. Or would she?

"Their decision," she demanded of Rafe at a whisper, in the mistaken hope that a low voice would mean less pain. It didn't.

Nodding, Rafe shifted on the bed so that they both faced the prelate. "My lord, given the chaos of the past quarter-hour, you'll forgive me if I need it confirmed. Tell me now. Is Bagot's daughter truly my wife?"

Annoyance washed over the churchman's narrow face, then died into testy acquiescence. "When I left Haydon, I'd have staked my life that nothing could convince me to accept this marriage as legal, no matter how many witnesses you paraded before me."

"We do have witnesses and a priest, my lord," Rafe offered, only to have the bishop wave him into silence.

"Of course you do, but it no longer matters, does it?" the churchman retorted. "Bagot's dead, and by royal decree the lady was free to marry where she pleased. And regardless of the devious way you came to own her, this marriage is best for her, for the shire and it would have been for Bagot, if he could but have seen that."

That said, the bishop's mouth took a bitter twist. "And now what do we do with Bagot's foul steward? I'd intended to give the man back to Bagot once this was resolved for whatever justice his master might have meted out. Now, Mary forgive me, but I find myself wishing the man would have the courtesy to drop dead like his noble master. If he won't, we'll have to present him to the sheriff, where he can tell his tale to all who listen."

Once again Bishop Robert pressed a hand to his temple to rub away an ache. Kate chewed her lip, recognizing the threat Warin still represented to the shire's peace and to her own happiness. Could what Warin knew force the bishop to change his mind about their marriage?

Only Rafe remained easy, a touch of a smile claiming his mouth. "My lord, with Bagot dead, what does prosecuting his steward serve save to further blacken a dead man's name? Were I you, I'd go to de Dapifer and warn him that word of his treachery will be spread from house to house. Within a month's time, there'll be no man in all England willing to offer him employment. Suggest to him that with his skills he'd be better bound for the wars in Poitou and Normandy, where"—it was hard amusement that came to life in Rafe's eyes—"he'll either die or make himself a living. Either way, your situation is resolved."

The annoyed expression on Bishop Robert's face melted from his features. No sour twist of the lips this time. Nay, it was a wide grin that claimed his mouth, displaying a goodly set of teeth for a man his age. "By God, lad, but you're good at this. I can't imagine why you haven't advanced further in our king's appreciation."

Kate watched her husband fight his own amusement, even as he shrugged away the backhanded compliment. "I fear I'm a rustic at heart, my lord. A home and loving wife to bear me sons was all I ever wanted. And that," he said, once more looking at the woman in his arms, "is what I have."

Epilogue

"**L**ady Godsol, that was a fine meal, indeed." Stephen de St. Valery's words rang in Glevering's hall.

So deeply had Kate been concentrating on scraping her own trencher clean that she started. Setting down her spoon, she looked at the knight. Sir Stephen had a curling thatch of dark brown hair and eyes as green as grass.

Almost all of Rafe's closest companions had come to bide with them that week. Seated beside Sir Stephen was Sir Simon de Kenifer, a slender man with pale brown hair and blue eyes. At the opposite table were Sir Josce, the scarred Sir Hugh d'Aincourt and the quiet, polite Sir Alan FitzOsbert. Kate found herself wishing that Gerard and Emma had come as well; she could have used another female as an ally against all these males. But Emma was battling the same temporary sickness that Kate had just surmounted and Gerard was unwilling to leave her side.

"My thanks, Sir Stephen," she said with a smile.

"Aye, my wife is an excellent housekeeper," Rafe said from his seat beside her at the high table, his voice warm with pride.

Kate shot him a happy but narrow sidelong look. "Fortunate for you that I am, since you never thought to ask after my housewifely skills when you took me for your own."

That made her husband laugh, naught but happiness in the sound of his amusement. Rafe caught her hand, his fingers twining in hers in a caress that Kate had come to know these past months as a reflection of the pride he felt for her. Kate couldn't help but smile. Mary save her, but she loved him so. That he still respected and cherished her despite the wrong they'd done before their vows were said still amazed her.

As he read her affection for him in her gaze, Rafe's dark eyes fairly glowed with pleasure. Lifting her hand, he brought her fingers to his lips to touch a kiss to her knuckles. Although the caress was but brief, there was more than a hint of the desire they both still shared for each other in that touch, enough to wake that flame at Kate's core.

Rafe's expression softened with the reflection of her own passion for him. Kate drew a sharp, pleased breath. There were times when she swore the heat they made between them would consume them both, but it never did.

Indeed, she had chosen well in her husband—if it had been her choice at all. More than once these past two months she'd told herself that the Lord must have planned their marriage, for there was no doubting the rightness of their union.

Keeping Kate's hand in his own, Rafe turned his gaze out into Glevering's hall and eyed his friends. "Enough chitchat, Stephen, until my wife is finished with her meal," he warned the knight. "This last week I've learned it's dangerous to come between her and her meat. I vow that child of mine gnaws a hole in her gullet."

"Rafe!" Kate cried, both amused and piqued by his comment. It was true. Who could have guessed that a babe in her womb could make her so hungry, especially after the sick misery of those first weeks?

Stephen sent his host a cheeky grin as his eyes glowed with mischief. "I cannot speak for the rest of us," the lift of his hands indicated the other men in the room, "but I'm not surprised that any child of yours, Rafe, born or unborn, might have fierce appetites."

Beside Stephen, Sir Simon choked as he sipped his wine, his face reddening as he fought to laugh and breathe in the same instant. At the opposite table, Sir Josce, Sir Hugh and Sir Alan all howled.

Kate shot a glance at her mate. Rafe was watching her, a touch of concern in his gaze. She nearly snorted. As if she cared a fig for what he might have done prior to their union. Nay, she knew well enough that she owned him now, body and soul, and that was all that mattered.

It was her two months as Rafe's wife that gave Kate the confidence to speak as she would. "I see you all know my husband very well, indeed," she called out, then screwed her face into an expression of innocence. "What say you? Shall we fill these evening hours trading tales of my husband's past? Perhaps, you'll tell me of those appetites of his."

Beside her, Rafe blanched. His eyes were round as he considered the wisdom of inviting his past into his present. Taking pity on him, Kate tightened her fingers around his hand, then brought their joined hands to her lips. In the presence of his friends, she staked her claim of ownership by pressing a kiss to his fingers.

"And I," she went on, stifling her urge to laugh, "will tell you how I've tamed whatever wild urges he might once have harbored to turn a young lion into a toothless married beast."

A moment's breathless silence held in the room. Rafe's astonishment at this tweak was so complete that his jaw dropped. Reaching out, Kate placed gentle fingers beneath his chin and urged his mouth to close.

"Poor dear. See how he suffers," she called to the men in the hall. "Be warned, all of you. This is what happens to a man when he loses the taste for all but one dish."

Her brows lifted. Her mouth quivered, so hard did she fight her smile. Even as laughter brightened Rafe's eyes, they narrowed. No warning of his could have stopped her.

"Oh, but Lord, how he craves that dish," she said, her words breaking with laughter.

Sir Josce roared at his friend's expense. Sir Alan pounded the table in approval, while Sir Hugh held his sides. At the other table, Kate's words had so astounded Sir Stephen that he came straight up off his bench, knocking it and Sir Simon into the rushes as he did so. Poor Simon could do nothing but lie on his back and laugh.

Beside her, Rafe growled. Kate shrieked and pretended to resist as her husband snatched her into his lap. All thought of avoiding him ended as Rafe's mouth came to rest against hers, even as he still laughed.

"Shall I show them with this kiss just how much I crave you?" he murmured against her lips, taunting.

It didn't matter that his friends watched. Kate's arms slipped up until she joined her hands at her husband's nape. Rather than reply, Kate caught his lips with hers and showed him what he already knew. Rafe's arms tightened around her. Against her hip, Kate could feel his shaft's reaction.

His friends hooted and whistled. Rafe's mouth smiled against hers. Giggles overtook Kate. Bracing his brow against hers, Rafe looked down into her face.

"They approve of you, but then I never doubted

that they would, since you are the only wife for me," he whispered, happiness shining from his face. "God help me, but how I love you."

Just as always happened when he told her this, her heart melted. "As I do you, husband," Kate replied, touching a tiny kiss to his lips, then slipping off his lap.

With Rafe's friends still hooting and throwing comments at their newly wedded comrade, Kate stood to shake out her skirts. As she prepared to sit again, her glance caught Dame Joan standing near the hall door. Both Ernulf and Joan had found life at Glevering under its new master too pleasant to resist. Since then, Kate had taken Joan into her heart. It would be the bailiff's wife and no one else in her birthing chamber some seven months hence.

Behind Joan stood a single travel-stained man. Kate frowned her question. Joan's hand lifted. That's all it took to convey the message. Whatever word that man carried, it was important.

"Rafe," Kate hissed to her husband, directing his attention to the newcomer.

With a gesture, Rafe bade the man come into the room. Their interest piqued by this diversion, his friends sobered. Sir Josce sat suddenly straighter as recognition flashed over his face. Dread followed.

"Arnold of Haydon," he called. "Why come you here, when you should be at Lady Haydon's side during my lord sire's absence?" Lord Haydon was escorting his middle daughters back to their convent school.

Grief twisted the messenger's face. He dropped

to his knee before his lord's bastard son. "It's terrible news, sir," he cried. "Your lady stepmother bids me bring you home to her. Your sire is dead."

**Look for Denise Hampton's next
utterly romantic love story—
as Josce meets his match—
coming in Spring 2002 from Avon Romance**

Are they married or aren't they?

Years ago, Lady Roselyn Grant left Sir Spencer
Thornton at the altar . . . now, her abandoned fiancé
has come back into her life and enters into a sensual
game of revenge in an unforgettable romance of
Elizabethan England

HIS BETROTHED
By
Gayle Callen

He's a Native American . . . a man as rough and
untamed as the land he claims as his . . .

Rafe Aigner has learned the hard way to make a
living as best as he can . . . and to beat others on his
terms. So when he wins ownership of Madeleine
Calhoun's newspaper in a game of chance, he's not
about to give it up—or to let her out of his sight . . .

THE RENEGADES: RAFE
By
Genell Dellin

ARM 0501